AUTUMN'S TRAITOR

HANNAH PARKER

AUTUMN'S TRAITOR

HANNAH PARKER

COUNTERPOISE
PRESS

For Mom and Dad

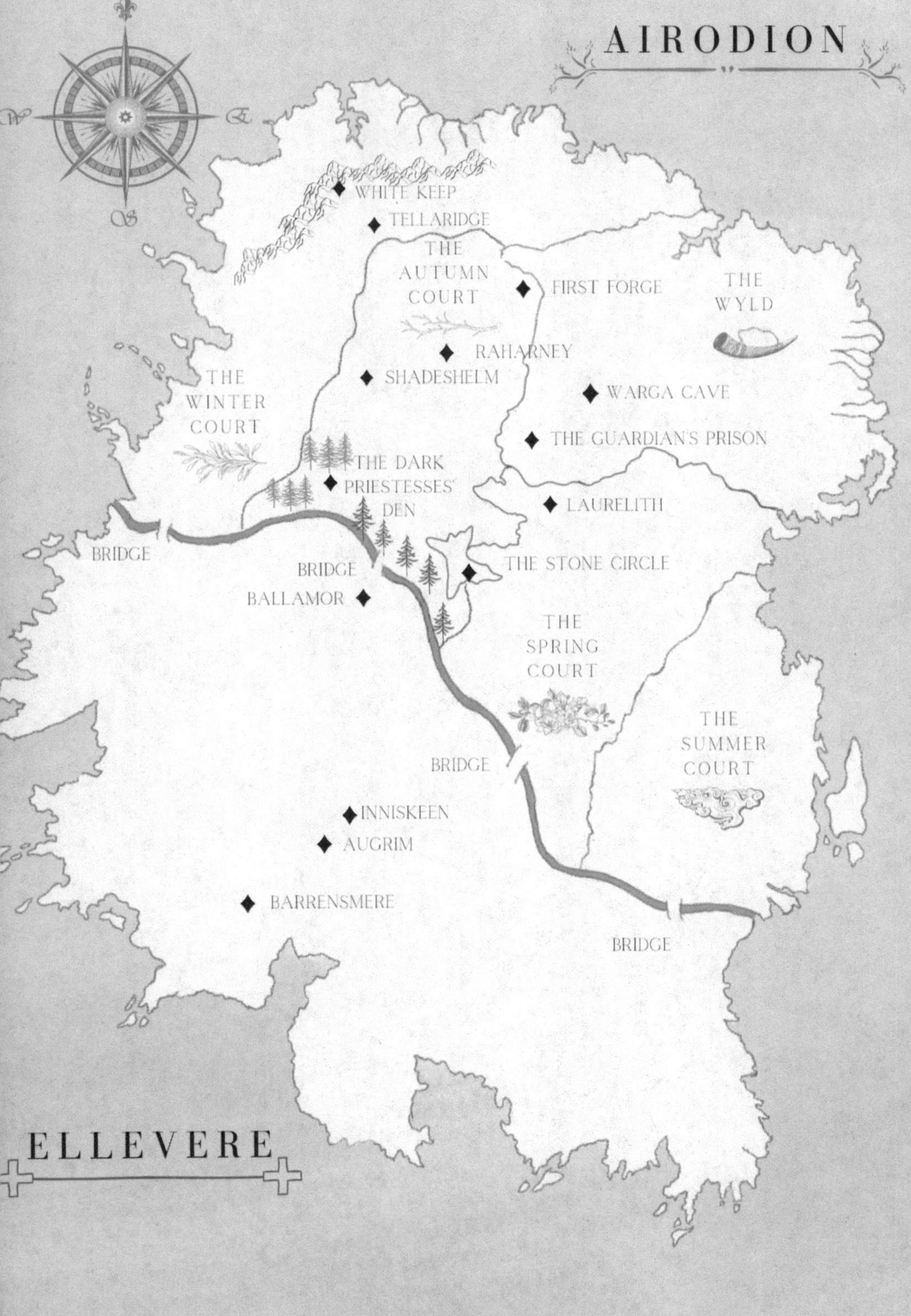

AIRODION
ELLEVERE
WHITE KEEP
TELLARIDGE
THE AUTUMN COURT
FIRST FORGE
THE WYLD
RAHARNEY
THE WINTER COURT
SHADESHELM
WARGA CAVE
THE GUARDIAN'S PRISON
THE DARK PRIESTESSES' DEN
LAURELITH
BRIDGE
BRIDGE
THE STONE CIRCLE
BALLAMOR
THE SPRING COURT
THE SUMMER COURT
BRIDGE
INNISKEEN
AUGRIM
BARRENSMERE
BRIDGE

THE EVENTS OF BOOK ONE

Seventeen-year-old Larken lives in a village visited by the fey every year. Her story begins on the day of the Choosing Ceremony, when the fey come to select a human girl to bring back with them, from which the girls never return. They need the girl for an unnamed "special task", and in return, the fey reward both her family and the villagers. Larken's friend Brigid was Chosen last year, and ever since Larken has dreamt of reuniting with her. The Prince of the Autumn Court, Finder, arrives, and chooses the butcher's daughter instead.

Castor, a disgraced member of the Black Guard, soldiers who prevent humans from entering the faery realm, raves that the fey are killing the girls. Larken meets with Castor because she is worried about Brigid, and Castor convinces her that the fey use the girls for some nefarious purpose —and that a deal has been struck between human rulers and the fey allowing this to happen. Larken enters the faery realm hoping to save Brigid, the butcher's girl, and discover the truth about the "special task." She catches up with the butcher's girl and the fey as they stumble into a pack of monsters. The butcher's girl dies, but Larken saves Finder's life. Finder explains that a life debt was created between them. Until he saves her life in return, they are bound. Larken cannot return home, and if either of them dies or is harmed, the same will happen to the other. Finder explains that the faery king, the Starveling, demands a tithe every year from each of the faery courts: a human heart. Finder now has no tithe and the Starveling will punish Finder's court and Larken's people. Unable and unwilling to use Larken instead, Finder suggests to his faery companions and Larken that they work together to overthrow the Starveling. Larken begrudgingly agrees.

Dahey, Finder's companion and cousin, suggests seeking help from the Dark Priestesses, who tell them that the Starveling can be killed. Two of the three Priestesses attack, claiming they had orders to kill anyone who seeks to bring down the king. But the third Priestess gives Finder a magical knife and urges him to find the Guardian who will give the knife its power. Larken was bitten by one of the Priestesses and she falls ill to its poison. They seek help from a pack of female wolf shapeshifters known as the Warga. Afterwards, Larken and her companions reach the Guardian's domain. The Guardian demands that Finder speak an incantation when he kills the Starveling and claims that the words restore the knife to its full power. Finder is suspicious of the true meaning of the words, but fears he has no other option.

They cross through the Spring Court, battling threats lurking in a labyrinth and withstanding torture by Etain, Princess of the Spring Court. Although they escape, one of their companions, Madden, dies. They reach the Starveling. During the battle, Finder saves Larken and ends their life debt. He speaks the words demanded by the Guardian and kills the Starveling. After the Starveling falls, a memory curse is lifted from the court rulers. Finder remembers that the Guardian had been imprisoned by the Starveling, the Dark Priestesses and the court rulers long ago after wreaking havoc with a magical language he created. By using the knife, speaking the words and killing the Starveling, the Guardian is now free.

Finder urges Larken to return home while he and Dahey return to the Autumn Court. One of their companions, Saja, accompanies Larken. They encounter a group of Fomari who seem determined to trap them in the human realm. During the fight, Saja senses through the *dornán* bond that Finder is hurt. The Fomari claim that Dahey is now their master, and Saja and Larken piece together that Dahey has concocted a plan to take Finder's place as ruler with the help of the Dark Priestesses and the Guardian. He commanded the Fomari that killed Finder's tithe and pushed Finder to seek the Guardian. Dahey plans on taking Finder back to the Autumn Court and imprisoning him for treason and to take his powers by force using the Guardian's magic. Larken and Saja return to the faery realm to save Finder.

PART I

ALLIES AND ENEMIES

1

DAHEY

Airodion

Two sides of the same coin, people had always said about him and Finder. They looked more alike than their twin fathers. Yet as a boy, Dahey had longed to look more like his cousin. He would have given anything to have Finder's green eyes and dark auburn curls instead of his own brown gaze and light red hair. Everything Finder did, Dahey also wanted to do.

But they were not boys any longer.

Finder stood on a raised dais in the middle of the throne room. The Weeping Metal chains wrapped around his wrists and throat prevented him from moving—or using his powers. The skin beneath the metal was red and oozing. The white linen of his shirt was rumpled and dirty from days in the dungeon, and his red curls were matted with sweat and blood.

General Reddon shifted beside Dahey, where they sat with the rest of the council facing the dais. Dahey wasn't a member of the council, but they had invited him to participate in Finder's trial. Reddon's long black hair slipped over his breastplate. He was young but levelheaded, and it

3

hadn't surprised Dahey when he had been elected. He caught Dahey's gaze and inclined his head. Dahey and Reddon had trained together as swordsmen at the Autumn Court's military academy. Reddon's estate had fallen on hard times the previous year, and Dahey had offered to let him repay his debts to the crown by working as a swordmaster at the academy. Dahey had been close to Reddon ever since and knew the male was loyal to him.

Dahey gazed out at the crowd. The room was packed with hundreds of fey. They hovered between the double row of white marble columns running from the front of the room to the doors in the back. The columns were carved to look like massive tree trunks, their branches sweeping high into the domed ceiling. How many times had he and Finder played in this room as children, weaving between the columns, running their hands along the marble trunks—so lifelike they felt as rough as real tree bark? How many times had they laid beneath the branches, staring at leaves carved from stone and glass, light streaking through the orange and red hues?

General Pike droned on, going over the details of their journey, filling in the Autumn Court fey about the Starveling's death. Dahey's stomach was in knots, half from the trial's proceedings and half from the oath that pulled at his gut, demanding he return the knife to the Guardian.

The council had decided that he must give the knife of power to them. Anxiety had spiked through him at the thought of being separated from the knife, but he knew he would find a way to retrieve it, especially if the trial went as planned.

Soon, he told the oath.

Only a week had passed since Dahey had brought Finder to Shadeshelm. His gaze caught on the puckered wound marring the skin between Finder's collarbone and shoulder. The wound should have healed by now—after all, it wasn't meant to be a mortal wound—but the Weeping Metal hindered its progress. Dahey remembered pulling his sword from Finder's chest and his cousin's subsequent cry of pain.

Finder never wanted to rule, Dahey reminded himself firmly.

"...attacked by the Dark Priestesses. One of the three dark sisters gave

Finder a knife of great power and sent him to a being known as the Guardian."

The Guardian had assured Dahey that once Finder spoke the words, the knife's power would overwhelm him, and that Finder's powers would come to Dahey. And it had almost worked—until the human girl, Larken, had brought Finder back.

Dahey drummed his fingers on the table. Larken. A glimmer of respect flared to life in his gut. He had grown to care for the human girl, but he would not allow her to stand in his way.

Dahey wanted—no, *needed*, to rule the Autumn Court. He deserved it more than anyone. Until he could figure out how to take Finder's powers, however, his only hope was to rule as regent in his stead.

"Finder used the Guardian's knife to murder our king," Pike said.

A murmur rose from the crowd—they knew the Starveling was dead, but they hadn't heard the details of his demise until now.

Pike clasped Dahey's shoulder. "Dahey was right to bring this treasonous act to the council."

Dahey nodded, ignoring Finder's glare from the dais.

"May I speak in my defense before you decide my fate?" Finder asked softly. Pike extended his hand, gesturing for Finder to continue.

"Do not pretend that the Starveling was some benevolent king," Finder spat. "He never cared about the wellbeing of the Autumn Court. He only emerged from his den for the tithe—which was agonizing for all of the court rulers."

"Why did you kill him?" Reddon asked.

"As Pike already explained, I was tied in a life debt—"

"Yes, we know about Larken," Reddon waved a hand. "But even then, you could have gone to the Starveling and begged for his mercy."

"He demanded that we bring him the hearts of innocent girls," Finder growled. "Does he seem like a merciful being?"

"The sacrifice of so many young girls is... regrettable," Reddon said, "but the tithe was a burden you should have been willing to bear for your court. We don't need a ruler who shrinks from his responsibilities. And there is a matter of Embryn Navallen's death."

Dahey's breath caught. Embryn. Finder's dearest friend, who had died when they had tried to rise up against the Starveling once before. But she had been Dahey's friend, too. He remembered wisps of her dark hair, her crushed elderberry scent.

"Don't," Finder whispered.

"It is difficult to believe that this wasn't an act of revenge," Reddon finished. "A ploy that could have cost us all our lives."

Dahey smiled. His nerves melted away. His court was on his side.

"Enough. Let us vote," Pike said. "Those in favor of declaring Finder Fairburn unfit to rule—"

Every member of the council raised their hands. Shocked gasps rose from the crowd. The murmurs grew into a roar.

Pike stood. "Silence! For crimes of treason against his court and killing the Starveling, we declare Finder Fairburn unfit to rule. Finder, you will be imprisoned until your powers give us a new ruler. Dahey Fairburn will rule as regent in your stead."

Dahey closed his eyes, shutting out the look of rage that marred his cousin's face. But a smile still touched Dahey's lips. He was going to be regent. And once he figured out how to take Finder's powers, he would be king.

Despite it all, a tiny sigh of relief escaped him. There had been a chance the court would rule that Finder should be executed for his crimes. Dahey had never wanted to see his cousin dead; even when the knife had overpowered Finder, he had wanted his cousin to live. All he wanted were the powers.

"No," Finder snarled. "I'm the only one who knows the true history of the Guardian thanks to the breaking of the Starveling's memory curse. I will protect this court."

"Be quiet," Dahey snapped. His cousin had never cared about this court. Not like Dahey did.

"He's going to take the powers from me," Finder spat, jerking against the Weeping Metal chains.

More murmurs from the crowd. Dahey glanced around, his heart beating quicker in his chest.

"Impossible," Reddon snapped. Dahey's shoulders relaxed. "The magic chooses the ruler. You should know that more than anyone, seeing as how much you loathe ruling this court. We honor our rulers because the magic chooses them, and you have abused that privilege."

"Pray your powers leave you soon," Pike said. "We declared Osiron Fairburn unfit to rule, and soon after, the powers sought another. I suspect things will not be any different this time."

Dahey jerked at his father's name. He couldn't stop himself from searching for his face in the crowd, but his father wasn't there.

"I know how to use the powers. A new ruler will have to be trained," Finder said. "Dahey betrayed his *dornán* bond. Do you want a regent who would stoop so low to overthrow their prince?"

"Again, what you speak of is impossible," Pike snapped. "No one can break a *dornán* bond. Dahey already told us that you released him from his oath. And we will train any new ruler as we always have."

Dahey clenched his fists. It didn't matter that he needed to be trained. He would train day and night until he mastered the powers. It would be a joy to learn them. He would respect and use the magic, while Finder had only ever shunned it. His court needed a ruler who would use the powers to protect them, not someone who would hide them away.

"You need me," Finder said firmly.

"We need a ruler who wants to rule," Reddon said coldly.

The corner of Dahey's lip lifted.

Guards unlocked Finder's chains from the dais and began dragging him away. A pang of sadness struck Dahey's heart. His cousin would never be free of those chains again. Once Dahey took the magic, he would never allow Finder to go free, would never allow him to spread the word that Dahey had taken the powers by force, or go to the Guardian to try to get them back.

"Your greed will destroy this court," Finder snarled at Dahey.

"I'm going to save this court," Dahey said, smoothing his coat. "I've done everything for my people."

He knew he had to be strategic about how he took the magic. He couldn't let his court know it was possible to take a court ruler's powers, especially when it would already look suspicious that the powers had chosen another member of his family. It was why he had spent so long gaining his court's loyalty. Dahey couldn't risk their anger if they knew he had taken the magic by force.

He walked out of the throne room.

It was time to fulfill his oath to the Guardian.

2

KAISA

Ellevere

Kaisa gritted her teeth as her sword slammed against Hollis's blade. Luckily, the swords didn't make a sound due to the padded leather. They weren't allowed to be out past curfew without a pass, which, of course, they didn't have. The skin on her back twinged at the thought of the lashes they would get if they were found.

"Stop thinking about getting lashes," Hollis whacked her with his blade. "You never get them anyway."

Kaisa grinned. He was right—there had been many times when Kaisa had escaped punishment. She was at the top of all her classes. Her tutors adored her.

"The most skilled student they've seen in centuries," Jovanna called from where she sat cross-legged in the dirt, watching them spar. Kaisa's chambermate bared her teeth in a grin, and Kaisa smiled back. Jovanna might be her opposite in every way—pale skin to Kaisa's ebony, bone thin to Kaisa's soft curves, irresponsible to Kaisa's discipline, but she was one of her dearest friends.

The balmy night air brushed against Kaisa's sweat-soaked skin. Though they were outside, sobs could be heard from the open window of the Cradle girls' dormitory behind them. The cries always began after the girls were locked in for the night. The sound echoed against the unforgiving brick and stone walls of the Institute.

Kaisa remembered what it had been like as a Cradle at five years old, just learning the ways of the Order of the Twins. She hadn't appreciated it then. She hadn't known how good she'd had it. A roof over her head, a warm bed to sleep in, an education... and above all, being able to work for her two powerful gods Aleea and Asphalion, and the four Popes who spoke their will. If it hadn't been for the Order and for the Popes' generosity, she would be starving on the streets. Many children were. The Institute did not take everyone. Only those with potential. Only those who were blessed by the Twins. Her heart glowed at the thought.

And while *she* might not receive lashes, she didn't want Jovanna and Hollis to be punished. "We need to leave. They'll be checking the dormitories soon," Kaisa said.

The Institute was strict about children maintaining their virtue until they were eighteen years of age. Opposite sexes were not allowed in each other's chambers after nightfall. When a child became a student at the Institute of the Order, their body and soul were given in servitude to the Twins.

"Please, Kai, just awhile longer," Hollis begged. "I'll have to apply to the Black Guard once I'm Anointed, and I haven't got the time to practice. Baid's been working me to the bone. I've barely got time to oil and sharpen everything he wants. I don't have time for training."

All the students of the Institute went through the same training, but Baid, the Weapons' Maker, had taken a special interest in Hollis when he was a Cradle.

"I've told you, not at night. I'm exhausted, and I've got a long day tomorrow—"

"Please," Hollis begged, his brown eyes turning a nauseating shade of pitiful. "This is the only time I've got. If Baid knew I was applying, he'd have my hide. He wants me to take his place as Weapons' Maker after I'm Anointed."

"You still haven't told him?" Kaisa groaned.

"You know I'm rubbish at confronting people." Hollis crossed his arms. "If you want someone to stir the pot, ask Jovanna."

He jerked his head at their domineering, hot-headed friend. The three of them had been as thick as thieves since their Cradle year. They did everything together, including reaching their Scholar year. Only a select few made it to their final year, the rest being left to perform other servant duties.

Jovanna grinned, cracking her knuckles. "Let me be the one to tell Baid," she pleaded. "I'd give anything to see the look on his face when he realizes his prize student wants to leave."

"I don't know how to tell him that Weapons' Maker will be below my station once I'm Anointed," Hollis said. "There's no point of me telling him until I pass the test."

"Entries aren't a secret, Hollis. If you don't tell him, he'll hear it from someone else first," Kaisa pointed out.

"Well then, I have to be good enough to pass this test in order to deal with any of that, don't I? So you'll stay?"

Kaisa looked at Jovanna, who shrugged. "Lashes are good for the soul, as they say. Well, good for my soul, I suppose."

Kaisa rolled her eyes but picked up her blade once more. She and Hollis exchanged a few more blows.

"Why do you want to join the Black Guard anyway?" Kaisa whined. "Everything you ever need is here in Barrensmere, including me and Jo."

The Institute, the school that trained children to become members of the Order, resided within the palace in the city of Barrensmere and had been Kaisa's home since she was five years old. The Order might be strict, but it had given her everything. A family of tutors and friends when her own parents had turned their backs on her.

"You know I want to protect Ellevere from the fey," Hollis said, swinging his sword again.

Kaisa shifted to block him. "But I don't want you to go to the North," Kaisa moaned. She didn't want Hollis to be locked away for years, learning the lore of the fey and put through grueling trials only to be shipped off to the North. Not when they could make a life here after they were Anointed.

Hollis swatted her thigh with his blade, breaking her out of her thoughts. "Ouch," she hissed.

Hollis grinned. "Pay more attention."

They continued sparring, Hollis outmaneuvering her with skill that was almost terrifying. He was good—too good at fighting to have his skills wasted once he was Anointed. He needed to be in the Black Guard.

After a few stinging blows from Hollis, most of which she was too tired to block or dodge, she collapsed on the ground, her chest heaving. Hollis flopped to the ground beside her. He tugged at the strap holding back his hair and let it fall in sweaty tendrils to his shoulders. His eyes were a bit too far apart to be handsome, the rest of his features too pinched, but she loved every bit of him as much as her own flesh and blood. Hollis had been her first friend in her Cradle year. He had a large family in town, but they had no time for him, no food for another mouth.

"Mother!" Kaisa screamed as soldiers swathed in black and blood red fabric hauled Kaisa away. Silver coins falling into her mother's hands, so many that they spilled onto the cobblestones.

Kaisa shoved those thoughts away, ignoring the deep ache in her chest. Sold. She could never forget the true word for it. Their families had sold them.

Now they were each other's family. The three of them.

"Are you nervous?" Hollis asked, wiping sweat from his neck.

"About what?" Kaisa replied, though she already knew what he referred to.

"*About what*," Hollis mimicked, shoving her arm. "Oh, I don't know. Maybe about our Anointing? It's only two days away."

"I can't think about it." Kaisa scratched her nail in the dirt. The Anointing was the final test they took as Scholars. If they passed, they were inducted as full members of the Order, and they could apply for the highest-ranking jobs. Less than half of each Scholar class completed their Anointing, and the rest were carted off in the dead of night in disgrace, forced to perform servant's duties at one of the Order's many outpost colonies. "Thinking about it will interfere with my work."

She was so close to achieving all she had ever dreamed. She worked harder than any other student at the Institute. She was the most accomplished Scholar her tutors had ever seen.

Everyone in Ellevere worshipped the Twins, but only those who made it through the Institute were allowed to work within the Order. Boys who completed their lessons at the Institute became members of the Black Guard who guarded Ellevere from the fey, the Red Guard, who protected the Popes, or Teachers of the Faith, who could teach the ways of the Order. Girls became Sisters of the Order and taught at the Institute, or they could become members of the Black Guard if they were ruled barren. But Kaisa didn't want to become a Sister of the Order or a member of the Black Guard. No, Kaisa wanted to rise above them all and become a Pope's Page.

Her heart leapt at the thought. She would be the right hand of Pope Sersius, the ruler of Barrensmere. Higher in station than Sisters of the Order, Teachers of the Faith and even the Black and Red Guards, the Pope's Page was a revered position. And Kaisa wanted it more than anything.

"I wish I could master my mind like that," Jovanna muttered. "Order myself not to think about something."

It doesn't work all the time, Kaisa wanted to say. If it did, she wouldn't be plagued by her mother's face. Wouldn't see her delight reflected in her handfuls of silver coins as Kaisa was dragged away. She wouldn't be haunted by thoughts of the secretive Anointing ritual. Her stomach twisted.

"I'm going to prove it to them," she murmured, more to herself than Hollis and Jovanna. "I'm going to prove all of them wrong. That I can make it to my Anointing. That they were wrong to give me up."

"We were children, Kai," Hollis said softly. "It wasn't our fault they gave us up."

Kaisa rested her chin on her knees, wrapping her arms around her shins. Maybe—maybe if she had been a more obedient child, her parents wouldn't have given her up. A slow ache spread across her chest. She should have worked harder.

Your fault, a voice whispered in the back of her head.

Kaisa shoved her sadness down deep inside her. Thoughts like that would only distract her from her task.

"I've got to sleep," Kaisa said, hoisting herself upright. She hauled Hollis and Jovanna up as well. "I'm covering Rachael's shift tomorrow morning."

Pride swept through her. Kaisa had worked hard to be promoted to care for the Pope, a task only the most devoted Scholars were allowed to do. But that wasn't good enough for Kaisa. She needed to become his Page.

She and Jovanna rushed back to their room. A few Blights stopped Kaisa on the way back, asking her how to set up for the morning service. Kaisa explained it to them in detail, putting their minds at ease.

They finally made it back to their room. The brown walls were devoid of all warmth—the room only big enough to fit her and Jovanna's beds. Kaisa pulled back the taupe curtain that shielded her mattress. She froze. On the quilt lay a small card inscribed with delicate script.

Scholar Kaisa,
Congratulations on your Anointing.
May the Twins watch over you.
- Pope Sersius

Signed by the Pope himself. An honor she had never heard endowed upon any Scholar before. Kaisa fell to her knees, clasped her hands together and sent thanks to the Twins. In two days, she was going to be Anointed. She was going to be a true member of the Order. Not just some rat her parents had sold the first opportunity they'd had. No, the Twins had chosen her for something special. They had plucked her from the rabble and given her a choice: stay in the life she was born to or rise above.

Now she would rise.

3

LARKEN

Airodion

Larken's teeth chattered more from nerves than the chill.

Saja's breath billowed before him; snow still caked in his beard. Blue tiles lined the frosted stone walls, making the room glow faintly. A throne sat upon a raised dais, a huge slab of sharp ice. It cut upwards in a diagonal slash, every shade of blue and white imaginable marbled within. The jagged tips looked like blades, and Larken knew without a doubt that if she were to place a finger on one of the edges it would draw blood.

But it was the queen sitting upon the throne who they had come to see.

She radiated such power that it rippled through the air, filling the space to the vaulted ceiling. A tall, spiked crown of ice rested on her head. Despite its obvious weight, she bore it effortlessly. She tilted her head, her short white hair almost blue from the light of the crown. She sat upright on the throne, her hands loose on the armrests of the chair. Her gown was skintight, glittering as though it was made up of hundreds of shards of ice.

It had taken them what felt like an eternity to reach the Winter Court capital city, White Keep. Larken despised the constant cold, but she couldn't deny the beauty of the city.

Their journey through the Winter Court had given them all the information they needed: that Finder had been declared unfit to rule and was imprisoned at Shadeshelm.

And Dahey ruled as regent in his stead.

Larken's fists clenched at her sides.

Saja believed that Finder was relatively safe—for now. But they knew Dahey would not rest until he had the powers and that he would seek the Guardian's council to find out how to take them. They just had to hope that Dahey had not taken them already.

Saja approached the dais, Larken quickening her steps to keep pace with his longer strides. She had been at the big warrior's side for weeks—refusing to let him out of her sight. He was all she had left—her parents were in Ballamor, Madden was dead, Finder was imprisoned and Dahey had betrayed them. Her heartbeat quickened at the thought of losing Saja, at the thought of being alone in Airodion. She bit the inside of her cheek.

Focus, she reminded herself. Their footsteps were quiet on the marble, making Larken feel incredibly small. It was like walking through a snow-covered forest when a hush was draped over the entire world.

"Queen Isra," Saja bowed, and Larken hastily dropped into a curtsy.

Isra rose from her throne and approached them, sauntering down the steps.

"Saja Roak," Isra said warmly. Larken blinked—she hadn't heard Saja's surname before. Hadn't known that the fey even used surnames. Saja smiled, clasping forearms with the Winter Court Queen. Isra was more beautiful up close; she had a round, pale face and high cheekbones. Angular eyebrows framed light blue eyes. Her hair was a striking stark white, shaved almost to the scalp on the sides but longer on top. Shards of ice glittered throughout her hair, making the strands gleam in the light.

Larken's gut twisted in anticipation. Saja had said that Finder and the queen were old friends—but how could he be so certain that Isra wouldn't betray them?

We thought Dahey was our friend, too, she thought bitterly. His betrayal was still lodged in her heart like a blade. She felt it with every pulsing beat.

Still, the queen was their most powerful potential ally. She had the magic, resources and soldiers. They hoped that she would talk to Dahey and demand that he release Finder, and if that failed, lend them the soldiers they needed to free Finder by force.

Larken's heart sank. The plan had seemed so solid during their travels, but now, faced with the queen, Larken wondered if they had been fools to come here. Isra hadn't helped them in their battle against the Starveling, so why would she choose to help them now? But Larken had to cling to her last shred of hope.

"How does it feel to be a queen, my friend?" Saja asked.

"Damn good, I must say." Isra grinned. She looked as if she were about to say more, her eyes darkening, then she stopped herself, turning towards Larken instead. "Forgive me. My name is Isra, Queen of the Winter Court."

"I'm Larken McLeary. Erm, from Ballamor. In the human realm."

Isra took her hand and squeezed it gently. "Welcome to White Keep, Larken. Rumors have been flying through Airodion of late. That Finder has been put on trial for crimes against his court. They say his cousin Dahey has taken up the role as regent, and that he rules with a heavy heart."

"That's a lie," Larken spat. Isra's eyebrows rose. "Dahey planned this from the beginning. He always wanted to rule the Autumn Court."

"Larken, I understand your anger, but surely you know that even if Dahey wanted to be king, there is no way to guarantee that the powers would have passed to him. Why would he attempt to usurp Finder without the guarantee that he would become king in his stead?"

Larken bit the inside of her cheek. Isra knew about the Guardian's perverse language; surely, she could guess that it would be capable of such things.

"Finder has been put on trial unfairly," Saja said. "We've come to ask for your aide in freeing him."

Isra studied them. "He was put on trial for killing the Starveling. I have no idea why Finder would put his court at risk by staging a direct attack on our king."

Tied to the stones, unable to move. Finder, exploding with power. The flames, burning her, burning everything as she screamed and tried to escape—

Larken shook her head, ignoring the black spots swimming at the edges of her vision. Something was wrong with her. She could barely breathe around a flame, and she had made Saja douse their evening fires as they had travelled to the Winter Court more than once just because the scent of the smoke made her gag violently. Even talking about the night they had fought the Starveling caused her breath to hitch, and the other day when she and Saja had discussed it, she had nearly fainted on the back of Saja's horse, Arobhinn.

Finder will know some way to heal you, she told herself. *He healed your body from the flame. He can also heal your mind. Once you get him back, all your fears will disappear,* Larken told herself.

"He had no choice." A muscle jumped in Saja's jaw.

Larken shifted. They hadn't come here to reveal the exact details of why Finder overthrew the Starveling, or how the Guardian's knife came into play. Isra could still turn them over to Dahey and forge an alliance with the new regent.

"A shift of power so quickly after the Starveling's demise is not much cause for question, nor do I disagree with the fact that Finder put his court at risk by attacking him. That being said, I do believe there is something strange happening in the Autumn Court, as well as in all of Airodion," Isra said carefully. "I wish to speak with you both at length about it, as well as my fellow court rulers, before making any decisions. Finder has been my friend for many years. Beyond that, I believe he is a good ruler. I have no remorse for the Starveling's demise, as his tithe was taxing on me. Still, to involve the Winter Court could put my people at risk. I will think on your words, and we will talk later—over our evening meal, perhaps. For now, you have had a long journey, and I would be most pleased if you would stay in White Keep as my guests."

Larken's heart leapt into her throat. No, they had come all this way—Isra had to help them. "Please, my queen," Larken tried to keep the raw desperation from her voice. "We know of no one else who can help us."

Their only other allies were the Warga—a clan of female shapeshifters that had helped them on their journey to find the Guardian—but they lived far to the northeast in the Wyld. Larken had already suggested that they ask the leader of the Warga clan, Remira, for help, but Saja had told her that the wolf shifters held no sway in court politics and that their clan was too small to help them free Finder by force.

"I will not speak of this matter until later," Isra said, a touch of ice coating her words.

Larken's heart sank.

"It was a pleasure meeting you, Larken," Isra said as guards came in and ushered them from the throne room.

4

DAHEY

Airodion

Dahey's legs moved of their own accord, marching him towards the being he had sworn his oath to. Surprise rippled over him when his oath led him to the Stone Circle.

Well, if he thinks he can replace the Starveling, he'll realize how wrong he is, Dahey thought to himself. Without the Starveling, the court rulers had no checks on their power. Dahey would not serve under another king.

Dahey pressed his lips together, his hand drifting to the bundle of cloth wrapped at his belt. He knew there was more to the weapon than the Guardian let on, else he would not want it back so desperately. Dahey hadn't dared to touch the naked blade. The power was tempting, yes, but he'd seen how easily Finder had been overcome. Dahey remembered the power Finder had commanded as he wielded the knife against the Starveling. How his cousin had exploded into a pillar of pure fire.

No, Dahey would not touch the blade. He had no desire to perish beneath the flame. He wanted to *command* the flame.

A chittering sound made the hair on the back of his neck rise. A creature emerged from the slender trees. It was white and hairless with sagging, wrinkly skin. Spines protruded from its head and back. It opened its beak and emitted another chittering sound.

Master has returned, it said.

Dahey nodded stiffly at the Fomari. The Guardian had taught him how to make a deal with the creatures, and they had obeyed him, killing Finder's tithe girl and attempting to trap Saja and Larken at the bridge.

You owe us what was promised, the Fomari said. *Flesh.*

He had promised the creatures flesh, either human or fey. He had no faery flesh to give them—nor would he ever sacrifice members of his court to the Fomari, but the humans...the humans he didn't care about.

"The bridge is open," he said. "Take your kin to Ellevere and feast. But then our bargain is done." He had no desire to work with the foul creatures any longer.

The Fomari chittered happily. *As you command, Master.*

The Fomari disappeared into the trees, more shrieking calls echoing through the sickly forest. Dahey shoved down his guilt. They would surely go to Larken's village first, as it was closest to the bridge.

You owed them what was promised, he reminded himself. *It was human flesh or the flesh of your court, and you would never put your people at risk.*

Smoothing down his jacket, Dahey entered the Stone Circle. His mind jerked back to the last time he had seen the Guardian in the Wyld. Then, the sky had been dark with glamour. Then, Larken had been with them, and Saja.

And Madden.

Dahey's lip curled. How dare Finder take everything from him, put his *dornán* at risk? They had sworn to protect Finder, had tied their souls to him so they could feel when one of their companions was hurt or dead, and he had abused that power. It was Finder's fault that Madden was dead. Dahey swallowed around the ache in his throat. He didn't need Saja or Madden. He didn't need Finder. He didn't need anyone.

The Autumn Court is about to enter a new age. And I shall be the one to lead it.

Not his father. Not Finder. *Him.* Dahey would be the one to lead it to glory. His kin had never deserved the honor of being ruler of the Autumn Court. Neither of them had wanted it.

Trees, burning with flame. His father screaming, hands lifted to the sky as it rained ash.

"Father, please!" Dahey cried. He had woken up in the nursery alone, choking on the smoke. He thought the world was ending, but his father was the source of the blaze.

His father turned to him, his features cold and hard as cut glass.

"Please," Dahey whispered. "I'm scared."

His father knelt, his robes pooling beneath him. He opened his arms, and Dahey ran to him, shivering in his father's embrace. His father was cold, though the fire raged around them.

"I will make you strong," his father whispered. "I will burn the fear itself from inside you."

The cold that surrounded his father slowly ebbed, warming until his skin became hot to the touch. Dahey squirmed, but his father held him tight. Held him as the flames leapt from his skin, consuming Dahey with its touch. And then, all Dahey knew was blind agony as his father burned him.

Dahey screamed for his mother, screamed for Finder, but that night, as with so many others, no one had been there to save him.

Dahey had seen what power did to a weak mind. Saw how it turned his father to madness, and Finder into a fool. But the fire hadn't wanted his father—it had left once it realized how corrupt its vessel had become. It had chosen Finder instead, but it had chosen wrong. Finder feared the powers. Finder had constantly rebelled against his rule instead of treasuring it. If Dahey had gotten tangled in a life debt to a human as Finder had, he would have gone to the Starveling and begged for forgiveness. He would have died for his court if necessary.

But it had all worked out in Dahey's favor. The Starveling was dead, and now Dahey would have no limits to his power.

Finder thought he had suffered because of his powers, but he didn't know the true pain the flames could cause. Dahey did. He was the only one who understood. He was the only one who deserved and respected its power. He straightened his shoulders. Finder had rejected his power over fire and death, but Dahey would embrace it. Use it as Finder and his father never could—for the good of his court.

He didn't see the Guardian approach, but rather felt another presence join his. Dahey spun around.

"Little regent, come to see me at last."

Dahey frowned, trying not to let the title annoy him. He wondered briefly how the Guardian knew that he was regent. No matter. Likely, he had spies along with the rest.

The Guardian looked the same, his hood drawn low over his face, concealing his features. A voice that sounded like rocks sliding against each other. At least he was no longer cursed to speak in those wretched rhymes. The hairs on the back of Dahey's neck rose as did a fierce desire to discover what was under that hood.

"I will be king soon enough," Dahey said, aiming for what he hoped was a civil tone. He had no desire to fight with the Guardian. He simply wanted information, and then the Guardian could have his knife. He clenched his sweating palms. The oath demanded that he return the knife. Dahey could only beg for answers.

No. A king does not beg. A king demands.

"Have you come to fulfill our bargain?" The Guardian's hooded head tilted.

"Yes," Dahey replied smoothly, letting his hand rest on his scabbard. "Once you uphold your end of our agreement."

"Have I not given you everything you desire? You brought your cousin to his knees and dragged him away in chains. The Starveling is dead, and you rule the Autumn Court. Have I not done everything you've asked?"

"And yet, you just mentioned your own failure. You said the knife's magic would make Finder's powers choose me."

"I couldn't tell you everything, little regent. I didn't know if you would have the gall to go through with your plan. A need for answers ensured that you returned to me, even if your courage failed."

"You made me swear an oath," Dahey growled.

The Guardian chuckled. "Another precaution."

"Are you going to tell me or not?" Dahey seethed.

"There is a way to force the magic's hand," the Guardian said, "though it will not be pleasant. It has never been attempted by a faery before, but I am curious to know the results. It could be the beginning of something extraordinary."

"Tell me," Dahey snapped before he could help himself.

"Return my knife."

Dahey carefully untied the bundle from his belt. "And the powers can be forced without—" he swallowed. "Without Finder's death?"

"Yes." A smile touched the Guardian's words.

Dahey's heart began to pound. The language this being had created was unnatural. And it didn't slip Dahey's notice how easily the Guardian was offering up the information. Almost like he wanted Dahey to use it.

The second the Guardian lifted a finger against his court, Dahey would find a way to end him. But he needed the powers. He needed to be king. He had to protect his people, and this was the only way. He knew the Guardian believed he could manipulate him, but the Guardian had no idea who he was dealing with. Dahey knew how to stay one step ahead. Always.

He handed the bundle to the Guardian.

"Tell me what I have to do."

5

***

THE GUARDIAN

Airodion

The Guardian spoke his language, relishing the way his tongue curled around the words, flying through the phrases. He carved with his knife, parting flesh and making it anew.

It was like stretching a muscle that had been cramped in place for centuries. The Starveling had twisted the Guardian's words into a rhyming curse as punishment so he couldn't speak his beloved language. The Starveling had feared the Guardian's language, hated how he had given power to those his father deemed lesser. He had revolted against his father once and had failed. The Starveling, Dark Priestesses and the court rulers had imprisoned him.

But he was free now. Not that his father was alive to see it. His father had scorned him since he was a babe. His father had only ever cared for power and had seen him as weak.

He would show his father power.

The Guardian looked up from his work, breathing in deeply. The scent of rot and decay greeted him. Sharp stones and gnarled shrubs littered the ground. The trees were pale and sickly, their branches cold as ice. It was as if the earth had wanted to reject his father.

He had returned to his father's domain—the Stone Circle where the Starveling had called the tithe—to perform his work. Yes, he would take up his father's mantle of ruler, but he would become more than his father ever could have imagined.

The Guardian lifted his hands from his work. It had been a tree dryad once. Now it was something *more*. His language had transformed her into something great. Her face had flattened, her skin turning from molten tree bark to striped flesh. She raised her tattered wings.

The Furyons had all been killed in the second war. But now they would rise again. He would need flying beasts to spread his message.

The creature bowed. *Master*.

The Guardian smiled. In days of old, mind-speak was common between the ancients. He gave it as a gift to his creations.

Soon, all creatures will be equal. No more power dynamics, as things were with my father, he cooed to his new Furyon. His father had relished in the fact that he was the most powerful being in all of Airodion. Had seen everything and everyone as beneath him, even his own son. He had sucked power from the court rulers. The Starveling had controlled all under his rule, and punished all, even those who were obedient to him.

No kings, no court rulers, only power. For everyone.

The court rulers didn't concern him. Obsessed with their petty squabbles, they didn't have the strength to stand against him. Only when they combined their powers with the Starveling and the Dark Priestesses had they been able to imprison him.

A seedling of doubt crept into his mind. They could ally themselves with other creatures of old, beings who might have the strength to stand against him. The Guardian shook his head. No. He would go to his allies from the war first. The court rulers would fall in line, either by choice or by force. If they refused to join him, his army would sweep through and crush them. He had already turned his sights toward his first target. And once their court fell, the rest would submit.

He would free magic for all. Then none would have to suffer as he had. But he would keep just enough of the language to himself to ensure he was never imprisoned again.

The Guardian pulled a round, onyx stone from his robes.

His father's orb. Each of the court rulers had two orbs, one that could speak to their respective Pope and the other that could talk to the Starveling. Yet the Starveling possessed an orb that could communicate with any of the Popes and any of the court rulers simultaneously. The Guardian had already been in communication with the rulers of Ellevere and had told them about the Starveling's demise.

He placed his hand on the orb. "Have you accepted my offer?"

After a moment, a chorus of voices answered from the orb, all talking over one another. The Guardian swallowed his irritation. Yes, he would banish hierarchies, but the humans...they were far beneath him. Any who refused to join him would become fodder for his army.

"We need more time," one finally said. The Guardian recognized his voice—Pope Sersius.

"No waiting," the Guardian snapped. "I will have the human world as well—but until I can figure out how to heal the chasm, my Furyons will serve as my eyes and ears. Their presence will be...unpleasant. I suggest you use them as incentive for your people to join your army. Once you and your people join me, they will be safe. Until then, my Furyons will consume whomever they please."

He released the orb. He didn't need the Popes on his side—but if he was to take Ellevere it would make things easier. A second army, rallying the humans to his side so they didn't flock to the fey as they had during the first and second wars. He turned to his Furyon.

Fly, he commanded. And the beast took to the sky, wings pounding towards Ellevere.

He turned to the next dryad.

"Please," she begged, but he ignored her cries. He would build his army. Once he used his language on his creatures, they were completely devoted to him. His father had made the courts forget him, aside from the court rulers, so he would have to spend precious time building his army. But soon, all of Airodion and Ellevere would know him by his true name:

Ziegan.

6

LARKEN

Airodion

Larken sat on the snowy ground, watching the Cynyadas spin their webs.

She only left her room at White Keep to go on a freezing walk in the game park. To her delight, she found that the Winter Court had Cynyadas—the spider creatures that spun art in their webs. She and the rest of her companions had stumbled across them during their quest to find the Guardian. A bolt of pain shot through Larken's heart. Not long ago, she had spoken to another Cynyada with Finder at her side. He had wanted to show her something beautiful in Airodion. She glanced at the trees, almost able to hear her companions' laughter filtering through the boughs.

One grey-speckled Cynyada began a portrait of Larken. It captured her perfectly—round face, upturned nose, her mass of curly blonde hair, though in the web the strands were silver. The Cynyada paused, then began strumming frantically on its web. Larken watched as the threads vibrated, sending ripples to the web next to it. The neighboring Cynyada gave a little giggle and strummed something back.

An idea spiked through her, and Larken scrambled to her feet. "Can

30

you communicate with other Cynadas through your web?" Larken asked the grey-speckled Cynyada.

The tiny creature nodded.

Larken motioned to a web opposite them. "These messages, how far can they travel?"

"To any Cynyada web in Airodion," the Cynyada chirped, clearly pleased that Larken was happy.

She and Saja had been searching for a way to get a message to Finder but had no way to do so while Finder was in the Shadeshelm dungeons. But if there were Cynyadas in the Winter Court, there had to be some in the Autumn Court as well. She could let Finder know that they hadn't given up on him, that they were searching for a way to free him and that he just had to hold on a little while longer.

"Can you send a message for me?"

7
_____

KAISA

Ellevere

Jovanna didn't move when Kaisa woke the next morning. Kaisa had to be up earlier than normal for Rachael's shift. Students at the Institute had no days off, but whenever a student fell ill, Kaisa covered for them. While Rachael was a Scholar as well, she wasn't quite as distinguished as Kaisa, so she mainly cleaned and prepared prayer rooms and delivered food to the prisoners. Kaisa tried not to wrinkle her nose.

No task is menial when done in service to the Twins.

She hurried down to the palace kitchens, making a breakfast tray for Pope Sersius. The kitchen staff prepared the food, but they didn't make the tray. That was Kaisa's job, and she took it seriously.

Kaisa carefully filled the tray. Three strips of bacon. Soft boiled eggs. Brown bread with warm butter. One cake of black pudding. Tea with enough sugar to make her teeth hurt.

Once she became the Pope's Page, she could devote herself entirely to caring for Pope Sersius. Tasting his meals, dressing him, delivering messages, traveling with him—she would do it all until she or the Pope died. His last Page had died several years before, and now he had no one, not wanting anyone from the previous Scholar classes. Kaisa would prove that she was worth the wait.

"*You are everything he's been waiting for,*" her tutors told her. "*The Twins have given you a gift, you must not waste it.*"

Keeping the tray perfectly level, she climbed the stairs to the Pope's chambers. She left the tray outside the massive wrought iron door.

She breezed back to the kitchen, almost stumbling over a Cradle who darted out of one of the corridors.

"Kaisa?" The little girl blinked at her through long lashes.

Kaisa knelt before the girl. "Yes?" Kaisa had seen her once before—the first time the girl had set foot in the Institute after her parents had sold her.

The girl rubbed her toe into the polished stone floor. "I didn't know who else to go to." Her lip trembled. "I—I soiled my bed."

Kaisa's heart squeezed in her chest. If the girls were caught with a soiled bed, they had to sleep in it the following night.

Kaisa took her hand. "We'll take it to the laundry together," she said gently. The girl beamed up at her, and Kaisa's heart swelled.

After helping the Cradle girl with her sheets, Kaisa hurried back to the kitchens.

"Kaisa!" a voice boomed.

Kaisa's face broke out into a smile at her favorite tutor's voice. Sister Abitha had taught Kaisa during her Cradle year. She was strict—but kind.

"Sister Abitha," Kaisa greeted her.

The huge woman bustled towards Kaisa, pulling her into a tight hug. "I heard a whisper that one of my Cradles was looking for you." Sister Abitha eyed Kaisa. "Something about a soiled bed?"

Kaisa shrugged. "A girl asked for directions to the laundry. I did nothing more."

Sister Abitha squeezed Kaisa's arm. "You have a servant's heart, Kaisa," she murmured. "The Twins have truly blessed you. One of my brightest pupils..." She shook her head. "We need you as a Sister of the Order, teaching the next generation of young ones." She held up a hand before Kaisa could protest. "I know, I know. You wish to become a Pope's Page. And I can think of no one more worthy."

Kaisa squeezed the woman's hand. "Thank you, Sister Abitha."

Sister Abitha's eyes glistened. "Now, no more helping my Cradles out of their punishments, you hear?" she said gruffly. Still, she softened her tone with a wink.

Kaisa laughed, then hurried off to the kitchens to pick up the slop designated for the prisoners. She couldn't help her gag—this food wasn't worthy for the pigs. Moldy scraps scattered with maggots. She hefted the ladle and bucket, breathing through her mouth to avoid the stench.

The Order of the Twins centered on justice, not mercy. The palace dungeons reflected that core virtue. If she thought the stench from the buckets was bad... nothing compared to the reek that clung to the stones of the dungeons.

It had taken Kaisa years to get over her squeamish stomach. Like a gardener ripping out weeds by the roots to protect the tree, so did the Popes cull the non-believers to protect the faith. But everything they did, they did for the Twins. And the Twins blessed true believers beyond measure. Her heart jumped—only one more day until her Anointing. Then she would prove to everyone that she was worth something. That her parents were wrong to throw her away like garbage. She could barely breathe when she thought about it.

But she had a task to do now.

She ladled the food through a slot in the doors. She tried to ignore the moans and the sound of hands scraping slop from the floor. Kaisa let the sounds wash over her, let herself acknowledge their pain, and sent a prayer to the Twins for a speedy suffering. It was necessary for them to come to the light of the Twins. It was all necessary.

She almost screamed when the ladle caught, dragging her arm up through the slat nearly to her elbow.

"Stop," a voice croaked.

Kaisa released the handle and fell back. The ladle disappeared into the slat.

"No!" she cried, crawling as close to the slender opening as she dared. The prisoner could hurt himself, or a guard. Even she wouldn't be able to escape punishment for this.

"I just...want...to talk," the voice from the dark murmured, "to someone who isn't making me scream."

"Give me the ladle," she said, much calmer than she felt, "and I will."

The voice—a man's voice, chuckled. "This ladle is the most power I've had in months. I'm not giving it up yet."

Kaisa scowled but said nothing. If it was conversation he wanted, he wasn't about to get it.

"You aren't the usual girl," the voice mused. "Is she dead?"

"No!" Kaisa blurted, aghast.

The man chuckled again. "Force of habit. I'm used to death down here. Everyone dies in these cells eventually."

"That's not true," Kaisa said. "You can repent. Begin a new life in the light of the Twins."

Pope Sersius had many prisoners, but none of them were in the dungeons for long. The majority of prisoners were accused of heresy, which had an easy enough solution: confession, then repentance. After confession and depending on the seriousness of the crime, the accused could repent their crimes through various levels of pain. Ones who could not or would not repent were sentenced to death.

Most of the prisoners here were in the midst of their repentance. The confession process didn't take long.

"Start a new life without a couple of limbs, I'd reckon. Or teeth. Or a tongue."

Kaisa narrowed her eyes. "No one said repentance was easy. You have to mean it."

"Oh, I'm sure they all mean it when the branding irons and knives come out. I would know, I was trained in torture, same as all the members of the Black Guard."

Kaisa's stomach dropped. This man had been a member of the Black

Guard? To be in this dungeon meant he betrayed the Twins, or his sacred duty, in some way.

"How does a member of the Black Guard end up in Barrensmere's dungeon?" Kaisa asked, her curiosity getting the better of her.

"I found out a bit of information I shouldn't have. Then I tried to stop a bad thing from happening again. And I don't even know if I succeeded." The voice broke. "I know you won't heed my advice, but since I can't seem to learn my lesson, I'm going to tell you anyway: get out of here, girl. The Guard knows some of the darkest secrets of the Order, and no part of it is safe. No part of it."

"I'm to be an Anointed member," Kaisa bristled. "I came from nothing, and I will have everything. All of it is because of Pope Sersius, because of the Order."

"An Anointed member?" The man's voice turned sharp. "And do you know what happens during the Anointing? Have they told you that?"

"Of course not. Only those who have been Anointed know what occurs during the ritual."

"Why do you think they haven't told you?" the man hissed. "Because if people knew the truth about all these damn ceremonies, all these secrets, there wouldn't *be* an Order at all."

"Stop it!" Kaisa cried, scrambling to her feet. "You won't talk that way about my faith, heretic. You deserve to rot in this place."

Silence dropped over them, disturbed only by the muffled sobbing and moans of the other prisoners.

Nerves nipped at her. Her tutors had warned her that the task would be difficult. It was their final test, after all. But the Anointing couldn't be bad. They wouldn't punish the Scholars, not when they had made it so far. No, she would pass the test. She wouldn't be left to serve out her sentence at the outpost colonies in disgrace.

"Maybe I do," the voice finally said. "But I tried. I tried to make it right. And I can die with that knowledge. The question is, once *you* know the truth, can you live with it?"

Part of her wanted to run from the dungeon and never return. Part of her wanted to drop to her knees and beg the man to tell her what he believed to be the truth. For some part of his words had wormed its way into her brain, making her doubt herself. She wasn't blind, she knew of the Order's brutality. But she had always been exempt. What if her luck finally ran out during the Anointing? What if she failed?

Her heart dropped to her toes. She couldn't fail, not after she had come so far. Not when she was about to prove herself to her parents, her tutors, even Pope Sersius himself.

"No, I won't tell you, girl," the voice said. Her heart fell at his words. "I ruined one girl's life with the truth already. Just leave after if you can. Try to forget. Because once you start digging up secrets, you can't forget them. And this religion isn't kind to those who discover them. But if you can't escape, or if you don't want to leave this life behind..."

The ladle extended through the slot. "An Anointing gift. From Castor Longshanks."

8

LARKEN

Airodion

Larken and Saja followed a servant to Isra's private dining room, where they met alone with the queen. The room was gorgeous, slate grey with painted blue embellishments carved into swirling designs. The small dining table was made of glass. Isra sat at the head of the table with Larken and Saja on either side of her.

Larken twisted her hands in her lap. She had settled on a simple white gown that wrapped around her shoulders in an elegant twist. Her feet rested in jewel-encrusted shoes with a tiny heel. It was kind of the Winter Court Queen to allow Larken to borrow any clothes she needed.

Isra tilted her head, her crown placed regally on her short white hair. Tall and jagged, the crown had molten grey and white crystal carved into a beautiful castle. Larken squinted. It wasn't just a castle—it was an exact replica of White Keep. Isra noticed her stare and grinned.

"Do you like it?"

"It's incredible," Larken said.

Isra removed her crown and placed it on the table for Larken to inspect. The rim of the crown was the mountain range that surrounded

White Keep. In the center rose the citadel itself, complete with minuscule markets, roads and finally, the castle. Isra trailed a finger around the edges of the crown.

"It is comforting to me, to always have it with me. Whenever I leave White Keep, it is still with me. And it is quite literally always on my mind." She smiled a coy grin. "Even the weather is the same. Luckily, you came on a cloudless day, lest you would barely be able to see the details of the town. The worst are the snowstorms. I hear the wind howling day and night through the spokes." Isra pointed to the mountains, and Larken smiled.

"Is it glamour?" Larken asked.

Isra shook her head. "No. The crystal was mined from our mountains and contains magical properties. Long ago, the mines in the Winter Court mountains contained all kinds of magical oddities. When it was carved to look like White Keep, it took on the properties of the city of its own accord."

A servant leaned over her, placing a steaming platter of food on the table.

"Thank you," Larken said when he'd finished, smiling at him. The servant gave her a smile and a small nod in return.

The clattering of silver cutlery ensued as they helped themselves to the spread. Larken went immediately for the stew, hoping that something warm would help ward off the constant chill she felt in the palace. It brimmed with spices and salt, thick and creamy with chunks of potato and onion. She went for the bread next, a thick brown bram that would rival her father's baking. No meat was found anywhere on the table. Like the Autumn Court, the Winter Court fey did not eat meat.

After stuffing herself with bread, stew, lentil pastries, and three glasses of the hot, spiced wine, Larken thought she could eat and drink no more. That was, of course, until dessert was served: four-layer chocolate cake with peppermint icing.

Saja's eyes brightened, and Isra laughed, tipping her wine glass in a salute.

"I happen to know that Saja loves chocolate, and the Winter Court has the finest chocolate in all of Airodion." Isra smiled devilishly. "It's the only thing that makes him come back and visit me."

Larken smiled at the queen. She liked talking with Isra; she was open and easy to talk to. She knew that they had come to convince the queen to help free Finder, but perhaps... perhaps Isra could help Larken heal her mind. It felt personal, and after all, she didn't know the queen, but Larken was desperate for her fear of fire to go away. As a court ruler, Isra would have the power to heal. If Isra could help her, then she wouldn't have to wait for Finder.

Isra motioned for Larken to help herself to the cake, and Larken obliged her.

"I appreciate you dining with me." Isra smiled at them from behind the rim of her wine glass. She reached out to pour Larken another glass, but Larken covered the rim with her hand, shaking her head.

"Don't tempt me," she moaned. "I can already feel my head begin to pound."

Isra chuckled. "Faery wine can do marvelous things; and cause marvelous hangovers."

Larken smiled. "Thank you for preparing this meal for us. You've been so kind to allow us to stay here."

"I know you were... displeased at the end of our last meeting."

Larken fingered the rim of her glass. She tasted blood. Her tongue prodded the ruined flesh of her cheek—worn thin from constant chewing.

"We understand it will take time to sway you to our cause," Larken said. "What can we do to make you consider helping us?"

Isra's brows lowered thoughtfully. "You are a rather extraordinary girl, Larken," she murmured. "It is curious indeed that all of your fellow humans died that night of the tithe, yet you remain. It is also curious that you happened to be the chosen human when Finder decided to overthrow the Starveling. Almost as if it were meant to be. You and Finder are connected somehow, or else, why would you—a girl he chose to sacrifice—be here, pleading for his life?"

Larken's leg bounced beneath the table. Her soul had been tied to

Finder's after she had saved his life, tangling them both in a life debt. She could still feel the phantom tug of the golden thread of magic that had bound them together. When one was cut, the other bled. A part of her now felt empty without him. Though it had been a relief when their life debt had ended, a part of her missed her bond with Finder. How they were never alone.

"I'm nothing special," she said.

Isra leaned back, a slow smile crossing her lips. "Come now. I insist you elaborate on your extremely interesting story, or I will be forced to other conclusions. Perhaps you wooed Finder and now come to me to save your lover's life, and I'm afraid I will not risk the lives of my people for romantic whims."

"It's not like that," Larken insisted. Her breath caught as she remembered Finder pressing his head into the crook of her neck as they rode, drawing her closer. His scent of crushed autumn leaves and spices.

Saja cut in. "Do you really think I would help just any girl taken with Finder? You act as though tithe girls have never fallen in love with him before. You know this is different."

A dark flush crept up Larken's face. Of course, other girls would have been stricken with Finder. She could hardly blame them. But Larken had never thought of them before, never considered how she might not be the only one that found him so alluring. And oh, Twins, what if Brigid had felt that way about him? A pang of sadness struck her heart at the thought of her friend. It had only been a little over a year since Finder had chosen Brigid, and her dearest friend in the world had been taken from her. The Starveling's magic had forced Finder to choose the girl who was the happiest, and he had chosen Brigid.

And then, when the Starveling's magic had commanded him to, he had carved her heart from her chest.

Larken swallowed, guilt clawing at her. Finder had no choice but to kill Brigid—the Starveling's magic had forced him to. But she had grown so close to him during their travels. She had seen him for what he was and knew he was worth saving.

She would never forget Brigid. Would never fully forgive Finder for what he had done, but she still knew in the deepest part of her that he deserved to be saved. That he deserved to be king.

Isra waved a hand. "Oh, force my hand, will you. I must know what makes Larken so special."

Larken knew that she and Saja had to take a risk, or Isra would turn them away. She didn't trust Isra—she had learned the hard way not to be trusting of everyone she met, courtesy of Dahey. But it was a gamble she was going to have to take.

"I saved his life."

Saja turned to her, eyes wide. Isra's brows lifted. Larken took a deep breath.

"Finder didn't choose me, he chose another girl from my village." Larken brought up Rosin's face in her mind. Dark hair. Willowy frame. So like Brigid and yet...

"Last year, my dearest friend Brigid was taken. She was like a sister to me. I was determined to find her, so when I didn't get chosen, I followed Finder and Rosin across the bridge into Airodion. I caught up to them just as they were brutally attacked by the Fomari. The girl, Rosin, died. I saved Finder's life, and then he owed me a life debt."

How simple the story seemed as it poured out of her mouth. How everything that had happened to her, changed her, originated from one human girl crossing the bridge when she wasn't supposed to.

She swallowed, looked Isra straight in the eyes and told her everything.

Isra said nothing, allowing her to finish. Saja helped gaps in her story here and there, but for the most part, he remained silent too, letting her tell her story to the fullest. It felt cathartic to tell the story at last, and some deep tension in Larken eased. Despite her faery companions being with her almost constantly and sharing her experiences, she was still a human and was different from them. She told Isra her version of the story, the human version. How it felt to be mortal in the realm of the fey.

And she could breathe again.

"Dahey betrayed us," she finished. "He practically tried to have Saja and I killed, and he took Finder."

Isra remained quiet for a moment, her eyes pensive. Finally, she spoke.

"And yet, here you are, still trying to save him. The faery that had been murdering girls from your village. The faery that almost burned you to ashes."

Isra was right. Here she was, choosing the fey again. But Finder needed her. Though they had only known each other for a short while, whenever she had needed him, he had been there. And whenever he had needed her, she had been there too.

"It's Finder," Larken murmured. "He's worth saving."

She didn't look at Saja, but she could feel him looking at her. Knew that he felt the same. Everything was riding on Isra, if they failed, if she handed them over to Dahey...

Dahey could not rule the Autumn Court. She had traveled with him, seen his coldness. She had seen the love he had for Finder and his *dornán,* and he had still been willing to betray them. Finder had cared for the humans, had fought against the tithe. When the Starveling fell, the magic sealing the bridge had disappeared. Larken bit her lip. The humans needed to be protected, and Larken knew without a doubt that Dahey would do nothing. He cared only for his court, for the fey.

"I believe you, Larken."

Larken sagged against her chair. Isra closed her eyes briefly. "I believe you, but I cannot help you. Not yet."

Her heart crumpled.

"I know you must think me terribly cruel. I believe what you say about Dahey's betrayal. Truthfully, I would much rather have Finder on the throne. But that doesn't change our reality. If I send troops to the Autumn Court with the intention of freeing Finder, the Autumn Court will retaliate. We would be at war with them, and with good reason. If another court brought troops to my court to settle a sovereignty issue, I would be livid as well. We as separate courts do not like to meddle in each others' affairs. And the one good thing about being ruled by the Starveling was that we didn't have to. We were all equal as his subjects.

But now, with him gone, I have no doubt that certain courts will begin to vie for power."

Etain. Larken felt as though a great weight shoved down on her chest. What if the Spring Court Queen tried to take over Airodion? Larken desperately tried to shut out the image of the beautiful faery. Her hand clenched around the knife belted around her waist—a gift from Madden.

"Beyond that, the council ruled that Finder was unfit to rule. Things are not as simple as freeing Finder from Dahey's clutches. And if I launch an attack on the Autumn Court for Finder, it leaves my home exposed. Summer and Spring could decide to join forces and storm White Keep. Or just one of them could, and the damage would still be catastrophic. Autumn could ask for allies, and how would that look? We cannot take the risk for one faery. Betrayal or no, I would rather have Dahey on the throne than face a war between the courts. And worry not about Dahey taking the powers. That kind of magic is impossible."

"It's not impossible," Larken said firmly. "Not anymore. You know some of what the Guardian is capable of thanks to the breaking of the memory curse. You have to know what could be possible with his new magic."

"When the memory curse broke, it showed us that the Guardian—or Ziegan, as the court rulers now know his name to be, harnessed magic to language, a feat previously thought of as impossible in our world," Isra said.

Ziegan. The name seared into Larken's mind like a brand.

"He created new beings, altering them with his language and his knife, but if Ziegan had the power to take magic, why didn't he do so during the war? Why hasn't he taken the powers of the court rulers already?"

"Ziegan might be using Dahey to see if taking magic is possible," Saja said. "We cannot assume that his magic will be the same as it was during the war—he could be expanding it, pushing the bounds of what is possible." Saja placed his hand flat upon the table. "We must free Finder before that happens. A new ruler is not what we need on the eve of war. Isra, please, you must help us. Give us a small group of soldiers.

Anything. With just Larken and I, we have no chance. But with help, even—"

Isra shook her head. "I will not meddle in this. You speak of war with Ziegan, but a war between the courts is much more likely. I won't stop you from leaving. I will provide you with any supplies you need, any provisions. I will shelter you here for as long as you need. But I cannot help you."

"Finder is your friend," Saja snapped. "If your places were switched—"

"If our places were switched, Finder would do the same. When you are a ruler, your court comes first. Above your family. Above your friends. Above your life."

Saja fell silent, and Larken could practically hear the unspoken words on his lips, that Finder would give up everything to help his friends. Larken gazed blankly at the table. They had failed to sway Isra to their cause. And it was only a matter of time before Dahey took the powers. It didn't matter that Isra believed it impossible—she didn't know what the Guardian's language was capable of.

Larken opened her mouth to announce that she was returning to her room, but Isra held up her hand. "I will not help Finder now. However, all the court rulers are meeting in a few days. If I find out that Dahey's actions will endanger the Winter Court, then I might reconsider."

Larken bit her lip, hope flooding her chest. "The court rulers are meeting?"

Isra nodded. "To discuss what will happen to Airodion now that the Starveling is dead. I'm sure we will talk about Ziegan and... other matters. After hearing your story, I want you and Saja to accompany me to the meeting."

Larken's heart caught in her chest. Would Finder—

Isra seemed to follow her thoughts for she said: "Finder will not be attending the meeting, Larken. Dahey will be standing in his place as regent. I know you will have more questions," Isra said. "Save them for the meeting of the courts. I won't be making any other decisions until I speak with them at length. We suffered under the Starveling's rule, but he did unite us. I fear what will happen without him, but I must trust that for now, the court rulers are on the same side. We must unify our courts. And I suspect that there might be a way to do so..." Isra trailed off, lost in thought.

"Unify them how?" Larken asked, puzzled.

"I will say no more until I have discussed things with the other court rulers," Isra snapped. Larken flinched at her icy stare. Had she said something that offended Isra?

You'll never get Finder back. You'll never escape these thoughts. Larken's breathing quickened. A pool of despair slowly sucked her deeper and deeper into its depths. She curled inwards on herself, her shoulders tilting under some indescribable weight. Isra's icy gaze cut into her, and she wilted. She was nothing, no one. She would never be able to rescue Finder, and he would never be able to heal her. She would be trapped with these dark thoughts forever. Tears welled behind her eyelids, and her throat closed. She should let it drown her to escape the horrible feelings welling inside her—

"Isra," Saja said sharply.

The Winter Queen shook herself, and the feeling immediately disappeared. Larken gasped with relief. What had happened? Had Isra used glamour on her?

"Apologies," Isra said, smoothing her gown. Larken looked at her with new eyes laced with fear. "I think it would be best if we all retired for the night."

Larken had to force herself not to run from the dining hall—anything to get away from the Winter Queen.

"Did Isra use her glamour on me?" Larken asked as she and Saja walked back to their rooms.

Saja sighed. "You know that Finder has the power of death, just as Etain has the power of life. Well, the other court rulers have dual powers as well."

Larken gestured to the ice castle. "Well, I'm starting to put together that her elemental power is water," she said, her voice weakly stumbling over the joke. "But her other power is..." She thought back to how she felt in that moment. Terrified. Defeated. "Despair?"

Saja nodded. "In a way. Isra has control over all negative emotions. She can make people feel them at will. A powerful ability to have, but a taxing one."

Larken shuddered. "I could never imagine purposely making someone feel like that," she murmured.

"I'm surprised she used them on you under such menial circumstances. But perhaps she is just adjusting to her new powers now that she is free from the Starveling's shackles."

Well, any thoughts of the possibility of Isra healing her mind were now lost. She could never fully trust someone who could make others feel such utter despair.

"Isra and Finder bonded over their dark powers," Saja said. "While Valakais and Etain represent seasons of life, Finder and Isra represent the seasons of death."

"I pity them." Larken shook her head. "What a heavy burden to bear."

They continued on, and Larken hugged herself from the chill. It lingered everywhere here, even inside the castle walls. She knew it would drive her mad if she lived here. The heat she could deal with, but cold...

A memory struck her, fierce and violent. Finder, exploding into flames. Larken wrapping her arms around Finder and the agony of her flesh burning, the endless flames, not being able to move, choking on the smoke, dying—

Her vision tilted sideways, blackening around the edges, and she slumped into the wall. She splayed her hands out, catching herself against the wall before she careened into the floor. Saja made a concerned noise and reached out to steady her. He opened the door to their rooms. She stumbled in, almost collapsing against the door when she beheld the flames that roared in the fireplace.

Choking, she sank into one of the blue upholstered sofas. She squeezed her eyes shut. Nausea rolled within her. Her eyes watered. The smoke grew, reaching out blackened hands to choke her. The fire was going to consume her. It was going to rush out of the fireplace in a huge gust, and she would be trapped, burning and burning until there was nothing left—

"Larken."

Saja's voice cut through her terror, but she didn't open her eyes.

"Put it out," she rasped.

"It's out," Saja replied. He placed a hand on her shoulder, squeezing it gently. She cracked open an eye, letting the big warrior come into focus. He stared at her, his golden eyes glimmering with concern.

"It's out?" she whispered.

"Yes. I thought it might be what frightened you. I doused it." He rubbed his jaw, his scruff of a beard more grown out after their travels.

What *was* happening to her? All day she longed for warmth, for a fire to curl up by. Her burns were gone, Finder had healed her, and yet, all the memories remained. She remembered how the flames had leapt upon her, how Finder's power had eaten away at her. The smell of her skin burning. Bile rose in the back of her throat, and she squeezed Saja's arm.

"I see it. All the time," Larken breathed out. "The fire. Finder burning me. I see it whenever I close my eyes. Sometimes when they're open," she whispered. "And it's hard here, in this blasted cold, because all I *want* is a fire, the warmth of the flames. Yet every time I think about it, the memories return, and then the fear. Over and over."

She felt so alone, like she was the only one who had ever felt this way before. She was healed now—she shouldn't be afraid. Nothing was hurting her in the present moment, and yet she couldn't put the pain from the flames out of her mind once it began to spiral. She was being selfish. How many others would have died from those wounds? She was lucky to be alive. And it was her fault, anyway, she had brought it upon herself by saving Finder.

Larken's chest tightened. She would wrap her hands around that burning faery a thousand times if it meant saving him. Finder was her friend. She wouldn't have let him die. But what did that mean for her? Her thoughts circled. Fear of the flames. The knowledge that she would do it again, that she had been partially responsible for the damage. Tears stung her eyes, but she wiped them away. She didn't have time to be thinking like this.

Anger burned in her gut. This was all happening because Isra had refused to help them. If she had offered them aide, then they would be on their way to rescue Finder at this very moment.

This is all stress, she told herself firmly. *Once you get Finder back, he'll cure you and all of this will go away. He knew how to heal your body, didn't he? He can heal this too.*

Saja was quiet for a moment. "These kinds of traumatic memories are common for soldiers. You are not the first to suffer from them. Those who have experienced horrifying things are forever touched by them. It is nothing to be ashamed of."

"But it's over," Larken spat. "It isn't happening now. I shouldn't be afraid. That fire in the room wasn't hurting me at all." She glanced at the fireplace and shivered.

"Think of all you experienced in just a few weeks," Saja said gently. "Think of all the terror and pain you endured. Sometimes your mind needs awhile to catch up. It's not something that you can control or force. And it doesn't mean that there's anything wrong with you."

Tears welled in her eyes. She felt like her mind was not her own. Like it was some enemy that she had to fight, but she never knew when it would attack. An enemy she could never win against.

"Madden struggled for years after Senna and Ainsley's deaths. He never fully recovered."

She pushed away the thought that Saja had inadvertently placed in her head: that she would never recover. She was no help to anyone like this—falling to pieces at the thought of a flame. She was a burden to everyone around her. She had nearly fainted, for Twins' sakes. How could she rescue Finder like this? And if they didn't rescue Finder, then there would be no one to heal her.

If Finder could heal trauma in the mind, then why couldn't he heal Madden? Memories of Madden came flooding back. Her throat closed. She would endure countless hours trapped in one of Madden's illusions if only he would return to them. He would have been able to help her, even if he didn't have the ability to heal. He hadn't been able to overcome his own struggle, but he would have helped her.

"I miss him," Larken said, picking absentmindedly at the threads of the blanket.

"I see his death every night," Saja murmured. Larken looked up at him.

"I was the one Finder said he would sacrifice. I was the one Finder said he could stand to lose," Saja said. No bitterness laced his tone—he believed what Finder had said at the Dark Priestesses' den. That Saja was the weakest of Finder's *dornán*. He believed that Finder knew best and that he was right. Larken's heart nearly tore in two.

"It was supposed to be me instead of Madden. I should have died. But now he's gone, and I'm here, and I cannot stop thinking that I will never be enough for this *dornán*, for you," he finished, looking down at his lap.

Larken had no words. She squeezed his hand. She had known Finder's words had hurt him deeply, but she hadn't known just how deep those wounds went. She knew Saja probably thought the same about her fear of fire.

They just didn't know how to help each other.

9

KAISA

Ellevere

Kaisa sat with Jovanna and Hollis at their evening meal that night. It was after the main rush had left, but those with late shifts or odd jobs remained to catch a meal before curfew. Across from her, a few Scourges nursed wounds on their feet. Kaisa had made them some salve to numb the pain, and they had thanked her profusely. Scourge year was one of the most difficult years, meant to prepare them for their final year as Scholars. Even if the lashes on their feet were earned, a little salve wasn't a sin.

She lifted her head as a squadron of Red Guards marched from the dining hall, their armor freshly polished. Under the cover of darkness was the safest time to travel for one of the four highest members of the Order. She would be accompanying them soon as Pope Sersius's Page. She knew it.

Kaisa pushed the food around her plate, unable to keep Castor's words from her mind. Why did he have this affect on her? He had betrayed the Order in some way. Why should she trust his poisoned words? She needed advice from someone she trusted.

51

"Audra," she said, turning to a girl sitting a few seats away. She had been Anointed last year and was now a Sister of the Order, tasked with teaching lower classes at the Institute. Audra had been the first one to dry Kaisa's tears when she arrived at the Institute as a Cradle. She had been like an older sister to Kaisa.

Audra met her gaze. Kaisa winced at the look in the Sister's eyes. Audra hadn't been the same since her dearest friend Claire hadn't made it through her Anointing and had been sent to the colonies. Kaisa couldn't imagine if Jovanna and Hollis didn't make it through the Anointing, but she knew they would. The three of them had survived everything.

"Our Anointing is tomorrow. Can you tell me what to expect?" Kaisa's stomach pinched. So soon. She should be overjoyed, she *had* been overjoyed, curious about the Anointing, but not fearful. Not when so many had come before her, and none had revealed that it was an unpleasant experience. She knew it would be a test, and that the Order had a tendency to be harsh. But she had never been afraid.

"You know I can't tell you that," Audra replied. She returned to her meal, sure that the conversation was over.

"I need to know some part of it," Kaisa pressed. "Any detail you can tell me. You don't have to give away everything, but I can't go in blind, please." She paused, considering her next words carefully. "I'm afraid."

"Precious Kaisa is afraid?" a voice sneered from down the table. Kaisa turned to glare at Izzy. The slender redhead had hated Kaisa since their Scourge year, when Kaisa had turned her in for trying to run away from the palace. Their tutors had burned off the bottoms of Izzy's feet in punishment. "What would the Twins think of that fear? Sounds a bit heretical to me."

"Shut it, Izzy," Jovanna growled.

Kaisa ignored them. "What difference does a day make, Audra. Just tell me, please. To put my mind at ease."

Audra's hand froze on her spoon. Jovanna gave a surprised grunt. It was usually her that asked all the questions, not Kaisa.

"Kai," Hollis murmured. Students of the Institute learned not to push.

And she was pushing at something the rest of them knew to leave well enough alone. But Castor's words had gotten to her, and she couldn't let it go.

"The Anointing is a joyous experience." A slow smile spreaded across Audra's face. "The night that you will be joined with the Twins."

Kaisa wished she could make her mind forget that horrible smile. And the light that had gone out of Audra's eyes.

10

DAHEY

Airodion

Finder hung limply from his chains, a slow trail of blood leaking from his split lips.

Dahey waited for the *dornán* bond to pull at him, forcing him to help Finder. To free him. But the silence within was almost deafening. No bond. No oath to be kept.

The Guardian's words lingered in Dahey's mind, plaguing him. If he did what the Guardian suggested, there would be no turning back. It would be altering another faery's magic and twisting it to his will. But the time to take them was now. Isra had sent word that the court rulers were meeting. Dahey needed to have the powers by then in order to be seen as a fellow court ruler—not just a regent.

Finder jerked, coming to. He pulled weakly against the Weeping Metal chains, the cuffs moving to reveal the skin of his wrists where they lay strung up above his head. They hung limply as birds with broken wings, bruised from where he had pulled against his bonds. Red, chafed skin had sloughed away, leaving raw and bloodied flesh beneath.

Dahey's stomach roiled at the sight. He'd seen the chains at work before, though Finder had always hesitated to use them when he was prince, insisting that the Weeping Metal was unnatural, too brutal to be used even on their enemies. To prevent any being from using their magic was barbaric, his cousin had claimed. Finder had used it only on the most powerful creatures that landed in Shadeshelm's dungeons.

Dahey hadn't hesitated to use the chains as soon as they reached the city. Finder's refusal to use Weeping Metal was just a further demonstration of why he was unfit to rule. Dahey would use any means necessary to subdue enemies of the Autumn Court. Finder's noble heart had gotten him nowhere.

Dahey inhaled, the dark tang of the metal assaulting his senses. The need to get away, to put as much distance between himself and the metal was so strong that Dahey almost bolted, clawing his way out the Autumn Court dungeons and into the safety of his chambers. Dahey wasn't sure how Finder was able to keep his sanity with the pain of the Weeping Metal that constrained him.

He approached his cousin, reaching out and placing a gentle hand on the side of his face, making sure to stay away from the chains. Finder's face was greasy with grime and blood. How much did it pain Finder not to be able to clean himself? A small convulsion raked Finder's body at the touch.

"Cousin," Dahey murmured.

"I would have released you," came the broken rasp.

Dahey froze.

"I would have released you from the *dornàn* bond. I never would have forced you to stay. You could have come to me at any time, and I would have freed you."

Dahey's heart tightened, but he forced his features into a sneer. "Even after I stabbed you, would you have freed me then? Would you have relinquished the power over me that forced me to protect you?"

Finder's green eyes lifted, the pain in them so staggering that Dahey took a step back. "Even then."

Dahey looked away.

"I loved you the moment I held you as a babe. I loved you when you became my brother and then my soldier. And I love you now."

Dahey squeezed his eyes shut, unable to stop the tears from running down his face. "I betrayed you. I've taken *everything* from you. You can't love me."

"I do. The love pains me, but I feel it still." He paused. "You should have come to me. You should have come to me, and I would have protected you."

"Protected me?" Dahey faced Finder. "Where was your protection when my father beat me with hands made of fire? When he refused to heal me, and I was forced to walk around Shadeshelm with blistering handprints all over my body?"

Finder's face twisted into a grimace. "I had no power then, but I have power now."

Dahey chuckled darkly, wiping away his tears. He couldn't remember the last time he had allowed himself to cry. "When you became prince, I swore to protect *you*. Because by then it was too late for me. No one had ever protected me," he choked.

"You didn't deserve what happened to you, Dahey," Finder said quietly. "You were just a child. If I could have switched places with you, taken your pain, I would have. Let me go," Finder said. "I know you don't believe I care for this court, but I do. This is my responsibility, not yours. If you take the powers, you'll have to be trained, and we need to focus on the Guardian. Or Ziegan, I suppose I should call him." A muscle flickered in Finder's jaw.

"Tell me what you know about Ziegan," Dahey said, a chill slipping up his spine.

"I already told you everything I knew about him after the Starveling fell when I thought you remained loyal to me," Finder said, his voice laced with pain. "But even with the memory curse gone, we do not know everything he's capable of. And without the Starveling and the Dark Priestesses, I do not know how we will defeat him."

A flicker of fear raced through Dahey.

"We can get past this," Finder said. "I can help you."

Dahey couldn't listen to his cousin's words any longer. He shoved his emotions deep inside him until he could no longer feel them at all. "You wouldn't say that if you knew the whole truth of what I've done."

Finder's brow drew together. Then his eyes widened. "Where is she?"

Dahey didn't miss the slight quiver in Finder's voice. He knew how much it must pain him to ask about Larken. "I tried to trap them in the human realm but failed," Dahey couldn't keep the bitterness from his tone. "The Guardian—Ziegan, didn't see fit to tell me that the bridges' magic would end with the Starveling's death."

"Where is she now? Do they remain in Ellevere?" Finder's breath caught.

A pang twisted through Dahey's heart as the realization struck him: Finder had wanted them to be trapped in Ellevere. He didn't care about them coming to rescue him—he wanted them to be safe.

"Please," Dahey spat. "She returned to Airodion the moment she realized the bridge was open. If you thought she would do otherwise, you are a bigger fool than I thought." Dahey grabbed Finder's face. His cousin's eyes were lit with panic—but not for himself. For Larken. "We all saw how you two felt about each other. But this story will not have a happy ending. You will remain in chains. And if she steps one foot in the Autumn Court, she dies."

Finder launched himself at Dahey, the chains groaning. Dahey took a step back.

"Do not threaten her in my presence again," Finder's voice was so soft it sent a chill down Dahey's spine. He knew his cousin cared for Larken, but this...

"Or what?" Dahey snapped. "You would't use the powers to protect her. You murdered her dearest friend. You nearly melted the skin from her bones. She deserves better than you."

He ignored Finder's snarl of outrage. He smoothed out his jerkin—red velvet embroidered with golden autumn leaves. The colors of his court.

"Why are you resisting this?" Dahey asked. "You never cared about this court. Never wanted to rule. How many times did you come to me saying you wished the powers had chosen someone else? That they would leave you—like they did my father? Isn't this what you wanted? For someone to take this burden from you?"

Finder's brow furrowed. "You are right—I didn't want the burden of being a court ruler once. You don't know how it feels. You can love your court and still feel the weight of it all. I feared the powers, yes, but thought that staying away would help protect them. I destroyed Raharney when the powers first came to me. Razed the city and its inhabitants. I thought staying away, burying my powers inside me was what was best for the Autumn Court. I know how wrong I was now." Finder's gaze bored into Dahey's. "You must listen to me, Dahey. Ziegan is free, and you are not the only one at fault. I am as well. War is coming to Airodion once more. This is my responsibility, my burden to bear, not yours."

Dahey bristled. "If the powers left you of their own volition and chose another, you would be overjoyed. It is only because I wish to have them that you resist me so."

Finder's gaze hardened. "You've always been ambitious, ever since you were a boy. But I see a spark of your father's madness in you. I thought keeping you away from Osiron would help, but if you continue down this path, you will follow in your father's footsteps and send this court to ruin."

"You're wrong," Dahey hissed. "I am nothing like my father."

"Really?" Finder snarled. "You use pain to get what you want. You stabbed me, bound me in Weeping Metal chains. You'd torture me if it came to that. Tell me, how are you different from Osiron?"

"My father never cared for this court. He only cared for himself. Just like you," Dahey spat. "I did what I had to do to save the Autumn Court, no matter how much it pained me. My father only caused pain for his own pleasure."

Dahey turned away from his cousin, breathing deeply. He was going to save this court. All he had to do was speak the words, and the magic he so dearly coveted would be his forever. The kind of magic that allowed Finder to control the flame and death. With the Starveling dead, Dahey would have no checks on his power.

Except for Ziegan, a voice in the back of his mind hissed. The Starveling and two out of the three Dark Priestesses might be dead, but he and the other court rulers would find other allies if need be. Dahey had done censuses of the Autumn Court before. He had found the Dark Priestesses when their names had almost been lost to the winds of time. He would find a way to imprison Ziegan again, or he would train until he became strong enough to rival the being himself.

Fierce need built up in Dahey's chest. He was so close. He had come so far, given up so much. Finder had had his chance and ruined it.

A shiver ran through him. He was about to use magic that the Starveling had not been able to achieve: taking powers completely. Dahey was meant to be king. And now he would be.

Dahey paced around Finder.

His cousin jerked against his chains. "What are you doing?"

Ziegan had been clear with his instructions. Even the slightest mispronunciation could have devastating effects. Dahey had used the language before to call the Fomari and break his *dornán* bond, but he knew these words were more powerful. He had shuddered when Ziegan had placed the words inside his head and explained what they would do. He feared the dark being's language. Wielding a power like that, spreading it to other fey... it was unthinkable. He was no fool—he knew that Ziegan would eventually become a threat to the Autumn Court. But if they had managed to kill the Starveling, they would find a way to kill Ziegan, too.

Dahey unsheathed his knife and cut away Finder's shirt.

"Don't do this," Finder pleaded.

Dahey ignored him. Finder might be his blood, but the Autumn Court was his family too. Finder never wanted his court to rise, had no ambitions other than suffering through being prince. Dahey would use his powers to further the Autumn Court, to make it the most powerful court in Airodion. He would make the royal treasury overflow with gold. He would strengthen their military to defend their borders, to make them the most powerful army in Airodion. He would use his skills with a sword to fight alongside them.

It was time.

Dahey pressed his hands to Finder's chest and began the chant, slowly at first, then louder—until it was almost a scream. The words burned as they came out of his mouth, the taste of smoke and ashes coating his tongue. Pressure grew at his temples, turning into a stabbing pain. He could barely breathe, barely think, and yet, the words kept coming. He didn't think he could stop them even if he wanted to. But he could *feel* the magic inside him, feel it responding to the words, coming to its call, coming to him. His heart thundered in his chest, his blood roared through his veins, the words a shrieking cry at his lips. He screamed.

Finder's cries echoed his own. He writhed against the chains, his back arching in agony. But the words kept coming, pulled out of Dahey like tendrils of black smoke. He kept going, but then he faltered—stumbling over a phrase, a tiny, menial word, just a fraction of the spell. And still, he kept going.

And when Dahey looked down, his hands were engulfed in flame.

Dahey's eyes fluttered open. His cheek was pressed against something cool and hard—the floor of Finder's cell. His breath shuddered out of him in a groan as he pushed himself up.

Finder lay limp in his chains. His chest moved up and down rapidly, and Dahey almost sighed in relief. He was alive. They were both alive.

Once the ritual had begun, he almost thought they wouldn't survive. The way Finder had screamed, the way *he* had screamed, and the pain, the unbearable, unnatural pain... But here they both were, alive and breathing.

"What have you done?" Finder croaked.

Dahey flinched when Finder looked at him, when he beheld the agony in his eyes.

"What have you done?" he asked again.

Dahey looked away, unable to meet his kin's gaze. "I did what I had to."

Dahey closed his eyes, searching within himself. He could feel the current of magic that pulsed beneath Shadeshelm. He imagined himself placing his hand in the river, the current swirling against his fingers. His usual powers were there—summoning and glamour—but there was something else. Something akin to a chain made of golden links, buried in the water. He reached out to touch it and found it burning with energy.

He opened his eyes. Holding the image of his hand and the chain of magic in his mind, he gave the chain a sharp tug. A flame lighted at his fingertips. Agony took him. Finder groaned, veins in his neck bulging. Dahey rose slowly as the pain and nausea faded.

Horror engulfed Dahey. He found the chain in his mind's eye once more and tugged, feeling the burning links beneath the current. Fire sprang to life between his hands then evaporated as he doubled over.

No—this wasn't supposed to happen. The chain...

"*What have you done?*" Finder screamed.

Dahey looked down at his hands in horror.

Their magic was bound together.

11

KAISA

Ellevere

Kaisa dragged her feet up the steps leading to Pope Sersius's chambers, lugging her cleaning supplies along beside her. No guards on duty tonight—not while he was away. She usually wouldn't work this late, but Rachael's duties had added up, costing her more time than she planned. But she didn't mind saving Rachael the punishment she would get for not completing her work. Kaisa slipped the key in the lock.

She had to focus on her task. The Anointing was tomorrow night, and she couldn't make a mistake now. A tortured member of the Black Guard wasn't going to turn her from her path. And Audra... she trusted Audra, but she hadn't been the same since Claire was sent to the colonies.

Kaisa couldn't entertain these thoughts, or the Twins would know she'd doubted them. The thought of her gods being angry at her made her quiver. Her faith was all she had. It was all she knew. It was the only thing she believed in.

One by one, she removed the doubts from her mind. She had a job to do.

The room was unspeakably lavish. The black and blood red theme

62

was everywhere, from the thick curtains to the plush rugs. Vases made from solid gold decorated the mantle above the fireplace, a silver serving tray laying on the table.

One wall of the study had floor to ceiling bookshelves, undoubtedly filled with priceless tomes. Armed with a feather duster, Kaisa began cleaning the bookcase. After what felt like hours, she reached the bottom shelf. She sank to the floor, her back aching. She glanced back at the shelf to see if she missed any specks of dust, and her gaze snagged on a book that was slightly out of place on the middle shelf. Kaisa frowned, hauling herself to her feet. The book jutted out, perhaps knocked out of place by her aggressive cleaning. The spine read *Twelve Mysteries of the Order*. Her interest sparked, and she grabbed the book.

Click.

The entire shelf *moved*, swinging towards her. Kaisa's mouth fell open. She could see an oak desk and bookshelves filled with tomes. She grasped the edge of the open bookcase, ready to pull the door wider, but then she hesitated. She could claim that the room was already open, that she thought Pope Sersius wanted her to clean it. They would believe her.

And this room could provide her answers about the Anointing.

She pulled open the door and crept into the room.

The oak desk dominating the room was intricately carved with hunting scenes and religious motifs from the doctrine of the Twins. Asphalion and Aleea creating the two worlds, one for the fey and one for the humans. The war between the gods. Asphalion forgiving Aleea and allowing Chosen girls into the faery realm.

Kaisa lit a candle and crouched before the desk, pulling open the first drawer. It wasn't locked. Her jaw almost dropped at the sheer amounts listed on the financial sheets. There were records of things that no religious order need purchase. The entire drawer was filled with these records, the print microscopic, dating back years. Decades.

She pulled open the next drawer. More of the same. Records of the higher members of the Order, trips away, letters from foreign dignitaries. But nothing about the Institute's students, nothing about the Anointing.

She reached the final drawer. Her heart clenched when she read the tiny tab labelled *Anointings*. She flipped through the document.

Kaisa's gaze caught on Audra's name, listed with Claire's.

Kaisa scanned the page, her gaze falling on the "notes" section.

Audra was hesitant to perform the ritual. Claire begged her not to do it, sobbed, but eventually, Audra picked up the knife. I thought for a moment she would refuse. In the end, she slit Claire's throat. I congratulated her on completing her Anointing.

Kaisa's eyes glazed over. Her heart thundered in her chest as she read the notes again. And again.

No. It couldn't be—

Kaisa frantically tore through the pages. Her eyes scanned the pairs of Scholars who went into their Anointing, but only one came out. And for those who refused... both names were struck through. She tore through the pages again and finally reached the date for this year's Anointing.

To her and Jovanna's names written side-by-side.

All the pieces fell into place.

They were going to have her kill Jovanna.

12

DAHEY

Airodion

Finder wrapped the bandage around Dahey's arm.

Dahey winced, keeping his eyes trained on his cousin's face. Finder was still dressed for his tenth birthday celebration, wearing a beautiful crimson coat embroidered with golden leaves. Though only three years Dahey's senior, he looked much older.

Dahey hadn't been able to attend the celebration. His burns had been too severe. Father had refused to heal him, even for the party.

His eyes darted to the piece of cake Finder had brought him: lavender with lemon icing. Dahey's favorite. But the pain was too great for him to consider eating it. His lip trembled. That was the worst part about burns—they hurt just as much after as they did receiving them. "Is it bad?" he whispered.

Finder tied the bandage off. "They look worse than they are," he said gently. "You'll heal soon." His eyes hardened. "It angers me that Uncle Osiron treats you like this."

Dahey shrugged, used to his father's punishments. "He says it makes me stronger."

Finder brushed a hand through Dahey's hair. "You're much braver than me, cousin."

Dahey's heart swelled.

"And besides, you didn't miss much at the celebration." Finder shrugged. He helped Dahey into bed, leaving the cake on the nightstand. He turned to leave.

"Wait," Dahey called, biting his lip. "Will you—will you stay? Father never punishes me while you're here."

Finder's eyes softened. "Of course."

He curled into bed beside Dahey. Dahey turned to face him. "Do you think—do you think you'll leave the city when you're older?"

Finder nodded. "Uncle Osiron and my father both expect me to go to the military academy. But truthfully, I want to go. I want to help my court in whatever way I can." He smiled. "I just started my sword training. I'll teach you everything I know—I have a feeling you would be good at it."

Pride swept through him. He hardened his resolve. Wherever Finder went, he would go too. "I'm going with you."

Finder smiled again. "Of course. I need you."

Dahey bolted upright, coated in sweat. He threw off the linen sheets, gasping for breath. The dream still lingered behind his eyelids. He shoved away the memory of Finder.

Dahey stood, crossing over to the large wooden desk. He braced his knuckles against the wood.

What are you going to do?

He didn't know. He needed to speak to Ziegan. He had been putting it off, unable to tell Ziegan of his failure. But he had no choice. He had to have the full powers before the meeting of the court rulers. He had a horrible suspicion about how he could force the magic to him, but he had to make sure...

He opened the desk drawer to reveal the two black orbs nestled in velvet. One allowed him to speak with Ziegan—who now had the Starveling's orb. The other allowed him to speak with Pope Sersius in the human realm.

Dahey placed his hand on one of the orbs. "Ziegan."

Moments passed. Anxiety spiked through Dahey. What if he didn't answer?

"Dahey," came the gravelly purr.

Dahey swallowed. "I made a mistake. I—I misspoke the words you told me. The powers are now split between Finder and I."

Nothing. Then laughter poured from the orb.

"How delightful," Ziegan chuckled.

Dahey scowled. "Tell me the words I need to fix it." He paused. "Please."

More laughter poured from the orb. "There is no way to fix it."

Dahey's stomach dropped to his toes. "No," he breathed.

"The only way to solve your little dilemma is if one of you dies. That will force the powers to the other. Now, leave me be. I have work to do."

The connection severed. Dahey released his hand from the orb.

The only way to force the powers to him was if Finder died. Dahey's heart lurched in his chest. His suspicion had been correct, but Finder couldn't die. Dahey had never wanted him to die. He had just wanted the magic.

Dahey slammed his fists down on the desk, a broken gasp escaping his mouth.

You've come too far, a voice whispered in the back of his mind, *to give up now.*

Dahey raised his head. He had given up so much for the crown. Betrayed Finder, his *dornán*. Lied to his court. Taken the powers.

This was a test. The final test. To see how far he would go for his court. What he was willing to lose.

Dahey reached for his magic, searching for that golden chain. It burned brightly beneath the surface, waiting, begging him to pull it. But what about Finder's other powers? Finder had the power to heal and portal, like all court rulers, but one of his powers was over death itself. Dahey remembered how he had made the Fomari crumple up dead like autumn leaves. Where were those powers?

He imagined wrapping his hand around the chain and *pulled.*

He gasped as fire lit between his palms, then pain exploded in his abdomen. Gritting his teeth, he willed the fire away and searched deeper —for anything that felt different, that could signal that the other powers were there—linked to the chain.

Dahey held it for as long as he could. Fire kept trying to spark to life between his palms, but nothing more.

Dahey released the chain, spitting a curse. He grabbed a porcelain vase from his desk and threw it at the wall.

He didn't have access to the other powers. Wouldn't—until Finder's death.

Dahey swallowed. As boys, he had wanted to be more like Finder, look more like him, act more like him. He loved Finder dearly. But so did his father. Osiron wished Finder was his son instead. Finder was stronger. Smarter. Better in every way. Osiron had told Dahey that every chance he got.

So Dahey had tried to be better. He studied until he had better marks than Finder at the academy. He trained with a sword until he was more skilled than Finder, until he was the best swordsman the Autumn Court had ever seen. It still wasn't enough for Osiron.

No one expected the powers to stay within the Fairburn line. No one. When they chose Finder, Osiron had been ecstatic. The powers might have left him, but at least they chose the son he had always wished for. Dahey could train all he wanted. He could become smarter, stronger, better than Finder, but the powers were the one thing he could never have.

Until now.

He was so close to having everything he had ever dreamed of. He had suffered so much for these powers, what was a little more? He had survived his father. He would survive this too. In his own way, his father had trained him for this. Had forged Dahey like a blade. Plunging him into the fire again and again until he came out stronger.

Would he finally earn his father's approval once he had the powers? Dahey couldn't help the flicker of hope that spluttered to life in his chest. Perhaps this was the way to earn his father's favor.

Dahey wiped sweat from his forehead. Was he really doing this? He had never wanted Finder to die. But this was the only way to get the powers, Ziegan had said so himself. This was the only way to ensure he would become king. Dahey swallowed.

This is the only way. But he couldn't let his court know what he had done. He was doing this for them, but some might not understand. He had to be strategic.

And he had a feeling he knew exactly when that moment was coming. The meeting with the other court rulers would confirm it.

He would wait until after the meeting. Yes, he would be a mere regent in their eyes for now, but soon he would show them all what he had become.

Finder would die, and then the powers would be his.

13

LARKEN

Airodion

Saja and Larken rode Arobhinn through the game park. Larken held her breath as they approached the silvered strands of the webs. Saja had woken her days before, certain that something terrible had happened to Finder. He had felt the crippling distress through the *dornán* bond, but the Cynyadas had yet to return a message.

"Look," Larken gasped. For there, draped across the trees, were dozens of Cynyada webs depicting Finder and Dahey—a strange silvery rope binding them together. It looked as though a substance was being drawn out of both of them, tying them together.

They searched the web, and more depictions of the scene unfolded.

Then they saw one web that only depicted words.

Dahey tried to take the powers and failed.

Larken's breath caught. Her eyes darted to the next web.

The fire magic is now split between us.

Saja hissed in a breath behind her. She spun to look at him, her heart leaping into her throat. "What does it mean?"

"If part of the powers still reside in Finder, then Dahey still needs a way to take them," Saja said, his eyes filling with terror. "The language failed him, but he can try to force the rest of the powers to him another way."

Horror filled Larken's gut. "He wouldn't—"

"He's going to kill him," Saja whispered. "He'll need some sort of excuse—the council ruled to imprison him. But Dahey won't rest until he has the powers. We're running out of time," Saja's voice broke.

Larken balled her fists. "Then we have to convince the other court rulers to save him."

14

KAISA

Ellevere

Kaisa gripped the desk and tried to slow her breathing. This is what the Anointing was. Killing one's closest friend to show complete loyalty to the Order.

All of it had been a lie. The most important people in her life, her older peers, her mentors, every person in the Order who had ever spoken to her, encouraged her to reach her Anointing, had told her the ritual was a test, but a glorious thing... all of it had been a lie.

Her gaze scanned the page for Hollis's name. His name came first, then a boy he was friends with—Joseph, who also apprenticed with Baid. Even Izzy's name was listed first.

She couldn't wrap her mind around it. Every single Anointed member that she knew had murdered their dearest friend. No wonder the light had left Audra's eyes. Kaisa's chest heaved. They couldn't make her do this. She wanted to be a Pope's Page more than anything else in the world, but this... this was the one thing she couldn't do. Wouldn't do. She had always suspected that the Anointing might not be easy, that it would be a test of faith. But this was sheer cruelty.

But can you really give up on the life you dreamed about? This was the ultimate test. They paired a weaker member of the Order with a stronger one and expected the stronger one to do what was necessary. Like the gardeners the Order so often talked about, ripping out the weeds to save the flower. It was a few moments of suffering for a lifetime of happiness in the Order. With a secure job and more power than she ever could have dreamed.

How can you be so cruel? Anger boiled through her. No. She would not do this. The Order had given her much, most likely more than she ever would have been able to achieve on her own, but they had lied to her every step of the way. She would not hurt Jovanna. Ever.

She had to talk to Hollis and Jovanna. They had to flee. They would punish Hollis and Jovanna as well. Fear sparked within her. If they ran, then the Order would hunt them down. They would string them up before the palace gates. She had seen other students try it before, and few had succeeded. The Order had eyes everywhere.

She stuffed her papers into the open book on the desk. If anyone asked, she would say she was returning one of Pope Sersius's books to the library.

Kaisa hurried out of the room, clutching the book to her chest. She kicked the bookcase closed behind her. Heart climbing into her throat, she rushed into the hall outside the Pope's chambers.

She barely had time to look up before she crashed head-first into Izzy.

The papers fluttered to the ground. Izzy grabbed one before Kaisa could stop her. Izzy scanned the page, her eyes wide.

"Izzy, please—" Kaisa began.

"You stole these from Pope Sersius." Izzy's eyes practically bulged out of her head.

"Look at the papers. Look what they say. That's what the Anointing is. We have to kill our friends." She waited for the other girl to gasp, to fall apart as Kaisa had. Maybe they could help each other now that they both knew the truth. Kaisa held her breath.

Izzy shook her head. "You're lying. The Order would never make us do such a thing."

Kaisa gestured to the papers. "It's all there, Izzy. This is what the Anointing is."

Izzy jerked her head away. "I won't fall prey to your lies, Kaisa. You forged these papers somehow. You're using your position to try to fool the rest of us. You can't stand the thought of someone surpassing you, and you're making us doubt the Anointing so we don't go through with it. I always knew you were a worthless street urchin licking the boots of the Order to survive. But now I know you're a heretic too."

Kaisa thought her heart might stop beating.

Izzy looked up at her. "I'm going to tell everyone that you forged documents in Pope Sersius's name." Izzy rose to her feet, the papers clenched in her fist.

"Izzy, please," Kaisa gasped.

"I'm going to tell them Jovanna and Hollis helped you. That they knew about your heretical thoughts and did nothing. And then you will all suffer as I have suffered."

Kaisa reached for her arm, rage boiling in her throat, but Izzy was quicker, darting down one of the hallways and out of sight.

15

LARKEN

Airodion

Isra portalled herself, Larken and Saja to the Wyld, a neutral location for the meeting of the court rulers. Isra had explained that Dahey had left earlier to meet them since he was unable to portal. Larken's stomach had pinched in response. He couldn't portal yet, but once he killed Finder and took the powers...

Larken rubbed her sweating palms on her skirts at the thought of seeing Dahey again. Saja was wound so tight that Larken feared he might snap in two. Isra had spoken to them at length before their departure. Under no circumstances were they to attack Dahey.

"What if he attacks us?" Larken had asked, almost hoping he would so she could sink her fingernails into his arrogant face.

Isra regarded her. "I hope that we, the leaders of Airodion, can be civil towards each other for a few hours. Dahey must learn to keep his temper on a short leash if he wishes to rule."

Larken had wanted to point out that the Spring Court Queen, Etain, could hardly be described as keeping her temper on a short leash.

"You two are under my protection," Isra continued. "But if you attack

75

Dahey, it will be seen as an aggression from the Winter Court, which I will not tolerate." She stared them down like troublesome children. Larken and Saja nodded their consent.

Larken watched as Isra closed the ring of ice that hovered in the air, shimmering with magic. Larken knew that Isra must be drained after portalling them, but the Winter Court Queen looked as composed as ever.

Peering about, Larken took in their surroundings. She had been in the Wyld not long ago to meet Remira, and later, Ziegan. She shivered. Was Ziegan still here, somewhere in the Wyld? She had no idea where they were in relation to his former prison or Remira's cave, which made her skin itch. She despised portalling because it made her lose all sense of direction.

Before them was a large stone table, overrun with tree branches and moss. Stone benches lined the table, and while deep cracks marred their surface, they still stood without crumbling. A faint wind whispered through the trees, bringing with it the musky scent of the Wyld.

Isra gestured to the stone benches. "Sit. The others will be here soon."

Larken and Saja sat, their shoulders brushing. Saja's knee bounced beneath the table. Larken couldn't shake her hope that Finder would come, that Dahey would bring him to show off. If she could just see him...

Isra eventually came to sit beside Saja, and Larken could have sworn that the stone cooled beneath her touch.

Valakais, the ruler of the Summer Court, announced his arrival with a blast of air pouring from his portal. When he stepped down, his feet hovered slightly above the ground, air gushing from beneath him. Leaves and dirt flew from his path.

He was beautiful as all the fey were; tall and bulky with muscle. Smooth, umber skin framed high cheekbones and a straight, square jawline. He had a wide, flat nose and perfectly rosy lips. His curly brown hair was shorn to his skull, which only put his beautiful features in stark relief. Perfectly sculpted eyebrows lifted as he caught sight of her, a smile playing about his lips. Valakais had a face that looked as though it was in a perpetual smirk. He wore a sleeveless tunic that barely reached the middle of his thighs, though it framed the muscles of his legs. Larken could not look away. She had seen him briefly when they had fought the Starveling, but something about being so near him made her stomach flutter, and the heat spread... lower.

She blushed furiously. *What's wrong with you?*

Valakais approached, making her heart leap into her throat. He flashed her a smile. "Larken. Your name spreads through Airodion faster than wildfire."

How ironic, she wanted to say, but she held her tongue.

"My name is Valakais," he purred, taking her hand and kissing it. Larken could not withstand the small tremor in her hand as she returned it to her lap. Of course—she was experiencing Valakais's powers over positive emotions. Just as Isra had made her feel that unending despair, Valakais made her feel... good.

Valakais breezed past her to sit at the other side of the table. He chatted idly with the Winter Queen, but from time to time, he would glance over at Larken and give her a wink. Larken found herself desperately wanting to see more of his powers. She felt herself drawn to Valakais—happier when she was near him. She could use a bit more joy in her life.

Stop it, he's just using his powers on you—same as Isra did.

Dread filled her stomach at the thought of Dahey acquiring Finder's powers over death. She couldn't begin to imagine how much horror he would bring to Airodion with an untapped power such as that.

Dirt exploded in the air, accompanied by blooming roses. Larken braced herself for the arrival of the Queen of the Spring Court.

Etain emerged from her portal as gorgeous as ever. Her hair—the color of sunlight—fell in loose curls to the small of her back. She gave them a demure smile, but her eyes shimmered with cold malice.

Hatred for Etain boiled in Larken's chest.

"Isra, Valakais." She nodded to her fellow court rulers. Her gaze fell upon Larken and Saja. "Human scum. Brute." Her lip curled. "What are you doing here?"

"They are here at my request and under my protection," Isra replied coldly.

Etain said nothing, taking her place beside Valakais.

They waited in tense silence for Dahey for what felt like hours. Pounding hoofbeats warned them that he drew near. Larken grew tenser by the second, glad to have Saja beside her to face their betrayer.

Finally, Dahey emerged from the trees astride his white mare. His resemblance to his cousin made her heart ache for Finder. Dark circles marred the skin beneath his eyes, bringing her a savage pleasure. Still, Dahey's brown eyes were clear and fierce.

"Nice of you to join us," Etain said, twirling her finger in the moss growing on the table. It burst into budding white flowers. "Tell me, why is a regent attending a meeting for kings and queens?"

Dahey swung off his horse and sauntered towards the table, ever the picture of confidence. "Would you prefer that Finder join us after being deemed unfit to rule? We have more important matters to discuss." His brown gaze fell on Saja and Larken. "What are they doing here?"

Larken could have sworn a glimmer of fear passed through his expression.

"They are here as my guests," Isra responded. "And they have a rather interesting theory about how you came across your new role as regent."

Dahey clenched his jaw.

Isra beckoned to Larken and Saja. "Tell them," she commanded.

Larken and Saja exchanged a glance. They had discussed at length what they would say to the court rulers to convince them to remove Dahey from the throne, or at the very least demand that he free Finder.

"Your, erm, majesties," Larken began. "We've come to explain what exactly happened the night the Starveling was killed and the events that set that night into motion." Larken took a deep breath. Valakais looked curious, Etain viciously scrutinizing, and Dahey looked as though he wished he could kill her. His brown eyes never left hers as she told her story, but his expression was unreadable. Larken desperately wished he would show some kind of discomfort. Her palms began to sweat.

"Dahey led Finder to Ziegan so he would attack the Starveling, unwittingly freeing Ziegan—and his language." She glared triumphantly at Dahey. A small smile twitched at his lips, and Larken couldn't help but think she had made a mistake. "He's going to take Finder's powers by force using Ziegan's magic," she blurted.

Silence. Then Etain burst into laughter.

Larken's heart sank.

"Take his powers by force?" Etain chuckled. "Impossible. The magic chooses the ruler. Even Ziegan's magic is not capable of such a thing. And if Dahey could take the powers, why hasn't he already? He rode his donkey here, didn't he?"

Dahey scowled at her.

Frustration prickled over Larken's skin. "Anything is possible with Ziegan's new magic. You're all freed from the memory curse and know what he's capable of." How many times would she have to repeat herself before the court rulers took Ziegan and his magic seriously?

"Magic has never been taken," Valakais said. "Even the Starveling could only siphon off a portion of our magic, not take it completely."

"Make Dahey swear an oath, then," Larken said, clenching her fists. "Make him swear he won't take Finder's powers. That he hasn't already." Once a faery swore an oath, they couldn't lie, and they had to fulfill whatever they swore to do. It had to be enough to convince the other court rulers of Dahey's wrongdoing.

"Enough," Etain said sharply. "Swearing an oath is no small thing, and we will not force Dahey to give his word over such a trivial matter. As we've said before, that kind of magic is not possible."

"I'm afraid Larken and Saja are mistaken," came Dahey's cool voice. "They are correct that I sought out the Dark Priestesses and eventually Ziegan because I knew Finder was unfit to rule. You all know what happened when his powers claimed him. You all know he has been absent since Embryn's death. He is reckless and cares not for his court."

Larken clenched her jaw.

"I asked if there was a way to break the *dornán* bond. I no longer wanted to be a part of Finder's cadre. He failed me and his court. I told my court that he released me, but I will tell the truth to my fellow court rulers."

"Finder would have released you from your bond. You know that," Larken growled.

Dahey shook his head. "I didn't know for certain. My wish was to sever my bond to him, nothing more. When his tithe perished, I gave him another chance. I begged him to go to the Starveling, to beg for mercy to save his court, but he threw it all away for a human girl and the chance for vengeance."

"You control the Fomari!" Larken exploded. "You killed his tithe and gave him no other choice but to fight. My village and your precious court would have faced the Starveling's wrath."

"I will admit, Ziegan did tell me how to make a deal with the Fomari. They were intended to make me trust him, so I would help him in his nefarious plans. But they have returned to his side and obey me no longer."

How is he doing this? Larken wanted to scream.

"Of course I want the magic to choose me," Dahey pressed a hand to his chest. "You clearly think the worst of me, so you must realize that if I wanted to force the powers and knew a way to do so, I would have by now."

Larken opened her mouth, ready to tell the other court rulers about the message from the Cynyadas telling them that Finder and Dahey's powers were tied, but Saja squeezed her hand, giving her a tiny shake of his head. If they revealed that they knew Dahey had half the powers, then it might antagonize Dahey into killing Finder as soon as he returned to Shadeshelm.

"I admit that Dahey's methods for breaking his bond are troubling," Valakais said. "But he didn't force Finder to kill the Starveling, nor did he force his court to deem Finder unfit to rule and declare him regent.

"We as court rulers are often faced with perilous decisions. It is the burden that comes with ruling. And though we do not have a choice if the magic chooses us, we do have a choice to make the best of our situations and do what is best for our courts, not ourselves. I was once in a similar situation. My tithe girl died. I went to the Starveling, and you are right, he is not merciful. But because I went to him, he agreed to spare my court and ordered me to kill everyone that lived in the human village where the girl came from. So I did. Every last man, woman, and child. Dead by my hand. I do not regret the decision I made, though I often mourn for their lives. But better their lives than my people's."

Larken couldn't hide her gasp, disgust coiling through her. She had thought the Starveling had murdered the village, not Valakais.

"Finder destroyed an entire town when his powers took him," Valakais continued. "I destroyed an entire town of my own free will. Finder used that as an excuse to shy away from his duties as a ruler, and I used it as a reminder that I must always do whatever I can for my court. Whatever his methods, Dahey has shown more initiative to save his court than Finder ever has. He is a capable regent, and I hope that the powers do choose him. Dahey understands that being a court ruler is about duty."

Dahey bowed his head at Valakais, who extended his head back.

"Where is the knife of power?" Etain asked suddenly. "I wish to see it."

Dahey shifted. "I was under oath to return it to Ziegan. And I did. But since then, I have heard nothing from him. I can only hope he has decided to use his freedom wisely," Dahey said.

Larken wanted nothing more than to rip out fistfuls of her own hair. "You're seriously going to let him rule the Autumn Court when he freed Ziegan? You're all going to let Finder—your fellow court ruler, rot in a dungeon?"

"Technically, Dahey isn't ruling. He's just a regent." Etain waved a hand. Larken didn't know why she bothered with Etain. She had tortured Finder herself; clearly she didn't care about his wellbeing.

"Until we hear that Ziegan is stirring up trouble, I say we leave him be." Etain picked at her nails. "I doubt we would be able to track him down anyway, and he would be impossible to imprison once more without the Starveling, which makes me believe he would be even harder to kill. No one remembers him besides us—as long as it stays that way, we have nothing to fear for now. And who can say he won't be happy with his freedom and leave us well enough alone?"

Larken's mouth hung open. "You're saying do nothing. About Dahey and Ziegan."

"Larken, darling, beings worse than Ziegan roam Airodion unchecked. It is a dangerous place. As long as they don't wreak havoc, we leave them be," Etain said.

Larken couldn't believe what she was hearing. Etain knew what Ziegan was capable of thanks to the lifting of the memory curse, and she still believed that worse beings roamed Airodion?

"I am also on the side of not antagonizing him if he doesn't antagonize us," Isra said. "His language worries me." She glanced quickly at Larken. "You're right, Larken, we don't know the full extent of what it's capable of, and I don't wish to find out. As Etain said, we have no way to imprison him. Like it or not, he did assist in the Starveling's fall, so perhaps we can view him as an ally for the time being. Maybe all he desired was the Starveling's death."

Dahey nodded. "If he begins spreading his language to the courts, then we have something to worry about. But until then, I agree, we leave him alone."

The other court rulers nodded. Larken couldn't believe her eyes. They were treating Dahey like a court ruler.

"What about the humans?" Larken rasped. "The magic is gone, which means that the fey and humans can cross the bridge."

"The chasm still stands, which means that neither fey nor humans will be able to cross en masse," Dahey pointed out.

"Even one faery creature could kill dozens of humans," Larken snapped.

Isra frowned. "Larken is right. The humans don't deserve senseless death. We all must evaluate what life will look like without the Starveling —we must confer with our Popes."

"Can't you reinstate the magic on the bridges somehow?" Larken asked.

Isra shook her head. "That was the Starveling's doing."

"We can give Larken something," Valakais mused. "Guards at the bridges to prevent fey or humans from crossing until we can find something more permanent. She's right—I do not think our races need to mix. I do not want the Popes meddling in our affairs here, nor do I want powerful beings traveling into the human world and beyond our jurisdiction. It could get... messy."

"Thank you," she murmured.

"Fine," Etain drawled. "We're all in agreement about that. Now can we get back to our true reason for meeting? We all need to vote if the Tournament should take place this year."

Larken glanced at Saja, puzzled.

"The Tournament is one of the oldest and most revered celebrations of the courts," Saja murmured to her. "It happens only once every fifty years. Each of the courts takes the strongest being they have in their dungeons and throws them into the kill pit. The winner earns their freedom, and their court is seen as the most powerful."

Larken's stomach dropped, remembering how Isra had cryptically said she knew how to unite the courts. "You can't have it this year," she exclaimed.

"Enough!" Etain's eyes blazed. "I've had it with you speaking as though you are a ruler of the courts. Be quiet before I silence you forever."

Larken and Etain glared at each other.

"She's right, Larken," Isra said, laying a hand on her arm. "I invited you here as a guest, and you said your piece. Now we must discuss on our own."

"It is more important that we have one now than ever," Valakais stated. "With the Starveling gone, we must find a way to unify the courts and prove to *all* the fey that we are strong and still in control."

The other court rulers nodded.

Etain clapped her hands. "So it shall proceed as planned. And it seems to have fallen on Shadeshelm to host this year. Dahey, I hope you are prepared to hold a reverie like Airodion has never seen before."

"Oh, it shall be like nothing you have ever witnessed," Dahey promised, a gleam in his eyes.

Larken glared at Dahey. "You're going to use Finder as your prisoner."

"I can choose whomever I please," Dahey growled.

"Larken," Isra said sharply. "By law, Dahey is allowed to select any prisoner in his possession."

Dahey extended his head to her but said nothing.

"The Tournament will take place at Shadeshelm in just a few weeks," Isra continued. "Ready your prisoners, for this shall be a Tournament like none before." She bared a grin, reminding Larken just how savage a place Airodion was.

"The rules remain the same," Valakais said. "The champion wins their freedom, and the court they represent earns bragging rights." He grinned. "And might I remind you who the last champion was."

"I tire of this," Etain quipped. "We've said all we need to say."

"You're going to focus on throwing a party while the true ruler of the Autumn Court is imprisoned and Ziegan walks free?" Larken looked around at them desperately. "You can't let Dahey get away with this. Think of what would happen if your courts discovered that they could usurp you with a word. Think of how the power would shift then."

Finally, the rulers looked uncomfortable, even Dahey.

"And think of what a poor start to a new age it would be if courts began meddling in one another's private affairs," Dahey said softly. "Unless you wish to start a war."

"If you think Ziegan is a threat, Larken, then you should want a new ruler for the Autumn Court," Etain said. "New rulers have bursts of powers that are raw and unfiltered. Once they're trained, they don't risk that kind of power again. And Finder doesn't seem likely to use his powers at all—he never has. A new ruler is in everyone's best interest."

"An experienced ruler is a safer bet," Saja argued. "One who has been trained and knows how to control their powers. A burst of raw magic from a new ruler could harm their allies just as easily as it could their enemies."

Isra lifted a hand. "That's enough. Dahey, we will leave you to your affairs until after the Tournament. Your court has deemed Finder unfit to rule, and we will not question your position as regent. The transition of power from the Starveling has been difficult, but however we got here, and by whatever means, we must continue. But if we get word that you have taken the powers by force, or if Shadeshelm is falling apart at the seams during the Tournament, then we *will* intervene, for it affects us all. Dahey must pray that by some stroke of luck, the powers decide to choose yet another member of his family."

Valakais and Etain nodded their agreement, and Dahey bowed his head. "Your judgment is fair, Isra."

"Until the Tournament," Valakais said. Etain, Isra and Dahey echoed him.

Larken sat in a daze as Dahey mounted his horse and galloped off. Isra seemed to sense that Larken and Saja needed a moment alone, for she walked a few paces away.

Larken closed her eyes, an ache spreading through the back of her throat. They had failed, utterly and completely, to sway the court rulers to their cause. Taking a deep breath, she opened her eyes. At least they had agreed to help the humans in some small way, but Larken knew that guards wouldn't be enough. She needed to go to Ellevere to speak with her parents, make sure they were all right, and warn them that fey could be coming to Ballamor.

"Could Isra portal me to Ellevere to see my parents?" she asked.

Saja shook his head. "The court rulers can only portal within Airodion, and even then, there are restrictions. Isra couldn't portal us into the Shadeshelm dungeons, for example, for they are warded against such a thing."

A thought struck her then, and she frowned. "Finder portalled us to meet Remira, but when I followed you into Airodion, you were on foot, just before you called the horses. Why didn't Finder portal you to and from the border of Ellevere?"

"Finder didn't like using any of his powers, even to portal," Saja replied. "And the longer we were on foot or horseback, the longer we were away from court."

"We're trying so hard to free him, but does he want the throne back?" she asked quietly.

Saja rubbed his temples. "I don't know. For as long as I've known him, Finder has resented his position. He would have given anything to have the powers leave him and choose another. But he tried to do the best he could with the burden he was given. And the fact that it is Dahey who is trying to usurp him..." Saja sighed. "He might not want the powers, but he certainly doesn't want Dahey to have them. Doesn't want him sitting on the throne. Yet it's more complex than that. Finder was declared unfit to rule, and now the powers are split between them. It will be a struggle to take back the throne."

"I can't believe the other court rulers are doing nothing to stop this," Larken murmured.

"I can," Saja replied darkly.

"And that they will allow Finder to fight—if that is Dahey's plan. But if Finder wins, won't Dahey be forced to free him?" Larken asked, hope sparking in her chest once more. They had faced worse odds with the Starveling.

Saja's gaze met hers. "They didn't explain the rest of the rules of the Tournament. It is a test of brute strength alone—magic is not allowed. Did Finder ever explain to you what Weeping Metal is?"

Larken shook her head.

"Weeping Metal is infused with some kind of corrupt magic. It doesn't affect humans, but whenever a faery or magical creature comes into contact with Weeping Metal, they are stripped of their powers completely. Prisoners who possess magic are bound with Weeping Metal before they enter the kill ring."

Larken's mind filled with horror.

Saja lowered his head. "Finder will have no powers, no weapons, and no strength. If he enters that kill ring—he dies."

16

KAISA

Ellevere

Kaisa stood there, arm outstretched. She waded through her hazy thoughts, trying to make sense of what was happening. She needed to leave. She needed to leave *now*.

Kaisa stuffed the remaining papers back into the book and ran. She had to find Jovanna and Hollis and get them out of the palace. She could think of dozens of ways that the Order would punish her for this, and less than half ended up with her still alive by the end of them. Her status wouldn't protect her this time. Not to mention what would happen to Jovanna and Hollis. She was ruining their lives forever.

She flung herself up the stairs, up, up, up, until she reached her chamber. She ran straight to Jovanna's bed, yanking back the curtain.

"Jo, get up. We have to go. Now."

Jovanna moaned. "What in the Twins' name are you talking about?"

"I found something in Pope Sersius's chambers about the Anointing. Something I shouldn't have. Izzy found me and—and—we're all going to pay for it."

Jovanna didn't question her. She sprang out of bed and rushed around the room, stuffing extra clothes into their bags. Kaisa crammed the book filled with the documents inside her bag. "We don't have much time," Kaisa said.

"Hollis told me he was training tonight," Jovanna said.

They made their way through the palace slowly, careful not to draw unwanted attention to themselves. Still, it felt like a lifetime before they made it to the training yard. Sure enough, she could see Hollis's silhouette in the moonlight as he trained.

"Hollis," Kaisa called, as loud as she dared.

He turned, his brows lifting when he caught sight of Jovanna and their packs.

"We have to leave." Kaisa grabbed Hollis's arm. "I found out what happens at the Anointing." She glanced nervously at Jovanna. "We have to kill someone. Someone we're close to. They paired me and Jovanna."

"*What*?" Jovanna screeched.

"I'll explain everything later," Kaisa said. "I—I stole papers from Pope Sersius that prove it. I ran into Izzy, she said she would turn me in, turn you and Jovanna in, and she ran off with some of the documents before I could stop her," the words spilled out of Kaisa.

Hollis shook his head. "What are you talking about?"

"We can't stay here." Her throat closed. "I'm so sorry, Hollis. I've ruined everything for you and Jovanna. But I can't let you get hurt because of me. We have to leave."

"Where would we go?" Hollis asked. "I have a job here and a future with the Black Guard. I can't leave."

"Didn't you hear me? They've paired you with Joseph, are you honestly saying you'd kill him to stay in the Order?" Kaisa said incredulously. This was the boy who made Jovanna kill spiders for him. He would never harm Joseph—never. Not even for a chance to join the Black Guard.

"Your connection to Kaisa is too strong," Jovanna said. "Once they discover she and I have fled, they'll never allow you to become Anointed."

Hollis took a step back. His eyes darkened. "I told you. I can't leave. I want to be a member of the Black Guard. I'll survive my Anointing. If Joseph has to die—so be it."

"Hollis, how can you say that?" Kaisa said. Horror filled her. Hollis knew what went into the Anointing ritual, and he still wanted to do it? Joseph was his friend—one of his closest friends, aside from her and Jovanna.

"Don't be a fool, Hollis," Jovanna snapped. "They know we're friends. They'll think you know where we went."

"I'll have Baid catch me out here, and he'll be able to tell everyone I was training. I'll convince them that I knew nothing of Kaisa's plan."

Kaisa flinched, her stomach hollowing out. Jovanna had stood by her side unwaveringly, even when she knew that Kaisa had been sentenced to kill her. Hollis was willing to murder Joseph for the chance of a life in the Order.

"If you were the boy I thought you were, you wouldn't leave your friends. You wouldn't kill an innocent boy," Jovanna snarled.

Hollis gave her a sad smile. "I know you're angry because you're worried. But I'll be fine."

"Hollis, please," Kaisa begged, grabbing his hand. "You're one of my dearest friends. I can't let you do this. This—this isn't you. You're better than this."

Hollis squeezed her hand. "You know I love you. But I would suffer more if I left. This is how we show our true loyalty to the Order." He squared his shoulders. "I understand that you and Jovanna cannot complete the ritual, but I will not be swayed from my faith. You and Jovanna will be fine out there. And I will be fine here." He sheathed his sword, real steel tonight, and unbuckled his sword belt. "I'm sorry, Kai. But I can't give up on my dreams." He rebuckled the belt around her waist.

Kaisa stood there, frozen. He was going to kill someone. His *friend*. "Please, Hollis."

He kissed her swiftly on the forehead. "Go." He crossed over to Jovanna, pressing her to his chest. She didn't return the embrace.

Jovanna stepped away. "This is your last chance, Hollis. Is this what you want?"

Hollis nodded. "It is. I don't want to do it, but the Twins have chosen this path for me. Now, both of you, go. Before it's too late."

Kaisa and Jovanna reached the stables, saddling up two geldings. They flew through the city, passing shop after shop, then the slums on the outer skirts of the city and, finally, into the farmlands beyond.

The nearest town, Augrim, was miles from the Barrensmere. She and Hollis had visited there during last year's Feast of Asphalion to get out of the city. It was a small town, known only for a few artisanal embroidery shops. Though it was close, she doubted anyone would suspect her and Jovanna of going there due to its small size. Later they would flee north, as far from the Popes' grasp as they could get.

They had ridden for hours by the time firelight from the village became visible. She slowed her gelding to a trot, finally coming to a halt before the wooden gates surrounding the village. Torches hung on either side, but no guards.

She and Jovanna guided their horses through the gates and walked through the quiet town. The few shops were dark, and every modest house was dark as well. The air smelled of smoke and straw and sweet night air. The town was vaguely familiar from her time with Hollis, and that comforted her.

They turned off the main road, though truly, it was the only road at all and found a small patch of trees away from the shops and houses. They unsaddled the horses and tied their reins to a low hanging branch. She and Jovanna curled up against their saddles.

"I can't believe Hollis stayed," Kaisa whispered.

"I know," Jovanna murmured. "Out of all of us, I was certain that you were the most steadfast in your faith. That you would do anything for the Order." Her friend's chin jutted out, but her lip quivered slightly.

"I would have said the same once," Kaisa said slowly. "But I would never hurt you, kill you," her voice stumbled over the words, but she pushed on, "for a place in the Order. Never. And I'm so sorry, Jo. I'm so sorry that the Order wanted to pit us against each other."

Jovanna said nothing, but Kaisa caught a glimpse of silver misting her eyes. Her gut clenched. Jovanna never cried.

"How are you feeling?" Kaisa asked. "I can't believe this is happening. I was so close to having everything I wanted, and now—now it's all over."

"They were going to have you kill me, Kaisa," Jovanna said, a sharp bite in her tone. "I know you wanted to be a Pope's Page, and that dream was taken from you, but imagine how I feel. I might not have been the chosen one, but I loved the Order too, as twisted as that may seem. I didn't have the same ambitions as you, but it was my dream to become a Sister of the Order. I worked so hard for them," her voice broke, "and I was worth so little to them that they would have sacrificed me. For *you*."

"I'm so sorry," Kaisa whispered. Shame burned through her. It was true, she had been so caught up in her own dreams being dashed that she had barely had time to think about how Jovanna felt. She had known that Jovanna had wanted to become a Sister of the Order, but she hadn't thought that Jovanna had been that serious about her studies. Not like Kaisa had been. She didn't think that Jovanna had the drive and ambition. But she realized now that her friend had been trying, had been striving towards her goals, and the Order had thrown her away. Treated her like livestock that had to perish for the greater good.

"You're my family, Jo," Kaisa said. "All I have left. I saw your name on that page, and I knew I would leave the Order behind for you. Nothing will tear us apart. Ever."

Jovanna lifted her head to meet Kaisa's gaze. She leaned over and squeezed Kaisa's arm.

"I'm glad you're here," Kaisa whispered.

"Me too," Jovanna whispered back. She took a deep breath. "I want to see the papers," she said, her voice shaking slightly.

Kaisa pulled them out of her pack and handed them to Jovanna.

Her friend scanned the page, fingering her lip. "They were going to have you slaughter me. Like a pig."

"Even with the Order's cruelty, I never expected this," Kaisa said. She wrapped her arms around her knees, hugging them close.

Jovanna's gaze turned upwards. "How could the Twins do this to us? How could they tell the Popes that this is their will? Killing children?"

Kaisa looked up and the stars scattered across the sky. A deep ache spread across her chest. She shook her head, looking down at her knees. "I don't know. But they aren't gods I want to worship. Not anymore."

Jovanna flinched. "Don't say that, Kai. The Twins are good. It's the Order and the Popes who did this—twisted the will of the Twins into something horrid."

Kaisa swallowed around a lump in her throat. She didn't know what to believe anymore. Perhaps the Popes twisted the Twins' will, but the Twins were all powerful gods. How had they allowed this to happen?

She leaned back against her saddle. Eventually, Jovanna drifted off to sleep, her breathing turning slow. But Kaisa stayed awake, staring out blankly into the night. It felt as though a piece of her soul was missing.

She had left the Order, but she couldn't help feeling as though the Twins had abandoned her as well.

17

LARKEN

Airodion

Larken and Saja ate their evening meal alone that night. They had no desire to see or speak to Isra after the disaster of the meeting of the courts.

Larken clutched a mug of warmed chocolate, hoping that the drink would ease her fears. "What now?" she asked, her voice small. "We haven't made a single ally since coming here."

"Now that the Tournament is confirmed and we know Dahey will use Finder as his prisoner, Dahey will suspect that we will try to free Finder before it begins," Saja said.

"And we can't allow him to fight," Larken murmured.

Saja's brow furrowed, and his lips pressed together. "I don't know if we can get him out of this," he whispered. He blinked rapidly. She forced down the wave of panic that threatened to drown her at the sight of Saja's despair. If he faltered, she would crumble completely.

"We can figure this out," she said. "We killed the Starveling, for Twins' sake. We can handle a Tournament. What about the party?" Saja had

93

already explained that before the Tournament a reverie took place from dusk till dawn, and once the sun rose, the Tournament began.

Saja shook his head. "Finder will undoubtedly be at the reverie. Dahey will want him on display to humiliate him. But getting him out unseen in front of hordes of gentry from all four courts and within Shadeshelm's walls is impossible."

"How can we be sure that Dahey won't execute Finder before the Tournament begins?"

"If Dahey gets Finder in the kill ring, Finder will die—and Dahey's hands will remain clean in the eyes of his court. Dahey loses everything if the Autumn Court discovers that he is forcing the power's hand, and killing Finder directly would only arouse suspicion. The Tournament is the perfect excuse."

Larken rubbed her temples. "So we have until the Tournament, at least. But it seems as though we are unable to free him before or during." She paused, a horrible thought creeping into her mind. "What if... what if we killed Dahey?" She had no love for the faery, but her stomach still roiled at the thought.

"I've already thought about it," Saja said quietly. "We wouldn't be able to get close to him. And the Autumn Court would surely suspect that Finder had some part in it, and then he would have no hope of reclaiming the throne."

"What if he doesn't want to take back the throne?" Larken bit her lip.

Saja's hand clenched into a fist. "Then I will help him place the blade into Dahey's heart myself. But we must focus on freeing Finder. There will be a time before the reverie when Autumn Court fey will be pouring into Shadeshelm. Dahey will be at his most vulnerable and stressed with preparations. That will be the time to strike.

"The Tournament is still weeks away, and we will need all the time we can get to figure out how we will get through the Autumn Court without drawing attention. Until then, we lay low here. I need to keep my skills up, and the Winter Court's fighting style will keep me sharp."

"I want to train, too," Larken said. Saja looked at her in surprise. "Maybe not fighting," she amended, "but I want to do something that could help free Finder. I can't afford to be a burden to you." She would have to face the Autumn Court and its flames eventually. "You said you've seen soldiers struggle with memories. Can you help me with mine?" the last part came out as barely a whisper.

Saja's gaze softened. "Of course, Larken. We will train together until the Tournament."

PART II

TOURNAMENTS AND TREASON

18

DAHEY

Airodion

"The Roaks still refuse to give the coin they owe to the crown," Nessa said, delicately scratching notes with her quill. Dahey lifted his eyes from the rim of his wine glass and scowled at the female faery before him. Her short blonde curls framed her face perfectly, accentuating her pointed ears. Dahey could imagine that even in battle, Nessa didn't have a hair out of place.

They sat together at the private dining table in Dahey's quarters. Sunlight filtered through the crimson curtains, staining the red, gold and orange accented room. Steps led down to the other part of the room, and a canopied bed dominated the space. These had been Finder's chambers once. Now they were his.

"Why not?" he growled.

Nessa met his gaze. Her warm brown eyes were wary. "You know why. They say they will not pledge loyalty to a king with no powers. And until they learn the whereabouts of their son, they will not make any decisions."

Dahey set his wine glass down, afraid his fists would shatter it. "I already told them I don't know where their son is." Saja's parents were difficult to manage, as strong and stubborn as their son. And he did have the powers, at least partially—his court just didn't know it yet. Not when the magic made him double over in agony every time he tried to use it. Not when he had no way to train, no way to learn how to master the powers.

He just had to wait a little longer. Just until the Tournament. He picked at the skin surrounding his nails until they were raw and bloody. He couldn't let the other court rulers know he had taken the powers.

But if Finder died, it would be much more believable that the magic had come to him of its own volition. A muscle twitched in his back.

Nessa was silent. Dahey studied her for a moment. She was loyal to the crown—one of the first generals to stand at his side. Many had followed her.

"Why did you join me?"

Nessa stopped scratching her quill. "Finder is kind and just. But a king who doesn't want to rule is no king at all," she murmured quietly. "Dark times loom ahead—we all can feel it. And we need a ruler who has our best interests at heart. I believe that could be you, Dahey."

Warmth spread across his cheeks. "It doesn't matter if I want to rule or not if I can't get a single one of the noble families' loyalty."

Once he had full control of the magic, he would gain his people's trust. What lesson had his father beat into him since before he could walk? That if Dahey wanted anything in this world, he had to take it. Because he'd never be good enough to earn it.

"Send guards to collect Saja's father," Dahey said. "A few nights in the cells might change his mind."

"That would be unwise," Nessa said, resuming the scratching of her quill.

Dahey slammed his fist on the table. "What could you possibly be writing?"

The scratching stopped. "Notes," she replied.

Dahey rolled his eyes. "My father took what he wanted. So did Finder. If that's the way things are done, then I'll do it too."

"That may be true, but you want to change the way things are done around here, do you not? Don't you wish to be different from them? If you want to earn your people's trust, maybe you should try speaking to them. Not all are impressed by power. Some are impressed by what you choose to do with it."

Dahey swirled his wine. Perhaps Nessa had a point. Finder had never wanted to speak with their people. Not at court, anyway. Dahey had always been there to put minds at ease and take care of court matters. Like Reddon's situation. Finder had trusted Dahey to take care of things, and Dahey had. His people knew him, knew to come to him for advice and help. "Leave me," Dahey said, getting up from the table. "But don't... don't send for Roak."

"I think that is a wise choice, my lord," Nessa said. She paused by the doorway. "You might be surprised how many people want things done differently too," Nessa slipped out the door, leaving him in silence.

Dahey stared out at the intricately carved pillars of the Autumn Court throne room.

He squared his shoulders. He had every right to be there, just as any ruler did. Finder had always looked comfortable on the throne, but if one had known him, they would have noticed his subtle hints at discomfort. The way he would shift his weight, never fully at ease.

The differences between him and Finder had always been so catching, especially when one began to look. And the way they ruled would be different too.

Dahey laughed and joked with courtiers, beckoning them closer to speak with him. Finder and his father had never spent this much time with their people. Dahey had struggled at first, unsure how to talk to his people as regent instead of as a general. But he knew how to charm them. And though it was forced at first, it was slowly becoming more natural. He found he liked talking to his people. They had been there for him on difficult days, and he wanted to return the favor. He had spoken with dozens of fey today already, hearing their requests, offering to ease their burdens. He listened well, flashing smiles, standing firm whenever he had to make refusals while always being polite. The members of the Autumn Court fluttered around him like nervous butterflies deciding whether to land. And he was ready for them, his words as sweet as honey, drawing more of them in. They were curious about their new ruler, and he met them with open arms, asking about *laithnams* and children, crops and trade.

It was only the noble families who still looked at him glaringly from the edges of the room. The Roaks, especially. He didn't know if the families wanted Finder back or just didn't want him. Dahey's father and mother were nowhere to be seen, nor were Finder's parents, not that they wanted to be seen during a time of such disgrace.

Dahey stayed in the throne room long into the night. And the day after that. He would stay as long as it took to win them over.

Every single one of them.

19

LARKEN

Airodion

Larken breathed in deeply, savoring the sharp, metallic scent of snow and ice. She surveyed the city before them, her breath hitching in her throat as it had the first time she had entered White Keep.

When they had first entered the tunnel into the mountain, Larken had expected some kind of cavern stronghold. Instead, the tunnel cut completely through the mountain, and on the other side, surrounded by towering peaks, was the city itself. Extending from the tunnel was a bridge of icy stone which led to a slab of rock, upon which sat the castle and sprawling city. It was as if they were looking at an island in the sea, yet the sea had fallen away, leaving the island in midair.

She and Saja stood on that island now, surveying White Keep. Larken was still painfully aware that surrounding them was a precarious drop to the forest floor thousands of feet below. Torches and fires burned everywhere, sending brilliant embers into the sky, the burning flakes of orange mixing with the fluttering snow. She looked away from the dancing flames. The buildings were all made of the same grey and white stone, yet instead of giving off a cold, intimidating feel, Larken felt strangely at home. It reminded her of the cold winter nights when she, Mama and Papa would pile themselves under mountains of fur.

Shame burned in her. She would find a way to send word to her parents soon. The fey used messenger birds, but Saja had already explained that they didn't know locations in Ellevere. And the Cynyadas only lived in Airodion, so sending a message through their webs was impossible.

Vendors shouted from the streets. Steaming mugs of mulled wine and loaves of bread shaped like bears called to her, though she couldn't imagine buying them as they reminded her of Papa. He would have delighted in all the faery confections, and the wine as well.

Yet the most popular thing amongst the vendors' stalls weren't baked goods or wine or clothes—no, it was weapons. Swords, knives, bows, anything a faery could wish for could be found at one stall or another. The steel gleamed in the sunlight.

Catching her gaze, Saja nodded towards the weapons. "The Winter Court is unable to produce much of their own crops, but what they lack in agriculture they make up for in weapon production. Mining and smithing—all specialities of the Winter Court."

Further into the city, the vendors stalls disappeared, replaced with prim storefronts. More exquisite weapons hung behind the windows, polished to perfection. Taverns, cleaner and less unruly than any tavern Larken had seen in Ballamor, boasted warm drinks and rooms for rent.

A child darted out in front of them, shrieking with laughter as his father tried to keep up with him. Larken smiled, but her her stomach twisted at the thought of the sheer drop that surrounded them. White Keep was an island of stone within the mountain. Larken assumed that children would grow up knowing the dangers of the edges of their city. She had seen little to no barriers separating them from the drop, but then again, the fey were not human. Perhaps they would have no fear of a clumsy maneuver sending them careening over the edge.

"This seems to be a dangerous city for children," Larken said quietly, angling her head towards Saja.

"Indeed," Saja replied, "so much of Airodion is. Children are extremely precious to the fey, and their parents serve as their most dedicated guardians. Females can only bear one child in their lifetime," Saja said.

Larken blinked in surprise. To be able to have only one child... it was unheard of in Ballamor. Villagers raised many children to help on the rural farms. Larken was a rare exception to be an only child. She frowned, another thought occurring to her. "What about Finder and Dahey?"

"It was an occurrence that has only been recorded in our written history a handful of times," Saja said. "Dahey and Finder's fathers were twin brothers."

To have siblings and cousins be so rare, and to have that cousin betray the other... the pain Finder felt must be unbearable.

"Finder's father and uncle had a complicated relationship. They were praised above all others and seen as two rare gems that could be placed on display. When they each had a son, it made sense for the two boys to have a tight bond, for only they could truly understand the situation they were in.

"But their family was special even beyond that. Dahey's father, Osiron Fairburn, became ruler, elevating their family to royalty. And then the magic passed to Finder."

Finder Fairburn. Larken let the words roll around her tongue and couldn't help her blush. She had never heard Finder's surname before.

"Resentment grew from the Autumn Court fey. They didn't believe that a family could be so lucky. First with twins, and now with two rulers from the same family. It was unheard of."

Larken opened her mouth to reply, but a loud huffing noise made her turn. Her jaw dropped.

Three white bears lumbered through the streets, headed straight toward them.

The bears were massive, nearly twice the size of a horse and almost three times as broad.

A faery sat on the back of each bear, long spears clutched in their hands. Weapons gleamed on their backs, some sort of war hammer with a large spike at the opposite end. Each of the guards also had a thick piece of fur draped around their shoulders. The fey's legs were almost buried beneath their bears' fur. Snow collected on the bears' backs in great clumps, but the beasts didn't seem to mind. One of the bears was slightly smaller than the others, but they were all pure white.

Yet the most astonishing thing about the bears were their huge horns, curled back from their heads like a mountain goat's. Small, furred ears hid behind them, sheltered from the wind and cold.

The male faery leading them slid off the smaller bear's back. He was a full head shorter than Saja with a lithe build. A mass of curly brown hair fell across his forehead. His nose was long with a gentle slope, and his hazel eyes were warm when he met her gaze. He wore one of the most dazzling smiles Larken had ever seen.

Saja broke into a grin. "Roone," he called, making an accompanying gesture with his hands. The two soldiers embraced, smiles nearly splitting their faces in two.

The Winter Court soldier—Roone, made a series of gestures with both of his hands but didn't speak. Saja laughed and made more gestures back. Larken glanced back and forth between Saja and Roone in confusion.

"Apologies, Larken, we should have explained ourselves," Saja said, continuing to move his hands as he spoke. "Roone is deaf. He uses hand-speak to communicate."

Roone gestured to one of the female guards who accompanied him, his dark brows furrowed.

The guard nodded. "Roone asked me to translate their hand-speak for you," she said. "My name is Saoirse."

Larken nodded, mystified.

Roone smiled at her and began using hand-speak again, his fingers flying through the air.

Larken looked back to Saoirse as she translated for Roone, but the guard shook her head. "Look at Roone as if he was speaking," Saoirse corrected gently. "I am merely voicing the words so you can understand him."

Roone began his gestures once more.

Simultaneously, Saoirse began to translate. "I apologize for our rudeness. Saja knows hand-speak, but he's too out of practice to translate for me. We are old friends, though we haven't seen each another in quite awhile." It was strange at first, seeing Roone's movements and then Saoirse's voice, but Larken grew accustomed to it faster than she expected. "My name is Roone Delaney, and I am a part of Isra's *dornán*."

Ah, so other court rulers have dornáns *as well*, Larken thought to herself.

Roone paused, eyebrows lifted, waiting for her to introduce herself.

Larken resisted the urge to look at Saoirse. "My name is Larken McLeary. I'm afraid I don't have any fancy titles." She swallowed, but Roone gave a small chuckle as his eyes followed the guard's hands as she translated Larken's words into hand-speak. "I'm from Ballamor in the human realm."

"It's a pleasure to meet you, Larken," Saoirse supplied for Roone. "I must ask you what it was like traveling alone with Saja. I have spent years trying to crack that stoic exterior to no avail."

Larken chuckled at Saja's flustered expression. "Once he warms up to you, he becomes very chatty."

Roone lifted an eyebrow.

"I envy the time you got to spend with him, then. Separated from Finder for once, and he still doesn't have time to catch up with me."

Larken exchanged a glance with Saja; sadness reflected in both of their eyes. Roone's face fell when he caught their expressions.

"I shouldn't have mentioned Finder, please forgive me. I should have known that some business surrounding his imprisonment brought you here."

Larken swallowed. As a member of Isra's *dornán*, Roone was close to the queen. If they could get Roone on their side, they had a better chance of getting Isra to join them too. Especially since he seemed to like Saja so much.

"I must get on with my shift," Saorsie translated as Roone climbed back onto his bear. "But you are welcome to spar with me anytime you wish, Saja. It will be good for you to learn skills from a master." He grinned, and he and his two guards lumbered off on their bears.

Larken hid her smile, saying nothing at the pink that colored Saja's cheeks.

20

KAISA

Ellevere

"We can't stay here long," Kaisa said the next morning. "The Order will be coming for us soon."

Jovanna nodded. "You're right. We'll stay long enough to gather provisions, and then we'll head north."

Kaisa leaned against her saddle bags but shifted as something dug into her back. She frowned, pulling the object out.

The book she had stolen from Pope Sersius. She hadn't noticed how strange it was before, but here, in the sunlight, she realized how rare the book must be. It was made from a strange, scaled leather that was velvety soft from age. She sat up.

"Jo," she breathed. "Look at this."

"Maybe it will have answers," Jovanna said shakily. "Something about why the Anointings have to happen."

Kaisa opened the book. The title page read *The Beings and Beasts of Airodion*. But jutting out from the page was a folded piece of parchment. Kaisa frowned, opening the paper. Her eyes widened,

"What does it say?" Jovanna prompted.

"Pope Sersius," Kaisa read. "So good to hear from you, my brother in faith. I'm glad to see you have accepted the offer as well. The Furyons will be difficult to deal with, of course, but it is a price we must be willing to pay. We can stand to lose a few farming villages, and when the time is right, we will swoop in with the light of the Twins to save them. If what Ziegan says is true, soon we will be rich beyond measure with his new magic. Think of what we shall accomplish then. As soon as I receive the signal, I will move. Let me know what your next play shall be. Signed, Pope Galba."

Jovanna frowned. "What in the Twins' Hell is a Furyon? And who is Ziegan?"

Kaisa closed her eyes, rage pooling within her. She put the letter down, afraid she would crumple it with her fists. The Popes were willing to sacrifice farming villages, and then somehow use the Twins to bring more people to the faith.

"I don't know," Kaisa said. "But whoever Ziegan is, he promised to give magic to the Popes."

"This Ziegan being must be from the faery realm," Jovanna breathed. "See if the book says anything about him or the Furyons."

Kaisa flipped through the pages, coming to a map of Ellevere and the faery realm above, labeled, AIRODION.

Kaisa sucked in a breath. This was a book about the faery realm. And for Pope Sersius to be reading it... She flipped through the book until she came to the name Pope Galba had mentioned in his letter.

"Here," she breathed. "The Furyons are hunters who feast on the fear of their victims as much as their flesh," she read aloud. "They keep them alive as long as possible while they eat them, inflicting as much pain and misery as possible. They appeared in Airodion shortly before the second war and were thoroughly hunted, deemed by the court rulers as unfit to live in Airodion. None have been seen since."

Jovanna pressed a hand to her temple. "Second war? Court rulers? What does this book speak of?"

Kaisa shook her head, baffled. "I don't know. And why does Pope Sersius believe that the Furyons are coming here? The boarder between

Ellevere and the faery realm—or Airodion as I suppose it's called—is sealed until the next Choosing Ceremony. Could some of them have managed to get past the Black Guard when the bridges were open for the Ceremony a few weeks ago?"

"How strange that this was on his desk," Jovanna said, frowning. "It's almost as if he was researching these faery creatures."

Kaisa stroked her hand down the worn leather of the book, her fingers trembling slightly. This was a priceless tome; she was sure of it. And if the Order ever discovered that she had taken it... she shuddered.

Jovanna reached over and placed a hand on her arm. "Let us put it from our minds for now. Let's go into town and see if we can find any provisions for our journey."

They tacked their horses. Kaisa's gelding was a gorgeous beast in the sunlight, a light bay with a white mark on the center of his forehead.

"I'm going to call you Sorreno," she whispered to him, patting him on the neck.

They rode together through the city, taking in the sights and smells. Kaisa tried to convince herself that she and Jovanna would be safe there for a time. They would leave as soon as they gathered the supplies they needed. They hadn't been able to muster up much food when they had fled the Institute, but they would be able to find all they needed in Augrim.

Kaisa wound her shaking hands in Sorreno's mane. She tried to focus on the sensation, but nothing felt real. Had she truly left the Institute behind forever? The Order had taken her in, given her everything. She had been a shining star amongst her classmates, adored by her tutors.

"You have a servant's heart," Sister Abitha's words rang in her head. A servant to the Twins. A servant to the Popes and the Order. Those words had meant everything to Kaisa once. She had relished her tutor's praise, had thought that becoming a Pope's Page would mean that every struggle in her life would have been worth it.

But was that what she wanted to be? A servant? She loved helping people—but she had been blind to the ways of the Order. Numbed to the pain it caused. Shame burned in her heart. It was easy to overlook the

Order's wrongdoings when she had always been exempt from punishment.

But who was she if she was no longer their servant?

She and Jovanna paused in the village square. A clump of villagers stood off to the side, muttering to themselves. Kaisa and Jovanna exchanged glances, then positioned themselves close enough to eavesdrop, making sure not to bring attention to themselves.

"...my brother says. Big as horses. With wings."

"Wings?" another man growled. "Piss off, that's a bedtime story to scare children."

"Would my brother come all the way from Ballamor just to tell us a bedtime story?" The first man clasped a similar looking man on the shoulder, his brother, presumably.

The man looked deeply shaken. Dark circles hooded his eyes, and his whole face had a sunken appearance, like he was starving.

"Doesn't make sense," the man muttered, his hands twitching. "Shouldn't exist—"

"Speak up!"

"Tell us for yourself!"

"He's in no shape to tell!" The first man shielded his brother from the growing din of the group. "Look at him, he's scared out of his wits."

"They came in the night," the man whispered. "Descending from the sky like dark birds. They set upon Ballamor like demons from the Twins' Hell. They wanted meat. They wanted us."

Some of the other men looked unsure now, either from the man's words or his terrified facial expression.

"They took some of our people into the sky, and then away into the trees. We could hear them screaming. For hours and hours, they screamed, as though the beasts feasted on them while they still lived." The man's eyes were wide and bloodshot. "I think the beasts wanted us to hear them. They wanted us to know we were helpless."

"How many did they take?"

"Five—three men, two women. But they will be back. We see them circling, waiting for their next attack."

"You're sure it wasn't some other creature?" an older woman asked.

"With wings? No, I'm certain. I had never seen the likes of this creature before, nor had anyone else in my village. Furyons, people are calling them. From the old legends."

Kaisa's mouth hung open. She turned to Jovanna, who wore an equal expression of horror.

"A punishment from the Twins for some sin the town committed," one man scoffed. "Nothing more. Repent, and they will leave you."

Kaisa's finger twitched, the first time she had moved since she began listening to the men speak. How often had she heard that excuse? How often had she blamed herself for something that was just sheer bad luck? The Order loved to escape blame and place it on its people instead. The man and his village would suffer, and people of the faith would shun them, claiming it was a just punishment.

"Other creatures have come as well," the man said, "huge white monsters with spines and beaks. Please, you must help us. Please—I'm begging you." The man fell against his brother, shaking madly.

"You expect us to travel that far north on mere rumors?" a big man said harshly.

"We cannot abandon our village for yours," another woman said in a kinder tone. "It must be a punishment from the Twins."

The man curled into himself, pressing into his brother. He began to sob. Slowly, the villagers left, leaving the two brothers alone.

Kaisa pressed her shoulder into Jovanna's side as they huddled by their campfire that night.

"I pity that man and his village," Kaisa said. She knew how it felt to be blamed, she knew how heartless the Order could be. "The Order was willing to let me murder my dearest friend, and now the Popes will let these monsters terrorize the farming villages. I don't understand how anyone can still have faith in divine beings who would send monsters to punish that man's village, or a religion that would leave them to die."

"I know it's difficult, but you must separate the Order from the Twins," Jovanna said softly. "I know we were taught that the Popes speak the Twins' will, and for a time, I believed that to be true. But I wasn't blind to the horrors of the Order. I wasn't exempt from punishment. I started to believe that maybe—maybe the Popes' will and the Twins' will were different things. I had to believe that to make it through the Institute with my faith still intact. These people could learn the same thing. That the Order and the Twins can be separated. That their gods haven't forsaken them, even if the Popes have."

"But what if the Twins don't exist?" Kaisa said, her voice quaking. She never thought she would say such a thing.

"These people just lost their homes, Kai. They don't need to be stripped of their faith as well. Not if it can bring them comfort during these dark times." Jovanna squeezed her hand. "We need to rest while we can—we should leave soon. Stay on the move since we don't know when and where these attacks will come next."

Kaisa bit her lip, nodding. As she settled down to sleep, she tried sending a quick prayer to Aleea and Asphalion. But the prayer felt forced.

It felt like shouting words across a chasm, with no one on the other side to reply. She had always heard her gods' voices so clearly, and now there was only silence. She hugged herself, tears welling in her eyes. She felt so alone, though Jovanna was right beside her. She didn't understand how Jovanna hadn't lost her faith and how Kaisa had lost hers so quickly, like it had been cleaved from her soul.

21

LARKEN

Airodion

A magnificent buffet lined the back wall of one of White Keep's dining halls, packed with every type of food Larken could imagine. Half of the table was laden with different kinds of bread, some sweet and studded with fruits and nuts, others thick and brown like the bram she was used to in Ballamor. Sweet syrup and jam sat in dainty glass containers along the edge of the table. Pastries, fried potatoes, and grilled vegetables crowded the rest of the table. A massive pot of porridge sat in a bed of coals in the fireplace, four tea kettles nestled nearby to keep warm.

Larken shoveled down her fried potatoes while Saja drank his morning tea. She managed to get through three cinnamon buns before her stomach began to ache.

Saja was eyeing her with a strange expression. She narrowed her eyes at him. "What?" she asked.

"Do you feel older?" he asked, swirling a spoon in his tea.

"How did you know it was my birthday?" Larken asked flatly.

"My excellent conversational skills weaseled it out of you on our journey here." Saja shook his head. "Eighteen. Sometimes I forget how young you are."

Truthfully, with the whirlwind that was her life in Airodion, she had nearly forgotten it was her birthday. Eighteen, a year she had dreaded since Brigid had been Chosen because it marked the year that she was no longer eligible, and therefore would never be able to reunite with her friend.

The thought saddened her. Looking back and seeing what she had feared then, and how differently events had played out.

"It is a bit strange," Larken admitted. "This is my first birthday I've ever spent away from home." Thoughts of her parents pushed their way into her mind, and a deep well of sadness opened inside her. They had no idea what had become of her, or where she was now.

Saja pulled out a simple wooden box. "I know Airodion hasn't been kind to you, but I hope this helps in some small way."

Larken opened the box, peering inside. "Saja," she gasped.

"Maps," Saja said, suddenly shy. "I found them in the library and asked Roone if I could purchase a few of them." His honey eyes lit up with his smile.

Larken ran her hands over the different parchments. Some were thick and stained, others were delicate as moth wings. "They're beautiful," she murmured.

"A few pre-date the Starveling," Saja said. "It was difficult to find ones that documented the human realm as well, but I found a few that do."

Larken couldn't tear her gaze away from the charts. Her fingertips tingled. She couldn't wait to lay out the maps across her floor and study them, learn the techniques of the faery cartographers.

"And I made you this," Saja said. He handed her another box.

She lifted the lid. Inside was a daintily frosted vanilla cake.

"Cake for breakfast?" she laughed.

Saja's brow furrowed. "Should I have made it a different flavor? I already tossed three out last night."

Larken squeezed Saja's hand. "It's perfect. Thank you." She picked up her fork, ready to stab it into the cake.

"I should have brought it out sooner," Saja worried. "Now you're probably full—"

Larken chuckled. "I'm never too full for cake."

But when the first bite hit her tongue, it turned to ashes. A pit of dread opened in her stomach. They were still no closer to rescuing Finder. She didn't deserve to feel this bit of happiness while he rotted away in the Shadeshelm dungeons. Her mind was a tangled mess of emotions—worse than she had ever felt in her life, even after her fight with Brigid. What if she felt this way forever? What if she never overcame her fear of the flames and felt her fear every day, all the time?

Tears welled in her eyes, spilling down her cheeks. Shame burned in her. She didn't want to cry in front of Saja. Not when he had done all of this for her.

He placed his hand over hers. "We're going to figure this out," he said gently. "It's a difficult thing to be afraid of one's own thoughts, but you aren't alone."

She nodded, swallowing hard. She wasn't alone, Saja was here with her.

Larken flipped through the pages of the massive book, her eyes nearly glazing over as they tried to decipher the minuscule text. The book, titled *The Beings and Beasts of Airodion*, listed nearly all of the known creatures in the faery realm.

She drew her fur drape tighter around her shoulders. The library of White Keep was like nothing she had ever seen. The entire building was made completely of ice, down to the shelves themselves. The blue panes of ice were so clear they resembled glass. Massive, scalloped archways filled the center of the space, columns flanking either side. Tucked away beneath the columns were interior chambers for private reading. Sunlight streamed in from skylights on the ceiling, but the direct sunlight never touched the books themselves, hidden away on their icy shelves.

But Larken's favorite part of the library was the cerulean blue canals that flowed through the space for quick access to the huge expanse of books. Small wooden boats with white sails were docked beneath the alcoves of the private reading areas, allowing visitors an easy way to travel to the shelves. Librarians manned several of the boats, ready to assist anyone who needed help. Larken had taken one look at the library and decided that she could happily spend the rest of her life there.

She forced her gaze away from the arched window in her private reading room and made herself return to her book. She'd started out by reading a book about past Tournaments but had quickly given up as she didn't know half of the creatures it referred to, which is why she now studied a book about the creatures of Airodion.

Etain hadn't been lying when she said that creatures worse than the Guardian roamed the faery realm. True, they might not know the full extent of what Ziegan was capable of, but many of the creatures mentioned in the book made her skin crawl.

Larken was determined to find out all she could about the Tournament and the reverie so she and Saja could form the best plan for rescuing Finder. She didn't want to focus on her mind. She could help by doing this.

Sooner or later, you'll have to face the flame.

She pushed the thought away, flipping through the razor thin pages of the book. It was far more than a thousand pages, and she only had a few weeks to learn everything she could. Hunching over the text, she began reading once more.

22

KAISA

Ellevere

Eventually, their city hideout was discovered by locals who demanded that the vagrants vacate the premises, so she and Jovanna were forced to spend their coin at the local inn.

They hadn't heard any rumors that the Order was searching for two girls that had escaped the Institute, but that didn't mean anything. They wouldn't plaster the news around that two people had escaped the Order. They would find them and punish them soon enough—no need to spread rumors. Kaisa knew they had to leave for the North soon, but it was difficult to leave behind the familiar in Augrim. Truthfully the North scared her—it was known as being a more lawless place, filled with heretics.

Though, I suppose you are one of those now, Kaisa thought to herself. She would miss the familiarity of Augrim. She knew Jovanna felt the same, as they kept making excuses that they needed to gather more provisions and let the horses rest before their long journey.

Ever since they had entered Augrim, some strange sadness had sucked the life from Kaisa's bones. As much as she hated to admit it, she

119

missed the routine of the Institute. She missed having a purpose to her days, a structure that she could follow. Though it meant hard work, and punishments for her failings, this strange, unstructured life did not suit her. But the more she missed the Institute, the more she hated herself.

Jovanna was settling into her newfound freedom well. She had been spending her days in the tavern down the road, keeping her head down but finding out what information she could. She asked Kaisa to come with her several times, but Kaisa could barely get herself out of bed.

Kaisa spent her time flipping through *The Beings and Beasts of Airodion*. Each beast chilled her more than the last, and those were just what the author considered monsters. She found descriptions of the other beasts the man from Ballamor had seen as well—the Fomari. And the other 'beings' were just as horrifying. Fey—who had the magic of deception. And their rulers, capable of wielding the elements themselves. Kaisa could barely believe her eyes, was all of this real? Could these beings share her world, separated only by a chasm? She rubbed her eyes.

The humans knew about the existence of the fey, of course. The Choosing Ceremony was a glorious ritual where each of the four faery lords came and selected a human girl to return with them. The girls lived a magical life in the faery realm, though they were never seen from again. The Popes claimed that this was a glorious affair.

Kaisa had believed that once. But now, she knew better than to believe those who were carted off in the dead of night were safe. The Scholars supposedly sent to the outpost colonies were murdered during their Anointing. Kaisa could only imagine that the girls sent to the faery realm shared a similar fate.

Jovanna returned, pulling her cloak back to reveal her shorn hair.

"Get up," Jovanna said, tossing Kaisa her cloak. "Word has it there's a town gathering tonight—and they don't want just anyone knowing. But I think it's about the attacks on the other towns. We should go."

Word had been pouring in as of late about the recent attacks. They came from all over Ellevere, not just the North, though those were the most prevalent.

Kaisa bit her lip, hesitating. What could she and Jovanna do to help?

She glanced at her pillow, at the book hidden beneath it. They had information. Information that could help people. They no longer had the protection of the Order, and neither did these people, being left to defend themselves against the Furyons. A warm glow burned in her chest, burning away some of the sadness.

She had helped people at the Institute. She could help people here too.

She nodded at Jovanna. "Let's go."

The town meeting was held in a loft above one of the storerooms.

Kaisa and Jovanna huddled together, hoods pulled low over their faces. They weren't the only ones trying not to draw attention to themselves.

A woman rocked a crying baby. Kaisa watched them. Had her mother held her like that, once? Her parents had sold her to the Institute. Of course, they wouldn't have known how bad the Anointing was, but they had still gambled on strangers. Kaisa could only hope that they had wanted the best for her. But look where it had gotten her.

"Quiet!" an older woman yelled from the front of the room. She was a plump woman with grey hair that fell to her waist in a thick, knotted braid. A handsome boy stood at her side, tall with light brown eyes and dark brown curls. He glanced around the room, his eyes watchful.

"You all know why we're here," the old woman said in a gruff voice. This must be the leader of the town. The woman commanded the room with her presence. "We've all heard about the attacks. It's not long before we're targeted—they're drawn to the farming towns. And while Barrensmere is within pissing distance of Augrim, we haven't heard a peep out of them. We can't expect any help from the Order."

Kaisa lifted her head. Other members of the crowd stirred, murmuring their assent. So this was common talk in the town—they were used to heretical ideas. Some part of her was surprised. The North was known for being particularly rebellious, some openly dissenting the

Order. But not the South, the crown of the Order. Here the beatings were frequent, the burnings commonplace. Nothing burned like a heretic, and in the South, they burned, and they burned, and they burned.

But this woman spoke freely amongst her people. Freely among Kaisa and Jovanna, though someone would have had to have recognized them as outsiders. Kaisa didn't know what to think. Either the woman was stupid for being so trusting, or cunning enough to know that anyone spending that long at the inn with their heads down, anyone who had dared come to this meeting, had a quarrel with the Order. And some part of Kaisa felt a kinship with this woman, who had welcomed them into this small herd of dissenters. They didn't trust the Order, and neither did she.

"We must decide what to do. The Popes haven't lifted a finger to help the souls in those other farming towns. We know they aren't a curse sent from the Twins, they come from that blasted faery realm—and if they're crossing the borders in the numbers they are, then the Black Guard isn't doing anything to stop it. We must assume that the bridges have fallen, and that the fey can enter Ellevere at will. The Popes are complacent. The Order is complacent. But we won't be. We won't roll over and show our bellies to these foul beasts. When they come for us, we need to be ready."

"We should leave," one voice cried.

"What can we do against these monsters? They'll tear us apart!" another wailed.

"Maybe if we go to the Order they'll help us," a man said firmly.

The old woman raised her hand, and the cries fell silent. "The Order knows what's going on, they would be fools not to, and still, they haven't sent help. And our lives are here—we can't expect everyone to pack up and leave. This is our home; we need to defend it. These beasts are just that—beasts. We can figure out a way to kill them."

Voices chimed in from the crowd, suggesting preparations that could be made.

Kaisa wanted to tell them about the book, but she knew it would only lead to questions. Where it came from, how she got it—questions she and Jo didn't need to be answering. The book could be a death sentence. For this whole town, maybe, if Pope Sersius realized they had it. That kind of information about the faery realm was not meant to be shared.

But then again, the woman before her just held a meeting and slandered the Popes and the Order in front of a crowd.

But more voices rose from the crowd, not all in agreement with the old woman. Some were frightened enough to want to seek the Order's help. Others wanted to leave.

"Silence!" the old woman cried. "We will start fortifying the town. What have we heard about these creatures of darkness? They fear the light. Everyone, keep candles burning in your homes."

No, no, no. The book claimed that only great bonfires could keep the Furyons away. Too much light frightened them off, but too little only drew them in like moths to a flame.

She bit her lip. A book like *The Beings and Beasts of Airodion* could fetch a high price from the Order—or from other bidders. She didn't want to draw that kind of unwanted attention to her and Jo, but she couldn't leave these people to die.

"No!" Kaisa blurted out. All eyes turned to her.

"What are you doing?" Jovanna hissed.

Kaisa slowly stood. "I had a dream last night about these hideous beasts," she lied. "Aleea came to me and told me that they are beings of the night, yes, but candles will only draw them in. We need huge fires to scare them off."

"A vision sent by the Twins," someone murmured.

The old woman's eyes narrowed. "A dream, you say? And what if your dream was wrong, girl?"

Kaisa swallowed. "Then I'll die alongside you." She held the woman's stare. Finally, the old woman nodded.

"Fair enough. Tell us what else Aleea warned you about these monsters."

23

LARKEN

Airodion

Two groups of Winter Court soldiers faced off in White Keep's icy training yard. Larken had joined Saja after one of her library sessions and sat beside him in the stands flanking either side of the yard. Sweat glistened on Saja's brow—proof that he had been working hard while sparring with Roone before she had arrived. The Winter Court faery sat astride his massive horned bear, using hand-speak to communicate with the soldiers. Larken had quickly picked up on the fact that nearly all of White Keep used hand-speak, especially in the presence of Roone.

"How do you know Roone?" Larken asked Saja. "And how long did it take you to learn hand-speak?" Roone must have been a close friend of Saja's if he had taken the time to learn Roone's language.

"We met during a Tournament many years back," Saja replied. "And the military school that Finder, Madden and I attended required that we learn many languages, hand-speak being one of them."

Larken didn't fail to notice that Saja had excluded Dahey from his list of companions.

"It's incredibly helpful for soldiers to have a form of non-verbal communication," Saja continued. "You can't always hear in the thick of battle. We don't use it much in Shadeshelm, but here, everyone uses it to honor Roone."

Isra was revered by her court, but Roone was positively adored. They couldn't walk anywhere with Roone without being stopped to chat. His constant smile and cheery attitude were intoxicating.

Roone gave another signal, and the two groups charged, swinging at each other with swords and axes. Roone watched from atop his bear until finally, he held up a hand. The two groups pulled apart immediately. Roone gave them what Larken could only guess were pointers about their skill before he nodded to another soldier, who took his place as instructor.

Roone approached them on his bear, smiling widely. His hands flowed like water as they made their way through the movements of hand-speak.

"Roone is asking me to translate for him," Saja said.

Roone gave a big smile and said something else in hand-speak.

Saja scowled. "Now he's saying that I need to take private hand-speaking lessons with him so he can teach me how to use my hands properly."

Larken hid her smile. Roone winked at her.

"Saja, I think Roone wants to spend time with you." Larken elbowed him.

Saja froze, gaping at Roone.

"I want both of you to teach me hand-speak," Larken continued, Saja translating beside her. She wanted to be able to use hand-speak herself and communicate with Roone on her own.

Roone's face lit up, his hands flying into motion.

"It would be an honor to teach you, Larken," Saja translated. He turned to her. "I told Roone about your struggle with the memories."

Larken tensed, not sure if she wanted Roone knowing such a personal thing about her, but the Winter Court faery's eyes were gentle.

"He thinks he has a way to help, and I have a couple ideas as well."

Saja's hands continued to translate his words for Roone. "We can begin as soon as tomorrow."

"We have many breathing techniques we can try," Saja translated for Roone. "And when you're tired of me re-teaching you to breathe, I'll re-teach you to speak. I must clarify that was supposed to be a joke—I get the feeling that Saja does not translate my tone." Saja scowled as he realized what he was saying, causing Larken and Roone to burst into laughter.

"I look forward to it," Larken said.

24

KAISA

Ellevere

News of the Furyon attacks spread. The monsters had attacked all the towns a few miles north of Augrim. The villagers all assumed that they would be next and expected the attacks to come any day now.

Kaisa and Jo sat at the tavern, The Dancing Toad. Warm brown wood and stone made up the interior, a large painting of a toad spinning around on its back legs occupying the back wall. The scent of sweet ale and fresh loaves of bread lingered in the air, and the gentle hum of conversation from other patrons settled over her.

"I think we should just hand over the book and be done with it," Jo growled. "We need to head north—we won't be safe here much longer."

"We have nowhere to go, now," Kaisa argued. "The attacks are all coming from the North. We have a way to help these people. We can protect them and ourselves. And if we help them, then they won't be as likely to hand us over to the Order. They could protect us, too." She almost said more but held her tongue. The book was special. She wasn't meant to have it, and part of that felt good. Like she had stolen something precious from the Order. It would never repay all they had taken from her, but it was something.

Jovanna bit her lip. "I don't like this, Kai."

Kaisa leaned forward, placing her hand on Jovanna's arm. "Trust me. We'll try to help them. If it turns out the book was wrong—we'll flee, and we'll just try to dodge the attacks as best we can. But it doesn't feel right abandoning these people to their fate—not when we have a way to help them."

Jovanna reluctantly nodded. "Fine. But if these attacks prove too much for us to handle, we run, agreed?"

Kaisa nodded. "Agreed."

Kaisa and Jovanna helped the villagers with preparations, using wood to fortify the city walls, making great stacks of wood that would be set alight each night.

Of course, once news spread that Augrim was fortifying their walls, members of the Order arrived in town to investigate, making sure some kind of rebellion wasn't brewing. Kaisa and Jovanna kept their heads down. Kaisa simmered in her own rage. The Order refused to send help, but as soon as they saw the town trying to save themselves, they suspected them of wrongdoing.

Refugees from other towns trickled in, seeking what shelter they could. Kaisa sat near the street outside the inn, watching the latest batch of survivors stagger into town. A few children had made it, she was glad to see, though still so few. Her heart ached at their blood-stained little faces. How many had lost parents and were now alone in the world?

One of the members of the Order peeled himself from an alleyway and made his way to the group of stragglers. "Greetings!" He steepled his hands out in front of him. "I can see that tragedy has befallen you, and yet here you stand, by the Twins' mercy!"

The people stared at him hopefully, likely praying that he was about to offer them food and shelter on behalf of the Order.

"I can see that you are special in the eyes of the Twins," the man said, his eyes glittering with malicious intent as he took in the refugees. "And because the Twins are merciful, I will offer you a deal." He pulled out his coin purse. "I will take the little ones for two gold coins each."

The children stared at him with wide, solemn eyes. A few hid behind their mothers' skirts, but most stood alone.

"All you have to do is sign a few documents for your child and a portion of their wages earned at Pope Sersius's palace will be sent to you. If you cannot read, I'm happy to read the document for you," he breezed on, whipping out pieces of parchment from his bag. "We can't have vagrant children on the streets. They'll have to come with me if they can't be cared for. No paperwork required for those without parents, of course. Can't have a child sign a document!" he chuckled to himself.

Blood roared in Kaisa's ears. How dare this man come and try to profit off these children's trauma? He would stoop so low as to try to make some quick coin off what these people had endured. These people had suffered, and they didn't know any better. They probably thought their children, especially the orphaned ones, would be better off living a life in the palace. After all, they would have access to food, clothing and wages.

And the Anointing.

No. No more. Kaisa might not be able to stop the Anointings from happening. She might not be able to prevent other children from being sold. But she would never allow it to happen in front of her. She would not sit by.

"Elija?" she called out the first male name she could think of. She hurried up to the group of refugees, grabbing the shoulders of one of the little boys with the same dark skin as hers and leaning down to hug him.

Keep quiet if you know what's good for you, she begged. She arched her brow, pretending to recognize another one of the lone little girls. "Sera?" She pulled the little girl in next.

Kaisa gestured to the children. "My sister's children. I can't believe—" she forced a hiccup. "I can't believe what happened to their poor town."

The other townspeople looked at her warily.

"What joyous news!" the member of the Order cried. "Now I have someone to sign the paperwork. Here are the documents."

Kaisa shook her head, pulling the children close. "Oh, no, sir, they'll be staying with me. They'll be well taken care of, I promise. Being chosen for the Institute is a huge honor, of course, but I couldn't stand the thought of them going to live with strangers, where I'd never be able to see them again." She tried not to raise her voice at the last part. She prayed that the refugees were paying attention. "Their wages can't compare to the care and love of their family members, and I can't stand to think about them alone with all those other children with only teachers to guide them."

Some nods came from the other refugees, and they pulled their children close, away from the man. Kaisa breathed a tiny sigh of relief.

The man's eyes narrowed. "You know a lot about the Institute, girl."

Kaisa waved a hand, forcing it not to shake.

What happened to keeping your head down?

"I had a bastard brother. He was taken in and we were so distraught that the man who recruited him told us all about the life he would have to soothe us. But I swore then that I could never part with another family member. We are weak, denying an opportunity from the Twins. But we swear to repent and serve in other ways."

The man gave her a once over, and Kaisa held her breath. Finally, he looked away, back toward the other refugees. "And you? Will you reject this opportunity from the Twins? How will you care for your children when you have no jobs, no coin and no homes? They will be better off with me."

Some of the other refugees exchanged glances.

"The town has been pitching in to help newcomers," Kaisa blurted. A lie, but she couldn't let a single child go with him. She couldn't.

The man turned back to her. "Are they now? Where are your lodgings, girl? I do not know if I can trust these children into your care, seeing as they are not even yours."

You've really buried yourself deep, haven't you? She opened her mouth to reply, but a strong voice interrupted her.

"That won't be necessary." A boy sauntered up to the group, his hands in his pockets. Kaisa recognized him from the town meeting.

"Who are you?" the man snapped.

"My grandmother leads this town," the boy replied cooly. "This is my dear friend." He gestured to Kaisa. "Her family has lived here for generations. And you will not insult her. You are a member of the Order, but our guest here."

The member reluctantly nodded after a moment. "Fine," he seethed. "Last chance to get some coin," he called to the crowd.

"These children are not for sale," the boy growled, his fists clenching at his sides. The member of the Order slunk off.

"What about the food she promised?" one woman called. "Is the town going to provide for us?"

"We will do what we can to care for you until you get back on your feet," the boy said gently. "There are makeshift beds set up in the outer barn. Keep following this road until you see it," he said. The refugees all thanked him, and he nodded. They shuffled off.

The little boy and girl that Kaisa had hugged stayed behind. "Are you really my aunt?" the little boy asked, his eyes wide.

Kaisa's heart broke, and she sank to her knees in front of him. "No, little one. I'm so sorry. But I didn't want that bad man to take you away."

The little boy bit his lip and nodded, and Kaisa could tell he was holding back tears with all his strength.

"Are the monsters going to come here?" the little girl asked. "It was loud when they came. Will it be loud here?"

Kaisa's brow furrowed in confusion.

"Will it be loud here?" the girl repeated. "I don't like it when they scream."

Kaisa didn't know if she was referring to the monsters or the townspeople, but she didn't want to find out.

"The monsters might come," Kaisa said. "But I'm going to stop them. I stopped the bad man from taking you, didn't I? So trust me. I'm not going to let the monsters hurt you. Or anyone in this town, if I can help it."

The two children threw themselves into her arms. Her heart ached. "Stay with the others," she whispered. "Family isn't always blood. Sometimes you find it. You'll find it again, I promise."

The children ran back to their people, and Kaisa turned to the boy, who had been watching everything unfold with a curious expression.

"Thank you," she told him. "I know what happens to children who go to the Institute, and I just couldn't bear to see any more of them taken."

Shut your mouth before you say too much, she warned herself.

The boy tilted his head. "You know what happens to children at the Institute. And you know about the monsters. It seems I was right to save you." He gave her a lopsided grin, and she scowled.

"You didn't save me." She crossed her arms. "A few more clever words, and I would have been fine."

"Hmm," the boy said, crossing his arms. Kaisa narrowed her eyes. Was he mocking her? "Because you're just so clever, are you?"

She narrowed her eyes further. "You didn't see me referring to my grandmother as the leader of this town, did you?"

The boy chuckled, shaking his head. "Clever and beautiful. Was there ever a more dangerous combination?"

Kaisa blushed, caught off guard. He smiled, clearly liking her reaction. "My name is Ishan."

"Kaisa," she returned warily. "Well, I best be going. Thanks for your meager help, Ishan," she turned on her heel and left, but not without peeking at him one last time over her shoulder.

He was still looking at her. He began to walk backwards, away from her. "I'll be looking for you when the monsters come, clever Kaisa," he called, spreading his arms.

She hurried back to the inn, her heart pounding louder than it had during her encounter with the man of the Order.

25

LARKEN

Airodion

"Imagine each thought that enters your mind leaves on a gentle river." Saja instructed her from the chair opposite her in the training yard. It was empty today—Roone and his soldiers were out practicing drills with their bears.

Larken tried to focus, but the harder she tried to think about not thinking, the more thoughts entered her mind. Had Finder ever practiced this technique at military school? Had Dahey been different then, before Finder had become prince? Was the Weeping Metal eating away at Finder's skin at this very moment until nothing remained? She squirmed.

"Distance yourself from your physical body," Saja said. She opened her eyes and squinted at him. How did he always know when she moved if his eyes were closed?

"And keep your eyes closed. Limit as many distractions as possible."

Larken rolled her eyes but did as she was told.

They'd been practicing meditation for the past few days, starting at just a few minutes, but Larken had barely improved. It was easy enough to count her breaths and inhale and exhale deeply, but what caused her the most trouble was her mind wandering. As soon as she took a moment to relax, to just focus on her breath, her mind scrambled away from her, dredging up every thought imaginable, both mundane and horrific. She quickly grew to hate her sessions with Saja as it meant she had to slow down and face her thoughts. She would much rather be rushing around from place to place, cramming her mind with books about the history of Airodion or going to hand-speak lessons with Roone.

She had always thought Saja would be a gentle, soft-spoken teacher, but during his sessions, he turned into the strict general that had served the Autumn Court. He treated her like a soldier—scolding her when she didn't breathe properly or when she didn't achieve his standard of perfection.

Roone, on the other hand, was an absolute joy to be around. She had been meeting with him for a few hours every day to learn hand-speak. Their sessions so far had been one-on-one, and they had communicated through writing down their thoughts on a piece of parchment and passing it back and forth. Roone had begun by teaching her how to introduce herself and had quickly moved on to every inappropriate word in hand-speak that he could think of that she might need to know. He had nearly made her cry from laughter during all their lessons, and it was a bright spot of her day.

Saja forcing her to sit in silence with her own thoughts did nothing but make her want to run away and keep running until even her dark thoughts could not keep up.

"I can't do this anymore." Larken stood up, brushing off her fur-lined pants.

Saja opened his honey eyes. "You can't even hold your concentration for a full five minutes yet."

"This isn't working," she snapped. "I don't have time to relax and breathe while Finder rots in a cell and Dahey plans the party that will send him to his death."

Liar. Her darkest thoughts didn't lead her to Finder's imprisonment. Her darkest thoughts led her to the fire, to the burning. To the searing agony and her flesh blistering under incredible heat. Her muscles trembled slightly.

"You cannot run from this, Larken," Saja said. "Though you can distract your mind until you forget for a time, your body will make you remember." His eyes fell to her shaking hands. "You must face the memories, or you will never fully heal."

She ignored the truth in his words, the ones that reminded her that she had nearly fainted at the sight and smell of the fireplace in her rooms. "This might have worked on soldiers, but it doesn't work on me."

"You aren't a failure because you haven't healed overnight." Saja stood as well, towering over her. "These things take time." He jerked his head. "But I can't make you do anything. Go. But please, come back tomorrow. Keep coming back."

Guilt swept in. "Tomorrow," she agreed.

Larken's feet crunched through the heavy layer of snow, the chill nipping at her. The staggering pine trees were wreathed in snow. It was a bright, clear day, and the sun cast radiant sunlight spilling across the white. There were usually other courtiers out, and once or twice, she had seen Isra and Roone, but today she was alone.

Larken savored the quiet. Despite everything, it was impossible not to enjoy the wintery landscape. She thought again to how desperately she wanted to visit Shadeshelm in the Autumn Court, if only to experience more of autumn's glory. Her heart ached at the thought of exploring it with Finder.

Larken reached down, sinking her gloved hand into the powdery snow.

"Careful, or you'll lose your fingers as well as your toes."

Larken smiled up at Saja. He looked splendid in a heavy black coat with brilliant gold clasps across the chest.

"Whenever it snowed in Ballamor, my father and I would make rabbits from it. We would sneak out early in the morning while the snow was still coming down and fill the grass with dozens of them." Larken stood, brushing the snow from her hands. "Rabbits are Mama's favorite animal—she'd wake in the morning to a yard full of them."

"They'll be all right," Saja murmured, but Larken's throat had already closed, and she looked away hastily before he could see the hot tears well in her eyes.

"They probably think I'm dead," Larken whispered. "I abandoned them to go after Brigid. They don't even know the truth."

Stupid, Larken told herself. *You should have gone back to Ballamor to warn your parents. To tell them the bridge was down and why.* But she had chosen someone else over them. Again.

"The guards posted at the bridge will help protect them," Saja reassured her.

"Like that's worked before," Larken muttered.

"No fey or creatures will be able to cross in great numbers," Saja pointed out. "That gives us time to figure this out and come up with a permanent solution. I know you worry for them, Larken, but Ballamor is filled with members of the Black Guard. They know about the fey, and they will be able to protect your family."

They don't know enough, Larken wanted to cry. Castor had told her how little the Guard actually knew. But Saja was right. She had made her choice, and traveling to Ballamor on horseback would take weeks— weeks they didn't have this close to the Tournament. She just had to hope that her parents would be safe a little while longer.

It seemed all she could do of late was hope.

She awoke to a hand shaking her.

"Larken." Saja's face loomed over her, and Larken blinked up at him sleepily. He held a candle, the flickering warmth lingering on her cheeks. He immediately moved it away from her face. "Put your cloak on and come quickly."

They rushed through the castle, Larken bundled in fleece slippers and a heavy dressing gown. Nerves tingled through her, fear making her legs quicken. She had given up asking Saja where they were going after the tenth try. The stoic warrior revealed nothing.

Saja finally slowed to a stop outside the doors leading to the park. He blew out the candle and pushed the doors open, letting the moon and stars light their way.

"Look," he whispered, turning his golden eyes upon her. She turned towards the yard, and instantly, all her fear melted away.

Covering the lawn were hundreds of snow rabbits. They spread out across the lawn and disappeared into the trees, all shapes and sizes imaginable. Larken turned towards Saja, her mouth agape. She couldn't form the words to express the gratitude brimming over in her heart.

"Roone and I made them. It's a reminder that you and your father will make them again." Saja gestured out into the yard. "And that I'll be at your side until you do, *a cara*."

Larken threw herself on him, squeezing him into the tightest hug she could manage while shaking with tears.

26

KAISA

Ellevere

Thud.

Kaisa's eyes flew open at the noise.

Thud.

Dust fluttered down from the ceiling. Kaisa sat up. Jovanna stirred in her bed. Kaisa motioned for her to be silent, and Jovanna stilled, her eyes wide.

A strange, echoing growl sounded above them. *Thud. Thud. Thud.* Kaisa's eyes tracked the ceiling, following the noise.

The Furyons were here.

The bonfires should have kept them away. Why were they here? Kaisa slipped out of bed and tiptoed to the window. She pressed herself into the wall, barely peeking out.

The bonfires had burned down to ashes, their guards asleep at their posts.

No, no, no, Kaisa thought desperately. The guards must have become complacent, sure that the bonfires would burn through the night.

The monsters were perched on every rooftop. They peered into windows, their strange, echoing growls rippling through the night.

Jovanna appeared at her side, her gaze widening as she saw the ashy remains of the bonfires. "We have to relight them," she breathed.

A few of the creatures crawled down the street, lurching along the cobblestones. They looked into windows as a human would. Kaisa shuddered. They were eerily intelligent.

"Keep quiet and follow me," Kaisa whispered, headed for the door. They had to make it to the bonfires before—

A scream rang through the night. Kaisa and Jovanna dashed back to the window just in time to see a Furyon smash into the window next-door, glass exploding in the air.

Kaisa drew Hollis's sword and threw herself down the stairs. She had to relight those bonfires *now*.

The streets were chaos. People fled their homes as the monsters crashed through their windows and tore through their roofs. And then the Furyons fell upon them in the streets.

Kaisa cut into all the Furyons she could, maiming their wings so they couldn't fly off with their prey. But she couldn't be everywhere at once. All too soon, horrible screams tore through the night as the beasts carried their prey off into the darkness.

Blood splattered her as she cut through monster after monster. She caught glimpses of others fighting, but none of them were trained soldiers. They wouldn't be able to do this for long. There were too many of them.

Kaisa stabbed another monster through the eye, screaming in frustration. The book claimed that these creatures also hated music, but how could music do anything to these beasts?

Before long, she had made it to the town square. She caught a glimpse of Ishan, fending off a Furyon with his sword. Kaisa eyed him with a newfound respect. He was trying to save his people.

She cut her way over to him.

"Clever Kaisa!" he called, cutting through the arm of a creature trying to haul him into the air. "Any more ideas on how to get rid of these beasts?"

She did have an idea, but a crazy one. "I do, but you're not going to like it."

"Try me."

Kaisa ducked as a Furyon hauled a screaming man away in its claws.

"Where can I find a musical instrument? Any kind will do."

"My chambers," Ishan called, and the boy even had the audacity to wink at her amidst the chaos.

But Kaisa was too dumfounded to notice. "You play?"

The boy nodded. "Violin."

"Your roof—is it thatched?"

Ishan narrowed his eyes. "Oh, I'm really not going to like this plan, am I?"

Kaisa gave a mirthless grin. "Not in the slightest."

They ran through the streets to Ishan's home, tearing up the stairs to the upper level. He grabbed the stringed instrument, and Kaisa grabbed a lighting stone.

"Start playing," she commanded, then she straddled the windowsill.

"What are you talking about? Where are you going?" Ishan demanded, grabbing her arm.

"They hate music," she explained, grabbing the stone walls of his house. She hoisted herself up. "And we need light. *Now.*"

His eyes widened as he glanced at her lighting stone. "No. People's homes will be destroyed. Their livelihoods. There has to be another way."

Kaisa shook her head. "We won't make it until dawn. Start playing."

He hesitated, then put his bow to the strings and began to play. And Kaisa began to climb.

As the violin notes coursed through the air, the creatures shrieked. They scattered away from Ishan, but it wasn't enough to get them away from a guaranteed meal. They screeched in anger.

More, they needed more. Unless a whole troupe of musicians descended from the woodwork, it wouldn't be enough. They needed light.

Kaisa struck the flint and set fire to Ishan's thatched roof.

She scrambled back down into Ishan's open window. "We need to get out of here. But keep playing."

He did, and together they fled the house as smoke began to filter in from the roof. The creatures scattered further away. Before long, other roofs caught fire. People screamed.

"Come on," Kaisa breathed. The fire blazed, bright and insistent. More of the monsters took to the skies, some abandoning their prey.

"It's working," Ishan gasped, and Kaisa nodded. It was working. Her plan was working.

Finally, the last of the monsters took to the air. They were safe for now. She doubted that the creatures would return for some time, but they had to be ready. And they couldn't set the houses on fire every time.

"We were right to trust you," Ishan said, his eyes glowing from the light of the fire. "Your vision from the Twins was a true blessing indeed."

Kaisa met his gaze. "I don't think this is the end of the attacks. And I think more beasts are coming."

Ishan studied her. "It's a good thing we have you, then."

27

LARKEN

Airodion

Water lapped at the sides of her boat as Larken slowly drifted down the library canal. The librarians told her that she didn't have to return the books herself, but Larken didn't mind. It gave her more time to explore the shelves.

Turning her boat off the main canal, she paddled down one of the many side streams that seemed to serve as hallways for the magnificent library building.

She docked her boat and walked up the stairs that led to the shelves flanking the canal. She returned one of the books she had been reading but kept *The Beings and Beasts of Airodion* and the other book that detailed the history of the Tournament.

She leafed through the book about the Tournament. It repeated much of what the other books had said: that no prisoner who had ever won the trial had ever been denied their freedom, that the winner brought honor and glory to their court, and that no prisoner picked for the trial had ever not competed. And though it was mainly a faery competition, any race could join the Tournament with a prisoner of their

142

own. She sighed. None of them mentioned the party that occurred before the Tournament, so she couldn't find any information on when it would be best to free Finder.

She walked back to her boat but couldn't make herself return to her reading alcove yet. Letting her boat drift down one of the many side canals, she entered the darkest part of the library she had seen yet. The more precious tomes were kept away from the light, and here it had nearly disappeared entirely. It wasn't long before Larken could only see a few feet in front of her.

Glancing at the unlit torch that hung at the foot of her boat, she took a shuddering breath. She took the flint out of its ornate box by the torch and struck it. The torch sparked to life and Larken scrambled back, her heart pounding. She imagined the sparks burning her, setting her whole boat aflame. She had to get out. She had to put the fire out. But she couldn't bring herself to get any closer to the flames.

Larken clutched the edge of the boat, gasping for air as her throat tightened. She was trapped. She was going to burn to death, and Finder wouldn't be able to save her.

When the memories come, return to your breathing. Saja's words came to her. *Remind yourself that you are here in the present, not in the past.*

Larken dug her nails into the boat, trying to focus on the physical sensation. But she couldn't stop imagining the wood becoming engulfed in flames. So she plunged her hand in the water instead, gasping when the icy water numbed her hand almost instantly.

The cold drove the fire from her mind, and Larken was able to take a few deep breaths. Her heart rate slowed.

You're in the library of White Keep, Larken reminded herself. She opened her eyes, taking up her oar. She had never seen these shelves before, and somewhere in these rare books might be something that could help Finder. She dipped her paddle in the water and continued onward.

It was the strange lock that brought Larken's attention to the door on the side of the canal. Water lapped against it, the canal continuing beneath the door.

Larken could think of dozens of reasons why a library would need a locked door. Secret, rare, or dangerous books could lie within. She paddled closer, glancing about, but even with the light of her torch, she could see that she was alone.

The circular lock was deeply engraved and resembled a small maze. Pushing thoughts of Etain and the labyrinth that guarded the Spring Court from her mind, Larken picked up the lock. It resembled a maze, but there was no entrance or exit. Larken frowned, inspecting a series of grooves along the edge of the lock. She dug her fingers into the center of the maze and twisted, moving it to realign with a notch along the side.

Snick. A tiny exit to the maze appeared. Larken grinned. Now for the entrance. She frowned. This one would be more difficult, as moving the maze again would cause the exit to be lost. She examined the grooves carefully, but there was no way to achieve both an entrance and exit in one move. She tried anyway, moving the labyrinth almost one full turn. Neither exit nor entrance aligned.

Clank. Larken winced. Some part of her knew she wouldn't get another try. If she failed her third turn, she would be locked out with no way of knowing when, or if ever, the lock would be reset.

Larken dug her fingers into the maze once more, holding her breath. She twisted the maze one half turn to the right, then back nearly a full turn to the left. The notches along the side moved along with the maze. Larken squeezed her eyes shut, unable to look.

Snick. Snick. Larken opened her eyes with a grin. The door glided open before her.

Larken paddled down the dark tunnel, nearly convinced she had gone to the trouble of unlocking the door just to have it end up being a drain after all. But eventually, she reached a circular room. Her boat bumped into steps that led to a raised dais.

Larken walked up the steps, raising her torch to see. Scrolls lined the shelves from floor to ceiling.

She didn't hesitate. She pulled down scroll after scroll, her eyes flying over the parchment. Each one revealed a new kind of record from the Winter Court. Some recorded dark creatures' whereabouts, some listed the inventory of the treasury at White Keep, and one listed every Winter Court ruler, their family, and their history. Even more exciting were the several maps she found of the mountain range and surrounding area of the Winter Court. Larken made herself put that one back lest she waste all her time studying it.

But the dates on the scrolls were old, they hadn't been updated in decades if not centuries. Larken pulled one of the ladders built into the shelves towards her, climbing higher. The dates grew more recent.

Her eye caught on a scroll that wasn't covered in a fine layer of dust. It had been put here recently. She pulled it down, her eyes glancing over the title. *Current Prisoners of White Keep.*

Her eyes flew over the paper. The prisoners' known names were listed, their species, their powers, what they were imprisoned for, their cell location, and for how long they were to serve. But Larken's eye caught on the prisoner listed at the bottom, with a date of imprisonment of just a few weeks ago. An infuriating smudge marked out its species, and most of the information was blank, but the entry was circled and a small note to the side read *Cell: 600. TOURNAMENT.*

Isra had chosen her prisoner.

28

KAISA

Ellevere

"Quiet!" Ishan called.

Kaisa and Jovanna sat side-by-side at another town meeting, surrounded by the people of Augrim. Ishan had called the town meeting as soon as they could after the attack, though this one was not a secret. The members of the Order had fled long before the attack upon realizing they wouldn't receive more coin for the children. Better to go to the next town, wait for the refugees to pour in and try their luck again.

Ishan's grandmother had gone missing during the attack. Some accused her of fleeing, but Ishan insisted that she would never abandon them. Kaisa had been with him as they searched the ashy buildings. They had finally found her in the trees.

She hadn't survived.

Ishan's parents had died when he was young, and his grandmother had raised him. He had no one left and a town to lead.

"What are we going to do now?" one man demanded. "Our homes were burned to the ground!"

"It was your homes or your lives," Ishan said sharply. "We have Kaisa

146

to thank for saving us." He gestured to her, and she nodded. She would make sure that Augrim was more prepared for the next attack. She would make sure they didn't lose as many lives.

"Roofs can be rebuilt," Ishan continued. "But we have bigger things to worry about. We can't assume the Furyons are gone for good—and we must assume that more dangerous creatures than them could come."

"What do you mean? What other monsters are there?" another man cried.

Kaisa stood. "If the Furyons can enter Ellevere, then other monsters can as well. The man from Ballamor already spoke of other monsters crossing the bridge. We must be ready."

"What about the newcomers? How will we feed them?" a woman asked.

People had been streaming into Augrim, and not just refugees. Word had spread quickly that Kaisa had found a way to warn off the monsters, and people had come seeking her protection. Kaisa's heart quickened at the thought. They were there for her—for her help.

"We will make do," Ishan said. "We will pull from our cellars, anything to scrape by. We will be all right for a time, and the present is all we can afford to think about until we figure out why these monsters have come and why the Order does nothing to stop it."

Murmurs of agreement swept through the crowd.

"We know how to scare off these monsters, but what about the others?" a boy her age asked.

Kaisa took a deep breath. She couldn't tell them about the book. It was still too dangerous. But Kaisa would make sure they were ready for the next attack. The book knew how to kill these beasts, and Kaisa would teach them. "We will train to fight these monsters. I will teach you."

Gasps rose from the crowd. Ishan's eyes narrowed. She hadn't told him about her plans, as she knew questions regarding her knowledge about the monsters would come up.

"The Twins have smiled upon Augrim," Ishan said. "They sent Kaisa with her knowledge to protect us." Ishan lifted his hand to gesture towards her. "A girl chosen by the gods. Blessed by the Twins."

Unease trickled through her. She wasn't chosen by the Twins. She had started losing her faith the moment she saw Jovanna's name on that paper, and it had been stripped from her bit by bit until she wasn't sure there was anything left.

But these people needed her, looked to her for guidance and protection. What did it matter they thought she was chosen by the Twins?

Because it's not true, a voice in the back of her mind whispered, but she ignored it. Better for them to think she was chosen by the Twins and follow her then for them to poke holes in her story and learn that all her knowledge came from a stolen book.

"We will fight," Kaisa declared. She hesitated before adding: "We have the power of the Twins on our side."

She didn't know what she believed in anymore. But she knew these people believed in the Twins, and she had to use what they knew to guide them.

"Kaisa! The Savior of Augrim!" Ishan cheered, and the crowd soon rose to take up his chant.

Kaisa beamed, though it faltered slightly when she caught Jovanna looking at her, her friend's gaze filled with disappointment.

Kaisa and Jovanna sat across from each other at The Dancing Toad that night. Jovanna kept her eyes on her cup of ale, and Kaisa couldn't stop glancing at her over her cup of tea.

"I think we should leave Augrim," Jovanna said. "We helped these people, and we can help the other towns we travel to as well, but staying here is foolish. The Order has already been sniffing around Augrim. It's only a matter of time before they find us."

Kaisa's heart sped up. "No," she blurted out. "No," she repeated more firmly. "We can do more to help Augrim. We need bigger bonfires, and I can teach them how to fight."

Jovanna bit her lip. "I don't know, Kai. I still think we should leave. You know as well as I do what will happen if the Order catches us."

"Augrim has more reason to protect us now," Kaisa pushed. "And it's not just me who's helping them. You can help them too. You can show them how to separate their faith from the Order."

Jovanna paused, taking a long drink from her mug. Finally, she set it down. "Fine," she said. "We will stay awhile longer. But you need to be careful. I know you want to help these people, but we've seen what the Order can do. How it uses people for power." She lowered her voice. "What Ishan said about you, about you being blessed by the Twins... you need to make sure you aren't manipulating these people. Using their faith against them."

A twist of irritation knotted in Kaisa's gut. "I'm not manipulating them," she snapped. She immediately regretted her tone. "I'm just using what they know."

The door to the Dancing Toad opened, making them both glance up. Ishan pulled down the hood of his cloak. He grinned at Kaisa, and Kaisa couldn't help her blush.

He strolled over to their table. "Kaisa," he said. "I've been looking for you." He smiled again, extending a hand to her. "I wanted to take you on a tour of the town, to show you around your new home."

Kaisa blinked. Could this be her new home? She knew Jovanna was right, that it would be safer to keep moving. But she was growing comfortable in Augrim. She knew there was more she could do to help.

She glanced at Jovanna. She wanted to keep talking with her. But at the same time, she didn't want to hear any further criticism from her friend.

"Go." Jovanna nodded to her and Ishan. "I'll see you back at our room."

Kaisa stood and took Ishan's hand.

29

LARKEN

Airodion

Larken hurried to meet Roone and Saja for their evening meal. She had read the information about the prisoner until she had committed it to memory, and then she had put the scroll back. She couldn't risk raising the alert by stealing the scroll, especially one that was so obviously related to the Tournament.

Larken burst into Roone's private dining room. Saja and Roone sat together at the end of the table. Roone had both of Saja's hands in his own, moving Saja's hands into some complicated phrase in hand-speak. Larken's breath caught at the intimacy of the moment. Saja looked up when he heard her come in, pulling his hands away from Roone.

"Sorry I'm late," she said, taking a seat across from Roone and Saja. She shoved down her jealousy. Saja deserved moments of happiness with Roone. It wasn't their fault it made her think of Finder. She wanted those kinds of moments with him—where things were just easy and simple.

Saja translated what she said to Roone. While she was starting to get better at hand-speak, she still couldn't keep up with their quick conversations and needed Saja's help to translate. Her movements still felt clunky and awkward.

"It's all right," Saja translated for Roone. "We didn't start our meal without you."

They ate, chatting idly about their day. Larken picked up on a few new military gestures in hand-speak as Roone and Saja talked about their sparring.

"There aren't many books on the history of the Tournament. How did it come to be?" Larken asked.

"It began long ago when one of the first Spring Court rulers began bragging about some beast they had captured," Saja said, hand-speak accompanying his words. "They claimed that their prisoner was the most powerful; therefore, their court was the strongest. The other courts heard about Spring's boast and saw it as the perfect opportunity to prove their own courts' strength. Better still, it was to be a spectacle for all the people to see, and to ensure that the prisoners fought at full strength, they offered freedom as the reward. Over time, they realized that allowing the prisoners to fight with magic was too dangerous, as was offering powerful magical beings their freedom, so they changed it to a contest of brute strength instead. It also serves as a way for courts to release tension without actually going to war."

Larken frowned. "What's stopping court rulers from locking up every powerful being they encounter just to save them for the next Tournament?"

"To lock up an immortal being is no simple task," Saja translated for Roone. "For a faery or another being of Airodion to be imprisoned, they have to commit a truly heinous act, and others must agree. Of course, there are always political prisoners who get thrown in the mix, but it's rare. The Tournament has strict rules and is considered a sacred rite. The rules are clear, and the courts want to win with honor to show their true strength. Each court ruler must bring records stating why the prisoner was taken captive, and if any of the information appears suspicious, they will be disqualified from competing, which would be devastating for their people. The fey may be fickle, but they respect the rite. Still, you must keep in mind that many of the prisoners presented at the Tournament are not the most dangerous beings held in a court's dungeons. They are simply the most likely to win through strength alone."

"You said that the courts must bring records of why they chose their prisoner—will the other courts allow Finder to compete?" Larken asked.

"The other courts know Dahey didn't imprison Finder for the Tournament because he didn't know for certain that it was going to occur. Of course, the council would have had a say in his imprisonment as well. More than that, the other courts want a show, and seeing a former Autumn Court ruler brought so low will only bolster their own courts," Saja said.

"Has the winning prisoner ever been denied their freedom?" Larken asked, biting her lip.

Roone shook his head.

"No," Saja translated for him. "The winner has always been given their freedom. Beyond that, the champion is forgiven of all their past sins and can start anew with honor."

"And it must be a fight to the death?" she asked quietly.

"Alliances have been formed in the past, but only one may earn their freedom," Saja translated for Roone. Then he frowned.

"Not always, Roone. There has been one recorded instance when two allies, Cassilus and Nestor, two prisoners from Autumn and Winter, reached the end of the Tournament but laid down their weapons rather than fight each other. They faced returning to their dungeons for an eternity. The crowd was so moved that they demanded an appeal, and both males walked free."

Roone waved a hand. Saja translated for him: "The Appeal has only been enacted once in a thousand years. Most fey don't know it exists."

"But it does," Saja insisted. "It's listed in the official rules, albeit a bit buried in the jargon."

Larken suppressed her smile. It sounded as if Saja were arguing with himself. "Where can I see a full list of rules?" she asked. An idea was forming in the back of her mind. Saja wanted to free Finder before the Tournament, but Roone said himself that winning absolved the champion of all their sins. What if Finder won and regained his honor in the eyes of his court? Wouldn't he have a better chance of getting back his throne from Dahey if he was crowned victor rather than if they freed him?

Roone grinned. "More library time for you," Saja translated for him. "I'll have the book waiting for you. But you better practice hand-speak with the librarians if you plan on cutting our lessons short."

Larken smiled back. "I wouldn't dream of it."

30

KAISA

Ellevere

For a town of farmers, the people of Augrim began their training with a surprising amount of force.

The smithy worked long hours making weapons while Kaisa, Ishan and Jovanna trained them with blunt sticks. By the time the rest of the weapons were made, the people were ready to begin training in full.

Every day, Kaisa trained the people of Augrim. And every night, she devoured the contents of the book. There were many magical creatures listed in the tome that she knew the humans would stand no chance against. But many of the monsters had weak points that she and her fellow humans could target. They made their bonfires larger and kept them burning through the night. The musicians of the town kept their instruments close, as much a weapon in their eyes as swords and bows.

Kaisa's main strategy was to keep any monster they encountered at bay with bows. Allowing them to get close usually meant the end, as the creatures were stronger and faster than humans.

When the Furyons returned, Augrim was ready, the bonfires burning strongly. Ishan even set fire to a huge ring of brush they had set up to encircle the town.

A few of the creatures were hungry—or angry—enough to snatch up a few people as they fled. People fired their bows, but none of them reached their target.

Ishan strode towards her once it was over, pulling her into a crushing hug. "How many did we lose?" he growled in her ear.

Kaisa returned his embrace, but disappointment still gnawed at her. "Too many," she said. Her heart ached as the cries of the broken families reached her.

Her plan was working, they had survived the Furyons twice now. The people of Augrim might not be skilled enough yet with weapons, but they would learn. They had to work harder, train harder, until they could fend off these monsters for good. And she would not rest until they made it through an attack without losing anyone.

"I want to show you something," Ishan said days later, pulling at her hand.

Kaisa grinned. She and Ishan had been spending most of their time together and had just finished their evening meal. It felt so strange to be alone with him. Yes, she had spent time with Hollis, but she had never seen him as anything other than a friend. She ignored the bitter sting in her throat whenever she thought about Hollis. He would have completed his Anointing by now. A twinge went down her spine. It felt wrong to hope he had passed when it meant an innocent life had been taken. But as angry as she was with Hollis, he was still like a brother to her. In the quiet moments where it was just her and Jovanna, she missed him fiercely. But things with Ishan were different. Warmth bloomed in her stomach.

"Where are we going?" Kaisa giggled.

"You'll see," he grinned. He led her to one of the barns on the outskirts of town.

"Up you go." He shooed her up the ladder to the upper level. She pulled herself up, falling into a pile of hay, laughing. She couldn't keep the smile and laughter from her lips whenever they were together.

Ishan collapsed into the hay next to her. He propped himself up on his elbow, straw sticking out of his brown curls. He shook his head, and straw rained down around them. They both laughed, and he bent his head towards her. She giggled, carefully pulling out the strands of hay.

He traced his hand along her cheek. Her heart stuttered in her chest. She desperately wanted him to kiss her, but nerves nipped at her thoughts. She had dreamed about her first kiss for so long, wondered who it would be with. The Order had been strict about the mixing of opposite sexes. She always assumed that the Order would match her with a husband, and her first kiss wouldn't be until her wedding day.

Anger burned within her. The Order had tried to control every part of her, but now she was free. She would decide her fate.

She leaned forward and pressed her lips to Ishan's. His mouth was warm beneath hers. Fear coursed through her. What if she was horrible at kissing? What if she did something wrong? Ishan's mouth gaped open in surprise. She shoved her fear aside, deepening the kiss. Her tongue traced his bottom lip lightly, and he groaned. He slid his arms around her shoulder blades, hugging her close. A tingle spread all the way to her toes, and she opened her mouth, fully letting him in.

"The Savior of Augrim," Ishan whispered, pressing kisses into her neck. "You're mine," he growled.

Kaisa forgot the way the word 'mine' grated against her when he pressed his lips to hers once more. She gasped against his mouth, desperate for air. Desperate for the moment to last forever.

31

LARKEN

Airodion

Saja's gift of the maps for her birthday proved more useful than she could have imagined.

One of them happened to be an old blueprint of White Keep. A peculiar passageway shot straight down into the keep. She followed the map to the tunnel and realized with delight that it was a back passageway into the dungeons.

The bitter cold ate at her bare skin. It smelled of stone and ice. Larken pulled her fur wrap closer. How had it gotten colder? Two torches flanked either side of the tunnel, and Larken pulled one free before venturing a few more steps deeper into the dungeon.

Never thought I would despise torches so fiercely, she thought to herself, holding the torch as far away from her body as possible. Still, her desire to find the prisoner slightly overpowered her fear of the fire. She walked quickly, wincing at the noise her boots made on the stone.

Before long, the tunnel straightened out. Larken passed beneath an archway into a huge, cavernous space. She stepped onto a wide, stone ledge. Three staircases led down from the platform. Larken swallowed.

The two staircases on either side of the platform were built into the wall, but the center staircase featured a terrifying drop into darkness on either side.

Larken peered down the staircase to her left. She could see that far below, it connected to a perpendicular wall of stone with cells built into the side. The staircase to her right featured something similar. But the staircase before her led to darkness, presumably to more cells below.

Larken had no doubt that the most vicious prisoners were down there in the dark, which meant that was where she had to go. Taking a deep breath, Larken raised her torch and began down the steps.

Down, down, down, she descended, her knees beginning to ache. The stones were incredibly steep and shallow, and Larken's foot slipped on the frost more than once, making her gasp. The air was so cold it hurt to breathe. When she looked up, she could just barely make out the stone platform.

Finally, after she wondered if she had climbed all the way to the bottom of the mountain, Larken reached the end of the staircase. She stepped onto the icy floor, the colossal space eating away the sound almost instantly. Her skin crawled. She couldn't shake the feeling that she was being watched.

She hurried on, eager to find more of the cells, but the cavern floor seemed to stretch on endlessly into darkness. Eventually, she stopped, faced with a massive stone wall—the end of the dungeon. But no, Larken realized, drawing closer. A towering archway led to... another tunnel.

Etchings on the wall read: *cells 500-600*.

She entered the tunnel, praying for once that her torch didn't go out, lest she be lost in this place forever.

Larken's breath fogged before her. No sounds came from the cells— the only noises that could be heard were her own footfalls and breathing. It was eerie down here alone. Or, at least, she thought she was alone based on the quietness of the cells, but she couldn't be sure. Larken quickened her pace, eager to complete her task. All she needed to do was get a good look at the prisoner. That was all.

Her hand traced the wall, her fingers brushing against the etchings. *550. 551. 552.*

Her hand shook on the torch. Her heart climbed higher and higher into her throat, choking her until she could barely breathe. She forced herself to stop, to take some deep breaths. She was fine. She wasn't a prisoner; she could leave this place. She wasn't trapped. She was on the other side of the doors marking the cells. She was fine. She wouldn't turn back, wouldn't let Finder down. She had faced worse than this. Forcing a lid on her panic, Larken pushed on, determination replacing her fear.

597. 598. 599.

Her breath caught. She was close. She left the tunnel behind and entered another smaller cavern.

600.

It had a lower ceiling and went deep enough that her torch light did not expose all of it, the edges fading away into darkness. She clenched her hand around the torch handle. Where were the bars? This was no cell. She groaned in frustration. Were there more cells beyond this cave?

She hurried on. The only sound echoing around the cavern was her own breathing. She just had to keep going, to see what was at the end of the cave. The wall marking said 600. If it didn't lead to more cells, then she would be forced to return empty handed.

Her foot caught on something beneath her, sending her sprawling. She hissed in pain, scrambling to her feet and looked to see what she had tripped on.

Chains, thicker around than her thigh.

Another set of lungs joined hers.

Larken froze, fear sneaking along her spine. She listened hard, and just when she thought she had been imagining things, the sound of a deep inhale and exhale came from up ahead. The breathing grew louder, and Larken could hear the shifting of some great weight being dragged across the floor.

It began with a whisper, like sandpaper sliding across stone. Then, the chains began to move, pulled back into the darkness. Larken's mouth went dry. A strange clicking noise began, like horse hooves against cobblestones.

A red snout came out of the shadows first, then a huge, scaly head and a winding neck. Long, white claws attached to four scaled feet. Lips pull back over pointed teeth. A low growl rippled through the air, and Larken turned and *ran*. Her feet tangled in the chain, and she fell backwards. The torch thudded to the ground behind her, flickering weakly, but she could see well enough to know what was before her.

For there, exposed in the light, was a firedrake.

32

KAISA

Ellevere

Kaisa rode Sorreno through the streets of Augrim, a smile never leaving her lips.

Whenever people caught sight of her, they stopped what they were doing to call out greetings and well wishes. Kaisa beamed at them, pulling Sorreno to a halt when children rushed up to her, bringing her little trinkets and flowers that she tucked into her saddle bags.

"Come, let us finish our ride," Ishan called.

Kaisa glanced over at him. "In a moment," she said. She wanted to spend this time with her people, basking in the fact that she had helped them when no one else could. A muscle flickered in Ishan's jaw, but he said nothing, just crossed his arms atop his horse and waited for the children to leave.

They continued their ride through town. Ishan held her hand for a time before she pulled it from his grasp to clasp hands with more people who had filed into the streets to see her.

"...the Twins would never condone what occurred in these towns!" a man's voice cut through the din of Augrim.

161

Kaisa lifted her head, searching for the source of the voice.

A small crowd of people stood in a clearing between buildings, all with their backs turned to her, watching a man standing on a crate.

He was older, perhaps in his mid-thirties, with stubble lining his jaw. His brown hair fell in waves to his shoulders, his light skin tanned from the sun.

A few people came up to Kaisa, but she was only half-listening to them as she took in the man preaching from his wooden crate.

"The Order has perverted the sacred nature of the Twins. We should not blame our gods, but the Order. The Popes!"

Cries of agreement rose from the crowd. Kaisa frowned. He sounded like Jovanna.

Jealousy rippled through her. Was it so easy for everyone to separate the Twins from the Order? She could not think of one without the other. Could not separate their cruelties.

"It is time we say that we will not tolerate this any longer. The Popes torture, maim and kill innocents in the Twins' name. They allow no one to question them. Is that the kind of religion you want? Or would you rather learn the Twins' teachings for yourself instead of being told? Would you rather connect with the Twins themselves instead of the Popes?"

More cries of favor rose from the crowd.

"I speak of a New Order." The man spread his hands. "A place where all are welcome. A place where there are real teachers of faith, not tyrants. A true place for the Savior of Augrim."

Kaisa froze as the man's gaze met hers. He gave her a small smile, extending his head. Then his gaze returned to the crowd. "I ask that all of you consider joining the New Order. But no one will force your hand. It is your choice."

He jumped down, and people surrounded him, eagerly asking questions. He smiled and shook hands, putting everyone at ease instantly as he chatted with them as equals.

Envy sank into her. The people were drawn to him. "Who is that man?" Kaisa murmured to Ishan. "Where did he come from?"

"I heard his name is Tarrio," Ishan said. "He came from one of the neighboring towns. He's one of the leaders of the New Order, a reformed version of the faith." He tracked Tarrio with his brown gaze. "I'm eager to hear what he has to say. I cannot call myself a member of the Order of the Twins when the Popes have so clearly forsaken us, but I still want to worship my gods."

"I wish to speak to him as well," Kaisa said, wheeling Sorreno around. *For different reasons.* "Set up a meeting between us."

Ishan's eyes narrowed. "Perhaps someone more equipped for scheduling meetings can take care of it. I have business in town."

Kaisa frowned. "I thought we were spending the day together."

Ishan kicked his horse away from her. "I wanted to spend time with you alone, not this." He cantered off.

Kaisa watched him go, then looked back to where Tarrio chatted with her people. The New Order would spread, she could feel it. But she could either use it to her advantage or be swept under the tide.

33

LARKEN

Airodion

Larken scrambled back. Her breath came in ragged gasps, her heart pounding furiously in her chest. A firedrake. Finder would have to fight a firedrake.

And now I shall burn to death with that knowledge. It just had to be fire, didn't it? she sighed internally, glaring at the firedrake.

The firedrake snaked its head back, looking at her. "I have seen many cower in fear, but none quite so defiantly as you."

The firedrake was talking to her. Her mouth gaped open.

"Oh, get up. I'm not going to hurt you," the drake continued. "I'm desperate for conversation, if you must know. These court guards have no manners." Its, no, *his* voice was deeper than any human or faery voice she had ever heard, excluding the Guardian. The firedrake's voice was different, low, but smooth.

"You're not going to burn me then eat me?" Larken blurted.

"As if I would eat the only living being who has talked to me in weeks," the drake scoffed. "My mind is starved of intellectual conversation. And besides, I couldn't burn you even if I wanted to." He lifted his head, revealing a large metal collar at the base of his neck. The scales around the collar were rubbed raw. "I cannot use my fire while this blasted metal is touching me."

Weeping Metal, Larken realized. She believed that he could not use his flames, else he would have cooked the Winter Court guards by now, but a tremor of fear still marred her hands. She imagined the drake's maw opening and fire pouring out, consuming her, just as Finder's had done.

Larken clenched her fists, slowly getting to her feet. Her torch lay abandoned where she had left it, miraculously still lit. She lifted it, finally able to take in the drake in full.

He was large, though not as large as Larken had originally thought. He was about as long as two draft horses, excluding his tail. His scales were not just red, but the color of a living ember, gold and orange and crimson spun into one. A golden mane of hair coated his neck. Straight white horns jutted back from his skull, and the small ears beneath them perked in her direction as she came closer. Bony ridges stuck out above his eyes like brows, but Larken had to hold in a gasp at what lingered beneath.

The creature's eyes, which Larken guessed had once been a beautiful, rich amber were now streaked red with blood. The lids were almost swollen shut over a mass of torn flesh. It looked as though claws had raked through them. Puss oozed down the creature's snout, and some of it had already dried into a crusty dark mess. Larken's eyes watered just at the sight, at the idea of the pain.

The drake sniffed at her, and Larken was shocked to see a fleshy pink nose similar to a cat's. "You smell strange," the drake noted. "I can tell you are no faery." He curled his tail around his feet, evidently pleased with himself for figuring it out. His long claws had disappeared—retracted back into the paw.

How interesting. She was wrong to assume the drakes would be reptilian, instead, they were much more similar to cats. She almost laughed.

"I'm human," she replied.

"Human." The drake settled down, lowering himself onto his belly. He tucked his paws beneath his chest and stretched his long neck out to get as close to Larken as the chains would allow. Larken resisted the urge to step back.

"I've heard of humans, but I've never seen one before. What is your name, human?"

"Larken," she replied. "And what is your name, drake?"

"My name is Fynvarra." The drake cocked his head. "If I did not know what kind of creature you were, how did you know what I am?"

"I've been traveling through Airodion with my faery companions. They told me about the trading system they have with the firedrakes."

"And your companions are from the Autumn Court."

"How did you—"

"The firedrakes only have trade negotiations with the Autumn Court."

Larken frowned, tucking away the information. "Then why are you here, locked in the Winter Court dungeons?"

The drake turned away, clearly uncomfortable. "I made a mistake. I was caught somewhere I wasn't supposed to be, and I paid the price for it."

"You're really just being held captive for trespassing?" Larken asked, her brows lifting.

"Well, no. I might have killed a few Winter Court soldiers." The drake turned away, then continued. "I didn't mean to kill them. I was injured. My eyes." Fynvarra stopped, a small choking noise coming from the back of his throat. "My eyes had suffered quite a blow before I entered the Winter Court. I heard there was something here that could heal them, but my vision quickly began to fail. I landed in the mountains, and a patrol found me. I was scared. I thought I was under attack—so I fought back. I killed many of them. But finally, they overwhelmed me. Next thing I knew, I was here." Fynvarra shifted uncomfortably. "Still, they cannot keep me here forever, else they would risk the wrath of the firedrakes. Erm, if they ever find out I'm trapped here, that is."

Larken didn't want to depress him further and tell him he was slotted to fight for the Winter Court in the Tournament. "Why do the drakes only trade with the Autumn Court?"

"Their prince, Finder, gave us sanctuary in his realm and away from the Wyld where we previously lived. Finder thought all the beings of Airodion would be safest if we resided in the Autumn Court, where Finder could put out our fires with his magic if need be. We agreed to a trading system in his honor."

Larken felt as though she had been punched in the gut. "He was one of the companions who told me about the firedrakes," she whispered.

"Finder is a good faery." The drake nodded. "I have always had a soft spot for him." He perked up. "You mentioned that he was one of your companions? Could you send word to him? Perhaps he could help me."

Larken choked back a dry laugh. "I'm afraid he's rather indisposed at the moment. There have been some... changes in Airodion. The Starveling has been overthrown. Finder should be king, but—"

"Finder is not the ruler of Autumn anymore?" Fynvarra asked sharply.

"No. I mean, yes. He still is, but not for long. Dahey—the regent— wants the crown, and he'll do anything to get it."

Fynvarra hung his head. "That saddens me. Finder was a good ruler."

Well, you'll get to see him again soon, Larken wanted to say. *To fight each other to the death.* But something held her back from telling the drake. His sightless eyes peered around his cell, and Larken found she didn't have the heart to tell him about the Tournament.

A door slammed somewhere off in the distance. Larken scrambled to her feet. "I've got to go. I can't be found down here."

"Wait, wait." Fynvarra rose, chains clanking. "Come back. Please. I need someone to talk to."

Larken hesitated. This was the being Finder would have to fight. She needed to get word to the Cynyadas to warn him what he was up against. She shook her head slightly. She couldn't take a liking to this beast. She would come back, but only to get more information to help Finder.

"I'll come back," she said, swallowing around her guilt.

34

LARKEN

Airodion

Larken had sent a message to Finder telling him that he would have to fight Fynvarra in the ring, but he hadn't sent a response.

To keep her mind occupied, she had accepted Roone's invitation to visit the great horned bears. Directly in front of them was a large, spacious center area filled with fey on the move. Servants and warriors alike carried buckets of water, bales of hay and huge slabs of raw meat. They darted in and out of the rooms to the right of the common area and over to the many smaller caves carved into the wall on the opposite side.

"Tack and armor room, grooming supplies and meat room," Roone said, Saja again helping her translate the hand-speak she didn't know. Larken tried to focus on Roone's gestures and not gape at her surroundings.

The most stunning part of the caves wasn't the spectacular architecture or delicate carvings chiseled into the ice. No, the most breathtaking part of the caverns were the horned bears that lived there. Most of the bears were a pristine white, but others had fur ranging from silver to molten grey. Larken could hear the scrape of their long claws on the icy floor, and yet, they were incredibly gentle beasts. One bear lay with his paw upon a faery's knee to be trimmed. Though the claws were incredibly long and sharp, they rested delicately on the faery's leg. Another bear took a slab of meat from a faery with teeth that could have severed the faery's arm from her shoulder as easily as Larken could snap a twig in half.

In the common area, a faery brushed the smaller, slender she-bear with a hard-bristled comb. When he reached her back, the bear's hind leg lifted, pounding the floor like a dog.

Roone tapped her on the arm, and she blushed, embarrassed that she hadn't been paying attention to him. But Roone seemed to understand. *"Would you like to meet one?"* he asked in hand-speak.

Larken nodded eagerly. Roone put his hands together and blew, a strange, hooting whistle coming out. The she-bear the servant had been brushing turned and, upon seeing Roone, lumbered eagerly up to meet them.

"I've told you, the servants have better things to do than sit around and brush you all day," Roone scolded her. She hung her head and let out a low groan. Larken broke into a smile. Roone reached out and scratched the she-bear behind one of her horns. Though she was smaller than some of the other bears, she was still huge, and Roone's head barely peaked over her shoulder.

"The servants only care for the bears who have no riders or whose riders are away," Roone explained, shoving the bear's muzzle away as she began intently sniffing his pockets. *"Riders are always the sole caretakers of their bears, unless, of course, you have a selfish brute who needs attention like Una."* Una put her huge, square head down and butted him gently.

Roone rolled his eyes and pulled three flaky biscuits from his coat pocket, holding them out on a flat palm to the bear. She gave a snort of happiness and took them gently from his hand.

"She's beautiful," Larken said clumsily. She was getting better at understanding hand-speak, but it was still difficult for her to master her own gestures. Larken stuffed her hands in her pockets. If she left them out any longer, she would have her hands fist deep in Una's beautiful fur.

"Come on, give her a pat." Roone grinned, jerking his head towards

Una. Larken squealed. She pulled off her glove and held out her hand for the bear to sniff. The fey horses had to give her permission to ride, so it made sense that she should also ask permission to touch the fey bears.

Una regarded her with warm brown eyes, extending her wet black nose to sniff at Larken. She lowered her head, exposing her horns. Larken tentatively reached out and scratched behind one of them, as Roone had done. The bear sighed in pleasure, and Larken beamed. Larken's hand brushed up against Una's horn. It was hard as metal. She ran her hand through the bear's silken fur next, marveling at how soft it was. So soft that it reminded her of her own fur-rimmed hood. She reached back to touch it, making the connection just as Roone gestured:

"Bear's fur." He pointed to his own coat, which had beautiful white fur springing from the neck. It was the exact same shade as Una's. *"We take the fur from the brushes and use it to line our garments. Riders always wear their bear's fur. All the extra hair is used for other garments."*

Una pressed a wet, fleshy nose to Larken's palm, and Larken beamed.

She loved the fey horses, but the bears might have a new special place in her heart.

"Where do the drakes live in the Autumn Court?" she asked Fynvarra when she visited him next.

"We have a great fortress, First Forge, half underground in the great forges and half in the sky in the eyrie." Fynvarra's eyes closed, his muscles relaxed. "It is incredible." His eyes flickered to the edges of his small cell, and pity washed over Larken. Fynvarra might be accustomed to being underground, but he wasn't used to being in a cage. The cave was large, but the Weeping Metal chains left him little room to move about. He shuffled his feathered wings, unable to extend them in the limited space.

The drake blinked, and a fat tear rolled down his scaly cheek. Larken's heart swelled painfully. She stared at Fynvarra's ruined eyes.

"What happened to your eyes?" Larken asked, forcing away her sympathy. *You need to learn more about his weaknesses to help Finder.*

"When the elder drakes think the previous ruler has become too old, they select a challenger, the strongest drake, to battle to the death against the old monarch for the throne. I was picked to be the challenger. I won, but the previous monarch blinded me. I flew here to find something to heal me and ended up here. The other drakes likely think I died from my wounds and have selected someone new." He hung his head. "They will be of no help to me now."

Larken gaped at him. "You're the king of the firedrakes?"

Fynvarra blinked hard. "I *was* the king. For a few hours, at least. But by now, I'm sure they have chosen another ruler. It saddens me. In truth, I was looking forward to ruling."

"Is there no way to heal your eyes?" she asked quietly.

"Maybe if I had found a healer when I was first injured, I could have saved them," he murmured. "But I did not. Isra tried to heal them but to no avail. I'm not sure why she bothered." His tail scraped against the stones, curling around him.

Larken shifted, unable to say, *because she's going to use you in the Tournament.*

"I still remember what it feels like," he whispered. "To fly and see the whole world below me, to see great patchworks of green and brown. To spy my prey hundreds of feet in the air and bring it down. Now, I am left in darkness.

"For the first few days, I could still see. It hurt to keep my eyes open, but I did. I was scared that if I closed them, I would be lost in that darkness forever. It went slowly. It almost drove me mad. I couldn't tell if I was losing my sight or if it was just dark in the cave. It was when I couldn't see my own paw in front of my face that I realized my vision was gone."

Larken hesitated, then she placed a hand on Fynvarra's neck, feeling the smooth, cool scales and the hard twist of muscles beneath. Then she began to speak, and suddenly, the words began to pour out of her— Brigid, the Choosing Ceremony, Ziegan, everything. How she had grown to love Finder, grown to love all the *dornán*, and then Dahey had tried to take everything away. How angry she was at Finder for burning her, how she could barely stand to see an open flame.

When it was all said and done, Fynvarra had no words. So they just sat together, her hand on his scaly snout, his slow breath huffing into her palm, comforting her.

35

LARKEN

Airodion

Larken visited Fynvarra nearly every day while Saja went out patrolling with Roone. She and the drake loved to exchange stories. Fynvarra's tended to be about flying and hunting, but she didn't mind.

"I wish I could fly," Larken picked at the ground with her fingernail. "None of my problems would exist up there."

Fynvarra gave her a curious look. "What if I could show you what it was like?"

Larken frowned. "What do you mean?"

A strange throbbing began at her temple. It wasn't painful, merely different. Then, a slippery presence bumped up against her mind.

Mmmm. Human minds are weak, aren't they?

"Fynvarra," she gasped. His voice sounded the same but tinged with an echo.

Obviously. And try not to think while you speak. It sounds like you're stuttering.

Larken almost opened her mouth to reply, then stopped.

HOW ARE YOU DOING THIS? She stared intently at the drake, trying to project her thoughts towards him.

Fynvarra flinched. *Larken, don't scream at me. Don't concentrate so much. Just think what you wish to say to me, and I'll hear it.*

CAN YOU HEAR EVERYTHING I'M THINKING?

Fynvarra winced. *Because you are inexperienced, yes. It's the same as if you spoke every thought in your head out loud. With time, you will be able to say what you wish but close your mind to the rest. Now concentrate.*

She tried very hard not to yell. *Can all firedrakes do this?*

Yes. It is called mind-speak.

"You've never done it with me before!" she blurted.

Unsurprising, as you are so bad at it.

Larken scowled. *Stupid worm.*

Ignorant human.

I didn't mean for you to hear that.

Then don't think it.

How do I only allow you to hear certain things?

Imagine that your mind is a fortress, completely closed off. Whatever you wish to say, envision it streaming out through the front gate, then have it close once the words are released.

Larken nodded, her face scrunching up in concentration. *Like this?* She let the words slip out, then quickly envisioned the fortress slamming closed.

Fynvarra flicked his tail, and the slippery feeling on her mind pressed against her again. Slowly, she lowered her fortress.

Yes, but you closed your mind before you could hear my reply. Your mind is not strong enough to withstand me. I could have forced my way in, but it would have been painful. Try this instead: whatever you wish for me to hear, project it towards me. Imagine your thoughts coming directly to me through the channel, and keep the rest of your thoughts back.

Larken tried again. *What about this?*

Fynvarra curled his tail over his paws. *Good.*

She quickly grasped how to "think" everything she wanted to say to Fynvarra while keeping the rest of her thoughts to herself.

What other beings can use mind-speak? The last creature that had spoken directly into her mind were the Fomari.

It's common in the ancient races—the Masters, the last of them being the Starveling, could use mind-speak, as can the Dark Priestesses and their kin. The creatures of old had the ability to send images to each other to communicate, then they learned the common tongue and could speak in words as well. But mind-speak is rare now.

What did you mean when you said you could show me how to fly?

Fynvarra extended a scaly paw to her. She took it.

Her vision went black. Then she was no longer in the dungeons of White Keep, no, she was soaring above the Autumn Court forest. And she was in Fynvarra's skin, not her own. She sucked in a deep breath, crisp autumn air filling her lungs. The wind billowed beneath her wings, lifting her higher—faster, until she plummeted into a dive, hurtling down—

She gasped as Fynvarra pulled away, and the connection abruptly broke.

We have to be touching for you to send images like that, she realized. So this is what the Dark Priestess and the Guardian—Ziegan, had done to Finder. The Dark Priestesses had projected the location of Ziegan's prison had shown Finder how to use his language. But Fynvarra said that the use of that kind of mind-speak was rare, so perhaps that was why Finder had been so surprised by their ability to project images into his mind.

Was that a memory? she asked.

Yes. You saw things through my eyes. Now, try to send me an image.

She thought for a moment, then took Fynvarra's paw once more. A low hum rumbled in his chest.

Home.

Larken startled. She'd sent him an image of the bakery. *How did you know it was my home?*

Some images are impossible to separate from the emotions you associate with them. Even when it is possible, it takes a great amount of practice. You sent me an image of a bakery, yes, but you also sent me the image of your home and the emotions you felt there. Happiness, safety, comfort.

Aching pain swept through her, but she didn't want to stop using mind-speak. She sent Fynvarra images of the Dark Priestesses, Etain and the Starveling. She showed him Rosin dying in Finder's arms. The last smile Brigid ever gave her before entering the land of the fey. But she sent him the beautiful things too. The Cynadas, Warga and her faery companions flashed through her mind in a swirling cascade of images, almost overflowing with emotions, laughter, wonder and love. They were bright, burning lights against the darkness.

I would never change my decision to come to Airodion. The beautiful, the terrible... all of it was worth it in the end. All of it has changed me.

You are a strange creature, Larken, Fynvarra said. *I have never met a human before, but if any of them are like you, then Airodion needs more of them.*

"*Think about hand-speak as a union of your mind and body,*" Roone instructed.

Larken squirmed. If only he knew how similar that sounded to mind-speak. She had to learn how to only send Fynvarra certain images and thoughts. With hand-speak, she had to concentrate to put her thoughts into motion, to think exactly how she wanted to express herself in the visual language. She still struggled to only send Fynvarra the images she wanted instead of anything that came into her mind.

Her lessons with Roone helped her focus on only one thought at a time and channeling it into a physical expression. She had come to love her lessons with Roone, as they gave her mind something to focus intently on. She had mastered the basics and was already moving on to more advanced levels of hand-speak. But she struggled with this next level, which frustrated her. She couldn't get her hands to speak the words she wanted in her mind.

"*How are your lessons with Saja?*" Roone asked.

Larken grimaced. She hated her lessons with him more than

anything. She despised that her body wouldn't listen to her, that her thoughts triggered such adverse reactions in her body.

"*Horrible,*" she admitted. "*I'd much rather be here with you.*" She rubbed the toe of her boot into the tiles of the library floor.

"*Your mind is not your enemy, Larken, nor is your body,*" Roone said. "*You still think of them as two separate entities fighting against one another. But both hold trauma. You must let them work together. It's why you haven't been able to progress in your hand-speak lessons, because your body and mind are not one. Your memories of the fire overwhelm your thoughts, causing a physical reaction in the body. You must work with Saja to learn to relax your body and mind to face the thoughts one at a time, as we have learned with hand-speak. One at a time so the body and mind can process and release.*"

Tears welled in her eyes, and Roone squeezed her hand. "*But I don't want to face the memories. Not even one.*"

"*I know,*" Roone replied. "*Keep working with Saja. He is a good teacher. Learn to calm the body and mind, so they can work together to process. Only then can you achieve real healing.*"

Larken nodded. "*I'll try.*"

36

LARKEN

Airodion

I want to show you something, Larken told Fynvarra. *Something that happened to me. I haven't been able to put it into words the way I want. But I want to show it to someone just so they can understand. But... but it's a bit traumatic*, she whispered.

I can handle it, Fynvarra said. *Show me.*

She took Fynvarra's paw and squeezed it.

She closed her eyes. *One thought at a time*, she told herself. She breathed deeply, like Saja had taught her. Her heart rate slowed. Fynvarra was here with her. She wasn't alone.

She forced her breathing to stay slow and even. She sent Fynvarra the image of her stepping into Finder's embrace. Then she let the image go. Then she sent him what she *felt*, the burning, the terror. Her breathing quickened, but she focused on the techniques Saja had taught her, and slowly, the panic ebbed from her veins. She let the feeling go. She let all of it go.

She opened her eyes, a triumphant smile spreading across her face. *I did it!*

Fynvarra pressed his nose into her hand. *You did it,* he agreed. *That was the best mind-speak you have done yet. You didn't overwhelm me or yourself.*

Larken bit her lip. She couldn't do this any longer, couldn't lie to Fynvarra. "I have to tell you something," she whispered. Fynvarra tilted his head.

"The Tournament is coming up in a few weeks. Dahey plans to use Finder, and Isra has chosen you."

Fynvarra reared back, letting out a roar that nearly shook the walls themselves. "I am not some beast meant for faery entertainment," Fynvarra snarled, landing back on his front paws with a crash. He lashed his tail, thrashing against the chains.

Larken took a step back, worried she would be trampled beneath the drake. "Wait, *wait,*" she cried. "You've said before that you cared for Finder, that he was a good ruler. I've been thinking... you two could become allies and win your freedom together."

Fynvarra paused his thrashing. "Even if I did decide to help him, human, only one may earn their freedom in the Tournament. And though I do care for Finder, I will not sacrifice my life for his."

"There is a way for both of you to gain your freedom. It has happened only once before, but two allies refused to fight each other, and the court fey demanded that they both be set free. If you and Finder can give them a worthy show, they'll release both of you."

Fynvarra sank onto his belly. "Why did you wait this long to tell me?" He lowered his snout to the floor.

"I'm so sorry," Larken whispered. "At first I just wanted to help Finder. But I care for you, Fynvarra. I want to help you both." She tentatively reached out and placed a hand on his paw.

"I will help Finder in the ring," Fynvarra said slowly. "But I require something in return. I came to the Winter Court for a reason. Hidden somewhere in these mountains lies a healing stone. It can cure any ailment for as long as the bearer wears it. Bring me the stone, and I will fight for you."

Larken frowned. She had never heard of such a stone. Why hadn't her companions mentioned it before? "How do I know once you have the stone that you won't turn on Finder to ensure your own freedom?"

"Finder is beloved by the firedrakes," Fynvarra said. "To turn on him when he has done so much for my kind could cause my kin to cast me out. My only desire is to return home, and I would not jeopardize that. Allying myself with Finder helps me as much as him. I do not wish to fight him."

"How do I find this stone?"

"I don't know. I hoped to discover more once I arrived, but all I know is it is hidden somewhere in these mountains. Healing stones are incredibly rare, and only a few remain in this world. It will be well hidden. But once you find it for me, I shall owe you a debt. Bring me the stone, and I will fight for you."

Larken bit her lip. "Deal." She paused, guilt gnawing on her stomach. "I'm sorry, Fynvarra. Please forgive me for not telling you about the Tournament sooner."

Fynvarra pressed his snout into her palm. "I forgive you, little human. I can't fault you for not trusting me, especially after you were betrayed by Dahey. You want to save Finder."

"I'm going to save you both," Larken said firmly.

Still, a low rumble began in his chest.

Larken moved her hand to touch the vibrating scales on his neck. *Are you... Purring?* A wry smile touched her lips. *Like a cat?*

Fynvarra growled. *Blasted cats copy everything we drakes do, and they get all the credit for starting it. Despicable.*

Larken braced herself for a battle in Saja's room.

The big warrior sat across from her in one of the twin armchairs in his room. She'd confessed that she was searching for a way to help Finder win the Tournament. She explained how they needed Finder to win his freedom fairly, or else Dahey and the other court rulers would never stop hunting him.

She told him how she had found the locked records room in the library that led her to the White Keep dungeons. How she had found Fynvarra and convinced him to fight with Finder as allies and he had agreed—if they could find the healing stone.

Saja scrubbed a hand over his face. "Well, now I know I can never leave you alone again. Look what kind of trouble you get into."

Larken grinned. Saja turned wearily towards the fireplace, exposing several dark marks on his neck. Larken's brows raised. It appeared that Saja and Roone had been enjoying each other's company. She swallowed, once again reminded of Finder. Heat crept up her neck as she imagined him kissing her, tracing blazing kisses up her neck—

"Do you know anything about this stone?" Larken asked.

Saja rubbed his jaw. "I thought healing stones were merely legends. It sounds too good to be true. Though, from what I remember, the stone only works when it is in contact with the bearer. As soon as it is removed, the ailment returns in full strength. It doesn't heal permanently. I've heard stories of fey using healing stones in battle, and when they removed the stone, sometimes even years later, they realized they had been dealt a mortal blow and died instantly."

Larken shook her head. "I don't want to get tangled up in more magic, but I don't think we have a choice. Fynvarra needs the stone to see and help Finder. We have to find it."

Saja nodded. "We'll find it. Though it might take another visit to the records room by our expert locksmith." He winked at her, and she smiled, but it quickly faded.

"What if this doesn't work?" she murmured. "What if we do all this and the courts refuse to call for the appeal and Finder and Fynvarra have to fight?"

Saja placed a hand on her knee. "I think you're right about the benefit of Finder winning with honor. Freeing Finder before the Tournament, if that is even possible, will only lead to Dahey hunting us. It will already be a struggle to win back the Autumn Court's favor and to evade the Tournament so dishonorably..." Saja shook his head. "Winning the Tournament is his only chance at true freedom—and getting his place back as rightful ruler of the Autumn Court. We'll find the stone."

Saja stood up and stretched. His muscles rippled under his loose shirt. He had so much power in his body, and yet, so much sickness. Saja's breathing had been more labored since they entered the Winter Court, the cold air aggravating his lungs. At least he hadn't had a breathing attack since arriving at White Keep, not one she had seen, but Larken kept herself wary. The attacks happened viciously and without warning, and she had to be ready to keep Saja safe however she could. She doubted that the Winter Court had yellow thorn, a plant that could ease his coughing fits, in this barren of a landscape.

"You're going to have to keep this from Roone," she said.

Saja chewed his bottom lip. "I don't want to, but you're right. We can't risk him going to Isra."

When Larken returned to her suite that night, she found warmth blooming in her chest. She and Saja were going to find a way to free Fynvarra and then Finder.

It took her a moment to realize the feeling was hope.

Larken peeled off her furred coat and collapsed onto the sofa. Saja made them each a mug of warmed chocolate before lounging at her side.

"What if Finder doesn't respond?" Larken asked. "What if he's so badly hurt he can't?" Worry knotted in her stomach.

"We must trust that the Cynyadas gave him the message. Fynvarra said he would ally himself with Finder. Even if Finder can't be warned before the Tournament, Fynvarra can tell him himself in the ring."

Larken stared dejectedly into her mug of warmed chocolate. They still weren't any nearer to finding the location of the stone, and time was slowly slipping from the hourglass. They'd been searching old books in the library, pouring over the maps every night, still to no avail. If the books mentioned healing stones at all, they claimed they no longer existed.

"It worries me, not knowing what Dahey is doing," Larken said.

Saja had explained that the courts became extremely secretive of their affairs during the time leading up to the Tournament.

"I know," Saja murmured. "And I don't mean to add to your troubles, but something happened while Roone and I were on patrol today." Saja leaned forward and placed his mug on the glass table before them. "We came across some dark creature that had worked its way into the mountain. We were able to capture it, but not before it killed a few soldiers." Saja's golden eyes flickered. "It was not a creature I had ever seen before. It reeked of putrid flesh and death."

A tremor of fear slid down Larken's lower back. Saja had lived for centuries, and for him to never have encountered this kind of creature before was a rare occurrence indeed.

"There are rumors. Creatures staining the land, the likes of which have never been seen before. Unnatural things."

His wording sparked some memory inside her. "Like the creatures in the war against the Guardian," Larken realized.

Saja nodded. "Roone and I believe that Ziegan is making his creatures once more. We fear he is building an army. Roone and his soldiers are questioning the creature now and hope to have more answers soon."

The thought of Roone torturing something made her skin crawl. It was easy to forget that her kindhearted teacher was still a warrior of the Winter Court. Part of Isra's *dornán*.

"You've been spending a lot of time with Roone," Larken commented.

Saja stared at his lap. "I care for Roone. But I fear it shall never go further than that. Romances between high members of the courts are forbidden."

Larken's heart twisted in sympathy. "Surely you two could find a way."

Saja brushed her off. "It doesn't matter how Roone and I feel. We are loyal to our courts, and that will never change." He stood abruptly and closed the door to his room without another word.

37

ROONE

Airodion

The creature writhed under Roone's instruments.

Roone never wished he could regain his hearing. He liked the quiet, the beautiful way he was able to communicate so visually with handspeak. He was able to keep calm in all situations. He stood like a stone in a river while the screams of his captives, the clamor of battle all parted before him. His silence was his sanctuary. Soldiers flocked to him, their minds put at ease in his presence.

Roone looked back to the creature. In a way, its striped skin was beautiful. It could fly, or rather, it had been able to fly before Roone had torn off its wings. He knew how to make the creature hurt. He wondered briefly what the screams sounded like during his interrogations, screams that made his generals grow clammy and vomit.

Other sounds made him curious as well. Una's roar, which shook the ground, or Saja's moans, but those Roone could *feel*, right down to his core. But he would not allow himself to think those things here. He kept everything that was good out of the walls of the interrogation room. This was a place of darkness and fear, a place that annihilated enemies of the Winter Court.

Roone pressed his knife into the creature's flesh, a shallow but agonizing wound. He would know. This move had been performed on him several times.

Isra was a just ruler. She required her guards trained in torture to experience the techniques on themselves. It prevented needless torture and abuse of power. Roone suffered it gladly. He knew the wounds that would cause the least amount of harm but also the most amount of pain, leading to a quick confession and a quick end for the prisoner.

He looked to Saoirse. Her piercing blue eyes were fixed on the creature. She had passed her training, where she had endured torture on her body, and now shadowed Roone during his interrogations. She hadn't looked away yet, even as she vomited. The creature spoke in mind-speak to Saoirse, as even in mind-speak, the creature could not communicate with Roone.

"*It says Ziegan is its master,*" Saoirse translated. "*It says it was told to come here.*"

"*Why?*"

Saoirse frowned. "*It doesn't know. I'm sorry, Roone.*"

"*You're doing a fine job,*" Roone assured her.

"*It just keeps saying the same phrase over and over now, no matter what you do.*"

"*What is it saying?*"

"*'Master is coming. Master is coming. Master is coming.'*"

Roone's heart quickened. "*When?*"

Saoirse's blue gaze met his. "*Soon.*"

Roone stood before his queen. He had told her everything the prisoner had told him. "*Ziegan is an undeniable threat now, Isra. We left him alone, and he has begun to raise an army against us. We must act.*"

"*One creature is not evidence of an army,*" Isra argued.

"The creature itself says that it was told to come here. That Ziegan is coming."

"The creature could have been sent here to spy, nothing more. And saying Ziegan is coming here could have been its desire to be rescued from your knife." She dug her nails into her icy throne. *"I am not a fool, Roone,"* she said. *"I know this creature is a threat. But we do not have enough information to fight Ziegan—not yet. None of us have faced him before. All we know is that the Starveling, Dark Priestesses, and court rulers all had to work together to imprison him. Attacking him now while Autumn still struggles to settle its power could destroy us all."*

"What about Finder?"

"Demanding that we free him could make Dahey and the Autumn Court turn on us."

Roone knew some of what Isra said was the truth. But he also knew that prisoners did not lie under his knife. The creature had been sent here, which meant others had been too. Ziegan was coming to the Winter Court. *"I have been in your* dornán *for many years, Isra,"* Roone said. *"And I have not led you astray. Waiting until after the Tournament to strike is the wrong path."*

"The Starveling and two of the three Dark Priestesses are dead," Isra said flatly. *"We have no idea what we are up against with his language and what it is capable of. I will not attack until I have more answers. If he comes here, so be it. White Keep has never fallen. And until then, we shall continue with the Tournament. The Tournament is the best way to show the citizens of the Winter Court that though the Starveling is dead, the court rulers are now in control. No one else. And certainly not Ziegan."*

A dark sadness spread across Roone's heart. Isra glared at him, and Roone felt her powers seep into him. He gritted his teeth, reminding himself that it was just Isra's power over those dark emotions. She was lashing out because she was afraid.

"Things cannot change," Isra whispered. *"When things change, I lose control. And I cannot lose control. You know what's happened before."*

Roone knew that Finder had lost control of his powers when he had first become prince and destroyed an entire town. Isra's had been much of the same when the powers over those dark emotions had claimed her and she had attacked her parents. She had put them into such a deep depression that they had nearly taken their own lives. They were now mere husks of themselves, permanently changed by her powers. Even Valakais hadn't been able to bring them back. Isra had never been able to forgive herself, no matter how many times Roone had told her that it was common for a court ruler's powers to make them lose control.

"Things will remain as they always have in the Winter Court," Isra said firmly. *"We have always held the Tournament, so that is what we will do. And if Ziegan becomes a threat, we will face it then. But for now, we are not treating things as if they are any different. The Tournament will go on."*

Roone bowed. *"As you wish, my queen."*

38

LARKEN

Airodion

Larken struggled to concentrate on the maps spread before her on the bed.

The past few nights had her desperately wishing that her room didn't connect to Saja's. Roone had taken Saja to bed nearly every night.

At first, Larken had thought it was sweet, but now she wanted to smack them both upside the head whenever she saw them. No one needed to be that loud and boastful about their lovemaking.

She sighed, forcing herself to study the maps once more. She'd asked Roone if he knew anything about healing stones during one of their hand-speak lessons, and he had assured her that they were nothing more than a myth. When she'd pressed him on the matter, he gave her a book about the legends of the Winter Court.

Larken turned to the chapter that mentioned healing stones. The author had spent several paragraphs describing them, which was more than many of the other books she had come across.

Healing stones possessed the ability to heal the ailments of any magical being they came into contact with. The stone did not possess true healing abilities, for as soon as the stone was removed from the wearer, the ailment returned in full. All of the healing stones were mined from the mountains of the Winter Court and were coveted by the fey in the era of the Masters. Many of them were fashioned into jewelry that the courtly fey could wear. These rare stones were particularly popular on the battlefield. Though many coveted the stones, the fey soon realized the undesirable advantage it gave to their enemies and one by one, the stones were destroyed or lost to the winds of time.

Larken frowned. *Well, we all know that things best left forgotten have a tendency to reappear,* she thought darkly. She flipped to the part of the book that described the mines where the healing stones were found.

It is said that the last known owner of one of the stones took her dying laithnam *to the mine in a desperate attempt to find another way to heal her beloved. The owner had suffered a mortal wound, and if she removed the stone, she would perish as well. But the mine had been empty for hundreds of years. Her* laithnam *perished, and in her grief, the last owner of the stone destroyed the mine. The outside of the mine is thought to still exist, though its interior is buried under rock and snow.*

Larken sat up. This was the first book to mention a mine, and the first to mention that part of it could still exist. She went back to her maps, three of which detailed the mountain range of the Winter Court. She pulled the first map closer, squinting hard to read the minuscule text.

Several locations were marked throughout the mountain range, cities surrounding White Keep and the locations of various ancient beasts that Larken was sure she didn't want to know about, but this map contained a small symbol for a cave. It was nearly indistinguishable from the shading of the mountains, and caverns weren't listed in the key, but Larken had studied enough maps that she knew what cavern markers looked like.

She pulled the second map over. This one was older but was still in the era of the Starveling. Again, the caverns were marked but not labeled.

Larken's brow furrowed. It was strange for the cartographer to have marked the location but not label the caves. As if he thought they were important but didn't quite know why.

Finally, she pulled out the third map. This one was so old it felt as though it could disintegrate into dust at any moment. She carefully scanned the stained parchment. This map pre-dated the Starveling. Her eyes widened when she saw a small dot near where the caverns were marked on the other maps. This map had no key, but a tiny sketch of a pickaxe adorned the dot. It was struck through, unlike the other symbols for mines she had come across.

Could it be one of the ancient mines?

She rushed across the sitting area to Saja's room, banging on the door and trying to ignore the sounds coming from within.

"Occupied," came Saja's gasp from within.

Larken scowled. "I've found something about the stone."

Blissful silence. Then the door opened. Saja stood before her wrapped in a bedsheet. Roone lounged in the bed behind him, not bothering to cover himself.

"*You know the entire palace can hear you,*" Larken said.

"*I didn't hear anything,*" Roone said innocently.

"*Lucky for you then,*" Larken said, making Saja chuckle. She turned so Saja was blocking Roone. "I think I've found the stone," she said. She felt guilty hiding it from Roone, but they didn't have a choice. They couldn't risk him alerting Isra.

Saja turned to Roone, giving some excuse in hand-speak, then turned back to her. "Show me."

Larken tore down the endless staircase into the dungeons.

"I've found it," Larken said, breathless.

Fynvarra, tucked into a scaly ball, lifted his head to peer at her. Larken grabbed his paw, too excited to speak, and poured everything she had found out from the books and the maps into him.

Fynvarra perked up. *You believe the stone could be there.*

I've found no other book that mentions the location of the stones, Larken said. *It has to be there. They couldn't consider the alternative. Saja and I will go there as soon as we can. We're running out of time. But once you have the stone...*

Fynvarra arched his scaly neck, his lips peeling back. *I will be a formidable enemy in the ring.* His nostrils flared, his sightless eyes gazing around his cave. *I smell...* he shook his head. *The Weeping Metal taints my senses. But I smell...* His eyes widened. *Someone is here!*

Larken whipped around just as Roone emerged from the shadows.

"Roone," Larken gasped, jerking away from Fynvarra. Fynvarra growled, low and deep, at the Winter Court faery.

"*It seems you have found our champion,*" Roone said. Larken couldn't read his expression, though his usual smile had disappeared. "*Though the real question is why? And how did you get down here?*"

Larken bit her lip. Roone was her friend and Saja's lover. But Roone loved his court. If he went to Isra, if Isra picked another prisoner, all would be lost.

"*I have maps of White Keep, and I went exploring—*"

"*Don't lie. I know someone broke into our records room. The scrolls were all in their right place but not rolled how I like them.*" Roone cocked an eyebrow. "*It was you, wasn't it? You found out that Isra has chosen the firedrake as her prisoner, and you came to see if it would help Finder in some way.*"

"*Yes, it was me who disturbed your scrolls,*" Larken admitted. "*Though I didn't exactly break in—I just unlocked the door. I have to save Finder. If we rescue him before the Tournament, he'll never be able to reclaim his throne with honor. You and Saja told me that allies have won before. Fynvarra,*" she gestured to the firedrake, who curled his lip at Roone, "*and Finder are going to fight together and win as allies.*"

Roone studied her for a moment.

"*Please don't tell Isra,*" Larken begged.

"*I'm not going to tell Isra,*" Roone said after a moment. "*I'm going to help you.*"

Larken's heart flew into her throat.

"Isra is refusing to face Ziegan until after the Tournament," Roone explained. *"She claims that she wants to wait until the court rulers are at full strength before they face him. She believes that after the Tournament, the Autumn Court will have a new ruler."*

Because Finder would be dead, and the powers would be forced to find another, Larken surmised.

"But this is unwise," Roone continued. *"A new court ruler is powerful, but they do not have control over their powers. That takes years, even decades, to learn. A new ruler is not what we need before a war, and it is a war I believe we are about to face."* Roone's hazel gaze darkened. *"We need Finder. And I believe you are right, this is the best, the only way to save him. And quite possibly the courts."*

Larken launched herself at Roone, crushing him into a hug. "Thank you," she whispered, though she knew he couldn't hear her. She stepped back so he could see her hand-speak. *"Thank you."*

Roone nodded. *"The one thing Isra despises above all else is change. But in this instance, I fear she will doom the Winter Court. It pains me to go behind her back like this, but it must be done. I will support you in this, in Fynvarra and Finder becoming allies."* He glanced at the drake. *"Though the firedrake is badly wounded. Even Isra could not fix his sight. How will he be of any help in the ring?"*

Fynvarra's tail tightened around her leg. She had kept her mind open to him while she and Roone were talking in hand-speak so he could understand. Larken smiled. "We have a plan for that."

39

KAISA

Ellevere

Kaisa and Ishan lay side by side in the barn, gazing at the stars through a broken slat in the roof.

Kaisa picked at the worn blanket beneath them. Ishan had been quiet tonight, and she could tell that he was still upset from their ride through town.

"Talk to me," she murmured, tracing small circles on his bare chest.

Ishan sighed, drawing her close. "I'm sorry for my harsh tone earlier," he said. "I've been struggling with leading Augrim as of late. My grandmother did so much for this town, and I feel I cannot live up to her legacy." His voice wobbled on the last note.

Kaisa cupped his cheek. "You are doing all you can for Augrim," she said. "You've trained alongside them, helped fortify the walls, spent time with the injured. Your grandmother would be proud."

Ishan ran his thumb along her bottom lip, making her shiver. "Thank you," he murmured. "We're both doing all we can for this town," he said. "I thank the Twins every day that I have you by my side, helping me lead them."

Kaisa shivered at his words. Was that truly what she was doing? Leading this town? It felt...good. Right. Like she was meant to do it. She would have thanked the Twins for such a blessing once. But now, now she felt as though she had earned it of her own volition, not theirs.

Ishan's arms moved beneath her, holding her close. She shivered when she felt his muscles flex against her.

Once, she would have been terrified to be held like this by a boy. If they had been caught doing this at Barrensmere... she shuddered. They would have been branded—or worse.

Kaisa pressed her nose to Ishan's neck. He smelled of sweat and musk, a heady scent that had her toes curling. They were not in Barrensmere. And she would do what she pleased.

She pulled herself onto his chest, straddling him. She leaned down and brushed a trail of kisses up his neck. He groaned, the vibration sending shivers down her spine.

Kaisa wasn't a part of the Order. She wasn't a Scholar about to reach her Anointing day. No, she was the Savior of Augrim. She was not some innocent child; she was now one of the leaders of this town.

She did not belong to the Order any longer. Her mind did not belong to the Order any longer. Her *body* did not belong to the Order any longer.

"I want you," she whispered.

Ishan sat up, crushing his lips to hers. She broke away, gasping for breath. "Tonight. All of you."

He flipped her onto her back, brown eyes questioning. "Are you sure?" he whispered.

She nodded, grazing his cheek with her hand. Then she gently pushed against him, pressing him down onto his back once more. She settled herself on top of him. He had said once that she was his.

But she belonged to no one. And tonight, he was hers.

She shrugged off her tunic. The light of the stars shined down through the broken slats of the roof, painting her dark skin in moonlight.

And when she took him, she felt power seep into her veins. She tossed her head back and laughed, laughed through the sharp pain and steady ache until there was no more.

Request for aide came the next day.

Some part of her swelled with pride when the bedraggled messenger arrived asking to speak to the Savior of Augrim. She had been eating her evening meal with Ishan when they heard the news. They hadn't left each other's sides since their moment in the barn the night before. She was glad they had spoken about their ride through town. It felt good to have him by her side. They were a team, joined now in more ways than one. She still felt giddy whenever she thought about it.

Inniskeen, a neighboring town not yet hit by Furyons, was calling for aide. They had heard about how Kaisa had fended off the monsters, and that she was training her people how to fight. They wanted her and her 'army', as the man had called her brigade of farmers and merchants, to come and help them defend Inniskeen.

She had told the messenger to rest in Augrim while they considered his request.

"This is a bad idea," Ishan warned.

Kaisa twirled her fork. She couldn't deny the warm feeling that had fluttered in her chest at the idea of being needed. The people of Inniskeen wanted her help—needed her help, and she was the only one who could.

"We should help them," Kaisa said. "You believe I have something special inside me. It's telling me that I should help."

"My people could die—*you* could die, and then we'd have no hope." Ishan's jaw clenched, and he pushed away his plate of food.

A flicker of guilt pulsed through her, disrupting her happiness at being needed. If she told everyone about the book, then they would still stand a chance even if she died.

But she wasn't ready to give it up yet. The book would raise too many questions about where she came from and how she got it. It would put her in more danger, and Augrim was already in danger. The people weren't ready for the knowledge about the fey—she was right to feed it to them piece by piece.

She shut out the voice claiming that if she gave up the book, she would be giving up her power.

"These creatures aren't going to stop. There will come a time when they overwhelm us. We need numbers and support. What better way to do that than helping other towns? Think of what we could do if we banded together. We could be a true army. The people of Augrim are ready to fight."

Ishan bit his lip, then finally bowed his head. "You're right," he murmured after a time. "It's greedy of me to hog you. You have a sacred path to follow, and I shouldn't hold you back."

Kaisa shifted at his words. Why did he always have to tie everything back to the Twins? Was it so hard to believe that she could be special on her own? But she could say nothing now.

A knock on the door startled them both.

"Come in," she and Ishan said at the same time.

A man entered the room. Kaisa's brows lifted in surprise. She knew this man—it was the member of the Order who had tried to buy the refugee children. She schooled her face into neutrality, trying not to outright glare at him until she knew what he wanted.

"Ishan. Kaisa." The man dipped his head to them both. "Forgive my awkwardness, I did not know if I should address you with any titles."

Kaisa ignored the insult. "What do you want?"

"News of your recent victory against the monsters has spread," the man began, folding his hands behind his back as he paced around the room. Kaisa tracked him with her eyes.

"These attacks grow more frequent, along with the common peoples' panic. They call you the Savior of Augrim, blessed by the Twins, and more," the man said. "They say the Popes have abandoned them, that the Order has forsaken them to these creatures, but you alone know how to save them."

Kaisa fought down the burst of pride that bloomed within her at his words. "I do not tell them to say such things," she said. "Perhaps you should be asking why they believe the Popes have forsaken them. Perhaps it is because the Popes have done nothing to help them against these creatures. Their armies lie dormant, the Order offers no aide," she practically spit out the last part.

"Oh, the Popes' armies are not dormant," the man purred. "They simply look towards bigger things."

Kaisa narrowed her eyes. "What is that supposed to mean?"

The greasy man gave a smile. "I digress. The Popes have sent me on their behalf to offer a truce of sorts. They know you abandoned your place at the Institute."

Kaisa's blood chilled, but she said nothing, refusing to glance at Ishan.

"They know you are spreading lies about the Order, feeding the people's fear that the Popes have abandoned them to these monsters," the man continued. "They are angry, of course, and while their human greed wants vengeance upon you, the Twins whisper in their ear: the Popes can use you to their advantage."

She felt Ishan's gaze upon her, but she didn't look away from the man.

"They offer you a deal: return to the palace with the Scholar Jovanna, and join forces with them. You will be sent out with a legion of the Popes' men to speak to the towns, convincing them that you are in the Popes' service and that they have not forsaken their people. The legion will protect you and the town from any of these creatures. Some will stay behind for a reasonable amount of time to make sure the peace is kept and to protect the town from any future attacks."

Kaisa stood up, bracing her fists on the table. "The Popes and their army already know how to fight these monsters, but they keep it a secret, allowing their people to die. Why? Why are they allowing these monsters to terrorize us?"

The man waved a hand. "Those things don't concern you, *girl*," he spat. "Take the offer. I'm afraid it is a one-time deal. If you do not realign yourself with the Popes, there will be consequences. For you, for this town, and any you associate yourself with."

"I'm *helping* people," Kaisa snarled. "The Popes abandoned them, but I will not. You can take that offer and shove it up your—"

"Deceitful woman," the man snarled. "This will be a death sentence. You are nothing. No one. History was not meant to remember you."

"Oh, I think it will," Kaisa said, lifting her chin. "Either as the Savior or as the Martyr. Now get out."

The man curled his lip but left without another word.

Kaisa waited for his footsteps to recede down the hall.

"Why didn't you tell me?" Ishan murmured. The look of mistrust in his eyes made her heart sink. In truth, she didn't know why she had kept it from him for so long. She trusted Ishan, but some part of her had always hesitated to tell him. Ishan saw her as blessed by the Twins. And while that might not be true, she couldn't help the little spark of happiness that occurred every time Ishan looked at her like she was something special. She didn't want that to change. She didn't want him to know that she had left the Order behind. That she didn't believe in the Twins anymore.

"I'm sorry," she whispered. "I didn't know how to tell you. That part of my life—it was ripped away from me. And now I don't know what to think."

Ishan took her hand. "I left the Order behind as well. We're the same, Kaisa. The Twins have called us to a higher path."

Kaisa gave him a wobbly smile, forcing a nod. "Yes, they have." Her heart twisted in her chest. She was still lying to him.

"I think the New Order could be good for this town," Ishan said excitedly. "We should speak to Tarrio and see what he has to say."

Kaisa swallowed. She didn't want their people talking to Tarrio. She didn't want them to believe in the Twins at all. As selfish as it made her, she wanted their faith to be stripped from them, just as it had been from her.

She squeezed his hand. "Later, perhaps. For now, we must set our sights on Inniskeen."

Kaisa stalked through town, irritated after her meeting with the man from the Order and hearing Ishan's comments about the New Order.

She stopped when she saw Jovanna near the town square, surrounded by a group of children.

Kaisa's heart clenched at the sight. Jovanna had wanted to be a Sister of the Order, tasked with teaching new members of the faith. Her friend might be tough as nails, but her demeanor softened around children. She knew how to be firm yet kind, guiding them with a gentle hand. Her dream had been ripped from her, but she had been spending the majority of her time with the village children, teaching them to read and write.

Kaisa drifted closer, a smile touching her lips.

"... and then Asphalion forgave his sister and invited girls into the magical realm of the fey. And so, the tithe was born."

The smile faded from Kaisa's face. Heat simmered beneath her skin.

"Kaisa," Jovanna said brightly, catching sight of her. The children turned, exclaiming in delight when they saw her.

Kaisa jerked her head at Jovanna. "I need to speak with you," Kaisa ground out.

Jovanna stood, dusting off her pants. "Practice your letters," she told the children, who dutifully began scratching marks in the dirt.

"What is it?" Jovanna asked, crossing her arms.

"What are you doing?" Kaisa growled. "You can't seriously be teaching them about the Twins."

Jovanna gave her a strange look. "It's their religion, Kai."

"The Order took everything from us," Kaisa hissed, gripping Jovanna's arm.

"I'm not teaching them about the Order," Jovanna snapped. "I'm teaching them about the Twins, there's a difference."

"You just can't give them up, can you?" Kaisa said. "You still want to be a Sister of the Order. You're *poisoning* their minds!"

"They can believe in the Twins and not the Order," Jovanna snapped, jerking out of Kaisa's grip. "And of course I don't want to be a Sister of the Order, are you mad? They tried to have me *killed*." She took a deep breath. "These children have lost so much. I'm not taking their faith, too."

"These are my people, and you won't speak to them of the Order or the Twins," Kaisa growled.

"I know you're struggling," Jovanna's tone softened. "You don't know who you are without your faith. And I know it goes against everything we were taught, but it's all right if you don't believe in the Twins anymore."

Kaisa blinked.

Jovanna took a deep breath. "But it's all right if these people do. You can't expect everyone to think the same way as you do. I know a small part of you wants them to suffer as you have suffered. I know that because I feel the same way. But no one will understand what we went through except us." She squeezed Kaisa's hand.

Tears filled Kaisa's eyes. She hadn't realized how badly she had needed to hear those words.

Jovanna squeezed her hand once more, then returned to her place amongst the children.

Kaisa watched Jovanna teach the children for a long while. Anger crept into her heart, steeping into her veins. Jovanna was wrong. The Twins could not be separated from the Order. And even if they could, what did it matter? The gods were not real. The gods could not help these people.

But Kaisa could. The gods hadn't saved them—she had. And she would continue to protect them as no one else could.

Kaisa watched the children for a moment more. Then she turned and walked away.

She had work to do.

40

LARKEN

Airodion

The wind screamed outside the cave, blistering any who came in its path.

Roone and Saja stood on either side of Larken as she surveyed the cavern before them. To her delight, they had ridden Una up to the cave. Larken unfurled the map clutched between her gloved fingers. "*Search everywhere,*" she said in hand-speak. "*I'm sure this place has been searched before, but part of the interior might still exist.*"

Larken knew the chances of the final healing stone being somewhere in the mine were small. But perhaps other owners of the stones had brought their stones here as well in search for more.

The Tournament was only days away. If they didn't find the stone, Fynvarra would be forced to fight without his vision.

They searched every inch of the walls of the cave, dug their nails into every crack and crevice. Una followed them around for a bit, intent on helping how she could. Then she found a particularly interesting rock to sniff in the corner until eventually she grew bored and curled up in a tight ball to sleep.

They searched for hours, but there were no rock pileups that would suggest that an interior part of the cave even existed. The cavern walls were smooth and coated in ice and snow.

Larken stared at her maps until her the space behind her eyes began to throb. There had to be something she missed, something she wasn't seeing.

"There's nothing here, Larken," Saja murmured after a time. "We should leave."

"It has to be here," Larken whispered.

"Others would have known about this cave and searched it," Saja said gently. "It was a good idea, and it is no fault of yours that the stone isn't here. We don't know if it ever was. Fynvarra is still a firedrake, injured or not. He'll still be able to help Finder."

"I need a moment," Larken gasped, her shaking fingers nearly tearing the map in two. Saja and Roone left the cave. Una, immediately sensing Roone's departure, lumbered out after him.

Larken sank to her knees in the middle of the cave. Tears spilled from her eyes, melting away the thin layer of snow on the floor drop by drop.

"I've failed both of them," she whispered, unable to keep the words inside of herself. "Finder is going to die, and there's nothing I can do. There's nothing I can do," she sobbed, digging her fingers into the icy stone. "He was part of my soul," she gasped. "I wish our life debt hadn't ended so I never would have left his side, and maybe I could have saved him from Dahey that night." Her entire body shook with her cries. "He took Brigid from me, he burned me, and I still can't hate him. I've never hated him. I—" she gasped. "And now I have to watch him die." She hung her head.

Movement flashed in the corner of her eye. Larken turned, her eyes widening as the rock in the corner unfurled. But wasn't a stone at all, but a faery—a faery coated in ice and snow.

Larken stood, her sorrow forgotten as she beheld the faery before her.

The female, for she was female, was completely naked and coated in a layer of snow and ice. Her body was tinged blue, and her cracked white lips moved as she spoke. "Why have you come for the stone?" she rasped in a voice that sounded like wind and dust.

Larken sensed this faery's ancient spirit and knew that the female was not here to harm her. She had asked for a story, so Larken told her one. Larken told her everything. About her life debt with Finder, Dahey's betrayal, the Tournament and Larken's desperate attempt to save both Finder and Fynvarra.

"Do you love him?" the faery asked finally. "Finder, do you love him?"

"Yes," Larken replied softly, and she shivered as the truth of the words settled over her skin. She had known for a while now, but hearing the words spoken aloud... "But the stone is not for him."

The thought had crossed her mind, of course, giving Finder the stone to protect him instead of Fynvarra. But while doing so might save him, it would certainly doom Fynvarra. She lifted her head. "I couldn't find the stone, but I will still save them both."

The faery studied her with eyes so blue they were almost clear, as though Larken could see straight through her. Her hair, perhaps another color once, was now made of ice shards, and her face was powdered with snow. "How did you know to come here?"

Larken frowned. "I read about it in a book. It said that after the final healing stone was destroyed, its owner took her dying *laithnam* to this mine in hopes of finding another stone. Her *laithnam* died, and in her grief, the last owner of the stone destroyed the mine."

"It seems history has forgotten much," the faery said. "The owner of the stone's name was Nix. Her *laithnam*, Koalin, was sick and needed the healing stone to live. But when Nix was fatally wounded in battle, Koalin begged Nix to take the stone. Nix refused, but Koalin convinced her to go with her to the mine in search of another stone. They went, but there were no stones to be found. Desperate to save her *laithnam*, Koalin took off the stone and gave it to Nix. Koalin died instantly, and Nix, in her grief, destroyed the mine. Only the outer most part remained, a mere cavern. Many have come to look for it and discovered that this is merely a cave. I have seen fey and beasts alike come here in a desperate attempt to save themselves or save a loved one from death."

The faery shook her head. "But using the stone to prevent death only prolongs suffering. Even the owners of the stones could not escape it forever. The stone cannot save both your friends, but it can give them a fighting chance together. You do not want to use the stone to prevent death, but to challenge it. And you would fight death just as fiercely without the stone."

The faery walked forward, pulling something from her breast. A necklace, caked in snow. She removed the narrow chain from around her neck, holding the necklace in her fist. "I have protected this stone for centuries." She sighed. "But I have grown tired. I give it to you now." The faery took one of Larken's hands and placed the necklace in her palm. "The stone is in good hands, Koalin," the faery whispered.

Larken's eyes widened as the faery's hand left hers, and Nix fell to the floor, dead.

Roone and Saja were dumbfounded, certain that the stone was merely a myth. Larken wore the necklace around her throat, hidden beneath her layers of clothing before she could find a way to get it to Fynvarra. Weapons weren't allowed during the Tournament, and Larken was sure healing stones would be banned as well, so they had to find a way to hide it on Fynvarra's body.

But they had it. She'd found it.

Now Finder and Fynvarra had to survive the Tournament.

41

LARKEN

Airodion

Those who wanted to attend the Tournament, and many Winter Court gentry did, had already left, leaving White Keep particularly barren. While the Autumn Court bordered the Winter Court, it was still a long journey down from the mountains. Nerves ran up and down her spine. Isra had portalled Fynvarra, Roone and her guards to Shadeshelm yesterday, then had retired to her chambers to rest. But soon, she would call for Larken and Saja to portal them as well. The reverie was that night, and at dawn, the Tournament.

Each court had its own arena where the Tournament was performed, and the prisoners would be stowed there until the fight began. Each of the courts brought their own guards to keep watch over their prisoner and ensure that there was no sabotage from other courts.

Larken had given the stone to Fynvarra before he left. She had tied the necklace into his golden mane, buried so deep within the fur that it disappeared completely. At once, the drake had sighed with relief and opened his amber eyes—completely cured.

"I can see," he sighed in a broken whisper.

Roone had warned them that Isra would come once more to try to heal Fynvarra's eyes. They instructed the drake to keep his eyes closed until Isra attempted to heal them, and then pretend as though she had cured him. They worried that it would arouse suspicion if Fynvarra's eyes were magically healed when Isra took him to Shadeshelm.

She and Saja had visited some of the shops in town to prepare for the reverie.

"It is customary for the fey to wear their court colors during the Tournament," Saja had explained when he caught Larken eyeing a rather drab, grey dress. "Autumn's colors are gold and red." Larken had reluctantly turned away from the grey dresses and towards the red, though it had never been her color. But to her surprise, she fell in love with a maroon gown. The shop owner had tailored it to fit, and Isra had graciously paid for it all.

A servant had come that afternoon to help Larken dress for the party. The servant painted her lips the same dark red as her dress and had dabbed her eyelids with kohl and powdered gold. Then she had dressed Larken in her gown.

The gauzy fabric was skin-tight from her sleeves to her waist, but then the dress flared into gentle waves to the floor. Two long slits ran along either side of her thigh, which Larken thought was rather revealing, but the dress maker assured her that it was quite fashionable.

But Larken's favorite part of her dress was her golden feather corset. Two golden wings encircled her, wrapping tightly around to cover each of her breasts and down to flare out around her hips. Each of the tiny metal feathers shifted with her, never pinching or digging into her. Larken never would have imagined that she would wear a dress so beautiful, never would have imagined that it would complement her body so well. The dress didn't try to hide her weight, it didn't try to disguise it under layers of fabric. No, it hugged each of her curves and displayed the contour of her body in gilded gold.

And when Larken first saw herself in the mirror, her first thought was pride. She had come so far in her body, in her journey to love and accept herself even on the hard days. She would wear this gown with her head held high, and she would save Fynvarra and Finder. She would face Dahey and every other faery there. She would not let them win.

Saja returned, dressed in a maroon tunic with gold leaf designs delicately stitched across his chest and sleeves.

His golden eyes widened as Larken stood. "You look stunning," he said, extending his hand to her. "Isra called for us."

Larken took his hand. "I'm ready."

42

KAISA

Ellevere

Kaisa sat astride her horse a short distance away from the gates of Inniskeen. Jovanna and Ishan were at her side, her small army of towns-people behind her.

Evening had fallen, cloaking everything in grey. It was late—later than she would have liked. There had been little time to prepare the town, but if the creatures attacked tonight, she was there. Her people had brought two torches each, and if they circled together, Kaisa was certain it would be enough light to warn off the Furyons.

Kaisa squinted as they drew closer. "Halt," she cried, and the people stopped.

She could make out two figures in red and black. Soldiers in the Popes' army. A strange, red cross hung on the gates. It looked like shredded cloth or meat, but Kaisa couldn't tell exactly what it was. Unease flickered through her. Why would soldiers be at the gates? Had the town somehow convinced the Popes to help them?

Kaisa summoned the messenger forward. "Why are there soldiers here?" she asked.

"I don't know," the man murmured. "They were not here when I left."

The feeling of unease did not let up as Kaisa led Jovanna, Ishan and the messenger closer to the gates.

"My name is Kaisa," she called. "I was summoned here by the people of Inniskeen. Let me and my people through—we are here to help defend the town against the fey."

The guards exchanged glances, and Kaisa caught a grin passing between them. Kaisa glanced at the red cross, still unable to figure out what it was.

"They don't need your help anymore," one of the soldiers shouted. "They have chosen the protection of Pope Sersius."

Kaisa shifted, wary. "All the same, I would like to enter the town. They have requested my presence, and I will not turn them away."

"You should have listened to the warning, girl," one of the guards snickered. He lifted his torch, illuminating the red cross.

It was a mass of torn flesh, nailed spread eagle to the gates. Blood dripped from the body from so many different wounds. It was a man, Kaisa could tell that much, and his head was shaved and hung down. He was dead—but Kaisa knew he hadn't been when these wounds had been inflicted upon him. She knew the Order's brutality.

"Don't cross the Order, girl," one of the guard's said, giving her a gap-toothed smile. He gripped the man by the forehead, pushing his head up.

It was Hollis.

It was what was left of Hollis.

Jovanna screamed beside her, falling forward on her horse's neck. Kaisa said nothing, but her body flashed hot and cold. She couldn't think, couldn't process that her childhood friend, one of the only two people she loved in the world, hung before her. Dead. And it was her fault. They had done this because of her.

She hadn't thought about him. The thought hadn't crossed her mind that they would hurt him if she refused the Popes' offer. In truth, she had been so wrapped up in her new life that she had barely thought about him at all. He had chosen the Order, and she and Jovanna had left.

Night fell, the shadows growing taller. A growl rippled through the night, echoing in the darkness.

"Kaisa," Ishan warned. "They're coming. What do you want to do?"

The soldier dropped Hollis and drew his sword. The other lifted his torch, and Kaisa could see the fear in their eyes.

Another growl rippled through the night, closer, this time. The flap of wings in the air.

Kaisa sat frozen atop Sorreno, her heart beating furiously in her chest.

They let the soldiers in, a voice said in the back of her mind. *They let this happen. They would have heard Hollis's cries and done nothing.*

Kaisa's grip tightened on the reins.

"Kaisa," Jovanna breathed. "There are innocent people in there, children—"

Could she really turn these people away? People who needed her help? But these people had chosen Pope Sersius—the guards had said so themselves.

Let them see what happens when they choose the Order. She had learned the harsh lesson that the Order would never protect her—now they could, too.

More growls tore through the air.

"Wait—wait!" one of the soldiers cried. "We were told the creatures wouldn't attack while we were here. We had a job to do. String up the boy and then wait for you. They said the creatures wouldn't come!"

The other guard raced to the gates. "We were just following orders. You said you were here to help; we'll open the gates. We're sorry, we didn't know—"

Kaisa didn't know what he was going to say next, for one of the Furyons swept out of the darkness and pinned him against the gate, splintering the wood. The man screamed and screamed as the creature tore into him and lifted him into the air. His screams didn't stop, and neither did the rain of blood from the sky.

Kaisa looked up, watching them disappear into darkness. Blood splattered her face.

"Please," the other guard begged. "Please!"

But then another creature was there, tackling him to the ground. Kaisa did not allow herself to look away. She forced herself to picture Hollis's screams in her mind. The soldier deserved this.

"Kaisa," Ishan murmured, "you can still save them."

Kaisa shook herself, blood dripping down from her hair. No. These people needed her help. It wasn't the town who had killed Hollis.

"Light the torches," she yelled.

Ishan and Jovanna lit their torches, the rest of her people doing the same. A Furyon descended from the sky, snatching one of her people off their horse. The man screamed as he was hauled off into the night. Kaisa's heart twisted.

"Quickly," she cried. "Band together."

Her people complied, forming a tight circle.

Kaisa lit her torch, wheeling Sorreno around to join them.

"We move as one into the city," she called. They entered through the gates.

Screams rose from the town. Glass shattered, wood splintered, and footsteps pounded.

"Light your torches," Kaisa screamed. "Light the roofs on fire if you must. Create as much light as you can!"

Wingbeats pulsed in the dark sky. Kaisa could make out the thrashing forms that were lifted into the air. But fire spread, people rushing to light their torches. Someone lit a wagon piled high with hay, and the bonfire sprang to life.

The Furyons shrieked with anger, but one by one took off into the night.

Kaisa's heartbeat slowed. They were safe now. Inniskeen was safe. A few of the townspeople reached out with shaking hands to stroke Sorreno. She clasped hands with several of them.

"Thank you," one murmured.

"Blessed by the Twins," said another.

"The Savior of Augrim! The Savior of Inniskeen!"

Kaisa closed her eyes, letting the praise wash over her.

Kaisa stayed at Inniskeen through the night, helping tend to the wounded. When the sun finally rose, she mounted Sorreno once more, anxious to see the state of Inniskeen in the sunlight.

The grey light of dawn mixed with the smoke and ruin of the town. Kaisa pressed her heels into Sorreno's sides, and he walked through town with Ishan and Jovanna flanking her.

The mangled bodies of the townspeople littered the streets, as did bodies of members of the Popes' army.

She guided Sorreno to the town square.

A hooded man approached her, stumbling a bit, pressing his hand into a wound at his side. Kaisa pulled Sorreno to a halt.

"Are you well?" she called. "Do you need a healer?"

"I only need one thing," the man rasped. He put his hand on Sorreno's neck. He sighed deeply, then pulled a dagger from inside his robes.

Kaisa cried out in alarm, reaching for her sword, but he grabbed her cloak, ready to pull her from Sorreno's back. Ishan and Jovanna called to her, but they were too slow.

The clattering of hooves shook the ground, and a sword flashed in the air, cutting the man down. Kaisa cried out again as blood sprayed her skin. Heart pounding in her ears, she looked down at herself, mercifully unscathed, and then at the body of the man before her.

She looked up, expecting to see Ishan, but it was Tarrio who sat astride his horse in front of her.

"You," she breathed.

"Me," he agreed, wiping his sword clean on his pants leg. "You should be more careful, little queen. Your enemies are watching." He trotted off.

Shaken, Kaisa turned Sorreno towards the town square once more. Had the man been an assassin from the Order? An angry townsperson? She would never know, she supposed, and that made it all the more terrifying.

She reached the town square. Her blood roared in her ears as she took in the dozens of crosses and the people tied spread eagle upon them.

"They didn't let the soldiers in," Jovanna murmured. "The soldiers took the town from them."

Kaisa couldn't look away from the bodies.

Shouts and the scuffle of footsteps made her turn her head. Her people dragged ten of the Popes' soldiers forward. Members of the Red Guard. Their clothes and armor were pristine, their weapons free from gore. She knew they had spent the battle in hiding. Rage simmered in her blood.

She slid from Sorreno's back, facing the people on the crossed wooden beams again. "Help me untie them," she murmured to Jovanna and Ishan. They nodded, following her to the posts.

Each of the crossed wooden beams was surrounded by piles of branches and kindling. These people—likely the leaders of the town, or anyone who resisted the town being taken by the soldiers, would have been burned, but the monsters came instead.

Kaisa cut the ties at the first woman's hands and feet with her sword. The woman's body collapsed onto her, and Kaisa grunted, hoisting her off the beams.

Eventually, other people began to help, and they cut down all of the poor souls.

Kaisa arranged their bodies, closed their eyes, and touched all of their faces. "Rest now," she said softly. They would bury them later.

She turned back to the members of the Red Guard. The men were spitting with anger as her people held them. Her chest heaved. Rage unlike anything she had ever known overcame her like a dark tide.

They had tortured Hollis to show her what would happen when she crossed the Order. Now, she would show the Order what would happen when they crossed her.

"Tie them to the beams," Kaisa said, jerking her head at the crosses.

Her people exchanged glances, but did as she commanded, forcing the struggling members of the Guard to the beams.

"Kaisa, what are you doing?" Jovanna hissed.

Kaisa ignored her. She pulled one of the lit torches free from one of the shops in the town square and returned to the men. She lifted the torch to each of their faces, illuminating them in the pre-dawn light.

"You all are members of the Order, yes?" she called.

A few grumbled answers rose from the men.

Kaisa narrowed her eyes. "Answer me," she commanded.

A few more cries of assent rose from the men.

She paced down the line. "Do not be afraid. You will not suffer the same fate as the innocents you strung up to these posts. I simply wish for a confession. Repent in the eyes of the Twins, and then you can go free."

The men stirred at her words, as did her people. Jovanna and Ishan watched her warily, but she ignored their questioning glances.

"Are you or are you not members of the Red Guard?" She knew their uniforms well enough—these were not common soldiers.

"We are," a few cried.

"And you left your soldiers and the people of this town to die?"

Silence.

"I would suggest that you answer." Kaisa lowered her torch precariously low to the branches surrounding the first man's feet. He gritted his teeth and said nothing.

"Bromm, just tell her," another man growled.

"Yes, we did," he cried. And others soon took up his words. Kaisa turned away, desperately trying to catch her breath.

"And, as members of the Red Guard, you know what happens at the Institute," she said. "You know what happens on Anointing day."

Again, she was met with silence. She whirled, clutching the torch in one hand and her sword in the other. "Did you allow children to kill each other," she screamed. "Tell me!"

Bromm curled his lip at her. "Yes."

"Confess." She pointed at the rest of them. "And all shall be forgiven."

More cries of agreement came from the men. Kaisa breathed in deeply.

"We played your game," Bromm snarled. "We confessed. Now let us go. You said you would before the Twins themselves."

Kaisa turned once more, meeting Bromm's gaze. She tilted her head at him. "Don't you know the only way to repent for your sins?"

The man glared at her, and she forced a laugh. "Come now, the Order teaches this lesson to the smallest children! Tell me the true way to repent."

Bromm said nothing, though sweat glistened on his brow.

"The only way to repent is through fire."

Bromm's eyes widened, a silent scream on his lips as she touched the torch to the kindling at his feet, and the fire roared to life.

Kaisa nodded to Ishan. He hesitated for a moment, then took his torch and lit the next member of the Guard on fire.

Kaisa swung herself up onto Sorreno's back, dropping her torch as the first light of dawn spilled across the town. The men screamed as they cooked in their armor, the bonfires growing brighter as it devoured the flesh of the Red Guard.

They knew how to save these people, and they refused to help them. They cowered while the townspeople died. They deserved this. They deserved this. They deserved this.

"People of Inniskeen," Kaisa cried, gesturing to the rest of the survivors of the town. "The dark night is over. I have come for you. You are welcome at Augrim, and we will care for you like we do our own people. Join us, please."

A few people bowed, then the rest of the people before her followed their lead, sinking to their knees. "Kaisa," they murmured. "Blessed by the Twins."

Kaisa shoved down her guilt. The Red Guard paid for what they did to this town and others. All would be well now.

"Look at how they bow for you," Ishan said, surprise coloring his words. Tarrio wouldn't look away, pinning her with his grey gaze. Jovanna wouldn't look at her.

"This is a victory," Kaisa said, leaning over to grip her hand.

"I know why you did this," Jovanna said. "But it makes you no better than the Order."

Kaisa pulled her hand away, ignoring the sting that accompanied Jovanna's words.

43

LARKEN

Airodion

They were surrounded by a forest of wood and stone. Massive trees, bigger than she had ever seen, enveloped them, but built into the forest was the city itself. Stone staircases led into the boughs, the buildings scaffolded to the trunks. The oranges, browns, yellows and reds of the leaves sparkled like jewels. The roads of the city twisted through the roots and stone archways.

"The City of Leaves," Saja said from beside her.

"This isn't what I imagined at all," Larken admitted. Her mind had conjured some dark place of black stone and fire. But this city was alive, it breathed, light and awash with color.

Saja smiled. "Only some of the palaces adhere to their ruler's elemental power, like Isra's."

Evening had already begun to fall, and the city fell into darkness, lit by torches. A tunneled archway of trees led to the palace itself, a massive building built onto the trunks of several trees. Endless glass windows adorned the palace, sporting what Larken could only assume was a gorgeous view of the city.

Larken, Saja, and Isra approached the palace. Two stone trees carved in stark relief flanked the arched wooden doors. The two guards moved aside, pulling the doors open and letting them enter.

They passed through a large great hall. Court gentry milled about. Larken was able to mark each faery by their court colors: Winter fey were garbed in silver and navy blue, Spring fey wore green and pink, and Summer wore orange and yellow. Male and female fey alike were extravagantly dressed, their sharp beauty only enhanced.

Autumn Court guards led them to a pair of great double doors large enough for Fynvarra to fit through. She marveled at the architecture, awestruck by the fact that they were inside a massive tree. The wood was akin to stone, petrified and hard. Decorations lined every surface, from flora and fauna motifs to mosaics and tapestries. All of them celebrated life in Shadeshelm and the Autumn Court. Fall, of course, was the main season presented, and it was clear that the fey loved their court. Horses were a central theme as well, as they were the mounts of the Autumn Court fey.

Music drew them up a grand staircase to a set of double doors thrown wide open. The throne room.

"The reverie always takes place in the ball room," Saja muttered. "Having it in the throne room must be Dahey's doing."

They entered the throne room, flanked by a double row of columns leading to a dais at the back of the hall. Larken couldn't resist reaching out a hand to feel the marble pillars. The branches curved and intertwined, tapering off into delicate twigs no wider than a finger. Streaks of orange, brown and red ran through the trunks and branches, setting the autumnal atmosphere perfectly. The wall to her right was made entirely of arched windows and several sets of doors led outside. Huge braziers near the windows roared with fire, bathing the throne room in hues of orange, red and yellow.

Plush couches and chairs lined the opposite wall, as did a few canopied beds with curtains that could be drawn closed. The chamber was filled with fey, talking and milling about.

Larken tore her gaze away, her eyes sliding to the end of the hall. A set of stairs led to a platform, and another set of stairs led to a raised dais upon which the throne sat. The throne itself was carved from white stone, with tree branches cradling it. The roots and branches encircled the chair, winding down the steps and back up the stone wall behind it.

Dahey lounged on the throne, wearing a maroon doublet with golden clasps lining his chest. His brown eyes met Larken's from across the room, and he smiled.

Isra went to join Valakais and Etain on the stairs. The court rulers surveyed the room before them. Dahey stood, sauntering down the steps to join them. He wore a magnificent, thick red cloak patterned with golden leaves and embellishments. It trailed on the ground behind him, and Larken's heart twisted. He looked like a king.

The music stopped as Dahey raised his hands. "Fey of my court," Dahey called, "esteemed guests. Welcome to Shadeshelm. You have been to many reveries before, but none shall match this night." A cheer rose from the crowd, making Dahey smile. "But first, a dance."

He swept his hands across the open space below the dais. The court gentry cleared the space as six dancers streamed in from between the columns, all dressed in gauzy white. The three female dancers took one side of the square dance floor, the three male dancers taking the other. They each sank into deep bows as servants brought four wooden chairs for Etain, Dahey, Isra, and Valakais. Larken was shocked that Dahey would leave his throne to sit with the others, but perhaps this was customary.

Once the court rulers had been seated, Dahey commanded, "Begin."

Servants doused a few of the roaring braziers. Darkness spread across the room. The musicians took up their instruments, and the dancers began.

The music was primal and dark and spoke not to the sophisticated gentry in the room, but the ancient, vindictive part of the fey. Raspy horns blew, stringed instruments playing out a near frantic, pulsing rhythm. Drums pounded, so loud Larken could feel them in her bones. One of the female musicians began to sing a song about a hunt for a monstrous beast that turned everything it touched to ashes. The dancers writhed with savage grace, their bodies trembling with the music. They formed a circle, then came together, each male and female paired. The males lifted their female counterparts, their movements wild. Their hands roamed each other, fisting in each others' hair and pulling back, exposing their necks. Larken's mind lulled, completely entranced by the music. The singer's voice grew more ominous by the second as she recounted how the hunters, now deep in the woods, realized the beast was the one hunting them. He would find them, and he would turn them all to ash. Dahey stood as the song reached a pulsing crescendo and raised his hands.

Flames roared to life, covering every inch of the dance floor. Icy horror spread over Larken, chilling her to the bone. Dahey had revealed that he had the fire to his people and the other court rulers—that was how certain he was that Finder would die tomorrow.

Isra and Valakais's mouths fell open. They exchanged worried glances but didn't get up from their seats. Etain gave a savage grin. The court fey leapt back, exclaiming in shock and delight, but the dancers didn't stop. Their bare feet danced upon the fire, but they did not burn. The singer cut off her song with a chilling howl. But the music continued, accompanying the singer's savage cries. The flames devoured the white fabric that wrapped around the dancers, burning it away. Only ashes remained, and the dancers smeared it across their bodies in ecstasy. The song spiraled downwards, and upon the final beat, the dancers spun towards the dais and knelt, their bodies completely prone upon the stone. The flames vanished.

Silence. Then the crowd roared with delight. Saja stood in mute horror beside her. Larken felt faintly sick as she watched the slow grin spread across Dahey's face as the other rulers leaned over to murmur their praises to him.

Larken couldn't tear her eyes away from the dancers where they lay, naked and breathing heavily upon the floor at Dahey's feet. *The beast in the song didn't kill them,* she thought numbly. *He let them join him.*

"The night has only just begun," Dahey promised with a grin. "Eat.

Dance. Enjoy each others' company. Make this a night you will not forget."

The fey cheered, and the music picked up again. The fey swept onto the dance floor and began to dance, their movements so beautiful Larken couldn't tear her gaze away. It shamed her to admit it, but she wanted to dance. She had never liked dancing before, but there was something about the music, the swaying movements of the gentry that made her want to lose herself.

"Come," Saja said, pulling her away from the dance floor. "Let's get something to drink."

They made their way to one of the laden banquet tables. Larken's eyes widened at the sheer number of silver plates and crystal decanters—all filled with every food and drink imaginable. Her stomach was tied in too many knots to consider food, but she reached for one of the bottles containing what looked like honey wine.

Saja grabbed her wrist gently. "Not that one," he said. "Try the lavender one instead."

Larken frowned. "I want to try this one."

"It isn't an ordinary wine," Saja said. "It makes you feel pleasure."

"Well, I'm even more sure I want it now. I could use a little happiness at a time like this," she muttered, reaching for the bottle again.

"*Pleasure*, Larken, not happiness," Saja said. She frowned again, but at his pointed look, she almost dropped the bottle.

"You didn't tell me it was that kind of party."

"Any faery party is that kind of party," Saja muttered. "Just stay close to me, and don't accept any food or drink until I tell you what it is." He nodded to the honey wine. "I didn't mean to stop you from trying it. You can if you wish. I'll just warn you that it will make you... *indisposed* for the rest of the night."

Larken sat the bottle down, intrigued as she was. "Another night then." She picked up the lavender wine instead. "Well, I still need a drink. Is this going to do something to me?"

Saja shook his head. "Just intoxicate you."

Larken uncorked the bottle. "Excellent."

44

LARKEN

Airodion

Larken and Saja stayed on the edges of the room, watching the reverie unfold. The fey talked, danced, and in the shadowy alcoves and couches, pleasured themselves and others.

"Let's dance," Saja said suddenly.

Larken shook her head. "I can't. It feels wrong knowing Finder is chained up somewhere in the palace, and we're here."

"Dahey wants us to cower in fear," Saja murmured. His golden eyes met hers.

Larken gave him a small smile. "It would be an honor to dance with you, my friend."

Saja swept her onto the dance floor. Though the warrior was huge, he was an excellent dancer. She leaned into his embrace, pressing her cheek into his chest. How had it come to this, only her and Saja left from their group of five?

Larken's eye caught on two couples locked in a dance. A woman with dark blonde hair, round cheeks and a gentle smile was clasped in the arms of a male faery with dark hair. While the female was soft—even her

221

brown eyes were warm and inviting—he was all sharp angles. He spun the female around with effortless precision.

The second couple danced around them, locked in the other couples' orbit. This female had red-blonde hair that hung in waves down her back and her face was dotted with freckles. Her blue gaze was kind. The male she was with had shining blonde curls. He held the red-haired female close, pressing her into the space between his neck and shoulder. They all looked to be in their early twenties, though Larken knew they were likely much older than that.

Larken tried to steal glances of them whenever she could. The longer she looked at them, the more familiar they seemed, as though she had met them all before. She couldn't tear her gaze away from the dark-haired male. His face was so devoid of feeling that Larken nearly shuddered. The soft female in his arms was quick to smile, speaking to the red-haired female as the four of them danced, but the dark-haired male did not speak. When the female laid a small hand on his face, it looked as though she was touching a statue, a being made of chilled stone.

Suddenly, the dark-haired faery looked up, locking gazes with Larken. Her grip tightened on Saja's shoulders. The dark-haired male whispered something to the female, causing her to look over at Larken as well. The four fey stopped dancing, standing still as the flurry of other dancers spun around them. The dark-haired faery broke out of the embrace of his female and strolled across the dance floor to where she and Saja stood. Saja followed her gaze to the dark-haired faery that approached them, and she could have sworn that he paled. The other fey parted before him.

The male halted in front of them. His short hair fell in tousled curls. He would have been so beautiful if not for the cold that seeped from him that Larken had only seen matched by Isra.

He was dressed nearly entirely in gold, with threads of red stitching woven throughout.

"May I have a dance," he asked, extending his hand to her. He didn't bother to lilt his voice into a question—it was a command. Larken swallowed, nodded, and placed her hand in his. She expected it to be as cold as the rest of him, but he was warm.

Larken placed one of her hands on his shoulder and the other in his outstretched hand. His shoulder was bony, and even the finery of his clothes could not hide how slender he was. He smelled strange. Like flowers with a tinge of rot beneath.

"You're not what I expected," he said, his voice slipping over her like silk. He had a lovely voice, but everything he said was cold. "I thought my nephew's tithe would have a bit more... fire." He smiled, and Larken's gaze widened.

Of course the faery looked so familiar. This was Dahey's father. The female he was with was Dahey's mother, and the other two fey had to be Finder's parents.

"It seems I had enough fire to be the only girl to survive the tithe," Larken said. She tried to rack her brain for anything her companions had said about Osiron Fairburn. Madden had once said that Dahey had been able to win his parent's pride but never his love. It didn't shock her that Osiron could be so cruel, but it surprised her that Dahey's mother could be when she looked so warm.

Osiron smiled, spinning her lazily about. Larken had never expected to feel so helpless during a dance, but Osiron's arms felt like a cage. "I must admit, I am curious about that night," he said. "Strange that a girl as plain as you was the only one to survive. And stranger still that Finder defeated the Starveling, and yet, my son now commands his fire. Does it hurt to see Finder brought so low?"

In the past, Osiron's words would have sliced into her, but now she felt nothing at all. Larken lifted an eyebrow. "Does it hurt to see your nephew and now your son command the powers that you once did? I have to wonder why the magic chose another, *two* others, in fact, while you still live." She was tired of faery games. If they wanted to throw words at her in hopes of tearing her down, then they would find that she was not so easily broken. She was not the girl she once was, and she would not roll over and take abuse any longer. If her companions' stories had told her anything, she owed the faery before her no kindness. Osiron had played a part in Dahey's fall.

Osiron stiffened. Then he bared his teeth at her. "You're a clever little thing. But clever won't be able to save Finder at the Tournament tomorrow. Nothing will." He glanced at where Dahey sat on the raised dais with the other court rulers. "My son is not a prince, he is a king. He was not raised to submit. Oh, I tried to beat it out of him as a child. I tried to cleanse him with my fire."

Larken's stomach roiled with disgust, with hatred for Osiron. "He was a child," she snarled. "He was your son. Didn't you love him?"

"I loved him as no one else could," Osiron snapped. "I made him into what he has become." Larken could swear she heard a hint of pride in his voice. "I made that boy bow until he realized he would do it no longer, that he was not built to cower. I made him want to fight back, to burn those who had hurt him, to take the throne that belongs to him. To me. To *my* line." His eyes turned to the throne where Dahey sat, every inch the ruler of the Autumn Court. "You should be afraid of the fire that burns inside him."

Larken spun away from Osiron, startling him, but she kept hold of his fingertips. She spun back into his embrace as the music hit its final beats. She lifted her chin to meet his gaze. "It is Dahey who should be afraid of me," she said, filling her voice with as much venom as she could muster. "As should you. For I have fire of my own now." She bowed. "Thank you for the dance. But now I must take my leave of you."

She spun around, but not before she saw his jaw fall open in disbelief. Larken smiled.

Roone returned from his guard duty sometime after her dance with Osiron. He and Saja fell into each others' arms, whisking each other across the dance floor. Same sex couples weren't uncommon, nor were couples from different courts, but Saja and Roone drew stares as high-level members of the Autumn and Winter Courts and because they danced with such simple passion and love, matching each other beat for beat, step for step. Their moves weren't erotic, as Dahey's dancers had been, or animalistic, as many of the fey's dancing had become. No, they danced with simple ease, melding together.

"He looks happy," a voice murmured from behind her. Larken froze.

"It almost sounds like you care," she replied coldly, turning to face

Dahey. She crossed her arms, the golden feathers of her dress shifting slightly.

"I do care," Dahey said, not taking his eyes off Saja. "I wanted you two occupied at the bridge, and for *you* to return home, not for either of you to die. I want Saja here with me, in the Autumn Court, supporting my rule, not Finder's." Dahey shook his head. "But he will never give up on him."

Larken caught the hint of jealously in his tone. Some part of her wanted to believe him, wanted to believe that he didn't send the Fomari to kill her and Saja outright. He had cried when Madden had died, after all. She knew he didn't hate the fellow members of his *dornán*. But she also knew that he would stop at nothing to keep his throne, and if that meant disposing of her and Saja, then he would.

She had thought about this moment alone with Dahey, about what she would want to say to him after all the lies he had told the other court rulers at the meeting. She thought she would want to ask him why he had done what he did, but watching him interact with the other court rulers, watching him here in Shadeshelm, had given her the answer. She knew exactly why he had done it. Finder as a ruler had been dragged down by his crown. Dahey as a ruler was radiant.

"I have something that belongs to you," Dahey said. "A white pony was found wandering the Autumn Court forests. It followed my guards back to Shadeshelm."

Larken gasped. "Snowfoot!" She had ridden him into Airodion, but he had thrown her off when they had encountered the Fomari. She hadn't seen him since and had assumed he was dead or had returned to Ellevere.

"He's gone absolutely feral," Dahey growled. "Won't let anyone ride him—even my most experienced riders. He'll only let the children on him."

Larken laughed despite herself. She desperately wanted to see Snowfoot, to escape this party and go to him.

"Dance with me," Dahey murmured, extending a hand to her. "Please."

She wanted to slap him. Rake her nails down those brown eyes, his mother's eyes, but she hesitated. Dahey's voice wasn't commanding, it was pleading. Vulnerable. And it shocked her enough that she placed her hand in his.

Dahey drew her close, and Larken's heart skittered in her chest when his palm splayed against her lower back. The contact between them, between her and this male she hated, felt too intimate. She had always thought him so cold, but after dancing with Osiron, Dahey practically radiated heat.

"I met your father," she said, not looking at Dahey, but tracking Saja and Roone with her eyes. She felt Dahey's gaze settle on her, and she returned it.

"My father is intrigued by the only human to survive the tithe in four hundred years," he said. "But his interest is never what you want."

"I'm sorry about what he did to you," Larken said, and she meant it. No child deserved what Dahey had gone through, and she knew she'd only heard pieces of what had happened to him.

"You don't think I deserved it?" Dahey said bitterly, but Larken caught the slight break in his voice.

Larken had thought all she would feel was anger. That she would want Dahey to die where he stood for everything he had done. But looking at him now, all she felt was pity. She knew Finder had struggled after he became prince, struggled with his powers, with Embryn's death, all of it. But Dahey had suffered his whole life. Dahey had everything he had ever wanted, but he was alone.

"Of course not," she whispered. She could have sworn that he pulled her closer.

"You'll change your mind when all of this is done," he said.

"It's not too late," Larken pleaded. He spun her away from him, and the fabric of her dress swirled around her. "You could let Finder go. Have another prisoner fight in the Tournament tomorrow."

"He would challenge me later. And things are... complicated."

Of course. He didn't know that she and Saja knew that the powers were split. And he had revealed to everyone that he had the powers now.

"You can't trust him," Larken murmured. "Every hour, Ziegan's powers grow."

Dahey lowered his gaze. "So do mine."

Larken dug her fingertips into the thick cloak covering Dahey's shoulder. "You'll really watch your cousin die? You love Finder, I know you do. There is still time. Saja and I can help you."

Dahey's eyes darkened. "If I let Finder go, my court will see me as weak. They won't support me as a ruler when they know he is still out there. There are those who still love him and would fight for him. I don't want him to die—" Dahey caught himself. "But I cannot let this go now, not when I have given up so much."

"Your father still lives, and he was a previous ruler," Larken argued.

"My father was loved, and then he was hated," Dahey said. "They say his powers left him because he had fallen into madness."

Larken looked across the room at Osiron. His blue eyes glittered with malice.

"I told you that you would hate me before the end." The music rose to a roar in the background. "There is nothing I won't do for the throne. I cut down my own flesh and blood, and now I will cast him into the pit at dawn. That is what this court needs, a ruler who will do anything for them, and after this, my people will know how loyal I am."

And when Larken caught his gaze again, it was not his mother's eyes that she saw. It was the cold, seething eyes of his father. And deep in that gaze, she saw the madness that was beginning to brew there.

"Then I hope your court is worth dying for," Larken said. "For if you go through with this, I will stop at nothing until I see you dead."

"You think you can defeat me?" Dahey clenched her hand, and blistering heat met her palm. Larken cried out, trying to pull away, but he held her fast, burning her hand with his fire. She bit her lip, tears welling in her eyes, but then it was over.

"You said it yourself," Larken gasped. "I am the first girl to survive the tithe in four hundred years. I think I will survive you too." She glared at him. "I *will*."

A hint of a smile touched Dahey's lips. "You haven't seen all the horrors Airodion has to offer yet."

The music came to an end. Larken bowed stiffly to Dahey, and he extended his head to her. He spun away from her, his golden cloak whispering across the ground, and he jogged up the steps of the dais, taking his place by the other court rulers. Valakais was entangled in the embrace of a male, kissing his neck for all to see.

Larken hovered by the banquet table, eyeing the honey wine and seriously considering taking it, wondering if it would make the night a more pleasant experience. Roone and Saja continued to dance. They broke apart only to exchange a few words in hand-speak. Saja's smiles made Larken's heart fill with both joy and sadness.

It had to be well past midnight, though it was hard to tell as time had taken on a rather meaningless feeling. Larken's nerves jangled together. At dawn, she would see Finder at last as he faced the Tournament. She had to hope that the stone was enough, that Fynvarra and Finder would work together.

She crammed a few cream puffs in her mouth, hoping they would do something to appease her nervous stomach. Dahey rose from the dais, and dread polled inside her, souring the cream puffs instantly. The musicians fell silent.

"I have a few more surprises in store for you tonight," Dahey said through his dazzling smile. "I promised you entertainment, and entertainment you shall have." He lifted his hands towards the back of the throne room.

Curious gazes followed and Larken craned her neck to see four soldiers enter the throne room. Gasps rose from the crowd, and Larken pressed her hands to her mouth.

For there, strung up between them, was Finder.

45

LARKEN

Airodion

He was stripped to the waist, a band of white cloth covering him with two long pieces of fabric in the front and back that fell to the floor. He was thinner—still lithe with muscle, but welts and scratches covered his torso. Someone had to have tended to him, for his face was clean shaven, and his dark auburn hair gleamed, cut to its usual length. His green eyes, once so warm and playful and tinged with sadness were now devoid of all feeling. Plates of gleaming metal encased his forearms, binding them together, and a collar similar to the one Fynvarra wore encircled his throat.

But most horrifying of all was the Weeping Metal mask that covered the lower half of Finder's face. Larken's gut twisted in horror. Of course—Dahey wouldn't want Finder to be able to speak, to be able to reveal the truth to his fellow court rulers and his people.

The crowd gasped, backing away and grimacing at the Weeping Metal. The chains connected to it must have been normal metal, for the guards clutched them tightly.

Saja cried out, pushing forward, but Roone grabbed his arm, holding

229

him back, exchanging a few frantic words in hand-speak. Saja relented, sinking back against his lover. Roone's hazel gaze followed the procession, his brows drawn together.

The crowd parted for Finder and the guards.

Valakais shooed away his companion. "What is the meaning of this?" he demanded.

"I thought I would treat the crowd to a gift," Dahey replied innocently. "They get to know who I have selected as my prisoner early. And I am giving Finder a gift as well. A farewell party." He smiled as Finder reached the bottom of the dais. "Release him." One of the guards unlocked his chains and then shoved Finder between the shoulder blades. Finder, unable to catch himself, hit his head upon the stairs with a *crack*.

Larken shoved her way through the crowd, earning hisses and curses. Bodies parted before her until, finally, she reached him. She fell to her knees, pressing her hands to Finder's face where it lay turned towards the stairs. He flinched away from her touch. She gently turned his cheek towards her, so he could see her face.

"It's all right," she breathed. She wiped away the blood on his forehead with her thumb.

"Touching, isn't it?" Dahey sneered. "Reunited at last with his human girl."

Larken helped Finder sit up. Saja appeared, gripping Finder's bicep. Finder leaned into his friend's touch.

"How about a dance," Dahey purred. "What do you say, Larken? Will you dance with Finder one last time?"

The crowd began to clap, exclaiming excitedly. Larken stared at them in hatred, shocked by their utter bloodlust for cruelty.

"Is this necessary?" Isra murmured.

Dahey ignored her. "Get. Up."

Larken took Finder's hand. "No. I won't be your entertainment for the night. And neither will he."

"It'll be worse for him if you refuse," Dahey said through his teeth.

Larken glowered at him before turning back to Finder. "Can you stand?" she murmured. Finder nodded.

Larken and Saja helped him to his feet. Finder groaned as the metal plates shifted, revealing blistered, oozing skin beneath. Larken glared at Dahey with all the venom she had. "You'll pay for this," she vowed.

"No, I don't think I will." Dahey smirked. "Play," he ordered the musicians.

The musicians took up a song. It was light and airy, full of strings, but with an undercurrent of strength. Dahey's eyes widened, and he whirled to the musicians. "That isn't what I told you to play," he hissed.

But the musicians played on, their eyes only for Finder, the broken faery before them. Dahey, unwilling to cause a scene to ruin his spectacle, merely scowled, sitting back upon the carved wooden chair on the dais.

Larken took Finder's hand, setting her other hand upon his shoulder. He wrapped his arm around her back, pulling her as close as he could, dipping his face to hide in her neck. He trembled slightly, too slightly for others to see, but he whisked her across the dance floor. They swept around in large circles, the crowd backing up to give them space. The stringed instruments continued, sad and hopeful at the same time. They had done this for them, ignored Dahey's request for a song and had honored Finder and Larken with their own.

"Listen to me," Larken said. It killed her that he couldn't speak to her. "Trust the firedrake. He'll protect you. Both of you are going to walk out of that ring tomorrow as allies. We'll come up with a plan to take back the throne. I know your powers are split, but we can use Ziegan's language to take them back. Can Dahey use your other powers?"

Finder shook his head. She sighed with relief. At least he could only use the fire.

The music swelled, and Finder lifted her at the waist, spinning her around. Though the Weeping Metal had to have drained him, he held her steady. She placed her hands on his biceps, her heart fluttering in her chest. A fierce protectiveness rose inside her. Dahey could not have him. He would not take Finder from her.

Finder set her down and grazed his fingers up her arms. She spun, parallel to him now, and they circled side by side before coming back together. Saja and Roone had taught her this dance, but even during moments when she and Finder were supposed to break apart, he refused to break their contact, his fingers never leaving her.

He drew her close again, and her heart beat wildly, matching the rhythm that thundered beneath Finder's bare chest.

She ignored the next steps of the dance and grabbed his face with her hands. "I haven't let you die yet, have I? Trust me," she breathed. His hands splayed against her hips, anchoring her.

The music reached its crescendo, and they picked up their dance again. Movement caught her eye, and Saja and Roone were there, dancing beside them. Saja gave her a nod. "We're here with you."

Dahey's eyes lit up with fury, and he dug his nails into the arms of his chair.

Isra and Valakais stepped down from the dais, taking up the dance as well. Finder's parents broke away from Osiron and Dahey's mother to join the dance as well. They danced around Larken and Finder, shielding them from the gazes of the other court gentry. Larken's heart nearly burst out of her chest. They were showing their support of Finder. Other members of the Autumn Court joined in, soldiers and gentry.

Larken pulled Finder's head down. "Don't give up. Promise me."

Finder's green eyes met hers. He nodded. She desperately wanted to hear him speak, to hear the soothing tenor of his voice.

The music ended, fading out beautifully.

"Take him," Dahey snarled. His guards poured in from both sides, shoving Finder's supporters out of the way.

"No," Larken cried. "*No.*" She clung to Finder, but the guards were too strong, ripping them apart. Finder groaned as the movement caused the Weeping Metal to chafe against his raw skin. The guards hissed at the metal, reattaching their chains and backing away as quickly as they could.

"String him up." Dahey jerked his head at the pillars. The guards yanked Finder between two of the columns, hanging him spread eagle across them. "No one speaks to him," Dahey ordered. "Rest up, cousin," he said to Finder. "Dawn will be here soon enough."

"You bastard," Larken snarled. "Rot in the Twins' Hell."

Dahey ignored her, taking his place on the dais. Isra and Valakais rejoined him. Larken glared at them. They would support Finder in a dance but nothing more. How fitting.

The gentry flooded the dance floor again, and the music picked back up. Saja and Larken stood near the pillars, watching Finder where he hung, head bent.

They stood like that until the dark hours of the morning, standing vigil for their king.

46

LARKEN

Airodion

Larken stood at the edge of a great pit, Saja and Roone flanking her. When the hour before dawn had struck, all the fey had been ushered from the throne room and directed to the arena. Four barred gates were cut into the walls of the arena, and a court ruler sat above each.

Larken clenched and unclenched her shaking fingers. The stands were built high around the arena, the seats packed with fey. It appeared all had come to enjoy the bloodlust. She, Saja and Roone stood closest to Isra's chair.

She should be exhausted, but her heart pounded in her chest. So many things could go wrong. Fynvarra could turn on Finder now that he had the stone, Finder might be too weak to fight, and the other prisoners might be more powerful than them both, even if they fought together.

Larken looked to Saja and Roone. Their hands were clasped, Roone rubbing his thumb over the back of Saja's hand. She looked away.

Trust Fynvarra, she told herself. *He'll be a powerful ally with the stone. He wants to help Finder.* She gripped the railing. She hissed—it was coated in frost. Was Isra nervous too?

For a moment, Larken wondered if they should have included Isra in their plan. But then she remembered how Isra had let Finder stay in Dahey's clutches not once, but twice.

Finally, dawn broke, the first rays of sunlight crossing the horizon.

The crowd fell silent, all eyes turning to Dahey. If the other court rulers were irritated by the fact that their people were looking to Dahey to guide them, they didn't show it. Or they didn't notice just how quickly Dahey was winning everyone over.

Dahey clapped his hands once. A loud grinding noise began, shaking the ground beneath Larken's feet. She looked over the railing and saw the gate beneath her begin to lift. Fynvarra's scaled body emerged. The gate crashed shut behind him. He was freed from his chains; only the collar of Weeping Metal around his throat remained, preventing him from using fire. He snarled, flaring his feathered wings.

"From the Winter Court, a firedrake," Isra announced.

The crowd gasped, some clapping appreciatively.

The gate below Etain opened next. A waif of a woman emerged, free of any Weeping Metal. The woman walked forward on her tip toes, lurching heavily from side to side. Her skin was pale with an almost grayish sheen. Lank, stringy black hair fell nearly to her feet.

Saja sucked in a breath just as Etain announced, "From the Spring Court, a Bean Sidhe."

Larken gasped as well. They had myths of Bean Sidhes in Ballamor, just as they did with the firedrakes. Larken had never imagined them to be real. In Ballamor, Bean Sidhes were beautiful women sent by Ashpalion and Aleea to usher the souls to the afterlife. She sensed that the Bean Sidhes in Airodion were different.

"Bean Sidhes are rare—and feared," Saja breathed. "Their cry can cripple you, and a touch of their hand marks you for death as soon as night falls. I don't know where Etain managed to find one."

Larken's stomach hollowed out. "Why isn't she wearing any Weeping Metal?"

"Because their killing magic isn't true magic, as Finder's is. Oftentimes, the death does not come by their hand, but fate itself. Their cry is the same—not magic, just loud."

"So Fynvarra's fire..."

"Is magic," Saja finished. "He might not be able to manipulate it once it leaves his body, but it is created through magic."

Their gazes turned to the next gate. Valakais steepled his fingers as his gate lifted. From the darkness emerged one of the most hideous creatures Larken had ever seen. This creature was huge, nearly double Fynvarra's size, and had a sloped back, beady eyes and huge front arms coiled with muscle. It seemed to have no neck, just one massive body trunk. It was a disgusting, brownish-yellow color. A long, spiked tail arched over its back, quivering.

"From the Summer Court, a sand troll," Valakais said.

The sand troll was free of Weeping Metal as well. Larken's heart sank. The troll and the Bean Sidhe would have an unfair advantage over Finder and Fynvarra—both of whom had to suffer the Weeping Metal.

Dahey's gate rumbled. Larken grasped the railing once more, ignoring the chill. Her breath caught in her throat as Finder stumbled from the tunnel. He was dressed in dark pants and boots with a white linen shirt, almost identical to the outfit she had first met him in. The gate crashed close behind him. Finder's gaze lifted, taking in his surroundings.

Weeping Metal still braced his arms and collared his neck. Thankfully, they had removed the mask that he had worn the night before. Still, he sported more metal than Fynvarra.

The prisoners all hovered by their gates, regarding each other warily. Even the troll, who Larken had first dismissed as an ignorant beast, had an intelligent, malicious glint in his eyes.

"You know the rules," Dahey said. "The last one standing earns their freedom." Fynvarra lowered himself into a crouch. Finder rocked back on his heels.

"Begin," Dahey ordered.

The troll and the Bean Sidhe rushed straight for Finder. Larken's heart thundered in her throat. Finder braced himself, raising his hands, instinctively trying to call the fire. Fynvarra leapt into the air, soaring over the Bean Sidhe and the troll to land before Finder with a snarl. Larken's fear nearly choked her, worried Fynvarra would end Finder then and there, but the firedrake whirled, smacking the Bean Sidhe with his tail when she got close enough. He grabbed Finder in his mouth like a mother cat with her kitten and jumped over the troll, flapping his wings up, up, almost to the top of the ring, but he smacked into some kind of invisible barrier at the top. He snarled and dropped back down.

He and Finder huddled together on the far side of the ring. Larken could tell they were talking but couldn't hear what they were saying. The Bean Sidhe opened her mouth into a large o-shape and began to scream. The sound somehow seemed muffled, whatever wards that covered the top of the arena protecting the viewers from the Bean Sidhe's cries. Fynvarra cowered, and Finder pressed his hands to his delicately pointed ears, doubling over.

The troll shook its head back and forth, roaring, and charged at the Bean Sidhe. She reached out a hand, palm limp, but the troll stopped before it could get too close and swung at her with its massive stinger tail. The Bean Sidhe ceased its wailing to roll out of the stinger's way. She stood, screaming directly into the troll's tiny ear. The beast bellowed, shying away from her, pawing at its ear. She darted away, heading straight for Finder again, her arms outstretched.

Larken bit down hard on her lip, struggling to watch but unable to tear her gaze away. Fynvarra snarled at the Bean Sidhe, but the female didn't stop. Finder ran to meet her, catching her by both wrists and forcing her arms outwards, bringing his knee up to slam into her jaw. The resounding *crack* echoed throughout the arena, and the crowd roared in approval.

The Bean Sidhe limped backwards, and Finder had his hands lifted, saying something to her. The troll had recovered and was barreling towards them. Fynvarra leapt into the air, and the two beasts crashed together, rolling again and again before coming to a slamming halt.

Fynvarra bit the troll's arm, but its skin was too thick to do any real damage. They tussled together in the dirt, the troll lunging again with its stinger, but Fynvarra was too quick.

The Bean Sidhe came for Finder again. She screamed, raising her hands. Finder cried out, backing away from her, his hands over his ears, his mouth open in a silent scream. He took a wrong step and fell, and at once, the Bean Sidhe was upon him, rushing forward, her hands outstretched.

A mass of feathers and scales crashed into her. Larken cried out as the Bean Sidhe's hands connected with Fynvarra's throat.

"No," Larken cried, her voice drowned by the cheering of the crowd, the masses from the Spring Court screaming enthusiastically for their champion.

"If he is the one to kill her, he will be able to break her curse," Saja said, but his voice was tight.

Fynvarra tried to dislodge the Bean Sidhe, but she had dug her fingers into the grooves of his scales. Fynvarra's paw caught her, finally tossing her free. He opened his jaws to end her.

"Look out!" Larken screamed, but it was too late. The troll grabbed Fynvarra by the tail, hauling him back with a bellow. Fynvarra roared in frustration. He turned back to the troll, snapping wildly. The troll gave a savage smile.

Then Finder was there, throwing himself on top of the Bean Sidhe. Larken hissed in a breath, but he forced his knees over the female's arms, pinning them in place. He took both hands and shoved them in her mouth and pulled, ripping her lower jaw free.

The Autumn Court fey went wild, screaming for Finder. Larken's stomach roiled with horror as Finder tossed the jaw aside, then punched his hand down the Bean Sidhe's throat, destroying her vocal cords. She turned and began to crawl away, her long hair dragging in the dirt. He sat back, panting and splattered with blood. The Autumn Court fey screamed at him to finish it, but he looked to where Fynvarra battled the troll. Fynvarra had to be the one to kill her, or else he would still be marked for death.

Fynvarra struggled with the troll, but finally got the beast onto its back. With a snarl, Fynvarra bit down on the creature's tail, ripping the stinger free. The troll bellowed in agony and fury. Finder called to Fynvarra, and the firedrake's head snapped up. The troll hit him with a massive arm, sending the drake flying into the wall.

Fynvarra hauled himself to his feet and hurled himself at the Bean Sidhe, fangs bared. He grabbed her around the middle and shook her until her bones snapped. The female went limp.

The Spring Court bellowed in anger, but the Winter Court fey screamed for their champion—even Roone let out a whoop for Fynvarra.

"One left," Saja breathed. "They can do this."

Larken gripped his hand on the railing, unable to reply. Finder and Fynvarra stood together, bracing for the troll. The beast stood, slightly off balance from the loss of his tail. His eyes gleamed with hatred for Fynvarra.

He stood on his back legs and ran at Fynvarra, swiping at Finder to get him out of the way. Finder flew, colliding with the other side of the pit. Larken's heart lurched, but she could still see the rise and fall of his chest.

The troll caught Fynvarra from the side, wrapping huge arms around Fynvarra's body, pinning his wings to his side. Fynvarra screamed as the beast squeezed him, the pressure threatening to break the delicate bones of his wings.

The troll shifted, grabbing both of Fynvarra's wings in one hand and the base of his neck in the other and slammed him into the ground. Larken cried out, but the troll wasn't trying to kill Fynvarra yet, he wanted him to suffer.

Fynvarra thrashed, and Larken's heart nearly stopped beating when the stone jostled free from its hiding place in Fynvarra's mane.

"The stone," she squeaked to Saja.

The big warrior squinted, then his eyes widened with horror. If anyone saw the stone, then Fynvarra would be disqualified, and it meant certain death.

The troll smashed Fynvarra down again. The stone was fully free of

Fynvarra's mane now, glinting in the sunlight. The troll stopped, then bent its gruesome head lower to inspect the shiny object.

"No," Larken breathed. But it was too late. The troll let go of Fynvarra's wings, grabbed the stone and yanked. Fynvarra's eyes immediately clouded—blind once more. The chain of the necklace snapped, and the troll clutched the tiny stone in its hand.

And then it clenched its fist, smashing the stone within.

Larken nearly sank to her knees. Saja cursed. Roone fisted his hands in his hair, his face turning white.

"Did he know what it was?" Larken whirled to Saja.

Saja shook his head. "I don't know. If he did, he didn't want to risk the advantage should it fall into Fynvarra or Finder's hands. And if he didn't, then he knew it was worth enough for Fynvarra to risk wearing it here, which meant it offered some sort of advantage."

Fynvarra buffeted his wings, feathers raining down. The frantic movement must have obscured the actions of the troll for anyone not looking closely. The crowd continued to cheer, oblivious that anything had happened, and the court rulers did nothing to alert them that anything was amiss.

Finder hauled himself to his feet, blood running down the side of his head from where it had struck the arena wall. He looked dazed, and he stumbled forward. Fynvarra backed away wildly from the troll, getting closer to Finder. Finder said something, holding his hands out, but Fynvarra didn't notice him. Larken could do nothing but watch as Fynvarra trampled Finder beneath his feet. Finder cried out as the claws slashed into his thigh.

The troll lumbered after Fynvarra, sensing weakness, a small grin on its face.

Larken bent over the railing. Fynvarra backed up against the wall beneath her, trembling, wings tucked into his sides. He was so close. Her heart pounded in her chest. Finder limped to the opposite wall, sinking down, his green gaze filled with defeat. The troll roared, sensing that victory was near.

Fynvarra stood no chance against the troll without his sight. He had barely held up against the monster when he was fully healed from the stone. The troll lumbered forward, taking its time, drool leaking from the side of its mouth. The sound of the crowd fell to a dull roar in the background.

Larken didn't allow herself to think. She threw herself over the railing, plummeting down to land on Fynvarra's back.

47

LARKEN

Airodion

Fynvarra didn't have time to roar in surprise before Larken connected them through mind-speak, joining her emotions to his, allowing him to see through her eyes.

Her legs weren't stretched painfully wide due to two large muscle divots where her legs, bent at the knee, could rest. His scales were tough, yet incredibly grippy. She felt secure on his back. Larken wound her fingers in his thick mane and clung to him.

I'm here, she said. Above her, the crowd screamed. She was sure she heard Saja's bellow, but she ignored him. Dahey, Isra, Valakais and Etain were standing, peering down into the pit, but they didn't stop her.

You're going to get us both disqualified and killed, Fynvarra growled, but gratitude flowed through their bond. *How did you get past the wards?*

The wards only keep the prisoners in. And humans aren't barred from competing—any race can join the Tournament with a prisoner of their own. I volunteered myself.

Fynvarra rose, his muscles surging beneath her. Larken squeezed her legs tight, clinging to the drake with all her strength. Fynvarra swept his tail back and forth, the furred tip making a *swooshing* noise against the dirt. Larken swallowed. She didn't allow herself to look at Finder, not yet. They had to focus on the troll.

Fynvarra bellowed his challenge. The troll narrowed its eyes at Larken, then continued to smile, dismissing her quickly.

Larken's world narrowed into a blur of bodies and teeth. Her bones shook as the troll's head rammed into Fynvarra's shoulder. Fynvarra snarled, his claws scrambling in the dirt. The troll thrusted out with his shoulders. Fynvarra toppled to the floor, shifting his body weight at the last second to avoid crushing her. Larken gasped for breath.

Fynvarra ducked as the troll made a swipe for his face. The beast's maw stretched wide before her as the troll roared, spit coating her face. He reached for her, determined to tear her from Fynvarra's back, somehow knowing that she and Fynvarra needed to be together.

Fynvarra lurched to his feet, snarling at the troll. He lunged, tackling the troll head on, knocking him off balance. They rolled in a ball of snapping fangs. Larken's stomach lurched as the world turned upside down. Fynvarra latched onto the side of the troll's face. Blood spewed from the wound, and the troll roared, shoving Fynvarra away with his two hind feet. Fynvarra groaned as the claws cut deep into his belly. Fear flooded down their bond.

Blood wept from the troll's mauled face.

"Larken, watch out!"

She barely had time to register Saja's bellow from above before the troll swiped at her. Fynvarra snapped up, his neck taking the brunt of the blow. He grunted as the troll's claws sank into him, and blood gushed from the wound.

He's onto us! she cried, tightening her grip on Fynvara's mane.

I can see that. Fynvarra dodged another one of the troll's blows.

Fynvarra swiped with his tail, making the troll step back. But the ugly beast was playing with them, biding his time before going for the kill.

He wants to play with us for as long as possible, Larken said.

Excellent news, Fynvarra growled.

No, it makes him sloppy. We have to use it against him. He won't go for killing blows yet—but we will.

The troll swiped lazily at Fynvarra, sure that he would flinch away, but Fynvarra lunged, taking a blow straight to the mouth. His jaws locked on the troll's clawed hand, making him howl. The troll beat Fynvarra's jaw with his other hand, forcing him to release. Fynvarra swung around to give Larken a bloody smile. Larken grinned back fiercely, trying to swallow around the pounding heart in her throat.

The troll limped backwards, curling his injured hand to his chest. The din from the crowd rose, but there weren't just chants for the troll. Some howled for Fynvarra.

They're cheering for you! Larken said.

Fynvarra's ears swung towards the crowd, and a ripple of pleasure went through their bond.

And then Finder was there, latching onto the back of the troll's arm. Larken screamed, but the troll smiled, grabbing Finder with his good hand and slamming him into the dirt.

"Help him," Larken cried, but Fynvarra was already there, sweeping Finder away as gently as he could with his tail before launching at the troll.

The troll turned away, and Fynvarra leapt at him, screeching as Fynvarra landed on top of him. Fynvarra swung at the troll's head with his tail, but the huge troll rolled, digging his claws deep into Fynvarra's sides and forcing him to roll with him. Fynvarra landed on his back, barely keeping himself upright enough so Larken wasn't crushed. The grip from Fynvarra's scales was the only thing keeping her on his back. Her hair brushed against the dirt.

The troll pressed his full weight down upon Fynvarra. A great head rose from over Fynvarra's shoulder. A snarl pulled his lips back from his teeth. Fynvarra growled, snapping at the claws that held his neck down.

Larken flinched away, powerless as the troll lunged for the kill. Fynvarra's wing came up to shield her. He howled as the troll's teeth sunk deep into the meat of his wing. The troll ripped its head away, enraged that it hadn't killed her, and spat out feathers and blood. Fynvarra screamed, but he was ready. When the troll's weight shifted, he threw himself upwards, ramming into his chest. His claws scraped the tough skin. He bit the troll anywhere he could, striking again and again, though the skin on its upper arms and body was tougher than layers of leather. The troll screeched, then bit Fynvarra's bad wing, inches from Larken's body. Fynvarra bellowed.

Don't stop! Larken cried.

The troll's beady black eye glared at her, the pupil reducing to slits. Larken curled her lip, and lunged, digging her fingers as hard as she could into the troll's eye.

The troll screamed, but he didn't let go of Fynvarra's wing. His eyelid tried to close, but her fingers were too deep. She gritted her teeth and forced her hands deeper, digging, searching through that pulpy mess until she could do no more. And then she pulled.

The eye came free, strings of muscles and nerves hanging down. The troll screamed, throwing his head back in agony. Fynvarra was ready. Faster than a snake, he darted his head out, catching the troll right beneath the jaw. The two beasts slammed into the ground, Larken's teeth knocking in her skull. The troll tried to push Fynvarra away, but his hind legs were trapped beneath him, and his front hand was injured. Fynvarra's jaws locked, blood gushing from the troll's neck. Too much blood. The troll kicked once, twice, and then was still. His neck slackened. Fynvarra gave him a shake, making sure he was dead, then released.

The crowd bellowed. Larken bent down Fynvarra's neck and hugged him, a sob racking her body.

"We did it," Fynvarra huffed.

"Not yet," Larken said. She slid from his back, rushing over to Finder. She helped him stand, letting him lean into her.

Now, the difficult part.

She swallowed, glancing up at the crowd. They screamed, some for Fynvarra and some for Finder, sure that the two were about to battle to the death.

"Fey of Airodion," Larken cried. The crowd fell silent, their confusion at her interruption palpable. "Your law decrees that two foes who declare themselves allies may both be awarded victory." She turned to Finder, whispering in his ear. "Say you take Fynvarra as your ally."

"I take Fynvarra of the Winter Court as my ally," Finder shouted, his voice raspy.

Fynvarra bent his head, his sightless eyes darting around. "And I take Finder of the Autumn Court as my ally."

Murmurs shifted through the crowd.

"Dahey claimed he would give you a spectacle." She gestured around. "Has he not delivered? He has given you something that has never been seen before in the history of Airodion."

The murmurs from the crowd increased.

"Humans are not allowed to fight," Isra said, filling Larken's heart with ice.

"That isn't true, my queen," came Saja's voice. He translated Roone's hand-speak for the crowd. "Nowhere in our laws does it say humans cannot participate."

Larken could see Isra turn red even from her place on the ground. "The representative cannot offer themselves to fight," Isra snarled.

"Also false," Saja translated. "Our laws do not specify if a representative can select themselves. No one has ever tried. Until now."

Larken's chest rose and fell heavily. Now was her last chance. "Fey of the courts, I might have helped my allies in this battle, but it is up to you to decide our fate. We have given you your entertainment, now I beg you to set my friends free." She turned to Finder. "Finder and I have survived so much. We took down the Starveling—together." Gasps rose from the crowd at the confirmation straight from her lips. "We were tied by the fates themselves, bound together. We were separated, but we have found our way back together, here, for you. And now we beg for your help."

"Three allies are not allowed," Dahey growled. "I forbid it."

"If one of us must die, then let it be me," Larken growled, placing a hand on Finder's chest. *Forgive me.* "But please, save the one I love."

Gasps of delight rose from the crowd. Finder's green eyes widened, his mouth falling open slightly.

You wanted a show, Dahey. So let me give it to you. Before she could hesitate any longer, she pressed her lips to Finder's.

The feral screams from the crowd faded away. Finder cupped his hands on either side of her face, and opened his mouth to her. She locked her hands in his curls, deepening the kiss. Finally, she broke away, unable to look at him.

That wasn't what I wanted our first kiss to be like, she fought the tears welling inside her. It was for him. It was to save him.

"Allies, allies, allies," the crowd chanted as one, banging their feet upon the stands. Valakais stood, placing his arm out, palm face up. The sign of acceptance. Larken's heart swelled. Isra rose next, placing her palm up as well. Then Etain. Larken's breath caught. But the Spring Court Queen held her palm up.

Dahey rose, his face twisted in anger.

Please, Dahey, she begged silently. *Give your people what they want.*

He placed his palm down. Larken's heart plummeted. He jerked his head. Guards poured out of the gates. Larken cried out, devastation threatening to crush her as they tore Finder away from her once more. Dahey leapt over the railing, landing on the floor of the pit in a crouch. He stalked towards them. Two guards restrained her, and she thrashed against them. Above, more guards had taken Saja and Roone, pinning them in place. Soldiers forced Fynvarra back with their spears. He hissed in anger.

"If you will die by no other, then you will die by my hand," Dahey snarled. He unsheathed his sword. The guards forced Finder to his knees.

"Dahey, don't," Larken begged. Terror poured down her spine. "*Please, Dahey, don't do this.*"

Dahey's hand shook ever so slightly as he placed the tip of his sword beneath Finder's chin. Fey shrieked in outrage. Isra and Valakais were shouting something, but she couldn't hear over the din of the crowd.

"Dahey," Finder said, lifting his hands. "You are my kin. Don't do this." Finder's voice lowered. "I can help you. We can figure this out without one of our deaths."

Dahey's eyes darted back and forth. His sword lowered ever so slightly, but then his eyes hardened once more.

A *crack* split the air, shaking the stadium. Fey cried out. Larken looked up, and there, perched on the railing of the ring, was Ziegan.

48

LARKEN

Airodion

Darkness spread across the sky. Dahey hissed in outrage at the sight of Ziegan. "You," he snarled.

Ziegan spread his hands, his hooded head tilting. "I have come with an invitation. Join me, and you will have as much power as you desire." He began to chant in his language. Fire flared to life between his outstretched palms. The crowd gasped. Ziegan summoned a sphere of water next, turning it to ice. Then a ball of earth. A gust of wind. The fey cried out in shock.

"The time of the court rulers is over," Ziegan said. "I have come to your foolish Tournament to inform you that while you have been playing games, I have been amassing my army. I grow tired of your dallying. Come and prepare to face me. I will bring Airodion into a new age, and I want you, my children, to join me.

Etain screamed, hurling a mass of stone at the Guardian. With a flick of his wrist, he deflected it, crumbling it to rubble. The crowd gasped, and Larken's eyes widened.

"With me, you can have everything you ever dreamed. Any magic you wished. All is possible with my language. Powers your court rulers could only dream of. Come to me, and I will teach you. Look at the tyranny before you. You, the people, have spoken, and one ruler has chosen to disregard you and do what serves him." The Guardian pointed a skeletal finger at Dahey. "Is that who you want as your ruler? Another Starveling? I will end tyranny," he vowed. "All will be equal in my realm. No being shall be ruled, no being shall be lesser. I will lead you to the better world, and then even I shall become like the rest of you. Equal.

"Take a few days to decide," he said, his voice surprisingly gentle. "My arms are always open. But know this: the time is coming when I shall take Airodion, and all those who stand against me and my children shall be destroyed."

He flicked his hand, speaking his language once more. Fynvarra and Finder's wounds closed, Fynvarra's wings snapping back into place. The Weeping Metal chains on Fynvarra and Finder cracked down the middle, falling away. The crowd gasped. The guards released Larken and Finder in their shock.

He can control Weeping Metal, the substance most detrimental to the fey.

"A gift," he said. Then he disappeared.

Larken grabbed Finder's hand, hauling him over to Fynvarra. She hurled herself onto the firedrake's back.

"Can you carry us both?" she asked, digging her finger's into his mane.

Fynvarra nodded. "I must. Just pray that Ziegan also broke the wards."

Chaos ensued beneath them as the court gentry surged for the gates, fleeing Ziegan. Etain, Valakais, and Isra screamed orders to their guards, who rushed to control the crowd.

But Fynvarra launched them into the air; Shadeshelm fading away behind them.

49

KAISA

Ellevere

Kaisa met with Tarrio at The Dancing Toad that night.

"I'm glad you agreed to meet with me," she said, unbuckling her cloak before sitting down at one of the wooden tables. She wrapped her hands around her mug of ale.

The man inspected her. "Of course. How could I not meet with the Savior of Augrim?"

Kaisa brushed off the compliment, if that's what it was. "I came to thank you for saving my life." She extended a hand to him, and he shook it with a smile. "But I don't want to play games. I think we have similar interests, you and I. We both hate the Order. We both want to bring people to our cause. Why not combine our efforts?"

Tarrio inspected her again, a slow smile spreading across his lips. "Do you hate the Order?"

Kaisa scowled. "Of course I do. They refuse to send aide despite the attacks. They know how to fight these monsters, and they do nothing. They force people to kill their friends, they kill innocents, they killed my friend just to get to me—" she stopped herself before she could say more. "Of course I hate them," she repeated finally, gritting her teeth.

"Do you want to know what I think?" Tarrio leaned forward on the table. Kaisa could smell the ale on his breath. "Maybe you did hate them once. But now you've become just like them."

Kaisa's face heated, but the man held up a finger before she could interject. "You use the Twins to promote your cause, but I don't think you hold true belief for them. Not anymore, at least. You nearly let Inniskeen fall because of what a few soldiers did to your friend." The man shook his head. "I can see what you were trying to do in the first place. You wanted to help people because the Order wasn't. You wanted them to choose you over the Popes. And I can respect that. But you've twisted religion to your own gain—just as they have. Calling yourself a Savior and blessed by the Twins. You tasted power—and now you're doing exactly what the Popes did. And that's not what I want for my people." The man took a bite of the stew sitting before him, smacking his lips loudly as he leaned back.

"You have no idea what I've experienced at the hands of the Order," Kaisa bristled. "If you did—"

"Oh, I'm sure I do know," Tarrio interrupted her. "You see, I was trained at Sersius's palace as well. I was a member of his Red Guard. I completed my Anointing, unlike you."

Kaisa stilled. This man had killed his dearest friend? He had to have been deeply loyal to the Order once.

"I know what the Order has done," Tarrio continued. "And I object deeply. But through it all, I have not lost my faith; I have learned to detest its organizers."

"What good is faith at a time like this?" Kaisa snarled. "You think powerful beings are controlling our every move, allowing all these bad things to happen? Of course not. People make these things happen, the Popes, the Order, *they* make it happen. People don't need faith. They need to realize who's pulling the strings—and fight back. And they need me to help them do it."

The man shook his head. "You're wrong. People don't need to abandon their religion. What good does that do them? It leaves them terrified and rudderless in a world where they already have so little control. Let them keep their faith but challenge the organization itself." He leaned forward again. "You aren't being clear with people about what you want. You aren't being honest. If you have no faith, fine, but don't try to twist others' beliefs to your advantage—then you're no better than the Popes. Plenty of people would follow you without your so called 'divine message.'"

How dare this man speak to her this way? She ignored how similar his words were to Jovanna's. "Like you preach any different?" Kaisa challenged. "I heard you in the square. You tell people to hate the Order. You tell people that you know the right path, and they flock to you."

The man shook his head. "The New Order wants a reformed Order of the Twins," he said. "I am not the only leader; there are many true teachers who wish to guide those who are dissatisfied with the Order. But we want them to keep their faith. And we want it to be their choice."

He stared at her so long that Kaisa finally looked away. Though she heard truth in his words, wisdom even, hatred still burned in her heart for the Order.

"I see something in you Kaisa," Tarrio said. "You are a good leader. You have saved many people, and I can tell they love you. And while I can see that you love the power they give you, enough so that you allow it to lead you astray, I can see that you love them too."

Kaisa stiffened.

"I want to work with you," the man said. "I can see that you are on a path to something great, one that you made for yourself. But I can tell that you are already going astray. Burning those members of the Order in the town square is going to cost you."

She shoved down her guilt. She couldn't dwell on that, couldn't admit that perhaps she'd made a mistake, or it would drag her down. And she couldn't stop now.

"Not to mention you've already had an attempt on your life. The reasons you began this journey are yours to tell, and I think at first you might have had the right reasons. But now you are doing this for the wrong ones, and your path is mirroring that of the Popes more than you know. And while I want me and my people to help you, I will not allow them to be dragged down your path to tyranny."

She glared at Tarrio as he took a long swig from his mug of ale.

"You said you wanted to work with me. So work with me." Kaisa growled. "Help me take down the Order."

The man shook his head. "We have different ways of achieving that goal. And I cannot follow your path. But if you wish to see mine, I will show you."

Kaisa ran her tongue along her teeth. His words had angered her, but she didn't need this man as her enemy. She took a deep breath, forcing her next words out. "Fine. But if this doesn't work..."

"We both have enough enemies as it is," Tarrio said. "Let's not create more before we need to. We are allies for now, but plan on impressing me." He gave her another infuriating smile. He raised his mug. "To new allies."

Kaisa reluctantly clinked her mug against his. "To new allies."

Kaisa rolled over in her bed, her skin itching at the tense silence brewing between her and Jovanna.

"I can't stand this, Jo," she murmured into the darkness. "Why can't you understand that we won a great victory in Inniskeen? I want you celebrating by my side."

Jovanna sat up in her bed. Kaisa turned over to face her. "I worry about this path you're on," Jovanna said carefully. "I already told you— what happened at Inniskeen wasn't a victory. You nearly left those people to die, and then you swept in and burned a few men to death and terrified the survivors even more."

Kaisa jerked upright. "That isn't true. I rid them of their tormentors. I rid them of the soldiers that took their town by force."

Jovanna shook her head. "Deciding who deserves to be punished and what that punishment should be makes you no better than the Order. Than the Institute."

"Well, it doesn't matter now," Kaisa replied coldly. "It's done. Their people chose me, and now I'm going to lead them on a path away from the Order. A path to freedom."

"This power—it's changing you," Jovanna said. "And sooner or later, your lies are going to catch up to you, and people are going to see you for who you really are."

"No," Kaisa growled. "I'm finally becoming who I was meant to be. My mother never would have sold me if she'd known who I would become. You're just jealous that I've found my place in this world and you haven't."

Jovanna was quiet for a moment. "You know what the worst part is?" Jovanna sucked in an angry breath. "The worst part is I know that for a moment you considered it—considered killing me to stay in the Order."

Kaisa's blood ran cold. "That's not true, Jo," Kaisa breathed. "I would never—"

"Save it," Jovanna snapped. "The real reason you left was because Izzy saw you." She shook her head. "I'm surprised you didn't try to kill her. And me. After all, isn't that what you do? Kill people who get in your way?"

Kaisa's heart sank to her toes. "Of course not—"

Jovanna scrambled out of bed, snatching her cloak. "I can't stay here," she muttered and left, slamming the door behind her.

Kaisa pressed the heels of her hands into her eyes. No. Jovanna was wrong. She didn't kill people who got in her way. She killed people who deserved it. Members of the Order who had tortured and killed in the name of the gods.

She wrapped shaking hands around her knees. She had killed them. She had taken their lives and snuffed them out like candle flames. Bile rose in her throat, but she swallowed hard, pushing away her nausea. They had deserved it. They had killed Hollis, likely killed countless others.

Kaisa took a deep breath. She had to be strong. She would bring justice to members of the Order. Every single one if need be. And no one was going to take that away from her.

No one.

50

DAHEY

Airodion

Dahey had broken six vases since noon. He glared at the carnage.

A headache pulsed at the back of his skull, threatening to overwhelm him. Finder was gone, which meant it was only a matter of time before his cousin came for his throne. Dahey had been so close to having everything he wanted. He had revealed that he had the powers. And now, Finder was gone.

Dahey gritted his teeth. Even though the Autumn Court would have lost the Tournament, at least he would have proven himself to the other courts. Now they would see him as a weakling who let Finder and Larken escape on that blasted firedrake. He had control over the fire, he had shown them, and it was all for nothing. And now Finder would be able to regain his strength. Would he tell everyone that the powers had split? Worse, would he go to Ziegan and try to take his powers back? And the other court rulers... if they found out that Dahey had taken the powers, they would surely find a way to punish him.

Ziegan... And what was he going to do about the Guardian? Dahey swallowed. Seeing his display of power at the Tournament had made

256

Dahey realize he had seriously underestimated him. Was it better to join forces with him? Maybe Ziegan would reward him for his loyalty. Maybe he would help Dahey turn the Autumn Court to the most powerful court in Airodion.

Dahey clenched his fists. No, Dahey would not serve under another king. And he didn't believe that Ziegan wanted equal power for everyone. He would always retain enough power to stay in control. Dahey had to focus on solidifying power in his court, and then he had to make allies out of Isra, Valakais and Etain. He had to convince them that the powers had chosen him willingly. But how would he explain that the powers had split? He dug at his nail beds until blood ran down his fingertips.

What if the other court rulers chose to side with Ziegan?

He had to be ready for anything.

He picked up another vase. It was beautiful—ancient from the looks of it. It reminded him of his mother.

With a howl, Dahey hurled the vase into the wall. It exploded into thousands of shards that rained down upon him. Dahey laughed bitterly. He had been so close to having everything. Now he had nothing.

No—he hadn't lost everything.

He snapped his fingers. A servant entered the room, her head bowed.

"Dress me." He jerked his head to the massive wardrobe occupying the far end of the room. He'd replaced all of Finder's clothes with his own. His cousin had no taste. "Black coat, gold clasps."

The faery fetched his coat, helping him into it and then doing up the clasps. She was careful not to touch his bare skin.

"Get out."

She scurried out of his chambers.

Dahey inspected himself in the mirror. The entirety of the outfit was black—down to his tall, polished boots. The golden buckles gleamed. But it needed more.

He buckled on a red half cloak that slung over one shoulder. The heavy fabric rippled down his back like a dark wound. Finally, he put on his crown.

His crown. The one he had fought and killed and betrayed for. The one he had earned. Giving himself one final look in the mirror, he swept away. He was the king. Now he must speak to his subjects.

He sat on the throne, his hands clasped in front of him. Before him milled hundreds of court gentry. Some of them murmured to themselves, others remained silent. Waiting.

"My friends." Dahey leaned back on the throne. The murmurs fell silent. "You all saw what happened at the Tournament."

Some whispers rose from the crowd. Dahey continued. "The human girl tricked you. Made you believe that she was in love with Finder. She was manipulating you as a ploy to get Finder back on the throne. She and Finder were willing to work with beasts. The firedrake could have destroyed all of Shadeshelm. Finder would have allowed that to happen. Would have wanted it to happen."

The whispers gave way to full on shouts. Dahey let them go for a time, and then held up a hand. They fell silent.

"Finder has abandoned his court. He might have won the Tournament, but he allied himself with beasts. He knew that the magic had chosen me. Not only that, but he allied himself with Ziegan, the dark conjurer. Finder has sided with that creature in an attempt to reclaim his throne. He cannot stand to know that the magic has chosen me, that all of you have chosen me."

Dahey spread his hands and flame roared to life between his palms. He let the magic go, fighting the urge to black out. He just had to hold on...

Gasps erupted from the crowd. Dahey smiled.

"Will you stand for this injustice?"

Shouts of anger came from the crowd.

"Finder fled. But I am here now. I fought for you. I put my feelings for my family aside in the pursuit of justice. We are about to enter a new world, and I will be the one to lead you to it. Not Finder. Not the traitor.

Not the coward. We will find him, and we will bring him to justice. Will you help me in that? Will you help me give you justice?"

"Yes!"

"All hail, King Dahey!" someone began the chant, and others joined them.

Dahey smiled.

51

LARKEN

Airodion

Fynvarra flew them straight to White Keep. Finder fell unconscious sometime along the way. Larken longed to sleep, but Fynvarra needed her sight. Her heart twisted. The last healing stone had been destroyed. Fynvarra would never see again, not without her help.

She and Fynvarra didn't speak, only exchanging brief touches of emotions that darted down the bond unbidden. Larken's face ached, her lips and cheeks chapped from the constant sting of the wind. Her hands were numb, and her entire body felt to be in the midst of a cramp. Though she had enjoyed the breathtaking sights from above, she was ready to have both her feet placed firmly on the ground.

They soared over the snowy trees of the Winter Court, finally coming to the huge icy gate that she and Saja had entered when they had first visited White Keep. Saja and Roone waited for them outside the gate. Isra must have portalled them back.

Larken slid off Fynvarra's back, gently lowering Finder onto the fire-drake's neck. He didn't wake.

"Will you stay with him?" she murmured to Fynvarra.

"He's safe with me," Fynvarra said. Larken touched Finder's face before turning back to Saja and Roone.

"The queen awaits," Saja said grimly.

"Honored guests," Isra greeted them stonily from the throne, accompanying her words with hand-speak. She sat stiffly upon her throne, her blue gaze hard as flint. Roone went to stand by Isra's side, but she held up a hand to stop him. Roone stepped back, a glimmer of fear in his eyes.

"Roone has told me everything," Isra said. Her eyes turned to Larken, unfathomably cold. "You broke into my records room and into my dungeons. Conspired with *my* prisoner behind my back. After I took you in, sheltered you, protected you from Dahey's wrath. I'm beginning to think I should have just turned you over to him."

She turned to Roone next. "You are not allowed to keep secrets from me," she hissed, her hand-speak movements jerky. "I trusted you above all others, and not only did you conspire behind my back, but you contradicted me in front of all the courts and their rulers. More than that, you've been flaunting around with the Autumn Court general for weeks, finally putting it all on display at the reverie."

Roone flinched.

"Now all will think the Autumn Court has attempted to seduce us and succeeded," Isra continued. "They will think I have sided with Finder's claim for the throne, and war is now more imminent than ever."

"Roone didn't just help us for Saja. He did what he believed was right," Larken interjected.

"I will not hear another word from you, girl," Isra bellowed. "You will leave my court. You and your beast are not welcome here. Neither is Finder or his whore of a general."

Larken glared at Isra in disgust. Roone brushed Saja's hand with his own.

Isra's eyes lit with fury. "Come here," she ordered him. "I will give you one last chance to repent for what you did. Swear to me right now that you will never see or speak to Saja again. You know the law. Nothing could ever happen between the two of you. Let him go, and I will know loyalty lies within you still."

Saja turned to Roone. "*You have to,*" he said in hand-speak.

Tears glimmered in Roone's eyes. "*I can't be without you.*"

"*Yes, you can,*" Saja said. He tried to smile, but a small sob came out instead.

Roone cupped Saja's cheek, pressing a kiss to his forehead. He turned back to Isra. "*I love you, my queen. I love my court. But you ask of me the one thing I cannot do. I will take whatever other punishment you desire. Flog me. Send me to the dungeons to serve as practice for the new soldiers training in torture. But to turn away from Saja is to turn away from the other half of my soul. He is my* laithnam."

Larken gasped. She'd known that Roone and Saja were close, in love even, but they were each other's *laithnam?*

Isra's lips pulled back in fury. "You have done more than betray me this day. You betrayed your entire court, the entire city of White Keep. You could have destroyed everything, destroyed peace with the Autumn Court, and have allowed yourself to become soul bound to a faery from another court. I can never trust you again. I do not wish to see you dead, but this I cannot forgive."

"*My liege,*" Roone tried.

"I release you from my *dornán.* From this day forward, you are banished from my lands."

Roone's eyes widened in horror.

"No," Saja cried. "Isra, please don't do this to him. He would do anything for his court, you know that."

"Not anymore," Isra replied, sweeping back up the steps to take her place on her throne. Roone stared at his queen with such broken, raw hurt Larken almost had to look away.

"Go with them." Isra jerked her head at Larken and Saja. "Or go wherever you desire. I do not care. From this day on, you are courtless. Get out of my sight, and do not return."

Roone fell to his knees, a keening wail tearing from his lips.

Courtless. Larken had never heard of such a thing. But from the agony that poured from Roone, it was devastating to a court fey.

"Now all of you, *get out.*"

52

KAISA

Ellevere

Ishan did not come to her bed that night, nor did Jovanna return to their room, so Kaisa spent the night alone.

Tarrio met her the next morning, insisting on shadowing her as she made her way through town.

"Good morning." Tarrio grinned, leaning onto the neck of his horse.

Kaisa forced herself to give him a polite nod, leading Sorreno out from the stables.

They rode together through the town. A crowd of people came up to her, but they greeted Tarrio as well, which made her grind her teeth. Some of her most loyal followers were drawn to him, asking him with bright eyes what plans he had for a reformed Order.

"What is the biggest export of crops that Augrim produces?" Tarrio asked as they rode on.

Kaisa frowned. Ishan had told her, once, but she couldn't remember. "I don't know," she answered, and truly it felt unimportant. Why did it matter what crops they produced?

"Hmm." Tarrio stroked his chin. "And is the town run by committee, or does a Reeve oversee it?"

Kaisa blinked. "Ishan—the boy I was with yesterday, he runs the town after his grandmother passed." She was oddly relieved that she knew an answer to the question and was brought back to her days as a Scholar, nervous when her tutors would call on her for fear that she would get an answer incorrect. The questions posed by Tarrio were the same, however much he annoyed her, she was still desperate to please him, to get the answers to his questions correct to impress him.

"Yes," Tarrio said slowly. "In many cases, these small farming towns have a central figurehead, but things are often discussed with a committee of respected people in the town. And more often than not, a Reeve oversees their work, collects taxes and whatnot."

Kaisa shifted in her saddle. "I've heard Ishan say that he wanted to discuss things with the elders of the town, but I've never heard him mention any kind of committee or Reeve. I think he would have told me if there was," she said, though doubt infused her words.

"If you want to lead these people, you need to understand who governs them," Tarrio said. "You are appealing to them as something new, but if you offer them change, you must make a new structure last, or it will fail."

Kaisa expected anger to wash over her, but all she felt was shame. She should know these things about her people, especially when she was demanding so much of them, urging them to fight back against the monsters, the Popes and the Order itself.

"I'll ask about it," she murmured. "It never crossed my mind, not with everything going on. I didn't expect things to go as far as they have. I refer to them as my people now. They say I have an army. I didn't expect to even live this long, not after the threats from the Order," she confessed.

Tarrio's expression softened. "It's a lot to take in. But they're not going to kill you. They can't risk igniting the people with a martyr. But I have no doubt at some point they will put all their efforts into taking you alive and changing your mind."

Kaisa knew what kind of efforts Tarrio spoke of. They would capture her alive and torture her until she wished she wasn't.

"You need to be vigilant," Tarrio said. "You need guards with you always, protecting you."

"What about now?" Kaisa said, lifting a brow.

Tarrio smiled devilishly at her. "You don't need guards when you're with me. I was trained as a member of the Red Guard, remember?"

A scuffle made both of their heads turn. A few townspeople dragged forward a man garbed in red and black. A member of the Order.

When they drew closer, Kaisa recognized the man. It was the same one who had tried to buy children from the refugees, who had spoken to her and Ishan and urged her to join the Popes.

"We found this one trying to buy more children, Kaisa," one man said breathlessly, holding the man from the Order by the collar. "We knew you would want him brought to you straight away."

"Why are you still here?" Kaisa snarled at the member of the Order.

"I'm trying to save these people from you and the blasphemous New Order," the man spat.

Tarrio said nothing at her side. He leaned back in his saddle, watching her. Kaisa couldn't help but feel like she was being tested, but she couldn't let it get to her. She would not let this man stain the streets of her city any longer.

"We burned your kin in Inniskeen," she said. "You will join them soon."

The crowd cried out in agreement.

"No," Tarrio said, gripping her arm.

Kaisa whirled, pulling it from his grasp. "You have no idea what this man has done. He's been trying to buy children, and I'm certain he had something to do with the soldiers taking over Inniskeen."

"You can't kill all who oppose you," Tarrio said. "You can't rule through fear. You didn't show mercy at Inniskeen. Show mercy now, and see where it gets you."

Kaisa paused. Maybe there was some truth to his words, though, as always, she hated admitting it. "What would you have me do with him then?"

Tarrio waved a hand. "Banish him. He'll return to the Popes, and we'll never have to hear from him again. You are stronger than him now," he added softly. "He can't harm you anymore. Let him go."

Kaisa pondered it for a moment. "A compromise, then. I will allow him to live, but not through banishment. He will be imprisoned here."

The man began to struggle at her words. "For how long?"

She stared down at him. "Indefinitely."

She glanced back over to Tarrio, who gave her a nod. She'd passed his test.

That night, she visited the small town dungeon, which was really just a cellar.

The man was chained to a wall, spitting obscenities at her.

She put her sword through his throat, ending his hateful words.

She wiped her sword clean on his clothes, sheathed it, and left him to hang there. She might have passed Tarrio's test, but he hadn't passed hers.

And she couldn't trust anyone who would allow her enemies to live.

53

LARKEN

Airodion

Fynvarra glided over the trees, Larken and Finder on his back.

They had left White Keep immediately, Saja half carrying Roone from the throne room. It had been decided that they would go to First Forge, the eyrie where the drakes lived in the Autumn Court. Larken had been fearful that Dahey would try to attack them, but Fynvarra had assured her that even Dahey wasn't foolish enough to attack an entire horde of firedrakes.

Fynvarra was clearly exhausted, having barely rested since his last flight from the Autumn Court, but he pushed on, determined to make it without stopping. Saja and Roone would ride their own mounts and arrive in a day or two.

Larken was still reeling from Roone admitting that Saja was his *laithnam*. Though she hated to admit it, jealousy had wormed its way into her heart. *Laithnams* had a magical bond that only the fey could experience, but the way her companions talked about it... She wondered if she would ever find anything like that.

Finder was still unconscious and seated before her. Larken brushed her fingers across his back. Her spine tingled. She had said she loved him in the arena. It was the truth. She wanted Finder. All of him. And now he was here with her, finally, after it all.

Fynvarra flew on, his powerful wings beating endlessly. Larken's ears popped as they descended at last, headed for a tower that jutted out above the tree line. The drake angled downwards, making her stomach drop.

A grassy plain stretched out before them, the entrance to the spiraling tower ahead. It had many entrances, huge holes cut from the rock, large enough for great beasts to crawl through. A tower built for drakes.

"First Forge," Fynvarra said.

Fynvarra soared through an arched opening in the tower, landing gracefully on his back legs. He lowered his neck so Larken could see their surroundings clearly for the first time.

They stood at the edge of a vast drop. The interior of the tower was open to the sky, the various openings for the drakes to fly through covering the interior walls of the tower like a honeycomb. Drakes perched and laid in the various openings. They were all shapes and sizes, all different shades of reds and orange. Only a few were pitch black.

She tugged her eyes away and looked down into a pit that stretched away into darkness below. Heat billowed from the hole every so often like a geyser, spitting steam into the tower.

"Our roost is above," Fynvarra said. "And our forges below."

Larken wasn't afraid of heights, but it made her stomach twist to not be able to see the bottom of the forges.

"Do you make weapons?"

"Make them?" Fynvarra chuckled. "No, we take them. Weapons, jewels, magical objects... we guard them all here. The forges are for the young ones to practice breathing fire."

Did they have weapons strong enough to defeat Ziegan?

A few drakes caught sight of Fynvarra, their gazes lighting with surprise.

"The king!"

"The king is back!"

Larken stilled. After all this time, she had nearly forgotten that Fynvarra was the king of the firedrakes. Would they take him back?

Many of the drakes flew to meet him, all holding their necks out, their chins tilted towards the sky.

"What are they doing?" Larken frowned.

Fynvarra nodded. "They bare their most vulnerable part to me. It is the deepest sign of respect."

Larken placed a hand on his neck. "Welcome home, little king."

Fynvarra purred in response.

Larken and Fynvarra left Finder in one of the many chambers to rest. She desperately hoped he would wake so she could speak with him, but she knew he needed to recover from his time in Dahey's clutches.

Fynvarra occupied a vast room in the eyrie that was partially open to the sky. A large opening led deeper into the eyrie while another large opening led outside—the forest visible hundreds of feet below. Hot rocks and steam from the forge heated the ground. Fynvarra's nest was on an elevated stone platform. The heat rising from the stones made the room cozy despite the cool autumn air billowing in from outside.

The drakes brought food to them—venison, pheasants, rabbits, fish, and other creatures Larken could not name. All of it was blackened to a crisp on the outside but tender and pink on the inside. Larken scarfed down the meat. She hadn't eaten any since they'd stayed with Remira at the Warga camp, and she wasn't about to waste it.

Fynvarra practically ate a deer whole before slowing down to savor his meals. "Wait until you see the kill pile," Fynvarra cracked a femur with his teeth, sucking the marrow out. "Each kill that our hunters make has to be placed in the pile, and a pecking order establishes who gets what. As king, I'll get all the best meals."

"So each firedrake has a job?"

"Oh, yes." Fynvarra crunched on three pheasants. "There's king, of course, and elders. Then there's the fighters, flyers, hunters, healers, and hatchlings. The hatchlings spend years shadowing each job to see what they have a knack for, and then they choose. Elders have to be nominated by the horde, and kings have to be challengers, of course."

So they weren't just beasts living in a cave. They had a whole society, a whole hierarchy to uphold.

"What were you before you became king?"

"Flyer," Fynvarra grunted. He coughed, hacking up a small bone. He resumed chewing on the hind leg of a deer.

"So you just... flew around?" Larken waved a hand.

Fynvarra rolled his sightless eyes. "No, human. I was a scout. Flyers mark our perimeters and monitor our territory. If something comes our way, we let the fighters know, and they take care of it." Fynvarra rustled his wings.

"I was the fastest flyer in the horde," Fynvarra murmured. "It's how I escaped the day I was attacked. Now I might never fly again."

Larken's heart twisted. "You have me now. I will give my sight to you whenever you want it. Any day. Any hour."

Fynvarra curled his tail around her.

They sat together afterwards, watching the sun melt beneath the horizon. Larken lent Fynvarra her sight for it. She felt he needed to see it. To know that they had made it another day and survived. And now he was king of the firedrakes. Drakes soared around the tower, their screeches and roars somehow becoming more familiar.

54

ZIEGAN

Airodion

Ziegan stood at the edge of the chasm. The Fomari, Furyons, and other creatures that had helped him during the second war stood behind him, drool pooling in their mouths. Some of his children had already entered Ellevere, but now more of his masses would cross. He had promised many of them human flesh in exchange for their allegiance. Others he had to offer more serious rewards—words and phrases in his language. But he gave it to them gladly. Soon, there would be no more courts, no more rulers, and all beings in this world would be equal. Though sacrifices had to be made along the way.

He lifted his hands and began to speak, the language pouring out of him. The ground shook fiercely, but then began to knit itself together. The bridges collapsed, the stones dropping away into nothingness. The chasm that his father had made four hundred years ago came to a close.

Ziegan smiled. He would not be satisfied with Airodion alone, no, not when untouched human lands lay across the chasm. The land smoothed over, completely healed.

He turned to his horde. "Feast, then return to me, my children. Fight for me, and this is only the beginning."

With screaming, ravenous cries, the beasts poured into Ellevere.

55

KAISA

Ellevere

The Furyons returned that night.

Augrim was stronger than ever, and they lit the bonfires with ease, the musicians picking up their instruments. The Furyons screamed, taking to the skies, but still they circled like a strange flock of crows.

Kaisa marched to the center of the town square, Tarrio by her side. Ishan was already there when they arrived, violin tucked against his chin. He looked at Kaisa, eyes sad, but said nothing as he began to play.

"Keep the fires going!" Kaisa roared. Why weren't the damned creatures leaving?

One of the creatures descended, a slender figure perched on its back. Kaisa frowned as the creature landed. Its eyes were closed, and it hissed in rage, swinging its head back and forth.

But what shocked Kaisa was the creature that crawled from the monster's back. At first, she thought it was a human, but then she caught sight of the female's pointed ears. She was fey.

Kaisa raised her sword, but Tarrio put a hand to her blade, pushing it down. "Wait. Hear what she has to say."

Kaisa scowled but lowered her blade. Unease rippled through her. She had never seen anyone riding these creatures before, hadn't known the monsters were even sentient enough to do so. She had read about the faery gentry in her book, and it couldn't be a good sign that they were here.

"Greetings!" the female cried. She was tall and slender, with a sheet of red hair that fell down her back. She was dressed in black, but Kaisa could see the glint of different weapons strapped to her body.

"I have come to speak to you on behalf of Ziegan. He apologizes for the recent attacks, but your leaders, the Popes, gave Ziegan whatever he desired when they joined forces with him, and Ziegan's creatures demanded flesh."

Confused murmurs rose from the crowd.

The name lit up a memory in the back of Kaisa's mind. Where had she heard that name before?

The realization struck her: the letter between Pope Galba and Pope Sersius.

"Who is Ziegan?" Kaisa called.

The faery woman turned to her, a smile on her lips. "There are things in motion that you do not understand, humans. Ziegan seeks to free the faery realm from tyranny, and he will do the same for the human realm if you join him."

More murmurs and shouts rose from the crowd.

"Join with the leader of the monsters that have been plaguing the human realm?" Kaisa scoffed. "Are you mad?"

The faery bent her head slightly. "Ziegan admits that it is regrettable that you have been tormented by his children, but they have been his loyal subjects since the second war, and he had to appease them. But now, he wants balance to be restored to the realm. These attacks will stop if you join us."

"We will never be on the same side as the Popes, the people who abandoned us to these monsters, or to Ziegan, who allowed his creatures to attack us," Kaisa spat.

A few cheers of agreement rose from the crowd.

The faery smiled again, stroking the monster's ugly head. "The winds are changing across our lands. Those who were once enemies are now allies, and all shall be equal through Ziegan. Just as he will offer clemency to his enemies, so must you forgive those who have wronged you to reach the better world. A balanced world, where all are equal."

"Never," Kaisa vowed. "The Popes abandoned us. No, worse, they offered us up to these monsters. We will never join Ziegan if he sides with the Popes."

The faery shook her head sadly. "You speak as though there is a choice. There is no choice. You will join Ziegan one way or another, either as allies, as slaves, or as sustenance for his army. You decide."

"We have held off your armies before," Tarrio called. "More people flock to Kaisa for she offers protection against the monsters. Why would we abandon her now for an unknown leader? We trust Kaisa to be able to fend off your kind."

Kaisa looked at Tarrio with shock. She couldn't believe that he had such favorable words to speak in her defense.

"Kaisa is not special," the woman sneered. "She gets her information from a book, a book that has been hidden from all humans save your Popes but that all faery children read." The woman drew something from her pack.

Horror filled Kaisa as she looked at the words on the spine: *The Beings and Beasts of Airodion*.

"Look familiar?" the faery cooed. She opened a page. "The Furyons. Repelled by music and light," she flipped a page. "The fey, possessing the power of glamour." She grinned, twisting a finger at Kaisa.

Kaisa yelped as a hundred spiders began crawling over her. "Get them off!" she screamed. "Get them off!"

The faery woman flicked her fingers again, and the spiders vanished. Kaisa's stomach filled with dread. She had been so sure that the spiders were real—but they were all a part of the faery woman's magic. "See for yourselves." The faery tossed the book to the ground before her. "What is rare here is common in Airodion. She has been lying to you this whole time. She is not special. She just knows how to read."

The woman mounted her dark creature. "If you must be convinced, then so be it. These creatures won't be found in your precious book, but they populate Ziegan's forces in great numbers."

People began to scream as new monsters descended from the town walls. Horrible, pale creatures with spindly legs and gaping mouths. The fire didn't bother them, neither did the music that the musicians began to frantically play.

"Please," Kaisa begged as the screams began. Tarrio grabbed her arm, ready to haul her away from the creatures.

"Not all will die," the faery woman assured her. "Just enough to convince you." She raised her voice before continuing. "Kaisa cannot save you from this war. Join Ziegan and live. Join your Popes and live."

She took off into the night sky. The other winged creatures left, leaving their spindly companions to their work. Kaisa lifted her sword, turning back-to-back with Tarrio.

"We will survive the night," he said, stabbing his sword into the nearest beast. "And then we will see what comes next. But focus on the now."

Kaisa tried, but nothing could stop the bitter pit of despair yawning inside her. She was completely helpless against these new creatures. She was a fraud, and now everyone would know it. She couldn't protect them, and now her people were going to die for it.

56

LARKEN

Airodion

Fynvarra spent most of his time attending to his new role as king. The drakes respected their law—whoever might have disagreed with Fynvarra becoming ruler put aside their anger. Another challenger wouldn't be chosen for another century. And until then, the drakes seemed content with their newly returned ruler.

Larken paced around the eyrie, waiting for Finder to wake. Finally, one of Fynvarra's flyers, Arox, came to her. He was small for a drake, even smaller than Fynvarra, with pitch black scales tinged with red.

"Finder is awake," Arox said. "He's in the forges."

Larken's heart jumped. She hurried down the many endless staircases to the forges below. The heat grew, making her face break out in sweat.

She paused before the wide archway that led to the forges. She forced her fists to relax. *It's Finder, not some stranger.*

Taking a deep breath, she walked into the forges.

Her eyes flew to Finder.

His shirt clung to his back with sweat. His brow glimmered, his red curls drenched. He lifted his arm high, bringing his metal hammer down upon a burning red sword. His back rippled with muscle as he brought down the hammer again and again. The drakes had no need for tools—Finder must have summoned everything he needed.

Larken's cheeks flushed, unable to look away from his toned arms. He had lost weight during his imprisonment, but he was still the most stunning male she had ever seen. Braziers filled with the drakes' fire burned around him. Larken waited for the wave of panic, but now that Finder was before her, all she could think about was him. The way his hair draped across his forehead, the way his muscles pulled against his white linen shirt.

"Finder," she said, her breath hitching ever so slightly in her throat.

He spun around, his grip slipping on the hammer. He caught it before it fell, and he placed it on the table before him. Larken could have sworn there was a tremor in his hand as he did so. Then he strode towards her, sweeping her up in his embrace. He crushed her against him. She hesitated, then threw her hands around his shoulders.

He was here. They were together.

Finder pressed his forehead to hers, panting slightly. Larken's breath matched his. She struggled to breathe as the fires of the forge raged around them.

She fought the blackness that crept into the edges of her vision at the thought of the flames. She would not faint. She would not let her fear ruin this moment, the moment she had waited so long for.

"I've missed you," she whispered.

Finder gave a shaky laugh. "I've missed you, too. More than you could possibly imagine."

She lowered her voice. "How are you?" She touched his wrists where the Weeping Metal had been. The skin was completely healed. "You still have your power over healing?"

Finder nodded. "Yes. Whatever phrase Dahey misspoke in Ziegan's language made it so that he only has power over the flame. But the fire magic feels different now. Before we were bound, my powers felt like separate currents." He took one of her hands, tracing lines on her palm as he described it. "I could reach into any with ease, pulling the magic to me. But now, with the fire, it no longer feels like a current. It feels like a chain." His mouth pulled downwards. "A chain binding me to Dahey. Whenever one of us tries to use the fire, the other feels agony."

"Have you tried to use your other powers since you've been freed from the Weeping Metal?"

"Only to heal myself. I didn't feel a chain—nor was I in any pain when I used them. The others feel the same, though I have had no need to use them."

Larken knew how much he detested using his powers over death, so she didn't push him. "What are we going to do about Dahey?" she whispered.

Finder sagged, leaning against the table. He scrubbed a hand over his face. "I do not know. I think—I think he was going to kill me in the ring. I saw something change in his eyes, a madness I have only seen once before in his father. I thought I could save him." His voice broke.

Larken's heart twisted. She could only imagine how much it hurt Finder that Dahey was willing to do this to him—his cousin, a previous member of his *dornán*. "I'm so sorry, Finder," she murmured.

"He must have spoken to Ziegan," Finder said. "If there was a way to correct what he did through his language, he would have done it already. The only way to force the powers now must be if one of us dies."

Larken squeezed his hand, at a loss for words.

Finder's face hardened, though his eyes remained haunted. "I tried to save him. I tried to help him. And he repaid me with a blade in my chest. I made many mistakes when I was prince, I know that now. But I have always cared for my people and tried to protect them. Ziegan won't rest until he takes all of Airodion. Chaos like we have never known will reign. Dahey believes he can stay one step ahead of Ziegan, use him for his language, but he is mistaken. Ziegan has only ever used Dahey for his own gain. Using Ziegan's language will have consequences that could lead to the Autumn Court's ruin. I will not allow my people to suffer. I will do whatever I must to take back the throne, and if Dahey stands in my way..." A muscle flickered in Finder's jaw. "Then I will do what I have to do."

Larken knew it would destroy Finder to kill Dahey. And she wondered if he would be able to follow through with it if it came down to it. But what choice did he have? He would already have to fight to get his throne back. Dahey was willing to free Ziegan, willing to use his dark magic, all for the crown. He would destroy the Autumn Court with his greed, and all of Airodion, and even Ellevere, would suffer for it.

She knew she needed to ask Finder to heal her. She knew they needed to talk about all that had happened before the Tournament and what she had said in the ring. She knew she needed to—

He tucked a curl behind her ear, and all thoughts fled from her mind.

"Larken!"

Larken and Finder jerked away from each other. Arox stood at the entrance to the forges. "The king requests your presence. He wishes to know if you want to fly with him to Ballamor."

Larken's mouth hung open slightly. Finder backed up a step. "Go," he said gently.

She nodded, running to find Fynvarra.

Home. She was finally going home.

57

LARKEN

Airodion

Larken clung to Fynvarra's mane as he soared through the air.

She was finally going to see her parents again. She would have to tell them everything—she hadn't had a chance to tell them she was going to find Brigid. So much had happened since then. Did they think she was dead? They had to have guessed that she went to the faery realm.

We're getting close to the chasm, Fynvarra said. Unease snaked its way through the bond.

Larken peered below, but she saw no rift in the earth. *We can't be close, or we'd be able to see it,* she pointed out.

The chasm is gone, Fynvarra said. Larken's hands twisted in his mane, feeling his fear as her own.

Larken's stomach clenched. *No. No, that cannot be—*

But Fynvarra was right. Even from above, she could recognize the pastures of Ballamor. They were in Ellevere already.

Ziegan, she realized. This had to be his doing. She raised a shaking hand to her chest. Ziegan had healed the chasm. She had seen him use earth magic at the Tournament.

282

His sights lay beyond Airodion, Fynvarra said.

Ziegan clearly planned to rule Ellevere. But the Popes would never submit to him. She shifted. The Popes had worked with the Starveling in exchange for riches and magical gifts. The Popes might not want to submit to a ruler such as Ziegan, but if he offered them magic... She bit her lip. Could humans use his language? She wasn't sure. Her stomach twisted at the thought of the humans siding with Ziegan. The humans wouldn't know what they were up against. She knew that many of the soldiers had been forced into the Popes' army by draft—few would be there of their own volition.

Faster, Fynvarra. Please, Larken begged. She had to get to her parents.

Fynvarra angled downwards.

Larken peered below, something catching her eye. There were no people on the streets. It was evening—people should have been milling about, closing their shops, returning to their homes. It was quiet.

"Something's wrong," she said. "Go down, Fynvarra, now!"

Fynvarra didn't hesitate, plunging into a dive. Larken's stomach hurled into her throat, and a feeling of weightlessness overtook her. Wind tore at her hair, her clothes, and she clung to Fynvarra's mane, afraid she would be ripped from his back.

Fynvarra fanned his wings and he landed gently. The streets were empty. A firedrake had just landed in Ballamor—there should have been an uproar. Larken gazed around at the shops, her eyes taking in new details for the first time. Charred exteriors. Broken glass. Doors broken in.

She slid down Fynvarra's shoulder, running to her family's bakery. Fynvarra hissed at his sudden loss of sight.

Larken pushed her way into the bakery. The door hung lopsided from its hinges, deep gouges scraping the wood. Some creature had been here.

Larken sobbed, her mind struggling to take in the state of the bakery. Bags of flour were ripped open; the white powder had exploded everywhere. The eggs and milk had spoiled, the sweet, creamy scent she associated with the bakery replaced with something rancid.

She called for Mama and Papa, but she knew they weren't there. It was a town of ghosts. She ran up the stairs to her family's living quarters above. Many of their belongings remained, but the clothes and blankets had been taken. By whom? Had some creature attacked Ballamor, and had the people fled?

Broken glass crunched under her feet from the broken windows. The maps she had drawn the night before the Choosing Ceremony remained on the floor where she had left them; her parents hadn't moved them. They were scuffed and torn but still there.

She couldn't stand to be in this place any longer. She hurried outside, her shock numbing her. Fynvarra crouched in the square, his wings puffed out to make him look bigger. Larken felt a stab of pity—she shouldn't have left him alone to fend for himself, not without more warning at least.

His nose twitched at her. "What did you find?"

"Nothing," Larken replied. "They're gone. The whole town is gone. Do you... do you think they're all dead?"

"No," Fynvarra said. "I smell death here, and found a few bodies—not your parents," he interjected before she could open her mouth, "I would have recognized their scent as similar to yours. But several others. All very old. The scents here are stale. Humans have not been here in a long while."

"They left?" Larken asked. "But what could have made them do that? Did the fey attack them? The Fomari?" Her blood chilled.

"I do not know," Fynvarra replied. "Some kind of creature from Airodion was here—that much I can tell. But the scents are so muddled I cannot tell anything else."

"Could you track the humans' scent?" Larken asked hopefully. She and Fynvarra could go and find her parents, make sure they were safe—

Fynvarra shook his head, crushing her. "The scents are most concentrated here, which is why I can smell them so clearly. Once they left this place, the scents became muddled and lost. But they got out. That much I know."

Tears welled in Larken's eyes. She had left her parents behind, and this had happened. If only she had stayed and had warned them the bridge was down instead of going back to Airodion with Saja.

Fynvarra hissed. "Something else lurks here. A scent I don't recognize..."

A blurry shape launched at her, scuttling out from behind one of the houses. It was a horrible creature with a smashed face and striped skin. Larken screamed, falling backwards. Fynvarra roared and the creature flinched. Then it opened its jaws and screeched back. Larken hauled herself onto Fynvarra's back. Her mind melded with his, and he threw himself at the creature, biting and snapping. Larken held his mane, praying she didn't get thrown from his back and into the creature's gaping jaws.

Fynvarra opened his mouth and Larken *felt* the fire rumble deep within him. Panic surged within her.

"No, Fynvarra, no fire," she gasped, her mind flying to that dark place. Her mind flew through the images, Finder succumbing to the flames, her hands reaching out to touch him, the scorching, blistering heat—

Her vision went black. She tried to breathe, tried to remember what Saja and Roone had told her, tried to leave her body behind, but everything was dark, dark, dark. She thought of the cold, the freezing cold, where the fire could never touch her, never harm her again.

Larken, stop! Fynvarra's words beat at the edges of her mind, but she cast him out, curling within her mind, shielding herself from the pain she knew was coming when Fynvarra breathed fire.

You're blocking me, Larken, stop, Fynvarra cried, but she could barely hear him. The creature squealed. Fynvarra was thrown backwards, and Larken released his mane. She rolled from his back, her head cracking on the ground.

The beasts roared as they fought. Larken moaned, holding her head, looking up to see Fynvarra shove the carcass of the creature off of him. Its neck was broken—he'd managed to kill it.

"You blocked me!" he growled. "Your panic was so strong that I was paralyzed along with you. I couldn't use my fire; I could barely kill that creature, and it's half my size."

"Don't use fire around me," Larken snarled. "You should have known better."

"I should have known better?" Fynvarra said incredulously. "You could have gotten both of us killed! You need to master your own mind before it's the death of you."

Larken crossed her arms. "I don't want to be here anymore." She sulked.

"And I don't trust you to fly. What if you block me again and my wings stop working?"

"Would you rather we walk back to First Forge?" She glared at the firedrake. Finally, Fynvarra huffed, turning his back to her. She climbed up, their minds stiffly weaving together.

She didn't want to think about blocking Fynvarra again and what would happen if she did. She had to focus on figuring out a way to get back to her parents. But for now, there was nothing she could do. She sucked in a breath, hopelessness spreading through her like a steady ache.

Fynvarra launched into the night.

58

KAISA

Ellevere

The strange, new monsters left at the first light of dawn, but the damage was already done. They hadn't killed everyone in the town, no, they had promised her that they wouldn't do that much, but they had killed plenty. Her people were terrified, they begged for her help, asked her to pray to the Twins for guidance. They still didn't know that Kaisa was just as helpless as they were.

Several people had come banging on her door, but she had locked herself within, and she sent them all away.

The one she couldn't send away was Tarrio, who sat outside her room with a constant *bang, bang, bang* of his fist on her door until she could take no more of it.

She yanked the door open. "What do you want?" She scowled.

He stood up, pushing past her into the room. "You can't hide in here all day. The people need you."

She didn't mistake how he had said "the people" instead of "her people." Tarrio's ranks had grown considerably in the past few days. Kaisa was jealous of the New Order's popularity.

"No, they don't." Kaisa crossed her arms. "What that faery said was true—none of what I knew was given to me by the gods. It all came from a book. Anyone could have read it and done what I did."

Ishan had already screamed his piece to her in the light of dawn after the creatures left.

"Anyone could have done what you did," he yelled. "You aren't special. You weren't meant to lead these people, I was. And you swept in with your divine mission, but it was all a lie. It all came from a book."

His voice lowered, breaking slightly. "I thought we were the same. I thought you had left the Order behind, but you still believed in the Twins. Tell me the truth, Kaisa. Do you still believe in the gods?"

Kaisa didn't have the strength to lie to him anymore. "No."

Ishan had backed up a step, eyes filled with horror. Then he had spun on his heel and left.

"Is this it?" Tarrio asked, lifting *The Beings and Beasts of Airodion* from her nightstand.

Kaisa nodded.

Tarrio flipped through the book, his eyes slowly growing wider. "Anyone could have read this book, and yet, I don't think anyone could have found it. Where did you come across such a priceless tome?"

"I stole it. From Pope Sersius's hidden chamber." Kaisa said. "But that doesn't matter. Any of the Scholars could have been cleaning his rooms. Any of them could have stumbled across that hidden chamber. Ishan's right. I'm nothing special." She swiped a hand under her eyes, hoping Tarrio hadn't heard her voice break.

Maybe she had gotten caught up in the fantasy of it all. It was nice to be needed, but more than that, appreciated for her work.

"But they didn't find the chamber. You did," Tarrio said gently. "Think of all the circumstances that had to align for that to happen. Not everyone would have made the choices you made that got you there. But you did. And I think that makes you special." He put the book back. "People aren't just drawn to your ability to protect them from the fey. They love you, Kaisa. You think if Ishan had stumbled across this book and given his people this information that he would have gained the following you have? I don't think so. And that's why I think he's so upset that your power comes from something that he could have had if only things had played out differently."

"It doesn't matter now," Kaisa said. "They know I lied. They know now that even with the book I can't protect them. I'm done. I'm leaving. I'll give the book to Ishan, but I can't stay here anymore." Her voice broke, but she stiffened her shoulders. She made her way to the half-packed satchel on her bed. She began cramming more of her clothes inside.

Tarrio grasped her arm, stopping her. "You must continue to lead. It isn't the Twins who chose this path for you, and it's not the people of this town either. It's *you*, Kaisa. You chose this life for yourself. Don't give up on it so easily." He let go of her arm.

Tears welled in her eyes before she could stop them. "I'm just a Scholar. I don't know how it came to all of this."

Tarrio smiled at her. "Oh, I think you have always been much more than that. Come. Let us talk to Ishan. It was a dark night, but dawn has come again. We will plan for what comes next together."

Kaisa hesitated. Perhaps... perhaps Tarrio was right. Maybe her people weren't as upset about the book as she thought. They had just wanted help, and she had given it to them. She could find a way to help them still, find a way to defeat these new monsters. She hardened her heart. She could do this. He took her hand and squeezed it. Together, they walked down the stairs of the inn.

Kaisa smiled at Tarrio, and he grinned back. Wiley as he might be, she was glad to have him in her corner. She needed him in her corner. They pushed open the doors to the inn.

The street beyond was filled with hundreds of soldiers of the Order.

Ishan stood in the middle of the street, talking with one of the soldiers. She couldn't comprehend what was happening. Why was Ishan talking to the Order's soldiers? Why hadn't he warned her, let her know about the incoming fight?

"What is the meaning of this?" Kaisa snarled. She unsheathed her sword, ready to stand by Ishan's side when the fighting broke out.

The soldier moved away as Ishan turned to her, his brown eyes cold.

"I'm sorry it had to come to this. But I had to do what was best for my people."

"What are you talking about?" she breathed.

"Your power comes from a book," Ishan said, his voice as chilling as his gaze. "You're nothing without it. And you can't protect these people any longer. Which is why I contacted the Order and told them that Augrim will join their army."

It felt as though a hand had reached into her chest and squeezed her heart. Horror filled her. "No," she whispered. Ishan wouldn't do that to her, not after everything—

"These aren't just your people," Tarrio cut in. "They're Kaisa's people too. And mine. We should have been consulted."

Kaisa lifted her head. "Is this what they wanted?"

"It's not up to them to decide," Ishan snarled. "You've never given them a choice before, so you can't start now. They need someone to speak for them, to protect them."

"You're really going to hand me over to them?" Kaisa said, her body going numb. "They wanted me alive for a reason. They'll torture me."

"Who said anything about handing you over?" Ishan said. "You mean nothing to them anymore. That's how far you've fallen. Taking your army is enough. You have no power anymore."

His words hit Kaisa like a blow to the gut. She wasn't even worth being taken prisoner.

"The New Order won't join their army," Tarrio growled.

"They will if they know what's best for them," Ishan snarled. "The Popes know the heretical New Order grows here, but since many of my people are members, I chose to protect them and said nothing about their leader. The Order wants numbers, and I promised them this town. I suggest you join them."

The muscles in Tarrio's jaw worked furiously, but he said nothing.

"You are no longer welcome here, Kaisa." Ishan turned away from her. "Leave before dawn."

"Ishan, please," Kaisa said, reaching for his hand. The sting of his betrayal cut deep, but faced with losing him now, she couldn't bear it. "I'm sorry I lied about the book, but it was still fate that I was the one who found it. These people need me and I—I need them." She stepped closer when he didn't pull away. "Please don't do this. We can still fight them. We can. I know this feels like the only way, but the Order isn't the answer."

Ishan stood still for a moment. "I didn't want this," he whispered. "I didn't want to choose the Order. But you saw yourself what happened last night. The Popes have allied themselves with these dark creatures, and you cannot protect us from them, even with your book." He turned back to look at her. "I won't deny that I'm angry about the tome. About you lying. But I'm more angry that you let your pride get to you, that you believed you were the only one who could protect these people. You aren't. And if choosing the enemy means my people get to live, then so be it. That's what a true leader does. And I know you wouldn't have been able to make that choice."

He was leaving her. Just like everyone else she had loved. The people who had come to rely on her, love her, were being taken away too.

Pain stabbed her heart, and she turned and ran.

59

KAISA

Ellevere

Kaisa sat in The Dancing Toad, nursing a cup of ale.

Tarrio sat across from her, eyeing her over his roast chicken. Most of the people of Augrim had left for Barrensmere, where Pope Sersius promised they would have a place to stay in the city.

Many members of the New Order had stayed, but Kaisa hadn't asked Tarrio what would happen or whether his people would join the army like Ishan had promised. In truth, she didn't care. She was too deep in her own despair to worry about the New Order.

Why can't you ever be good enough? Tears stung her eyes, the back of her throat growing painfully tight. She wasn't a good enough daughter. She wasn't a good enough leader. She wasn't a good enough friend. She wasn't a good enough lover. She was good at many things. But she had never been good enough.

The door banged open. A woman entered the tavern, pulling down her hood. Jovanna.

Kaisa's heart nearly burst seeing her. "Jo," she breathed, pushing back her chair. She rushed to her friend, pulling her into a rib-crushing hug.

Jovanna squeezed her back.

"I thought you left," Kaisa said.

Jovanna leaned back. "Of course not," she murmured. "I came here with you, remember? I'm not giving up on you that easily."

A tiny part of Kaisa's heart returned to her. "I thought you were upset with me." She assumed that Jovanna had left with Ishan. She hadn't seen her all day when many people left for Pope Sersius's city. All men over the age of eighteen were expected to be in the city in three days, fulfilling the number Ishan had promised. Those unable to fight were allowed to stay, though the Order could offer them no protection.

Jovanna chuckled darkly. "I was angry with you. I still am, in a way. What you did in Inniskeen..." She shook her head. "But I know you, Kai. I see the good inside you. Despite getting swept up in your status, you've helped people. I know it must be hard. And you can't be expected to make all the right decisions all the time. I still love you, and I'll still be by your side through it all."

They sat, Tarrio giving Jovanna a brief greeting as she situated herself at the table.

"There's more," Jovanna said, leaning forward. "I've been going around town, seeing who is still loyal to Kaisa. You still have a following. They stayed here for you and are waiting to hear your council."

Kaisa shook her head. "There's nothing I can do for them. Nothing I can give them. They're better off going to the Order's army with Ishan."

"She has more numbers than that," Tarrio said, ignoring her. "The New Order will never join the Popes' army. She has those people as well."

"I'll get them together," Jovanna said excitedly. "We'll come up with a plan. We'll have to leave, of course, for as soon as the Order realizes Ishan has promised them soldiers that never came, they'll return to this town and try to take people by force. We'll go to Inniskeen. I heard they've recovered greatly from their attack and haven't had any since."

"It's not a long-term solution," Tarrio agreed, "but it'll work for now. We need to buy time, find a way to grow Kaisa's following once more."

"No," Kaisa cut in. Both Jovanna and Tarrio looked at her. "You two aren't listening. I'm done. I'm leaving Augrim at dawn—alone. I'm not blessed by the Twins, I'm not a leader, I'm nothing. Tell the people foolish enough to want to keep following me that. And tell the New Order too." She looked at them both. "Save those people. Save yourselves. I'm done."

"You can't leave these people to the Order," Jovanna said. "Think about what you've accomplished so far, how hard you've worked to free those people. We escaped, and they can, too, with your help. What are you going to do on your own?" she growled.

"I lied to them just as much as the Order did!" Kaisa cried. "I used their religion for my own gain, just like the Popes. I'm no better than the Order."

"We talked about this," Tarrio pushed. "I told you that you found that book for a reason. You were ready to fight then. What changed?"

"An unknown beast came and murdered my people, the majority of who now left because they know I'm useless. My lover betrayed me, and now my people have sided with the Order, and there's nothing I can do to stop it," she said coldly.

"The faery woman said that there's a war brewing in her realm," Tarrio said. "If the Order and these dark fey are preparing for war, then that must mean there is resistance. We could find out who they are—join them."

The thought had crossed Kaisa's mind. The book spoke of court rulers with immense power. Though she had seen one faery ride the Furyon, perhaps some of the fey were against these dark creatures.

She shoved those thoughts away. She wanted no part in this war. Not anymore. She had always wanted to help people, but perhaps that was because that's what the Order had told her. To help get people into the Order. To train the new ranks. And in her fight for normalcy, once she had left the Order, she had done the same thing—tried to help people by bringing them to her cause. But how was she any different from the Order?

What do you want to do?

She wanted to leave. She wanted to be alone. She had spent her whole life terrified that she would be abandoned. First by her parents, then by the Order, even if it had been her own choice. And now her people were turning away from her.

She couldn't help people. She was only harming them. She had burned those soldiers at Inniskeen, put her sword through the throat of that man from the Order. She deserved to be punished. And the only way she could think to do that was to leave. To be alone.

Her heart quickened in terror. She had never been alone before. She didn't want to be alone, not when Tarrio and Jovanna were right there, offering her support. But she had to protect them. Staying with her put them at risk, and she couldn't live with herself if something happened to them, Jovanna especially.

"I told you," Kaisa repeated softly. "I'm done. Take the New Order north if you wish. Or join the Popes' army. I don't care. I'm leaving at first light."

"Then I'm coming with you," Jovanna said.

Kaisa shook her head. "No. I'm going alone."

"Kai—"

"I'm done," Kaisa whispered. "I tried. I tried to help people, but I can't. I'm going alone so I don't hurt anyone else."

Jovanna must have seen something on her face because her friend said nothing.

Tarrio stood. "I'm done trying to convince you," he said quietly. "I'm taking my people to Inniskeen. And then north, to the faery lands, if they'll have us. But I'll die before they join the Order. If you change your mind, come find us." He turned to leave, but then stopped, turning around to face her once more. "I fought to convince Kaisa the leader to stay with her people, to fight. But I won't fight for the person I see before me. This Kaisa is not one I recognize. And I don't want her leading anyone."

He left, and somehow, his words cut deeper than Ishan's had. Slow tears dripped down her face.

"Tell me to stay, and I will," Jovanna whispered.

Her courage wobbled. Of course she wanted Jovanna to stay. She was her sister in everything but blood. But she couldn't risk her friend getting hurt. Kaisa forced her face to harden. "I don't want to be around you anymore. You're just a reminder of the Order. Of my failure."

Jovanna stood. "I know you don't mean it," she said softly. "But I don't know how to convince you. So I'll give you what you want. I hope it's enough."

She left, and Kaisa was alone.

It was worse than she ever could have imagined. But she deserved it. Deserved to be hated by her people, by Ishan, by Tarrio and Jovanna. Because she could never be good enough for them.

Kaisa packed the rest of her belongings. She still had a few hours before dawn, but she wanted to leave now. She didn't know where she would go. She would just run from the war, she supposed, for as long as she could. Perhaps Tarrio and the New Order would find the good fey of Airodion and win the battles to come. Or perhaps the dark fey and the Popes' army would sweep over the land until she couldn't escape it.

Her gaze fell on *The Beings and Beasts of Airodion* where it sat on her nightstand, precisely where Tarrio had left it. She should have given it to him, or even Ishan. What good would it do in her hands?

She sat down on the bed and began flipping through the pages. She had read all of it, every single page. Except the last.

It was a short message from the author, one she had never bothered to read. It hadn't seemed important. But now, a part of her was curious. Reading the final page of the book before she left this life behind forever.

Dear reader,

I hope this book has assisted you in navigating Airodion and the strange beings and beasts that inhabit it. It was my goal as the author not just to document these creatures so you know how to avoid them or fight them (in the cases where that is possible), but instead, I hope it allows you to view these creatures with curiosity, not malice. It is my greatest wish that you can see them with empathy.

I have spent many years tracking down these creatures. I have encountered nearly all of them, some of which involved great peril to my life. But I don't regret it. In documenting these creatures, and sometimes speaking with them, I have learned a great deal, and I hope I can share even a small bit of knowledge with you.

Many wars have plagued Airodion over the years. From the first war with the Masters to the second that led to the tithe, and countless other battles that were lost to the winds of history. You may recognize some of the creatures in this book and wonder if I speak of them too when I beg you to see them with empathy. After all, how could I ask you to see monsters that fought against us in these wars with any shred of kindness? But I do ask that of you.

War inevitably comes to great lands such as ours for a multitude of different reasons. And I do not argue that those wars are futile. But in the end, when the peace comes (for it always does, in some form), we all must inhabit this world. So my plea is for you to have empathy. Have kindness. And think of peace. Every being and beast mentioned in this tome deserves those three things. And so do you, reader.

Kaisa read over the passage again and again until tears streamed down her cheeks. She couldn't figure out why the author's words touched her so deeply, but they did. Out of all the things the author could have said, they urged kindness. Empathy. Peace. In a book about monsters.

She flipped the book over, searching for the author's name. There were only two initials, N.F.

This author was a true leader. They had recorded all of this information, not in the hopes that someone would use it to fight, as she had, or to save lives, though Kaisa was sure it had. They had written it to help the beings and beasts featured within its pages. To help others see those creatures from a different point of view. The author wanted to help them all.

Kaisa clutched the book to her chest. Maybe she wasn't deserving of all that had happened to her. Kaisa had known what was right for her and chose her own path. She had left the Order. And yes, she had made mistakes as she tried to lead these people. She had started out wanting to help. Her intentions were good. But then she started caring more about her own status in the people's eyes than she did about protecting innocent lives. She'd let those intentions become corrupted.

She had spent so long agonizing over what others thought of her. Of disappointing them. She had believed that she had let her parents down in some way, and that was why they had sold her.

And maybe all of those things were true. But maybe none of them were. She wanted to help people, but she couldn't control them. She couldn't control what they did to her or anyone else. The only person she could control was herself. She had known her true path was leaving the Order. She knew her true path was leading people, though the power had led her astray.

But this book had opened her eyes in a way she had never expected. She had been using the book as a tool to gain power, power to defeat the monsters and also, power over her people. But that wasn't the purpose of the book.

She could help people without controlling them. She could help them and not have their choices reflect on her. She wasn't perfect, but that didn't mean she deserved the bad things that had happened to her. She didn't need to earn her existence in the eyes of her parents, or the Order, or the people she wanted to help. The book's author had seen worth in every creature. And all this time, she had been fighting to earn her place in this world. But maybe she was worthy just by being *her*. Just by being Kaisa.

This whole time, she had thought only of war. War against the monsters, against the Order itself. She had constantly thought of her against the Order, or her and her people against the monsters, but neither were evil. The monsters were doing what their instincts drove them to do. And the Order was made up of people, too. She couldn't ostracize everyone associated with it. She didn't know what brought them to fight for the Order. Perhaps the same desperation that caused her to fight against them. If she worked harder to understand them, then perhaps she could convince more to join her side. Or, if not, at least learn not to hate them so much. She wanted justice for the wrongs the Order had done. But all life had worth, and it wasn't her right to take it and dole out punishment however she pleased.

The book was right. War divided, but war was temporary. What came after was what mattered. Peace. Abandoning her people was not the answer. Enacting vengeance on anyone who wronged her was not the answer. She couldn't fight tyranny with more tyranny.

War was coming. The book had admitted that it was sometimes necessary. But not enough people focused on what came after.

She had thought the book had been meant to teach her about the monsters. But it hadn't. It had been meant to teach her this.

She knew what she had to do.

60

LARKEN

Airodion

Straw covered the room, littering the stone floor of Roone and Saja's chamber. Bits of it stuck out from Roone's hair, which, at another time, might have been comical, but now it just made Larken's heart ache.

Ziegan had taken White Keep. He and his swarm of creatures had overrun the palace.

Larken had never seen Roone lose his composure, but he had lost it completely when news of the attack on White Keep reached them. He had shredded the mattress with his knife, emitting a keening wail so heartbreaking Larken nearly had to leave the room.

With nothing left to destroy after the mattress, Roone had taken his knife to the walls themselves. Finally, Saja intervened, wrapping his huge arms around the Winter Court faery and sinking to the floor until Roone calmed.

"Isra said they had to fall back to Tellaridge," Saja said to Larken. "We could go there and help them."

Roone looked up. *"Did Isra send for me?"*

Saja brushed Roone's hair back from his face. *"No, my love."*

300

Roone bent his head, tears welling in his eyes. It must kill him to know that his court had been attacked, his queen had been attacked, but he could do nothing.

"He can't go with us," Saja said. *"Just as the bridge closed itself to you while you were bound to Finder, so too will the Winter Court close itself to Roone unless his banishment is lifted."*

Roone curled up on the floor with his back to them, clearly not wanting to partake in the conversation any longer.

"How could Isra do that to him?" Larken whispered.

"It is one of the cruelest fates a court ruler can bestow, especially to a high ranking court gentry." Saja shook his head. "But I do think we should go to Tellaridge. We could plead for Roone's reinstatement, and Isra might be more willing after the attack. And we should talk to Isra, see what she knows about Ziegan so we might predict where he will attack next."

"I want to come."

Saja and Larken whirled to see Finder standing in the doorway.

"I want to come," he repeated. "If I'm ever going to take back the throne, then I need to know what my people face."

61

DAHEY

Airodion

Dahey rubbed his temples, aching to get out of his seat.

He had been discussing the attack on White Keep with his advisors since the news had reached them. It chilled his blood to think that Ziegan and his followers had the power to occupy White Keep—to force their queen out. Isra and the surviving members of her court had fled to Tellaridge, which was closer to Shadeshelm than Dahey cared to think about. Both cities lay close to the border separating the Autumn and Winter Court.

His council advised him to wait and see where Ziegan's forces attacked next, to wait and see if White Keep was their only objective. But Dahey knew Ziegan. He sought to claim Airodion for his dark magic. It was only a matter of time before he swept across the Winter Court and claimed Tellaridge for himself. And by then, it would be too late for Shadeshelm.

And Shadeshelm could not withstand an attack. Not when Dahey only claimed part of the fire. No, if Ziegan attacked, Shadeshelm would fall.

He prayed that Finder hadn't spread rumors about the split power over the fire and that his court just assumed Dahey not wanting to use them just came from the time it took new rulers to adjust to their magic. But he knew he hadn't convinced them all. A new ruler should have more strength than he demonstrated. And on the brink of an attack, on the brink of war, Finder was looking like a better choice for ruler. "Just tell me what we need to do."

"What we need is a miracle. If we were attacked now, and if these new fey are as strong as we assume they must be to take White Keep, then Shadeshelm will be overrun. And we will be forced to retreat, as they were," one of his generals replied.

There were other towns they could retreat to in the Autumn Court, of course. But for how long? If Ziegan's goal was to take all of Airodion, then it was only a matter of time before they were pushed out of the Autumn Court itself. And Dahey would rather die than allow that to happen.

Dahey pressed the tips of his fingers together, leaning forward to look at the maps spread across the table. "Is he intent on claiming the citadels of the court rulers? So he can rule in our stead?"

A few of the generals exchanged uncomfortable glances.

"What?" Dahey asked flatly.

"We were able to recover some deserters who wished to join Ziegan," one of the generals began. "They revealed that Ziegan intends to take the cities to show his might and draw more to his side. But he will never force them to join him. He wants all to come to him of their own volition. He claims that court rulers who join him will be spared—as will their cities."

"He wants chaos," Dahey said slowly. "How could he allow the court rulers to continue ruling when he seeks anarchy?"

The general shook his head. "You misunderstand, my king. He will spare their lives, but they will not be allowed to rule. He claims that with his new magic, all is possible. That an average faery could have the powers of a court ruler."

All eyes turned to Dahey.

"That is impossible," Dahey said, resisting the urge to wipe the sweat from his temple. "You all know that is impossible."

"We all saw what Ziegan did at the Tournament," the general replied. "Perhaps things are changing."

The suspicion in their eyes didn't escape him. It seemed too convenient that Ziegan rose to power at the same time that the magic had come to Dahey.

"I will not yield Shadeshelm to him," Dahey growled. "And I will never fall prey to his dark magic." *Not again, at least.* "Which means we must prepare for an attack now, while Ziegan's sights are still set on Tellaridge."

If he joined forces with Ziegan, he would be giving up being king forever. Ziegan would rule over them as the Starveling had. Dahey would never bow before a king again. Not when he had given up so much.

Shouts and arguments broke out at the table. Dahey banged his fist down so hard it stung. The generals and war advisors of the council fell silent.

"Shadeshelm will not fall," he growled.

The group exploded into arguments again.

"Where will we go if the city should fall?"

"We must prepare to stop deserters, to prevent them from flooding to Ziegan's side."

Dahey sent a lick of flame down the table. He slammed both hands into the wood. "Quiet," he snarled softly. "I will not let Shadeshelm fall, and I will not let my people die. I will do whatever it takes. There is no end I would not go to for this court."

He knew he spoke the truth. And he knew what he had to do.

62

KAISA

Ellevere

Kaisa kicked Sorreno, begging him to go faster.

She had to make it to Inniskeen, had to find Tarrio and Jovanna before it was too late. She hoped they would forgive her. Hoped that she deserved their forgiveness. But if they didn't, she had to keep going, even if it meant she had to do it alone.

She tore into town, making for the nearest inn. She jumped off Sorreno, shoving the reins into the hands of a serving boy tossing a pail of water outside. At his mutter of protest, she threw him a coin. He shut his mouth and led he horse to the stables.

She hurried inside, heading straight to the barmaid manning the tables. "Is there someone by the name of Tarrio staying here? Or Jovanna?"

The barmaid looked at her warily. "What's it to you?"

"I'm a friend of theirs." Kaisa lowered her hood, biting her lip as she took the gamble. "My name is Kaisa. I've come to help."

The barmaid's eyes widened. "We heard you joined the Popes' army

305

after the recent attacks on Augrim. We thought you'd abandoned the cause."

Kaisa shook her head. "The previous leader of the town did what he thought was best for his people. He convinced many to join the army. But not all. And I'm not giving up, not yet."

The barmaid gripped her arm. "Thank you, Kaisa," she whispered.

Kaisa stilled at the name. Her name, not blessed by the Twins, not Savior. Just her name.

"They're upstairs." The barmaid jerked her head up the stairs. "Third room on the left."

Kaisa nodded her thanks and rushed up the stairs. She pounded on the door.

"Go away," came Jovanna's irritated voice. "I've told you once, and I'll tell you again, we're not paying that outrageous amount for ale."

"It's me," Kaisa said.

A few whispers came from behind the door. Footsteps. Then the door creaked open, and Jovanna peered out. She pulled the door open. "Why are you here?" she asked warily.

"I made a mistake," Kaisa said. "I know that now. Can I come in?"

Jovanna looked behind her.

"Oh, you better let her in," came Tarrio's amused voice.

Jovanna opened the door wider so Kaisa could enter, and she nodded at her friend before stepping inside. Tarrio lay shirtless on the bed. He raised an eyebrow at her, a smile playing about his lips.

She raised an eyebrow right back at him. "Having a bit of fun before the end of the world, are we?"

"Oh, please," Jovanna said, rolling her eyes.

"I've been trying all my charms to no avail," Tarrio said, his voice falsely mournful.

Kaisa chuckled, but she could feel the tension in the air like a hot wool blanket. They had let her in, but they were still wary of her.

"Why are you here?" Jovanna asked, sitting on the bed next to Tarrio.

"I made a mistake," Kaisa said. "My pride made me selfish." She took a deep breath. "I never would have called myself selfish before. Not at the

Institute. And not even after we left. But once I started using the book, once I started gaining power..." She sighed, rubbing her temples. "At first, I thought I wanted this responsibility. And then, when Ishan betrayed me, I thought I didn't want it anymore. But once you left, once my people left, and I was faced with being alone, I was able to figure out what I really wanted. And that's to lead. Not by fooling people but by learning what they need. Protecting them from the Order, as I first did when I came to Augrim and prevented those children from being sold to the Institute. When I used the book for good to protect the town. I know now I was wrong to try to strip them of their faith. And I don't want to lose myself along the way. I want to lead, and I want to deserve it this time. I'm not saying I won't make mistakes, but I want you two there guiding me. I need you by my side." Her voice broke, and she finally shut her jaw to keep the rest of the words from spilling out.

Jovanna smiled at her. "You're a good leader, Kai. You can be pig headed, that's for certain. But you're back now, and that's all that matters."

Tarrio nodded. "And you have us to help you. And the numbers of the New Order as well. Ishan might have taken Augrim to join the Popes, but that's only one town. And you have more followers than that. They will come to you once they hear you haven't joined with Ishan and the rest."

Kaisa smiled, tears stinging the back of her throat. How easily her friends had forgiven her. "I don't deserve you two," she whispered.

Jovanna crossed the room and crushed her into a hug. "Of course you do. You don't have to be perfect to deserve friends."

Tarrio grinned, hopping off the bed and pulling on a shirt. "So, my benevolent leader, what's next?" He took a seat at a small wooden table, urging Jovanna and Kaisa to join him.

The two girls sat. "I think we should go north," Kaisa said. "If the Popes have sided with these dark fey, then we need allies with magic and the skills to fight them."

"But how will we find them?" Jovanna asked. "We don't know anything about the faery realm—aside from what's in your book, and it doesn't exactly detail who we should be joining forces with."

Tarrio nodded. "I've been thinking about that too. I think we need to capture one of these beasties and see what they know. Surely, they know who they're fighting against and why."

Kaisa leaned forward. "I've been thinking the same thing. The book mentioned court rulers, and I think that's a safe bet, but we have no way to send word. I say we capture one of the beasts, or better, that faery rider we've seen, hopefully there are more. We get information."

A frantic knocking on the door made all three of them look up.

"Open the door!" a voice cried, and Kaisa recognized it as the voice of the barmaid. Jovanna and Tarrio stood while Kaisa went to open the door.

"What is it?" Kaisa asked.

"Soldiers at the gates," the barmaid said breathlessly. "The Popes' army is here. They're looking for the leader of the New Order—and you."

Kaisa whirled to look at Tarrio and Jovanna, who wore twin expressions of horror.

"Ishan said the New Order had days to join them and that I was free to go," she said, fear twisting like a snake in her gut. This town wasn't prepared to fight, and the people who might still be loyal to her were back at Augrim.

She turned to the barmaid. "Tell me what your people want. We can try to flee or, at least, fight by ourselves to try not to involve the people of Inniskeen."

The barmaid shook her head. "We survived a bulk of the attacks thanks to you—news spread about using fire and music. We won't join the Popes, not after they left us to die. I can't speak for everyone, but many will help your cause."

"How many soldiers are at the gates?" Tarrio asked, strapping on his weapons as Jovanna did the same.

"Two hundred."

"That's not that many," Tarrio said. He nodded at Kaisa. "We can take them. The people of this town and the New Order will help."

"But there's more." The woman bit her lip. "They have a monster. A great hulking beast with skin like hard leather and huge limbs that could rend a house in seconds. They claim it will destroy the town if we do not surrender."

"Show me," Kaisa said.

Together, she, Jovanna, Tarrio, and the barmaid hurried through the darkened streets towards the front gates. People filled the streets, some desperately clamoring for a way to escape. Children cried, and babies wailed.

"Head towards the back of the town!" Kaisa called. "Escape through the back gates if you can."

A few members of Tarrio's New Order rushed up to him, and he gave them a few brief instructions on getting people out of the town.

They finally made it to the front gates. The four of them climbed up to a platform lookout.

Kaisa's stomach sank as she beheld rows upon rows of torches from the Pope's army.

But what disturbed her most was the great ring of people in the center, each holding a length of chain tied to a central creature.

The beast was a massive creature with grey skin, beady eyes and hulking muscles. It thrashed and roared, and a few of its guards backed away, but the taught chains held firm.

Kaisa closed her eyes. "They have a troll."

A soldier walked through the ranks, coming to a stop before the legion.

"We have come for the soldiers we were promised by Ishan, leader of Augrim. And we have also come for Kaisa and Tarrio. Give us what we desire, and we will leave."

"Ishan said that the leader of the New Order and I were allowed to go free," Kaisa called.

The guard clasped his hands behind his back. "Ishan was mistaken. Give yourself up, girl. You can't win this fight." He turned and gestured proudly to the beast in chains. "We have a troll," he said smugly.

"And only two hundred soldiers," Kaisa called, forcing her tone to have a confidence she didn't feel.

"Not just any soldiers," the man replied. "The Red Guard, specially trained to protect the Pope."

Kaisa narrowed her eyes. "And you would let so many soldiers stray this far from Pope Sersius? Rather foolish of you."

A different man stepped forward. A general, Kaisa guessed, based on his ornate armor.

"Of course not." The man lifted his head.

Pope Sersius smiled.

63

LARKEN

Airodion

Tellaridge was a city of tents.

The main city couldn't possibly hold all the refugees from White Keep, so they had taken to putting up tents on the outskirts of the snowy woods surrounding the town.

"Stay away from the woods," Saja had warned her. "They call it the Blood Forest, and it's filled with dryads who thirst for it."

Larken, Finder, and Saja had arrived days ago with Fynvarra and a few of his flyers. They were helping in any way they could. Finder and Isra were running themselves into the ground trying to take away the Winter Court fey's pain.

Fynvarra sent Arox to Ellevere, and he had returned with more troubling news: the humans had sided with Ziegan. Larken had fallen to her knees in the snow, too stunned to shed a tear. The chasm had sealed. The humans had sided with Ziegan. War unlike anything she had ever known was coming. Larken threw herself into tending for the wounded. She would not fall apart. She couldn't.

Larken stood in Isra's tent now, Finder and Saja by her side. The tent was massive, populated with a four-poster bed, a large oak table filled with papers, and a dining area. Larken frowned at the extravagance. Isra wanted to stay with the refugees of White Keep instead of in the city itself, yet she had not forgone many of the luxuries of home.

Isra sat at the table, her eyes red-rimmed and dark. Her crown was destroyed. They had seen the queen often but hadn't had a chance to speak with her. She was scrambling to find a way to take back White Keep while settling her people here and healing the wounded.

All messages sent to White Keep had come back empty. The city had fallen. Many had fled the city as soon as the fighting got thick, but many had perished. Others had followed Isra here in hopes that she would be able to protect them.

"We need to send word to the other court rulers," Finder began, but Isra held up a hand.

"You are no longer a court ruler," she said. "You have no right to speak to me as one."

"Dahey is not king, not while I still live," Finder said quietly. He made a fist, and fire sprang to life around his knuckles. His breath turned shallow, and he paled.

Isra's eyes widened. She stood up. "Impossible," she breathed.

Finder dropped his hand, the flames dying out. The color faintly returned to his cheeks. Larken eyed him. She hadn't seen him use the flames. Not once, even after he was freed of the Weeping Metal chains. The pain his magic caused him was evident.

"Dahey used Ziegan's language to take my magic," Finder said. "But he misspoke, causing a flaw in the transfer of powers. He can only use the fire magic, though, when we use it, we cause each other pain. Neither of us is King. Not yet."

"The magic chooses the ruler," Isra said, disbelief still coloring her voice.

"Not anymore." Finder met her gaze. "We have severely underestimated Ziegan's power and those who would be drawn to it. Your people have paid the price for it."

Rage bloomed through Isra's features, but Finder wasn't finished yet.

"He is going to take Airodion if we don't stop him. We need to find out more about his magic, where it comes from, if it is different than ours, and where he will strike next. News of this attack will only spread, and more will flood to his cause. He has taken magic and bent it to his will. The things we once trusted to be true aren't any longer."

Larken stared at Finder, shocked at how much he sounded like a ruler.

"We cannot hope to defeat Ziegan if you and Dahey are bound," Isra said quietly. "One of you must end with the powers, or all is lost."

Finder nodded. "I am searching for a way to fix it. But while I have left the Autumn Court in disgrace, I have not abandoned my people."

A guard burst through the tent flaps. "My lady," she said breathlessly. "King Dahey is here."

Finder turned, a muscle flickering in his jaw. He stalked out of the tent.

Larken and Saja exchanged a worried glance before darting after him, Isra and her guards following close behind.

Finder didn't respond to a word Larken said as he tore through camp. They finally reached the end of the tents, coming before a great, snowy field. In the distance stood a frozen lake, the ice a deep cerulean blue.

Dahey sat astride his white mare. His dark clothes and shock of red hair stood out in the endless expanse of white. Hatred boiled within her. A platoon of soldiers was with him, all riding horses of their own. All dressed in armor.

Fynvarra, led by Arox, came and stood stiffly beside her and Finder. He snarled softly at Dahey. To the faery's credit, he didn't flinch.

"Larken, glad to see you," Dahey called out.

"Rot in the Twins' Hell," she said curtly.

Dahey chuckled. "Still angry, I see. Greetings, cousin."

Finder said nothing, though his hand curled around the hilt of his sword.

"What are you doing here, Dahey?" Isra called warily.

"Ziegan comes for you, Isra, you know he will. He wants to create chaos in Airodion, and we cannot allow that to happen. If Tellaridge falls, it is only a matter of time before Shadeshelm does as well."

"Tellaridge cannot withstand an attack from Ziegan," Isra said quietly. Her guards shifted behind her.

Dahey nodded. "I know. Neither can Shadeshelm, from what I have heard about the attack on White Keep. Which is why I have a proposal for you. You and your people are welcome at Shadeshelm, as are you, cousin, if you agree to bow before me and help defend the city."

Silence. Cold wind blistered across the field, numbing Larken's cheeks. Dahey wanted their help. Wanted *Finder's* help. He must believe that Shadeshelm was in danger.

"No," Finder said.

Larken glanced at him in alarm. He couldn't mean that. Dahey was offering them a truce of sorts. She didn't trust him, of course, but this could be a way for Finder to return with grace to his court and win them back by defending the city.

"Come now, Finder. You don't wish to see your court destroyed," Dahey scoffed. "Ziegan's forces are wicked. All the courts are at risk."

"I will help defend my people, but I will never bow to you."

"The magic chose me, cousin. Accept it."

"Liar!" Finder screamed.

Dahey's guards looked uncomfortable. Were any of them still loyal? Why hadn't they tried to help Finder when he had needed them?

"You never deserved to be king," Dahey spat.

Finder screamed, hurling a ball of fire at Dahey's face. Dahey's horse reared, and he clung to her neck. The flames dissipated. Dahey's eyes blazed with rage as he threw himself from his horse's back and stalked across the field towards them. Finder stumbled, the magic taking a toll.

"Both of you, stop!" Larken cried, but it was too late.

Dahey gritted his teeth and sent a whip of flame towards Finder. Dahey fell to his knees, and Finder's hand shot out, engulfing Dahey in fire. Finder screamed, sweat pouring down his brow. The snow melted around them.

"Stop it!" Larken ran towards Finder, but Fynvarra blocked her with his tail.

Do not interfere, he warned.

Larken bit her cheek, watching as Dahey and Finder fought. If one could even call it that. Each time they dealt a blow, they seemed to do more damage to themselves than their opponent.

They stayed a short distance away, hurling fire at each other from across the field. The fire didn't seem to be able to harm either of them, but even using the smallest bit of magic caused them agony. Dahey was gasping for breath, Finder's own breathing laborious. Sweat poured from both of them, and Dahey had to pause to vomit into the grass. It was horrifying to watch. Split between them, the fire was nowhere near as powerful as it had been with Finder. They had been reduced to this.

"Why can't you just let me have this?" Dahey screamed, his voice hoarse. "You never wanted to rule. If it was anyone else, you would have given up your powers in an instant."

"You stabbed me," Finder bellowed. "You tortured me. Bound my powers to you."

"You can't protect those you love. You can't, so I had to," Dahey seethed.

Finder shot another burning cylinder at Dahey, but Dahey brushed it away with a flick of his hand.

"You go on and on about Embryn. You fought the Starveling for her, you removed yourself from court because you couldn't bear to be reminded of her. You couldn't save her even with your powers. You are *weak*, Finder." Dahey's brown gaze lifted, and Larken was taken aback by the sheer malice that glimmered within them. Blood trickled from the corner of Dahey's mouth, and he wiped it away. "If I had your powers then, I would have been able to save her."

Finder screamed, tearing across the field and tackling his cousin around the middle. They thrashed in the grass, tearing and clawing into each other.

"They're going to kill each other," Isra said.

Larken's heart ached as she watched them fight. Dahey had suffered all his life, and the powers he could have used to free himself of his pain had been given to another. Someone who didn't want them. Someone who, in Dahey's eyes, had misused them at every turn and had failed.

She pushed Fynvarra's tail away and set out across the grass. No matter how much she hated Dahey, she understood him. And though their paths were wildly different, she knew how it felt when the person you loved most in the world was chosen for a better life and you were not. But she also knew that it rarely ever was a better life. And that everything came with a cost. Finder knew the price of his magic—Dahey did not. But she understood Dahey in that moment more than she ever had.

She waited for the jealously to come, expected it to burn inside her when Dahey's words about Embryn had set Finder off so drastically. But she didn't feel it. Finder loved Embryn, she knew that. But she also knew he hadn't lied to her when he said he only loved her as a friend.

Sheer heat poured from both males, rippling in the air. Finder had Dahey around the neck, choking him.

"Finder, stop." She grabbed him by the shoulders, trying to pull him back. Finder let go of Dahey. He whipped around faster than she could blink and shoved her, his hands colliding with her chest and face. She saw the flames that licked from his palms.

Pain seared across her face and chest, and she screamed, falling backwards. Fynvarra roared, hearing her anguish, and seconds later, Saja was by her side.

Larken cradled her cheek with shaking fingers.

Fire. Burn. Pain. Flesh. Agony. Darkness.

Tears streamed down her face as sobs racked her body. She was going to die. The fire was going to consume her, peel her flesh back from her bones and turn her to ash, but slowly, oh so slowly, to make sure she felt every second—

"What have you done?" Saja snarled. Her vision blurred with tears, but she could still see Finder's face wide with shock and regret. Dahey scrambled backwards, but he didn't flee.

"I'm sorry, Larken," Finder breathed, reaching a hand toward her. She sobbed harder, turning away from him, and his beautiful face twisted with agony.

"Don't touch her," Saja said. "You might hurt her again."

"I didn't know it was you," Finder moaned. "Let me heal you, love, please," he said, reaching for her again. She shook her head, twisting back in Saja's lap with a sob.

"Isra!" Saja called. The Winter Court Queen appeared a second later, crouching by Larken's side. She laid a cool hand on Larken's arm.

"No. I'm going to heal her," Finder said.

"You're the one who caused this, you fool," Isra snapped.

"I know," Finder said, his demeanor finally calming. "Which is why I must be the one to do it."

Larken clutched her face, her stomach roiling as she felt the blisters there. The pain would ebb for a mere second then explode once more in pulsating bursts. She slipped away into an abyss of her own pain. She didn't care who healed her. She just wanted the pain to end.

Finder passed a hand over her wounds. His hands shook, sweat glistening on his brow. Larken's back bowed, a silent scream on her lips as the blisters burst, new skin healing over them. Saja murmured apologies to her as his huge hands came to lay on either side of her neck, holding her still so Finder could work.

Finally, it was done. Larken sagged into Saja's embrace with a sob. Saja lifted her into his arms and carried her back to Isra's tent, leaving Finder and Dahey there in the dirt. He laid her on Isra's bed.

Fynvarra shoved his way into the tent, winding his lithe body around the bed. "I'm here," he said. "No one will disturb you. Rest now."

Her eyes closed, and she knew no more.

64

KAISA

Ellevere

Kaisa nearly tumbled from the platform, but Jovanna and Tarrio steadied her.

"What's he doing here?" Jovanna hissed in disbelief.

"Quashing this rebellion at its source," Tarrio muttered. "The New Order and Kaisa. Two birds with one stone. And he does it in front of an audience so they can spread the word about his might."

Kaisa knew firsthand how the Popes trained, she had seen it herself during her time at the Institute. Pope Sersius might have a legion of highly specialized Red Guards protecting him, but that didn't mean he let himself fall out of fighting shape. He was just as trained as the rest of them, perhaps even more so.

The first Popes had made a name for themselves and the Order of the Twins through crusading. Now, centuries later, the Popes kept up that fighting spirit, making sure they were always ready for the war against heresy.

"I heard you've taken something that belongs to me, Kaisa," Pope

318

Sersius called. "I would like it returned to me. Personally, if you would. Don't make this a struggle."

Boom. Boom. Boom. The crackling sound of splintering wood filled the air.

Only one thing could be making a noise like that. Screams rose, accompanied by the sound of pounding feet.

The troll was inside the city. She was out of time.

She drew her sword, throwing herself down the platform and charging out into the streets beyond.

Some people screamed, running away from the action while others brandished weapons and ran toward the fray. Kaisa's heart swelled as she took in these people that were willing to fight to save their town. She caught glimpses of New Order soldiers clashing with the Pope's Red Guard. Sersius wasn't among them, likely waiting for the troll to clear out as many of them as possible.

As though she had spoken it into being, the troll charged around the corner, smashing its boulder-like fists into every building it came across. It crashed into people, sending them flying, their broken bodies hitting buildings and cobblestones.

She had read about these creatures. Dull, lumbering beasts distracted by shiny objects. They had the sentience of toddlers. But what they lacked in brains, they made up for in brute strength.

"What can I do?" Tarrio cried, running up to her side.

"I need you with the New Order dealing with the Popes' men. If Sersius comes, avoid him at all costs. He might be a Pope, but he's a highly trained soldier."

"I won't leave you to face this alone," Tarrio growled.

"I'm not alone," Kaisa said, a small smile touching her lips. "I have Jovanna."

Jovanna nodded stiffly from her side, raising her weapon. Hollis and Kaisa had taught her, and she had trained along with the rest of the town.

Oh, Hollis, she thought. She might not believe in the Twins, but she hoped that if there was a life after death, that he was happy. He had made mistakes, but so had she.

She shook herself. She didn't have time to think about that now.

"You'll be most helpful to me elsewhere." She gripped Tarrio's arm, not taking her eyes off the troll as it lumbered closer, distracted by every torch and glint of metal. Good. The more distracted it was, the easier it would be to kill.

"Be careful," Tarrio warned, then he dashed into the crowd.

Jovanna pressed close to her side. "I don't know if sending him away was the best idea, Kai. I'm not the strongest fighter, and I don't want something to happen to you because of me."

Kaisa's heart clenched at the worry in Jovanna's voice. She looked at her friend, the one who had stood by her through everything. "I need you here with me. I have a plan. Both of us are making it out of this, okay?"

Jovanna gave her a determined nod.

Kaisa searched around until she found what she was looking for: a shield, likely abandoned by its bearer. She shoved the shield into Jovanna's arms.

"It's drawn to anything shiny," Kaisa said.

The troll was busy looking in one of the glass windows of a shop, drool coming out its mouth. It smashed a huge hand through the glass, pulling out a fistful of glittery cloth.

"Wave the shield around and make as much noise as you can," Kaisa said. "But keep out of the way. It's slow and clumsy, but it's strong. While it's distracted, I'll go for the killing blow."

She didn't mention that the most vulnerable part of a troll's body was on the back of its neck...twelve feet in the air. She would have to find a way to bring the beast to its knees or find a way to climb it.

"Ready?" she asked.

"Ready," Jovanna replied. "Come this way, beast," Jovanna yelled, beating her sword on her shield in an attempt to get the stupid creature's attention.

The troll turned, its deep eyes locking on Jovanna's shield. It dropped its fistful of glittery cloth and lumbered forward with a grunt. Kaisa ran, pressing herself against the buildings.

Jovanna kept pounding her sword on her shield, drawing the creature closer. Kaisa sucked in a breath as the troll lumbered past her, but the beast paid her no mind.

Around her, people screamed. She caught glimpses of the Order's soldiers in the midst, but they gave the troll a wide berth. Without the chains containing it, the creature was as likely to turn on them as the town. She thought she heard Tarrio shout. Members of the New Order poured into the streets, clashing with the soldiers.

Thankfully, none of that was enough to distract the troll, which was now on a mission to acquire the shiny object clutched in Jovanna's hands.

It roared, reaching for Jovanna, but she darted away. The troll spun, groaning angrily. Kaisa eased herself out of her hiding spot, staying directly behind the creature. Her eyes locked with her target: the soft patch of skin behind the beast's neck. But how would she get to it?

Jovanna darted away again, now screaming obscenities at the creature while banging her sword louder upon the shield. The beast swung an arm, howling, and Jovanna ducked, her face pale when she popped back up. Kaisa had to hurry—the beast might be slow, but it was only a matter of time before it got lucky and one of its blows landed.

The beast whirled, and Kaisa dove behind it. The beast reached for Jovanna again, and this time, Kaisa took her chance and stabbed her sword behind the beast's kneecap.

She expected the beast to fall, but to her horror, she realized that her sword had barely sunk into the creature's flesh. The beast roared, and before Kaisa could move, it backhanded her with a massive fist, sending her flying into the nearest building.

The air whooshed out of her as she crumpled to the ground. Everything hurt, and tears leaked down her face from shock. Her mouth gaped open as she struggled to breathe. The beast roared, shuffling closer, but Jovanna dove in front of her, raising her shield.

"Jovanna, no," Kaisa groaned, struggling to sit up.

The beast's eyes locked on the shield.

"Run, Kaisa!" Jovanna screamed. The beast lunged. Jovanna tried to dart away, but she was moments too slow. The beast caught her in one of its huge fists, howling triumphantly.

"No," Kaisa wheezed, horror engulfing her. She wouldn't watch Jovanna die. She couldn't. Not the one person who had chosen her repeatedly, even when she didn't deserve it.

Jovanna cried out as the beast squeezed her. The troll growled in confusion, shaking her, unsure where the shiny metal object it had been chasing went.

She didn't have much time. Kaisa hoisted herself to her feet. Her back spasmed, but she gritted her teeth, forcing one foot in front of the other.

"Here!" Kaisa shouted hoarsely. "Here, you stupid beast!"

But the troll had its prize in its clutches, and it would not be swayed. Kaisa shuffled closer, but her movements were too slow. "Here," she cried desperately.

Jovanna's gaze met hers, tears streaming down her friend's face as the troll squeezed her. "Run," Jovanna breathed.

The troll slammed her into the ground.

Kaisa screamed. The troll bent over Jovanna's body, peering down at it curiously. Kaisa ran at the beast, hurling herself onto its crouched back. The troll grunted in confusion, but Kaisa dug her nails into its knobby flesh, climbing up the creature's back. It straightened, swiping its hands behind its back in an attempt to reach her, but it wasn't flexible enough.

Kaisa reached the top of its bald head. Screaming, she plunged her sword into the soft patch of skin on the back of the creature's neck.

The beast gurgled, then slumped forward. Kaisa leapt off, circling around its great head. The troll's eyes were glassy. She'd done it. She had killed him.

But she could feel no joy. She rushed to Jovanna's side, falling to her knees in the dirt. Her friend's face was streaked with dirt and blood. The shield was clutched to her chest.

"Jo," Kaisa sobbed, gently touching her friend's face. Jovanna didn't move.

"I'm so sorry," Kaisa wailed. "I never should have asked you to do this. It's all my fault."

She buried her face in Jovanna's chest, letting the cold metal cut into her cheek. She had lost one of the last people she cared about, one of the only people who cared about her. She didn't deserve to be a leader. Not when she couldn't protect her friends, not when she sent them into danger so willingly.

"We did it," came Jovanna's hoarse whisper.

Kaisa jerked up, trying not to let hope flood her. But Jovanna's eyes were open, staring at her.

"Jo," Kaisa whispered, stroking her friend's hair. "How—I saw the troll —" She squeezed her eyes shut, not ready to relive that memory. Ever.

"He didn't slam me down that hard," Jovanna said with a smile. "Didn't want to damage his shiny present." She pushed the shield from her neck. "I'm okay, really. Just stunned."

"We did it," Kaisa whispered, unable to hold back her smile. "Just the two of us."

Jovanna nodded. "I didn't doubt us for a second."

Kaisa grinned and squeezed her friend's hand.

"Kaisa!"

Her head jerked up at Tarrio's shout. She helped Jovanna to her feet as the blood-stained leader of the New Order rushed towards them. "Find somewhere to rest," she murmured to Jovanna. "You're too weak to fight anymore."

Jovanna reluctantly nodded, which told Kaisa her injuries might be worse than she let on. "What is it?" she called to Tarrio.

"It's Pope Sersius," Tarrio panted. "He's entered the city. And he's looking for you."

Kaisa nodded grimly. She knew she would have to face the Pope eventually. And if it was to be this night, then so be it.

"Let's end this," she growled.

65

LARKEN

Airodion

Larken jolted awake in Isra's tent. She reached immediately for her face, but pain didn't meet her fingertips, only smooth skin. She was reminded horribly of waking up after Finder had burned her. No physical scars had remained, only the ones seared into her mind.

Finder was hunched over the bed, asleep, his hand outstretched. She wanted to feel some kind of tenderness toward him for laying by her side, watching over her, but she didn't. Heat simmered beneath her skin.

She tossed the covers aside, glancing around the room for a pitcher of water.

Finder stirred, lifting his auburn head. "Larken, You're all right."

Anger flared inside her, her desire for the water forgotten. "I am not *all right*," she snapped. "Every single day for weeks I have struggled with my fear of the flame. I can't see a damn torch anymore without feeling like I'm going to faint. Do you know how humiliating it is? How inconvenient? No." She shook her head. "Not inconvenient. It's terrifying. I see fire, and my mind starts spiraling before I can stop it. And it just keeps spiraling and spiraling until I feel I will drown in it, and I can't breathe. I

324

fear I will die from the flames even if they aren't touching me. Sometimes, I think I'll die from the fear alone."

Finder stood, his eyes glazed with pain. "I'm sorry."

"I aways try to get you out of that dark place when you go to it," Larken said hoarsely, "but I'm tired of going there when I get hurt too. And I'm not going to do it again." She hugged herself.

"I know," Finder said. "I know, Larken. And I hope you know I'm grateful for it. And I hope you know I wish you didn't have to pull me out of that dark place. But I'm glad you do."

Something pulled inside her chest, like a cramped muscle. "Where are you when I'm hurting? When I'm lost in the dark?" Tears spilled down her cheeks. "There's been no one to face the darkness with me. I'm alone. And sometimes I don't think I can do it."

Finder crossed the room in a few strides and cupped her cheeks. "I'm so sorry, Larken. It took me awhile to find myself again, but I'm here now."

Larken looked in his eyes, at the pain there. She looked for the faery she had come so fiercely to love. He might think he had escaped the darkness, but he hadn't. He was still struggling, still healing, just as she was.

She stepped back. "I've been trying. But when I felt the sear of your flames today, I was thrown deeper into that darkness. I shouldn't have gotten between you two. I know that. But you and Dahey were going to kill each other."

"That's how this has to end," Finder said coldly.

"Killing Dahey will destroy you," Larken said. "And it will destroy everyone around you. Dahey asked for help, your court needs your help, and you were willing to turn them away. You were so blinded in your attempt to cause him pain that you burned me."

"It was an accident," Finder pleaded.

Larken took a deep breath. She knew Finder hadn't meant to hurt her. And she knew she was partially to blame for getting between him and Dahey. She had come so far in her healing. She had experienced setbacks, yes, but she was trying. She needed Finder to try. They both couldn't stay in that dark place forever, and they couldn't rely on each other to get them out. They needed to face some battles, heal some of their wounds, alone.

Her heart climbed into her throat. She didn't want to face it alone. But all her lessons with Saja, Roone, and Fynvarra, had shown her that no one could do her healing for her.

She wanted to be with Finder. She had thought once they got him back things would be easy between them, that they could share all the tender moments that Saja and Roone had, all the easy intimacy. But she had work to do on her healing—she knew that. And Finder did too.

He had to mend some part of his relationship with Dahey.

"There has to be another way with Dahey," Larken insisted. "There must be a way to fix this without either of your deaths."

"No," Finder said, shaking his head. "No, Dahey will pay for what he did."

"He will," Larken said, stepping forward and placing her hands on his chest. "But not like this. Not with you killing him."

"You have no idea how it feels," Finder said, his voice lowering, "to have your own kin betray you. Dahey was like a brother to me."

"You must try to see things from his side," Larken pleaded.

Finder took a step back, pulling away from her touch. "You can't seriously be taking his side," he said incredulously.

Her stomach dropped. She didn't want Finder to think she was siding with Dahey. She wanted to see him punished almost as much as Finder did. "Of course not." Larken's brow furrowed, searching for the right words. "I'm only saying that the only way to move past this is to try to see his reasoning. You said yourself that you care for your court. War with Ziegan is coming. Like it or not, Dahey holds power in your court. Working with him is in your best interest, and it's in the best interest of your people. You can't cast them aside."

Finder wanted revenge; she knew that. She knew that Dahey deserved to be punished. But she knew Finder, and she knew that putting his blade through Dahey's heart would cleave his own in two. He would never be the same if he killed his kin.

"I will never move past this," Finder said quietly. He turned his back to her and walked out of the tent.

Larken's breath caught, anxiety spearing through her chest. "Finder, wait—"

But when she pulled back the tent flap, he had already disappeared.

Larken drank. She shoveled down as much of Isra's food as she could stomach. Perhaps she had been wrong. Perhaps Finder should just kill Dahey and be done with it. He wanted revenge, she could understand that.

But revenge wouldn't end his torment. He was truly in pain from the rift between them. And killing Dahey wouldn't resolve it.

Saja pulled back the tent flap, Fynvarra snaking his head in beside him. "I just saw Finder storming through camp. What happened?"

She told them what she had said about Dahey.

Saja sighed, scrubbing his beard. "There is some truth to your words, though I don't think Finder wished to hear it."

"I know," she murmured. She rubbed her arm absentmindedly. "But I think he needs to hear it from you as well."

Saja nodded. "I'll go find him."

He ducked out of the tent.

Fynvarra stayed, and the air grew tense. They hadn't spoken at length since she had blocked him from using the fire. Larken fidgeted, unsure what to say.

You shouldn't have come between him and Dahey, Fynvarra said at last.

I wasn't going to let them kill each other.

They don't need you meddling, Fynvarra said coldly.

Larken glared at him. *Just say what you truly mean. You're still angry with me after I blocked you from using the fire.*

Of course I am, he snarled. *That creature could have killed us both because of your fear of the flame. I rely on you, Larken. I have no choice. You need to work harder. You cannot let your fear control you like that—it affects us both.*

This isn't about you, Larken exploded. Tears sprang to her eyes. *How can you say I'm not trying? You know I am.* Her voice broke, even in mind-speak. Tears spilled down her cheeks, and she wiped them furiously away. She was still upset from her conversation with Finder. She knew she should tell Fynvarra that they should wait to speak until she had a chance to calm herself, but her heart was pounding too loud in her chest. Her breath quickened, and she clenched her fists.

When she looked at Fynvarra, all she felt was anger. Anger for the words he had spoken, yes, but anger at the fire he held inside him. The unquenchable flame that burned and took and could not be put out. She couldn't believe she had ever ridden him, ever trusted him with her life.

She couldn't risk being so near Fynvarra's fire. It would kill her. And if the flames didn't, then her fear would.

"I don't care where you go," Larken said, closing off her mind from him. "Go back to First Forge. Go help Shadeshelm. I don't care. I only needed you to save Finder. I don't need you anymore."

Fynvarra blew a puff of smoke toward her. The smell nearly choked her with fear. "You don't mean that."

"Leave," she gasped. She knew she should consider her words carefully, that she might say something she regretted, but she couldn't stop them from tumbling out of her. "I can't stand the sight of you. Knowing what you have inside you, the fire, how willing you are to use it—I can't bear it. I don't want to see you ever again."

"Larken—" Fynvarra gave a small whine. "I shouldn't have said those things. I was just angry about you blocking me. Fire is a part of me, but you know I would never hurt you, not even as Finder has."

"Get out," she said. She couldn't help it—the anger felt good. Better than fear. And she had been afraid for so long.

Fynvarra growled softly and left. Larken shoved down her guilt that he would have to call upon someone else to guide him around camp.

Night fell. She asked the guards for a tent of her own. The cold bit into her skin. She had become used to the Autumn Court climate during her time at First Forge. The chill here had seeped into her soul. Did being so near Isra cause her to feel this way? Or was she merely cursed to feel this pain forever? Larken wasn't sure. But she didn't think her pain was solely influenced by Isra. Not all of it, at least.

She had the guard lead her to her new tent. It was on the edge of the forest, a few paces away from the other tents, likely for privacy. She thanked the guard and collapsed on her sleeping roll. Tears welled in her eyes once more and she let them come, great sobbing gasps that racked her body.

Guilt gnawed at her heart. She had meant what she said about Dahey, but she should have searched for better words when she had spoken to Finder. And Fynvarra... She rubbed her hands over her face. She would find Fynvarrra in the morning and mend things with him. She had said things she didn't mean. She took a deep breath, exhaling through her mouth.

Twins, you really had to argue with everyone, didn't you? She sighed, rolling onto her side, utterly spent. She would face her troubles tomorrow. For now, she had to sleep.

Just as she began to drift off, hands grabbed her, startling her awake. She thrashed, trying to scream, but a gag was stuffed in her mouth, and a bag was thrown over her head. More hands dragged her out of her tent and into the snow beyond.

66

LARKEN

Airodion

"Hurry," a voice snarled.

"Help me with her arms," another grunted. There were several voices that sounded fey, Were they working for Ziegan? Had he come for her?

Larken thrashed, pushing against her captors, but it was no use. They were too strong. They hauled her through the snow. Larken shivered, her shift and cloak doing nothing to stop the chill.

The sounds from the camp quickly faded away. Fear rose in her throat, her heart pounding. Saja was looking for Finder, and she had pushed Fynvarra away. Now she was alone. Completely helpless without them.

A sob rose in her throat before she could stop it. She couldn't see where they were going, had no hope of finding her way back. What did they want from her?

Rough hands shoved her down. Her knees cracked against something hard—stone?

"You won't be needing this," a female voice cooed, ripping her cloak off. Larken shivered, resisting to the urge to cross her arms across her chest.

"Get the wood," one of the voices called. Footsteps shuffled around her. Larken twisted her head, though she knew she had no hope of seeing through the hood.

More scuffling and sounds she could not identify. She could not stop her trembling. She couldn't speak—couldn't ask them what they wanted or even beg them to let her go.

"Don't move," a voice snarled.

Larken clenched her trembling hands in her lap. Her teeth chattered around the gag.

"Remove your hood," another voice called, female this time.

Larken pulled off the hood and ripped the gag from her mouth. Her eyes widened as she took in the scene around her. She was encircled by a ring of branches, and seven fey stood outside the circle. Two pointed crossbows at her. The others held torches. Winter Court soldiers, judging by their uniforms.

She pressed her hands into the ground, no... not ground. She looked down, her stomach pooling with horror. Ice. Blue, even in the moonlight, streaked with silver cracks. The ice moaned, thin—too thin for her to be kneeling on.

She tried to rise, but the ice moaned in protest, the cracks spider-webbing beneath her feet.

"I wouldn't do that," the female called, suppressing a grin. She was beautiful with red hair and green eyes.

Larken swallowed. "What do you want?"

A male Winter Court soldier took a step forward. "It's your fault White Keep was destroyed."

Larken shook her head. "No, no—I had nothing to do with that. I wasn't even there."

"Our queen took you in, and you led Ziegan straight to her after you freed Finder during that show in the arena. You control the firedrake. He could have turned the tides, but you left us."

"I'm sorry," Larken said, lifting her hands. She had to bite through her tongue not to lash out at them and scream that it wasn't her job to protect White Keep, that she wasn't anyone special, that Isra had failed them, not her, but the fey before her were already so angry—she knew she had to hold her tongue.

"I'm sorry," she repeated. "Tell me what I can do to make it right. We came here—Finder and Fynvarra and I came here to help Isra, to help her reclaim White Keep. We can help you."

The male guard lifted his sword. "And where is the firedrake now?"

Larken swallowed. "Back at camp."

"Liar," he snarled. "Disgusting human filth. He left you to return to First Forge. He told the guards himself. And now you are ours to do with as we please." He set the torch to the branches.

Flames roared to life, encircling her. Larken choked. She scrambled backwards, but there was nowhere to go. The fey before her laughed. She wanted to scream, but she could barely breathe, could barely think.

The fire roared, but not loud enough to drown out the moans of the ice. Larken scrambled to her feet. The ice cracked beneath her, growing more unstable by the minute.

"Please," she gasped.

The fey just laughed, backing away.

She glanced around. The branches were so thick. The flames were so high. She would have to jump through it. She would have to try. Bracing herself, she prepared to run the last few steps to the burning branches.

The ice collapsed beneath her, plunging her into icy darkness.

67

LARKEN

Airodion

Pain flooded her, squeezing the air from her lungs.

The shock blinded her. She opened her mouth, desperate for air, but there was none. She could see nothing but the murky darkness of the lake.

I'm going to die. Panic sparked to life inside her, and she thrashed, trying to swim. But she could scarcely tell which way was up and which way was down.

The hole, look for the hole where you fell through. She glanced desperately at the surface, but she could find no discoloring, nothing to alert her of where she fell through.

There. A faint sliver of light. She kicked and kicked, forcing her arms to move. Her lungs burned and burned, the pain nearly blinding her. Her hands lifted up, up—

Slamming into the unforgiving sheet of ice above.

Larken cried out, unable to stop herself from losing precious air. She slammed her fists against the ice, but it was no use. The ice was unyielding. She slammed her fists against it again and again, but it would not break. It was as if her hands moved too slow in the water, and she could not make them go any faster.

Give up. There was no one coming to save her. There was a reason she had never been able to face anything alone in Airodion. It was because she was too weak. She needed the fey to protect her, help her, save her, and now they were gone. They were gone, and she would die for it.

Darkness ebbed at her vision. She didn't have long now. She should just take a breath, speed up the process. She had always thought drowning would be peaceful, but this was agony. Her empty lungs were full of knives and the cold sliced into her core.

Give up. Her fists slackened. She began to sink.

Her panic had ebbed, leaving her only with her thoughts. It was fitting, somehow, that it wasn't fire that killed her, but ice.

You were willing to try. You were willing to jump through the fire to save yourself a moment ago, and now you give up. Why?

Because it was easier. Because she was tired. Because she didn't want to live in the darkness anymore, didn't want to live with the panic every time she saw a flame, and now that the end was here, so plainly laid out before her, it felt like fate.

Her eyes drifted shut. She thought the cold would go away, but it hadn't left her, hadn't turned her numb. It reminded her that she was still alive. That the pain would be with her until the end.

Her head jerked. The pain hadn't left. It should enrage her; she should want a moment's peace before the end. Didn't she deserve that? But the pain hadn't left her.

She had spent weeks running from the fire. Hating it. Despising the way that something so ordinary could upend her entire life. How ashamed she was of her fear. Of her pain.

But she had been willing to run toward it. After all this time, she had been willing to run *toward* the fire to save herself. Because, while it might influence her life, make it difficult or painful at times, fear was not her whole life. It was only one part of it.

She had lost Brigid. Lost Madden. Lost Finder for a time and had been hurt by him. Faced her fears and failed. She had made mistakes.

But she had made friends here in Airodion. Friends who she now considered family. She'd saved Finder's life again. She had ridden on the back of a firedrake when no other human had.

There was more pain to come—she knew that. The pain she felt now was proof of it. But pain and fear did not make life not worth living. It was numbness she feared. For when no pain came at all, she knew her life was over.

She wanted to see her friends again. She wanted to see the skies from Fynvarra's back. She wanted to face the fire. The darkness might never leave her, but she could face it. Every day, she could face it. She wanted the pain. She wanted the joy. She wanted to live.

She kicked her legs, willing her lungs to hold on just a little longer. She swam towards a tiny patch of light visible on the surface.

She pounded her fists on the ice. She moved along the ice, following the light, pounding and pounding.

Until her fists finally broke through.

She thrashed and kicked like an animal until her head finally broke the surface, and she took lungful after lungful of air.

68

——————

LARKEN

Airodion

The reality of the cold caught up with her, making her veins turn sludgy with fear. She needed to get out of the water, or her decision to live would mean nothing.

She dug her nails into the ice, furiously kicking her legs, trying to wiggle her way out of the water. She squinted at the shoreline, but her captors were gone.

Crack. The chunk of ice she had been clinging to broke off, unable to support her weight. She cursed as frigid water splashed against her face. Huffing out a breath, she dug her fingers into the ice again. She kicked her legs so hard they burned. She pulled herself onto her elbows.

Crack. The ice split off again. Larken screamed in frustration, falling backwards into the water.

"Come on," she panted. She paddled herself forward once more. She dug her nails in so hard she feared they would break off. Gritting her teeth, she kicked her legs, pulling herself up—then shifted her weight to her forearms. The ice held.

Gasping, she slithered forward, still kicking her legs as hard as she

336

could. Inch by inch, she moved across the ice. She pulled one of her legs up onto the ice and then the other, scrambling forward. Sobbing, she crawled the rest of the way. She got shakily to her feet, half expecting the ice to crumble away to nothing. It held.

She ran, tearing across the ice as fast as she dared. Her bare feet thumped against the ice, shooting stabbing pains up her foot from the numbing cold.

Her feet hit land—snowy land—but still land. She collapsed where the line of trees began. She expected to feel some kind of immediate relief after getting out of the water, but the cold was just as furious as it had been before, cutting and biting into her.

Her teeth chattered. She was free of the water, but the danger hadn't passed yet. She had no idea how to get back to camp, her sense of direction muddled by the bag her captors had placed over her head. She had nothing on but a soaking wet shift.

She wrapped her arms around herself, walking further into the trees. She would just have to start walking and pray they hadn't taken her too far away from Tellaridge.

A glimmer of light caught her eye. She squinted, then her eyes widened.

Torches. Two of them, plunged into the ground like stakes. She forced herself to run, dropping to her knees before the torches. Why her captors had left them behind, Larken didn't know, but she was glad they did.

She would have to make a fire.

A skill you thought utterly pointless until now. She sucked in a breath through her teeth. She had to hurry. She wouldn't last the night in the state she was in.

She picked up one of the torches, trying not to hold her face so close to the heat that she burned herself. A small glimmer of pride bloomed in her chest. She wasn't afraid of the flame. She might never be able to forget or move on from what happened to her, but it wasn't choking her as it had before. And maybe that would change. But for now, she was grateful for the time she had without the fear.

She dragged as many dry branches as she could find to the center of the camp. Her foot caught on something. Her cloak. Larken picked it up, scarcely believing her eyes. She smiled.

She used her torch to light the logs. The fire sparked to life, growing into a steady blaze. Shrugging off her shift, she tossed it aside. Larken wrapped the cloak around herself, huddling down on a log. She tucked her feet in, desperately trying to rub warmth back into them.

Dark splatters in the snow caught her attention.

Blood.

Her stomach clenched. She stood, following the trail. She reached a clearing surrounded by slender, ice laden trees. Her eyes tracked the blood droplets to the center of the clearing, where it became a pool. To the heap of bodies.

Larken froze, her eyes widening. Her captors hadn't left the torches and her cloak there on accident—they had been attacked.

And they had lost—for their seven mutilated bodies lay in a heap before her. They lay perfectly surrounded by the trees, as though they had been artfully placed there.

Larken turned to run, but then the trees *moved*. Bodies peeled from the trunks, thick branches still connecting them to the base as they stepped into the snow, surrounding her.

Larken's chest heaved as she watched the tree fey surround her. They resembled the fey, though they were taller. Their skin resembled snowy tree bark, and they had a wild array of branches for hair. Plates of bark encased them like armor. But it was their faces that were most unsettling, twisted and knobbed like the trunk of a tree, with only a slit for a mouth. More tree-like than fey.

Their roots began to move, wrapping around the bodies, pulling limbs beneath the soil until they were half-buried. Larken swallowed. Would she be next? Survive the water only to be eaten by tree fey?

"Why did you kill them?" she asked slowly. Twins, her feet ached. They ached so much she could barely stand.

"We saw what they did to you," the tree before her rasped. The voice was neither male nor female, merely ancient. "We do not permit killing in the Blood Forest—only we are allowed to take lives here. It is our territory and our right. They knew the risk in coming here, and they chose to anyway. For that, their lives were forfeit."

"It's called the Blood Forest. You'd think they'd know to stay away," Larken muttered.

The tree faery tilted its head back slowly and laughed, the sound like the creaking of branches in the wind. "We do not kill all who come here. We mainly feast on animals, but those who bring violence to these woods are killed. They thought they would be able to get away with their crime. They were wrong."

"So you kill those who kill," Larken mused. "I suppose I should thank you for ending my tormentors." A tiny flash of guilt pierced her heart as she looked at the fey's half submerged bodies, at their glazed-over eyes. Did they deserve to die for trying to kill her? She was angry at them for what they had done, but the part of her that had saved Finder all that time ago was in her still. She didn't like senseless death, even for revenge.

She wrapped her arms around herself, willing her teeth to stop chattering enough for her to get her next words out. "Are you going to kill me?"

The tree shook its head slowly. "No, human. We know who you are. The girl who saved Finder and Fynvarra. You allied yourself with a drake, would not allow him to be sacrificed to save Finder. We saw you go into the water, and we saw you come out."

Another tree tromped closer, still attached to its trunk by several ropey branches. "Water is the sacred element of the Winter Court," it rasped. "It can heal, but it can also kill. Not all survive it, and those who do come out stronger."

The first tree turned its knobby eyes back to Larken. It reached out a hand, touching a long, branchy finger to her chest. Larken gasped at the contact.

The tree breathed in, its branches and trunk a few feet away trembling slightly. "We can sense your spirit. It is fierce, but more than that, it is kind. You have survived by your own merit, not by tearing down others."

"That's not true," Larken said. "I've hurt the people I love." Her heart squeezed at the thought of Fynvarra.

The tree tilted its head. "Mistakes do not change who you are inside. And mistakes can be forgiven when the heart is righted. You are not the same girl who went into the water."

No, she was not.

"We will return you to Tellaridge." The tree gestured to the pile of bodies. "Take their clothing. They will not need it any longer. We cannot offer you much, but we can offer you our blessing. Nothing will harm you."

"Our kin have been corrupted by Ziegan. He takes creatures and turns them in to what they are not. He has taken other dryads and turned them into monsters."

Larken tugged on the clothing of the dead fey. The trees returned to their trunks, stepping inside and pulling the bark closed like one would a curtain. They returned to their positions around the clearing, but their branches moved, pointing the way.

Larken listened to the trees, following their signs. The rattle of branches, the shape of the bark, the twist of the roots. All led her on a clear path, until she reached the outskirts of Tellaridge's camp.

She laid her palm on the trunk of the tree beside her. "Thank you," she whispered. The tree groaned in response.

She'd made it. Out of the water, out of the Blood Forest, out of it all. Now she had to make things right.

PART III

SEIGE AND SMOKE

69

KAISA

Ellevere

Kaisa and Tarrio ran through the streets.

Her lungs burned with effort, her body still aching from when the troll had thrown her into the wall, but rage fueled her forward. Pope Sersius had bought children and made them murder each other. Used religion as a weapon. Killed countless innocents. And let a troll into a town of his own people, without a care for their lives or the lives of his own men.

They paused outside one of the buildings. Members of the Red Guard stood watch by the door.

"He'll hide in there until he knows the troll is dead," Tarrio hissed. "He's hoping it takes care of his problems for him and ends the New Order and you along with it."

"Sorry to say he's mistaken," Kaisa growled.

"As soon as he knows the troll is gone, he'll come for you."

Kaisa unsheathed her sword. "No need. I'm coming to him." She gestured to the Guards. "Can you handle them?"

Tarrio grinned. "Of course." He leapt from their hiding place, charging at the Guards.

As soon as they were deep into the throes of battle, Kaisa slipped into the building.

It was quiet inside, the sounds of the battle muffled. A voice spoke up ahead.

"I don't understand why you won't answer me," Pope Sersius growled. "You are my court ruler, you must answer me!"

Kaisa peeked around the corner to see him hunched over a table. He kept muttering in disgust.

Kaisa raised her sword, creeping forward.

"Cowardly enough to strike a man while his back is turned?" Pope Sersius sneered, keeping his back to her.

She swung her sword. Sersius whirled, meeting her sword with his own. Shockwaves rippled down her arm, he was stronger than she thought.

He spun away. Kaisa glanced at the table, half expecting a tortured body to be laying upon it, but instead, it was a strange, dark orb.

The Pope swung at her again, forcing her to step back. "Talking to stones now, are we?" she taunted, keeping her sword aloft. "What will the people say when they discover their Pope has succumbed to madness?"

Pope Sersius curled his lip. "You are a child playing a game you do not understand."

Their swords collided, their bodies coming together and apart in a vicious dance. In the dim lighting, alone, Pope Sersius looked young. He was handsome, with dark hair and eyes that blazed blue even in the darkness.

"Then a child is doing more to protect your people than you ever could," Kaisa snarled.

The Pope laughed. Again and again, their blades crashed together. The Pope's feet were quick, and Kaisa struggled to match his pace. "And why should my people put their trust in a child?"

"Because this world made me, and you made this world," Kaisa said, spinning to meet his move. Twins, he was quick. And fit. Fitter than she was, especially after her troll encounter. But her anger kept her sharp instead of clouding her.

"You are nothing," Sersius scoffed. "You might have defeated a few monsters, but you have no idea what's coming. Armies are moving across Airodion, girl. While you try to colonize a few towns, cities bend to the power of the Order. We march to war."

"On the same side as the monsters who terrorize your people's villages, I know," Kaisa shot back.

Sersius shook his head. "You don't understand. We fight for a new world, one where humans and fey are rejoined and magic runs beneath Ellevere once more. Where even humans can have power they never expected."

Kaisa stumbled, and Sersius nicked her thigh. She hissed. "What do you mean, magic will run beneath Ellevere once more?" Sersius spoke as if the faery and human realms had once been together. But that was impossible. The gods had created them separately.

Sersius ignored her. "You see monsters, we see allies. Those creatures fight on behalf of Ziegan, a new king amongst the fey. And the power he has promised us is beyond your imagination."

"People will never agree to fight alongside monsters," Kaisa growled. "Not when they've decimated towns, families, *children*. You're supposed to keep innocents out of war, not offer them as collateral."

Sersius shrugged before swinging at her again. "A small price to pay."

Kaisa shook her head, disgusted. "People will always resist you. You say war is coming to Ellevere? Then my army marches as well. And we will stand with whoever opposes you and Ziegan."

She would find a way to end the Order's brutality without forcing people to lose their faith. She wouldn't rest until she did. But for now, she had to set her sights on the war brewing in the faery realm.

Pope Sersius chuckled again, and Kaisa felt heat color her cheeks. He knew exactly how to make her feel like an insolent child.

"The courts will fall. They don't know how to unite—not anymore."

Kaisa blinked, tucking away that bit of information in the back of her mind. Did that mean she was right, that the leaders of the courts wanted to fight against Ziegan and the Popes?

"It doesn't matter, anyway." Pope Sersius stalked forward. "Because you're not leaving this room."

Kaisa yelled, running to meet him. Their swords clashed. They parried and swung, until finally, she landed a blow on Sersius's arm. She cried out triumphantly until she saw his amused smile. Then she saw the ceiling as her back crashed into the floor.

She rolled as he brought his sword down. She desperately pulled herself away.

"Give up, girl," Sersius growled. He swiped again, nicking her leg. Her eyes blurred with pain. He was toying with her.

"You are nothing," he spat. "You came from nothing. Your own mother sold you for a handful of coins because you weren't worth the trouble."

Kaisa lifted her chin. *Don't listen to him.*

"You failed as a Scholar. You failed as a leader."

She glanced behind her, her eyes burning with hatred. Pope Sersius spread his arms wide, grinning. "How many of your people do you see here today? Your own people rejected you."

It was as though he had a hammer and nail to pound every one of his words into her heart. She stopped crawling.

Maybe he was right. Maybe she was nothing. Maybe her people had given up on her, maybe this was all futile.

But even if all of that was true, even if she had no people left to follow her, she wouldn't want to be anywhere else. She would still want to fight this man, right here, right now. For he had caused more suffering than she could imagine. He had created the institution that had held her captive for so many years.

She was here for herself. No one else. To prove to herself that she could fight evil on her own. With no one beside her.

She didn't need to be the hand of justice. But this was one man she couldn't resist killing.

She swung her sword at Pope Sersius's hip. He blinked, too

surprised at the move to block her. But she had been too far away for a killing blow, too far away to do any damage. Only enough to nick fabric.

He looked down at her. "You missed." He smiled, almost sympathetically. He began walking towards her again.

The tear in the fabric from where her sword had cut him ripped. The delicate threads snapped from where she had carefully placed her blow. A blow she knew would cause it to rip because she had mended those trousers as a favor for another student back at the Institute.

The pants slipped, catching on the Pope's boot. He tripped, falling forward, arms outstretched—

Directly onto her sword.

Blood sprayed her face.

"Impossible," Sersius gurgled. He braced his hands on either side of her, struggling to push himself off her sword.

She rose with him, keeping the hilt plunged deep. "Poor choice of last words." She shoved him off.

He gave a wet scream, reaching for her, then he finally went still.

Kaisa stared down at him, her mind strangely blank. Not so long ago, she had dreamed of being a Pope's Page. Thought she would have done anything to achieve that honor. And she had just killed the man she had wanted to serve.

She rose shakily to her feet just as Tarrio burst through the door. He was covered in blood and scrapes, but otherwise unscathed.

"Are you all right?" he said, grasping her by her forearms. "I tried to come as fast as I could, but those bloody Red Guards were more skilled than I thought."

Kaisa nodded, still dazed. She had killed a Pope. What would happen now? The Order was headed to war.

There would be no escaping what she had done. People would be hunting her. But somehow, the thought didn't terrify her. She was ready. Ready to take her army north.

But first, they had to find a way to rid the town of the rest of the Order's soldiers. "How is Inniskeen?" she asked, her knees trembling. She didn't know how much longer she could fight. The events of the night were catching up with her.

Tarrio gave her a small smile. "Come and see."

He helped her outside. The streets were filled with townspeople, more than Kaisa had seen before. She gasped. "Who are these people?"

"They're your people, Kaisa," Tarrio murmured gently. "They knew the Pope and his army were headed to Inniskeen, and they knew you had left the city. They knew you would be here and followed you to fight at your side. Those who left with Ishan to the palace abandoned him. They helped push the soldiers back."

He turned and raised his voice. "Pope Sersius is dead!"

The people roared for Kaisa.

70

LARKEN

Airodion

Larken trudged into camp in the boots of one of the Winter Court fey. They were too large, but she couldn't complain, not when they had likely saved her from losing her toes to the cold.

The camp had settled down for the night, but fey still bustled around. Larken blinked at the realization that she hadn't been gone that long. Yet so much had happened during her time in the water and the Blood Forest.

She made her way back to her tent, keeping her focus on placing one foot in front of the other. Weariness tugged at her, and she wanted nothing more than to curl up and sleep. Was she safe now? But even if more captors took her into the Blood Forest, she knew the trees would protect her. Despite their violence, she felt a sort of strange kinship with them.

She stopped when a flash of red caught her eye. She looked up.

Fynvarra lay curled around her tent. He lifted his head as he caught her scent, his sightless eyes darting back and forth.

Larken let out a choked sob. He hadn't left her. He hadn't gone back to

First Forge, as those soldiers had said. She ran to his side, falling to her knees and wrapping her arms around his neck. She joined her sight to his so he could see once more.

"I'm sorry," she whispered. "I'm so sorry, Fynvarra. I didn't mean what I said, I was hurting so badly, but I shouldn't have taken it out on you."

Fynvarra tucked his chin around her back, pulling her closer. "It's all right," he said gently. "I didn't mean what I said either. I know you're trying, little one."

Larken's breath caught the same moment she heard footsteps come to a halt behind her. She stood, turning. Saja and Finder stood before her.

Finder frowned. "Those aren't your clothes."

Larken threw herself into his arms. He wrapped his arms around her, anchoring her, easing her nerves. His scent flooded her, comforting her beyond words. Apples and leaves and spice.

"You're right," Finder murmured into her hair. "You're right about Dahey. I should have listened to you."

She squeezed him tighter. He rubbed small circles on her back and then paused. "But where are your clothes?"

She stilled. She still had to tell them about the kidnapping, about her time in the water. She stepped back. "While all of you were away, some Winter Court soldiers dragged me from my tent and took me to a lake in the Blood Forest."

Saja and Finder froze.

"They—uh, they tried to drown me. They thought I was partially responsible for the loss of White Keep."

"Tell me who did this to you," Finder said. "If you don't have their names, you will describe them to me." His voice was quiet, his muscles strained.

She shook her head. "I'm wearing what's left of them." She gave a low laugh, then stopped herself. "They were killed by the tree fey."

"Blood Forest dryads," Saja breathed. "How did you survive them?"

Finder hadn't moved, his fists still clenched.

"They helped me," Larken said. "They saw what the soldiers did to me, and they saw me emerge from the water." Some part of her hesitated to speak the rest, of what they had said about how she had changed. "They gave me their blessing and helped me return to camp," she finished instead.

"I never should have left you," Finder whispered.

"I shouldn't have either," Fynvarra said, hanging his head.

"I have a feeling they would have found a way to take me no matter what." She repressed a shudder. The image of sinking into the freezing water was terrifying, and the memories did instill fear in her, but not the terror and blind panic she had experienced with the flame. And now, the flame had saved her life after the water.

It was as though her temperature had slowly been rising, the heat inside her growing until she was burning from the inside out, and then she had been plunged into the cold.

Like a blade, forged anew and stronger.

Larken changed back into her clothes, anxious to rid herself of the dead soldier's things.

Finder had gone off in search of food, insisting that she have something to eat after her ordeal. Fynvarra lay curled around the tent, fast asleep. Saja stayed with her until Finder returned with a platter of dried fruits and nuts.

"Not much," he admitted sadly. He settled down beside her.

Saja gave her a knowing smile, bid them both goodnight, and left.

Larken ate as much as she could stomach, then curled her arms around her knees. Finder sat facing her, his arms draped around his legs as well. "Do you want to talk about what happened in the water?" he asked quietly.

"I thought I was going to die," Larken admitted. "I almost let myself. But in that moment, something about the water and my memories made me want to live."

"I'm sorry that happened to you," Finder said.

Larken bit her lip. "In a way, I'm not. I was drifting for so long; I didn't know how much longer I could until I lost myself. This woke me up."

She gave a small smile, her eyes drifting halfway closed. She was so exhausted.

Finder stood, brushing off his pants. "Sleep now. Saja and I will be outside, and I don't think anything could convince Fynvarra to go anywhere."

She nodded, rolling over onto her sleeping mat. Her heart beat wildly in her chest, wanting to ask him but too afraid—

"Will you stay with me?" she blurted. "Inside the tent, I mean. If you want to." She squeezed her eyes shut, her face burning.

A soft rustle. Disappointment flooded her—he was leaving.

But then she felt him lay down beside her. So close—as close as he could possibly get without touching her.

"Closer," she whispered. Her heart beat faster. "Please. I'm scared I'll never be warm again, that I won't remember what it feels like."

Silence. Her heart leapt into her throat. Had she gone too far?

A warm body pressed up against her back. A soft sigh tingled against her ear, and her cheeks warmed again as Finder shifted, pressing his body closer to her. His warmth seeped into her. His arms snaked around her, one shifting beneath her and pulling her head into his shoulder and the other wrapping around her waist.

"I will never let you forget what warmth feels like. Especially from me. You never have to ask," he said into her neck.

Her eyelids fluttered closed, tingles exploding into her core. Her heart beat louder. His scent was intoxicating.

His nose grazed her neck, his lips skimming over her skin. She couldn't stop her shiver. She felt him smile. "I can feel your heartbeat."

Biting her lip, she closed her eyes, willing her heart rate to slow. *Calm down. You can't spend all night like this.*

No, she could not. She flipped over. Finder's green eyes were luminous. She would have given anything to know what he was thinking.

"Ask," he said hoarsely. "Ask, and I will give it to you. Anything. Tell me what you want."

"I want to kiss you," she said.

Finder didn't hesitate. He lowered his lips to hers. He was gentle, so gentle, and when his mouth opened, coaxing hers open along with it, she followed him. He moved, cupping her cheek with his hand. She swept her tongue in, and he moaned, pulling her closer.

It was all the invitation she needed. She got on top of him, straddling his stomach. "Is this okay?" she asked breathily, half afraid her weight would hurt him.

He tugged her down, pressing her weight more fully upon him. "Yes."

Their lips met again, more frenzied this time. His hands began to move, taking advantage of her new position. They swept up her thighs, up her ribcage, then stopped. She broke away. He looked at her questioningly.

She took his hands in her own. She moved them up, her lips parting slightly. His hands skimmed her breasts. His eyes took on a wicked gleam. Her head tilted back, and she moaned.

"Shhh," Finder admonished with a smile. "I'm sure waking Fynvarra will have consequences."

"I need more," she gasped.

"With. Pleasure." Finder sat up sharply. The motion made her fall onto his lap. She blushed again at the exposed position, but she didn't want to stop. Finder met her lips, and she lost herself as his hands brushed up and down her body. She dug her fingers in his curls and pulled him closer.

She could do this for hours. Forever. After everything she had been through, this seemed like a bright light banishing the darkness.

But she still needed time. Time to know Finder, know him like this, before she could go any further.

"Stop," she breathed.

Finder stopped immediately. His hands didn't touch her. She missed their contact instantly. "Are you all right? Did I—"

"No!" She placed a hand on his chest, lowering her voice. "No, of course not. I just want to take things slow. I know you have more experience, and I want this..." Twins, why were the words so difficult. "I want more. Just not right now. I want time to—to know you."

Finder tucked a curl behind her ear. "Of course, Larken. And know that my experience has nothing to do with this. This is between us. We will learn from each other, teach each other what we like." He gave her a lopsided grin. "I liked this."

She blushed. "I did, too."

"Tell me what you want," he murmured. "Do you want me to leave?"

"No," she said quickly. "I want you to stay. To sleep here. But we can't lay facing each other. It's too tempting." She wiggled out of his lap. She thought for a moment. "We have to lay back to back," she said seriously.

Finder tried to hide his smile. "Back to back."

She spun a finger at him. He lifted his hands, smiling, and laid down, his back facing her. She wiggled up beside him, her back pressed against his. It was a different kind of touching, yes, but extremely comforting. She sighed, closing her eyes as his scent drifted over her.

"Laying this way won't prevent my inappropriate thoughts, you know," Finder said.

She bit her lip, smiling. She whacked him on the arm. Except it wasn't his arm—it was his thigh. Her face burned.

"Don't start something you can't finish," Finder said wryly.

"It was an accident," she grumbled. "Focus on keeping me warm." But she couldn't help her smile. Not even when she drifted off to sleep.

71

LARKEN

Airodion

She woke only once during the night. She was still pressed up against Finder's back. His chest moved up and down slowly with his breath. Fire blazed to life in her core, and a part of her desperately wanted to wake him up, to continue where they had stopped before, but she forced those thoughts away. There would be time for that later. Now she just wanted to enjoy being here with him. This quiet moment of intimacy. She fell back asleep with a smile on her lips.

Daylight spilled through the tent flaps, and the clamor from the camp outside had risen steadily in the past few hours. Larken rolled over, her eyes widening slightly as she came practically nose-to-nose with Finder.

He must have rolled over some time during the night, though his arms were curled under his head, inches from touching her. A part of her wished that he had wrapped his arms around her, waken her up in a different manner—

Stop it.

Finder's eyes fluttered open, stirred awake by her movement. "How did you sleep?" he murmured. He brushed the curls back from her face.

A wave of self-consciousness swept over her. Her hair was a mess, her face was unwashed—she was glad she didn't have a mirror just to confirm her fears.

She didn't know what had come over her. Finder had seen her in worse states than this during their journey to defeat the Starveling. They had ridden Rhylla together while she was coated in blood so old and dried her dress was stiff with it. Her face heated.

"Don't tell me you're having wicked thoughts," he purred, lifting himself up on his forearm.

"I'm not," Larken said quickly, but, emboldened by the look in his eyes, she added, "though I did have them in the middle of the night."

"Really?" Finder's gaze was practically sinful. It was so different, this side of him that she hadn't experienced before. But she was enjoying it far too immensely to stop. He lowered his head, his auburn curls dipping across his forehead. His lips grazed her neck. "Tell me more."

She arched her back and swallowed. "I wanted to—" she gasped as he began to suck. "I wanted to—" Twins, she couldn't think while he was doing that.

"Go on," Finder smiled against her neck.

Bastard is enjoying the effect he has on me. Larken scowled but couldn't keep it for long as Finder's kisses traced along her jaw.

"I wanted to wake you up and do *more*," she rushed out the words.

Finder pulled back, his eyes questioning. His shirt had pulled up slightly, revealing corded muscle beneath. She bit her lip, placing her palm against the exposed skin. Finder sucked in a breath.

She trailed her fingers up, taking the fabric with her. Finder's eyes fluttered closed, a low groan escaping him. "But then I came to my senses." She pulled his shirt back down, taking care to still trail her fingers down his skin.

He brushed his thumb against her lips and cheek. His green eyes were so gentle. "We have time. I'm in no rush."

She wrapped her arms around his chest, and he pulled her close, tucking her head beneath his chin. It felt so strange, this kind of intimacy. She had touched Finder before—many times even. It had been a part of their relationship as friends. But this was so different, so new to her. She had never kissed a boy before, not before the Tournament, and now this. She wanted Finder, she did. There was no denying it. But she had to get used to the feelings coursing through her. She had found Finder attractive when they had first met—how could she not? And had grown so close to him during their journey. With their souls tied, how could she have not grown to love him during that short time? And after, when Dahey had taken him, she had had weeks to simmer with her thoughts and emotions. Anger that he had burned her, fear for his wellbeing, and an almost obsession of him while he was away. Coming back together had been an adjustment, a rocky one with her healing. But now she felt whole, like a full human being again, not just a shell going through the motions. She finally felt whole enough to let Finder in. And exploring it was new and terrifying, but it thrilled and delighted her like nothing else.

But while her wounds were finally healed, or at least getting there, Finder still had so many that were raw and oozing. The trauma of receiving his powers and then having them taken away by his own kin. She couldn't help him resolve things with Dahey—nor did she know if they ever could be resolved. But Finder needed to forgive himself. Forgive himself for all the mistakes he made, either on accident or from a wrong choice. He deserved forgiveness. And she began to have an inkling of an idea of how to help with that.

"I want you to consider something," she said, tracing her fingertips along his cheekbone. Finder stilled. "You don't have to do it, but I think it will help you. But I don't want you to be upset with me when I tell you what it is."

"What is it?" Finder murmured. His eyes turned fearful.

She bit her lip. She might as well just say it. "I want you to go back to the town you destroyed when you became prince."

Finder squeezed his eyes shut. "No."

"I think it will help," she urged. "I know it's not the same, but the water changed something inside me. I knew I had to face the fire or die—and when I came out of that water, I was no longer afraid. Not like I once was. I think if you go back to face it, you'll be facing the biggest fear you've ever known. And then you can let go. You don't have to forget, but you can let go of some of that pain inside you."

Finder met her gaze. His eyes were drowning in fear. "I can't," Finder whispered. "I can't see that barren place I created. The death that lingers there. I see it every day in my mind."

"If you go back to the place where the worst thing that ever happened to you occurred, then you've faced and conquered the worst. What happened to you there will not happen again. Going there allows your mind to realize that that is the past, and this is now."

Finder bit his lip, his eyes downcast. She placed her palm on his cheek once more, brushing away the wetness. He didn't need to live with the weight of those memories any longer. "I'll be there with you," she said. "I might not be able to help, but I'll be there. You won't be alone."

Finder's breathing sped up, his chest billowing up and down. But finally, it slowed. "I'll do it," he said finally.

Larken knew he wasn't just doing it for her. He was doing this for *himself* because he wanted to heal from it, and he would take any suggestions she had—no matter how painful. Pride bloomed within her. He was changing.

"Fynvarra," she called.

A moment later, the drake's huge head pushed its way through the tent flaps. He sniffed the air. "I smell arousal in here." The drake paused, then added: "and tears."

Larken couldn't hide her grin. "What can I say? It's been a busy morning."

72

LARKEN

Airodion

Larken convinced Fynvarra to take them to Raharney, the town Finder had destroyed.

Finder was jittery with nerves. She had never seen him like this. Even when they had fought the Starveling, he hadn't been this anxious—or, at least, hadn't revealed his nerves to her.

"We're almost there," Finder murmured after a time. Fynvarra glided down, his claws sinking into the dirt. Larken glanced at the hills surrounding them. The town was concealed from view. She was nervous to see it as well. She knew the strength of Finder's powers before the Starveling fell—she had felt it when he used them. But seeing the destruction he had wrought when the powers had first taken him... Would it change how she saw Finder?

But she knew Finder. She knew he hadn't meant to hurt these fey. And she knew this would help him. Even though she knew seeing the charred husk of the city and its inhabitants would be difficult, it would help him. Like putting a corpse to rest at last.

"You don't have to, you know," she murmured, touching his arm. "No one is going to make you. And now that we're here, if you aren't ready, or if you never are, it's okay."

He looked at her. "You still stand by what you said? You think it will help?"

She nodded. "I do."

He stuck out his chin. "Then I want to do it. I think some part of me needs to see it after all this time."

They walked to the top of the hill, Fynvarra padding alongside them.

They reached the top, and Larken's breath caught in her throat.

The town was bustling with fey. Smoke rose from chimneys, from hearths and cookfires. It wasn't the sprawling grandeur of Shadeshelm, but a quiet, country town. It reminded her of Ballamor.

Finder's mouth hung open in awe.

"Did you know?" Larken asked softly. "Did you know they had rebuilt all of this? That it was here?"

Finder shook his head mutely, but his eyes glistened slightly. Her heart swelled and she touched his arm again.

They made their way down, Fynvarra insisting on accompanying them. He kept close to Larken so she could help him navigate.

Larken and Finder walked side-by-side down one of the main streets. Fey slowly came out of their houses, their shops, stopping whatever they were doing to watch the faery, human and firedrake pass through their streets.

Finally, an old female faery approached them. Larken was shocked by her appearance. She didn't know that the fey could look older than their twenties or thirties.

The female faery held out a hand to stop them. Her skin had the appearance of molten tree bark. Larken wondered if whatever type of faery she was could be related to the dryads she had met.

"My king," she said bowing slightly. "It is an honor to have you here."

Finder paled. "You know who I am?"

The female nodded. "Of course."

Fey surrounded them, so many of them filling the streets that Larken could not see the end of the crowd. Their gazes were curious, not hostile.

Finder drew his sword and dropped to his knees before the female, holding it out to her. Larken stared at him in surprise, and shocked murmurs drifted up from the crowd.

"I have come to beg for your forgiveness," Finder whispered. "When my powers came to me, I killed everyone who lived here. I razed this town to the ground." He bowed his head. "This place is tarnished land. It's filled with suffering because of me. I haven't been able to return because of the shame—because of the hatred I felt towards myself. But I've come here today to say I'm sorry. I'm so deeply sorry for what I did. I know there are no words that can ever ease what I've done, but I needed you to know. I offer my life to you, though I know the debt can never be paid."

"Finder, no," Larken gasped, but he ignored her. Stretched his hands out, bearing the sword to the female before him.

He couldn't do this. What had happened here wasn't his fault. He hadn't expected the powers to come to him, hadn't wanted them. It was an accident, and now they were going to kill him in retribution. Fynvarra growled.

The female took the sword from Finder's hands. Larken lunged forward, but Finder stopped her. "No, Larken. I have to do this."

She stepped back, her heart pounding in her throat. But some part of her knew she couldn't intervene. This was Finder's moment. This is what he needed to heal. He would give any part of himself—all of himself, to the female before him, to the leader of the new town. It was his choice, and she couldn't take it from him, not when that might destroy him.

The female glanced down at the sword in her palms. "We know what happened here. And we chose to rebuild." She lifted her gaze to her people, then back to Finder. "The dead are gone. We don't speak for them. But I speak for the living, the new life here. We know it was an accident. We know you would never cause your people harm. And I know you came here to heal some part of you that was broken." She threw down the sword. It clattered upon the stones. Finder stared at it wide-eyed as the female took his face between her palms. "We've been waiting for you," she said, her eyes warm, her smile like sunlight, "and we forgive you."

Finder lifted his head to the sky as tears streamed down his cheeks. The female helped him to his feet. She took his arm and flung it into the air. "The king has returned!"

Cheers rose from the crowd, turning into a dull roar. Fey reached out to touch Finder, and he smiled. He clasped arms, shook hands, and brushed fingertips as the crowd surged, all trying to touch him. Larken was stunned by the beauty of the moment, the forgiveness of these people, or beyond that, their desire to heal their king. And with every touch, with every joyful tear, Larken saw Finder grow stronger.

These people thought Finder was their king. They knew Dahey ruled as regent, but they had still chosen Finder. Perhaps there was some hope of him reclaiming his throne. All of his people hadn't abandoned him.

Finder turned to her, his green eyes lit by the rays of the sun. "It is Larken who deserves your praise," he said, holding out a hand to her. "The girl who saved my life again and again. The girl who saved my soul."

Larken's heart was near bursting when she took Finder's hand. They drifted through the crowd, every faery wanting to touch them. Gentle fingers brushed her hair, her face, her clothes, and with every touch, Larken felt herself grow lighter, filled with light from these strangers.

A female faery pushed her way through the crowd, a male child clutched in her arms. The little boy reached out and pressed his palm to Finder's cheek. Finder closed his eyes, covering the boy's hand with his own. Larken's throat closed.

They reached the end of the road. Finder lifted a hand to wave to the leader of the town. She raised her hand back.

"All of this is because of you," he whispered, pressing his forehead to hers. Larken squeezed his hand.

Finder helped her onto Fynvarra's back. "Now, to war."

73

DAHEY

Airodion

Ziegan took Tellaridge that night.

Isra and most of her people had left, streaming into the Autumn Court. Dahey knew the refugees would likely be here soon.

Dahey sank into his chair, anxiety twisting his stomach into knots. The walls of Shadeshelm pressed in around him, still as comforting as ever. He would do anything to save his home. He knew Ziegan was on his way, knew that there was no way to save the small outlying towns of the Autumn Court. He would take everything in his path, as he had been doing, without fail, without challenge.

"Did any of the other court rulers answer?" Dahey asked, lifting his head.

Nessa shook her head. "None so far, my king."

Dahey scrubbed his jaw, willing his hands not to shake in front of her.

The Winter Court refugees would fight when they arrived, if only because they knew that the Autumn Court surviving was one of their only chances to get their own court back. It enraged him that Summer

363

and Spring had not answered them when their courts would be next to face Ziegan's wrath. Unless they had chosen to side with him.

He didn't have control of the magic. He didn't have allies. Ziegan would be at their door soon, and Dahey would lose everything.

"Leave me," he gritted out. Nessa nodded solemnly. She turned to go.

"Wait," Dahey said. She paused. "Get your loved ones out of the city," he said. "Shadeshelm is no longer safe."

Nessa gave him a small smile. "You are kind, my lord, but they have nowhere to go. If Shadeshelm falls, it will only be a matter of time before the other cities and courts follow."

She left.

Dahey steepled his fingers. Was this what he deserved? It was he who had set everything in motion to free Ziegan. He had betrayed his cousin for the throne. His own father didn't care for him—why should Dahey sacrifice everything for this court when it hadn't been able to save him?

But what could his people have done against his father? No one challenged the court rulers, not when the magic itself picked them. But his people had been there to tend to his wounds, to teach him, to love him. To love him as his father should have. His people should not pay for his father's crimes. This was Dahey's home, despite the bad things that had happened here.

It wasn't your people who cared for you, a voice in the back of his mind whispered. *It was Finder.*

And now, sitting here in this chair, with only half of the fire magic and less than half of his people's support, he sympathized with Finder. Dahey still wanted to rule. But the part of him that had been so confident that he could do a better job than Finder was slipping away. For what good was being a king if he didn't have his cousin here beside him to offer his council? He had known that being king would mean that Finder would not be by his side. Worse, that Finder would be his enemy. And on the outside, Dahey had thought it would be worth it. But now, he wasn't so sure.

And he couldn't deny the relief that had poured over him when that damned human girl had saved Finder in the ring. Anger, yes, he had felt that too, but the relief had shocked him deeply. And the jealousy. The fear that no one would love him enough to do what Larken had done for Finder during the Tournament.

Nessa rushed back into the throne room, breathless. "My lord, there is someone here to see you."

Dahey stood. Could it be Valakais or Etain? Had they come to offer aide? Dahey couldn't help the spark of hope that flared to life in his chest.

Nessa threw open the doors. A roar shook the walls of the palace, nearly making Dahey take a step back.

He beheld the trio before him. The human girl, the firedrake, and Finder.

Finder held his head high, almost regal, and Larken stood at his side. A fierce fire burned in her eyes. And behind them—the firedrake.

Larken lifted her chin. "We've come to save Shadeshelm."

74

LARKEN

Airodion

The hum of battle pulsed around her as the fey prepared for war. Larken stood in the hallway, still as the motion streamed around her. They gathered weapons, placed more barriers against the walls and doors, and stopped to comfort each other when their nerves overtook them. Some part of it was beautiful, working together to protect their home. But remembering the battle to come had caused her to spend most of the day curled around an empty pitcher in case she needed to vomit.

Larken walked out onto the huge balcony overlooking the forest, Fynvarra at her side. The sun had already slipped behind the trees, and the shadows were long and skeletal in the twilight.

Fynvarra's drakes were perched in the trees below like a flock of peculiar birds. Fighters and flyers had followed their leader to the siege. The elder drakes hadn't protested when Fynvarra told them he was taking the drakes to the Autumn Court to help defend it against Ziegan. If anything, they seemed eager to test their king in battle. That, or they were just thirsty for blood. The drakes' blood ran hot, and squabbles between them grew more frequent as they grew excited about the coming violence.

A constant knot of tension resided in Larken's stomach. She peered below to the battlements. Lines of soldiers manned the walls, armed with bows. A mix of Autumn and Winter Court fey. Roone and Saja paced behind them, Roone using hand-speak while Saja called out orders. The drakes had flown Roone here at Larken and Saja's request.

A Winter Court soldier lifted his bow, his arms shaking. Roone took him by the shoulder, making gestures with his hands to breathe deeply. The soldier calmed under his gaze.

They knew Ziegan would attack from the sky and the ground. The drakes would take the brunt of the arial attack, and Dahey would lead the Autumn Court calvary on the ground. Isra would lead the few bears and soldiers she had to assist Dahey. They had no idea if Ziegan would make an appearance, but if he did, Dahey, Finder and Isra would band together to try to hold him off.

Their only goal was to keep the city from being overrun.

"I don't know if I can do this," Larken whispered. Fear roiled inside her. She touched her hand to Fynvarra's neck.

You are not alone, Larken, Fynvarra rumbled. *You have me. The city will not fall. Not with an army of firedrakes defending it.*

Larken tugged at the straps of her armor. "Doesn't feel right," she muttered.

Fynvarra tilted his head. *Have you tried tightening the straps?*

Larken glared at him. "Yes, Fynn, I've tried tightening the straps."

"Can I help?"

She turned. Finder stood in the archway of the armory. The clamor of the approaching battle faded away as she looked at him.

He was a vision. Shining gold armor covered every inch of him. His breastplate was adorned with two galloping horses—the sigil of the Autumn Court. He looked like a king.

She nodded and turned so Finder could help her with her armor. He tightened the straps on her back, and the ones that buckled behind her thighs. She tried not to blush.

"I'm worried about you," she said with her back still turned. "You won't be able to fight with the fire, and you don't like using your powers over death," she said, biting her lip. "I don't want you getting hurt."

Finder gently spun her around to meet his gaze. "I'll do what I have to."

He hugged her close, and she breathed in the scent of crushed leaves and spices. His armor dug into her, but she didn't care.

"I'm scared," she admitted.

Finder gave her a small grin. "I'd be more worried if you weren't," he said. "I'll tell you what I tell everyone in my legion. Take everything only one moment at a time."

She took a deep breath and nodded.

The drumbeats started, and warhorns blew.

"It's almost time." Finder glanced out over the trees.

Her heart nearly punched through her chest. She could hear Ziegan's forces approaching. The trees shuddered, and the flap of wings beat in the air. Hisses and shrieks and howls.

She climbed up onto Fynvarra's back, settling between his shoulder blades. She dug her hands into his mane. Finder tied her arms and legs in place with straps so she wouldn't fall.

Quit fidgeting, Fynvarra admonished. *And quit thinking about Finder. He's all I can see.*

Embarrassed, Larken tried to block Fynvarra from her mind.

Oi, not that much! Fynvarra cried as she severed their bond completely, blinding him.

Oops, sorry. She patted his neck. *Good lizard.*

I can bite you, you know.

She ignored him. The nerves crept back in. They just had to stick to the plan. Worry twisted in her belly, making her feel ill. What if something went wrong?

Calm your mind, Fynvarra rumbled. *You can never predict everything that will happen in battle so don't even try. Things will happen the way they were meant to.*

Larken tried to calm her breathing. The plan. They just had to stick to the plan.

And don't block my fire, he added.

Finder placed his hand on her leg. "I'll see you when this is over," he said.

She nodded, all the words she wanted to say to him stuck on her tongue. "Be careful," was all she could manage.

"I will," he said, drawing his sword. Larken feared for Finder. He could be so much stronger. And what if his powers could have turned the tide in the battle? She would never know. But she had to hope that the magic he shared with Dahey would be enough against Ziegan.

Finder left, leaving her alone with Fynvarra. Below, Roone and Saja fell into line with their soldiers, leveling their weapons. For a moment, everything was quiet. Still.

Then Ziegan's forces poured out of the trees like a tide, crashing into the calvary below.

Saja screamed commands to his soldiers, and their volley of arrows streamed into the air. Fynvarra roared, and his drakes roared in answer. Ziegan's winged creatures descended from the skies like carrion crows. The drakes raced to meet them, colliding midair and lighting up the sky with their fire.

Now, we fight. Fynvarra said. He ran and jumped into the air, circling the palace.

The massive oak came into view, the branches jutting straight up around its lower trunk like the parapet of a castle. Larken could see between the smaller trunks and she could make out a domed ceiling made of glass and woven branches. Light shone from within.

Let's try not to destroy too much of it with fire, she warned.

No promises, Fynvarra replied, pausing to hover.

Booms shattered the night, echoing alongside the beat of Fynvarra's wings. Larken peered over Fynvarra's shoulder, her stomach roiling. She had never seen anything like this. Fire lit up the night. From the drakes—or from Finder or Dahey? Her gut twisted at the thought of Finder in pain.

The screams of soldiers and beasts rose from below. She could see black and grey masses writhing beneath them, Ziegan's forces and court soldiers clashing in a fitful mess of noise and claws on flesh. Between the flashes of firelight, she saw Winter Court bears charging through the ranks.

Fynvarra roared again, his drakes calling back to him.

Are you ready?

She dug her hands into his mane in answer. She screamed as he plummeted, half from fear from the battle raging below, and half from the anger burning inside her.

Fynvarra opened his jaws. Larken felt the rumbling deep inside him and tensed, waiting for her panic to overcome her, but it never came. Fynvarra spewed Ziegan's masses with fire. The fey in his ranks shot arrows at them, but Fynvarra's scales deflected them.

Fynvarra lowered to a portion of the calvary that was completely surrounded. He landed, taking out a few of Ziegan's fey with his claws, and swept his tail, clearing a path for the horses and riders to rejoin the ranks of their comrades.

She could make Dahey out through the smoke, his red armor standing out against the coat of his white mare. The horse was streaked with ashes and blood.

Fynvarra launched back into the sky, spewing more fire at Ziegan's fey. Adrenaline pulsed through her, but she couldn't move, couldn't release it as she clung to Fynvarra's back. Her mind and throat clogged with smoke until her lungs and eyes burned.

And still, the battle raged around them.

Something caught her gaze. Fey were thrown backwards by gusts of wind. The earth split open and took Ziegan's creatures with it.

Spring and Summer had come. A flicker of hope flared to life inside her. Despite her hatred for Etain, Larken was glad she was here. That she and Valakais had come to help Shadeshelm.

The court rulers battled on the front lines, side-by-side with the Winter and Autumn Court soldiers. And when Fynvarra dipped lower again, she could see Finder in his golden armor, cutting down creatures from Rhylla's back. The horse's grey coat was splattered with black and red gore.

Ice, air, and earth magic lashed at the creatures. Stronger now without the Starveling's chains binding them, the court rulers reeked of power.

Slowly, the tide began to turn. The magic fell over Ziegan's forces, freezing them in place to be cut down, stealing the breath from their lungs or swallowing them whole into the earth. The calvary pushed forward, the bears helping cut deep paths through Ziegan's ranks.

"It's working," Larken breathed. Fynvarra roared in response, some of his drakes echoing his call.

A pulsing beat rang through the air. Quiet at first, growing steadily louder. At first, Larken thought it was the war drums of the fey, celebrating pushing the creatures back, but Larken could not see where the sound was coming from.

"What is that?" She frowned. Fynvarra took to the sky, angling towards Shadeshelm, flying lower, following the noise.

They rounded the corner. Below marched an army three thousand strong. They pounded their fists over their hearts, over their armor embossed with a double cross wreathed in flames.

"The Popes' army," Larken screamed. But she recognized the armor—recognized the metal that had held both Fynvarra and Finder captive.

The human army was wrapped in Weeping Metal armor.

75

DAHEY

Airodion

Dahey cut down monster after monster, and even a few fey, as the battle raged around him. Energy filled him, replenishing him as he realized that the tides were finally beginning to turn in their favor.

He barely noticed the strange smell that began to drift through the air. He wasn't one to feel sick before or during battle, but his stomach began to pain him, and his moves turned clumsy. Two fey were able to land a mark on him before he cut them down, which was unthinkable to him. A headache pulsed between his brows.

What's happening to me? A twinge of fear rose within him. He hadn't been using his magic for fear that it would make him ill, and now he felt sick all the same.

The smell grew stronger, sparking something at the edge of Dahey's memory. He turned towards the breeze where the smell was coming from, trying to find the source, and his blood ran cold.

An entire army of soldiers poured around Shadeshelm.

The Popes' army.

He grabbed one of his generals by the arm. "Tell everyone that we must be ready to fight from behind *now*."

He craned his neck, straining to see where Finder was. There—he could make out the shining golden armor. He watched the moment in slow motion as Finder caught scent of the metal as well. As he turned to face the human horde, his eyes glazing over with terror at the Weeping Metal. His sword slackened in his hand, falling to the ground beside Rhylla.

"Oh, you bloody fool," Dahey growled. He dug his heels into Sylvie's side and plowed through the creatures, desperate to make it to Finder in time. Finder sat motionless on Rhylla's back, staring at the humans. Rhylla whinnied in terror as the creatures swarmed her. She kicked out with her front legs, but without Finder cutting them down, it was only a matter of time before she was overrun.

Dahey drew another sword, a blade for each hand. He lowered the blades as Sylvie pounded over the earth, letting his blades slice into creature after creature on either side of them.

He made it to Finder, cutting down the creatures around Rhylla. Finder's eyes met him, filled with too many emotions to name. Anger at what Dahey had done to him, for torturing him with the metal that now rendered him powerless. But deep down, Dahey could swear he saw relief. Relief that Dahey was all right.

Dahey tossed Finder one of his swords. His father's blade, the hilt a band of gilded leaves.

Finder caught the blade. He gave Dahey a nod.

And together, they charged side by side into the horde.

76

LARKEN

Airodion

Larken cried out in despair. She had known that the humans had sided with Ziegan, but she thought she would have more time to figure out a solution—she didn't know that she would have to face her own people in battle so soon.

She could barely believe that the human army had made it all the way to Shadeshelm without detection. But the Weeping Metal must have deterred the fey. As soon as they sensed its unpleasantness, even if they didn't recognize it for what it was, they would have headed in the other direction.

The army streamed around the palace, moments away from ambushing Dahey's calvary from behind.

We have to warn them, she cried.

They already know, Fynvarra dipped his head, pointing. Firedrakes dropped from the skies to rain fire upon the soldiers, but it had little effect. Larken peered below. Blasts of air, ice and earth were pummeling the ranks of the Popes' army. But it still seemed to have a weakened effect. Valakais, Etain and Isra should have been able to wipe out hundreds of humans with no effort, yet their powers were barely dropping a few. And it only seemed to work when the ice, wind and earth struck a soldier at the same time.

Despair welled inside her. They couldn't defeat this. And worse than that, it would end in senseless human death. Her people were innocent.

Don't kill them, she wanted to beg. *They don't know what they're doing.*

But if they fought for Ziegan, willing or not, they were a threat to her friends. Larken's heart spasmed as she realized she was choosing the fey over her own people. Again. She hardened her heart. She would find a way to talk to the humans. Find a way to sway them to the fey's side, away from Ziegan. But first, she and her companions had to survive this battle.

She stared below, her eyes frantically searching for Finder. They had to find him, they had to fall back. They were going to lose Shadeshelm, but she couldn't allow him to die for it.

Two streaks of red and gold in a sea of black uniforms caught her gaze. Dahey and Finder, cutting their way through the ranks on the backs of their horses. Larken's breath caught as they seamlessly worked together, twin blades, twin flames, the opposite sides of a coin. They worked in tandem to cut through the armor with no magic, nothing but steel.

The realization came to her then, so clearly that it rippled down the bond to Fynvarra, making him flinch with shock. Finder and Dahey had been working so hard to master the fire, to master the power of the Autumn Court... but maybe that was the problem. They'd been fighting each other. *Blocking* each other, as she had done to Fynvarra.

Get me to him, she said. Fynvarra dove towards Finder. Fynvarra landed as close as he could, clawing and blasting the humans with his fire. The fire had much more of an impact at close range, and a circle formed around them. Fynvarra kept them back with his claws and the fire.

"Larken!" Finder cried. "Get out of here, *now.*"

Fynvarra came closer to Rhylla, doing his best to shield them from the chaos, keeping the humans away. Dahey took one look at her and must have known she was there for a good reason for he threw himself into the fray at Fynvarra's side, quelling the tide for a moment so Larken and Finder could speak.

"You and Dahey have been trying so hard to gain control of the powers," she had to scream to be heard over the din of the battle. "But it's not working. It's not working because you have to work together."

Was this not the lesson Saja and Roone had been trying to teach her? That her mind and body had to work together.

"I can't," Finder said, his teeth gritted. His eyes were filled with so much rage, so much hate.

Dahey's eyes gleamed, but with an emotion she couldn't place. Though they stood mere feet from each other, it was as if a sea chasm miles deep stood between them, within them, from all the pain they had endured.

"A court ruler's magic is powerful, but think of what you could achieve together. Valakais, Etain and Isra are doing what they can. But they need the fire. *Your* fire. And Dahey's."

His green eyes lifted to hers. "I don't know if I can," he whispered.

"You're stronger now," she said, her body moving with Fynvarra's rhythm as he clawed the soldiers before him. "We both are. Humans and fey are not so different." She gave him a smile. "We are capable of forgiveness. I forgave you for all of it. The town forgave you for all of it. And you don't have to forgive Dahey fully—not yet. Just enough to work together."

He held her gaze for a moment, then nodded. "We need to get to the other court rulers."

Larken gripped Fynvarra's mane. "We'll help you."

Fynvarra launched into the sky. Finder shouted something at Dahey, who fell in beside him. Together, they charged back toward the other court rulers. Fynvarra flew higher into the sky, breathing fire below, trying his best to clear a path for Dahey and Finder.

This has to work, she prayed.

Something whistled through the air. Larken frowned, her confusion turning to horror. Spears from below.

"Fynvarra, look out," she cried.

Another spear came, and Fynvarra squealed, his body hurling to the left.

"Fynvarra!" Larken screamed. The drake let out a hoarse whine. Larken leaned over, and her breath caught.

The spear had gone straight through Fynvarra's neck.

He gave a few mighty flaps of his wings, pulling them as far away from the army below as he could. But he was flying too slow, too straight, to avoid the next volley of spears. Chest. Wings. Blood poured from Fynvarra's wounds.

"*Fynvarra*," she screamed, with her voice and with her mind.

I'm sorry, he said, and then he fell from the sky.

77

DAHEY

Airodion

Dahey watched the drake fall from the sky, his wings fluttering in the wind.

Finder screamed when he saw his human girl, still strapped to the firedrake, plummet toward her death alongside him.

He and Finder were close to the other court rulers now, and Finder screamed for Valakais. The dark-skinned faery looked up.

"I don't know if I can save them both," he cried. "She must untie herself from him."

Finder's eyes tore to the sky, powerless as Larken and Fynvarra fell. "Undo the straps!" Finder screamed, and Dahey knew there was no point in telling him that Larken couldn't hear him.

Valakais lifted his hands, a great gust of wind hurling towards Fynvarra and Larken. It slowed their fall, but only just.

"What can I do?" Dahey asked.

"Keep the soldiers away from me, as much room as you can give me," Valakais grunted. "The Weeping Metal isn't doing me any favors."

Dahey nodded, grabbing Finder by the arm. "Watching her isn't going to make her fall any slower. But Valakais can. Fight, now."

He and Finder cut a path around Valakais. Seconds stretched long as Fynvarra and Larken seemed to fall in slow motion from the sky. Valakais gritted his teeth, his hands raised and trembling.

"Come on, Larken," Dahey muttered as he cut down another solider. "Cut the damn straps."

78

LARKEN

Airodion

Her connection with Fynvarra flickered as he drifted in and out of consciousness. The ground grew ever closer, but somehow, Larken thought they should have landed by now. She hoped she didn't feel it. Hoped she was just plunged into darkness.

She was scared, terrified beyond her wits, but once she reached that point, there was a moment of calm.

I'm here, Fynvarra, she told him. *I need you to wake up. Wake up and open your wings.*

Tired... Fynvarra murmured through the bond. Their connection flickered like a spluttering candle.

I know.

Hurts...

I know. She dug her hands into his mane. *I'm here with you. You can do this. Open your wings. We don't have much time.*

Wind howled around them, more than should have been possible. When Larken glanced below, she saw a tiny speck—Valakais, using his wind magic to try to break their fall.

If you open your wings, Valakais can save us, she said. She wasn't certain, but at least he could break their fall. He slowed their descent, but not enough.

Undo the straps, Fynvarra said.

No. They were in this together. She had chosen to fly with him into battle. If he fell, so did she.

Undo the straps. He can save you.

I'm not leaving you. Tears streamed down her face, torn away by the wind.

I love you, Larken. Fynvarra hooked a claw around the straps binding her to him and snapped them in two. Larken screamed as she was ripped from his back by the wind. She screamed until the cry became the wind itself. Fynvarra rolled onto his back, plummeting away from her. He unfurled his wings, lifting them to break her fall however he could.

Valakais' magic lifted her away from Fynvarra. Her tears, her voice, all of it lost to the wind.

They crashed into the ground.

Larken opened her eyes. She glanced around frantically for Fynvarra. He lay crumpled next to her. She crawled to him, blood, dust and smoke on her tongue. Every inch of her was shaking, but she was alive. She felt like she had been trampled by a few dozen horses, but nothing seemed broken.

Fynvarra wasn't moving. His belly moved up and down slowly—he was breathing.

She fell across his great head. "You stupid lizard," she cried, sobs racking her aching body. "You cut the straps to save me when all you had to do was open your wings. *Which you did anyway.*" She pressed her forehead into his scaly cheek. "Why did you do that? *Why?*"

Fynvarra didn't move. She tried to connect them through their bond —but there was nothing. Was his neck broken? Had his spine snapped when they landed?

Her tears dripped onto his scales. "Please, not you. I can't lose you." She stroked his cheek.

I'm still here. He cracked open an amber eye. *I'm still here.*

Larken sobbed and flung herself on Fynvarra's neck, trying not to crush him with her hug. Fynvarra lifted his head, letting out a low growl.

The Weeping Metal soldiers, previously occupied with Finder and Dahey and likely thinking her and Fynvarra dead, were now taking notice. Larken hoisted herself to her feet, but horror filled her as the soldiers closed rank around them.

79

DAHEY

Airodion

Finder screamed when Larken hit the earth.

"She's alive!" Dahey gripped Finder by the shoulder. "I saw her move. But they're in a bad position, the soldiers are starting to notice."

Valakais had returned his efforts to taking down soldiers with Etain and Isra, but their magic was missing its final counterpart.

"We can save her," Dahey murmured to Finder.

An arrow whistled through the air, barreling towards Dahey's neck. Finder grabbed him by the front of his chainmail and hauled him forward, lifting his shield to block. The arrow *pinged* against Finder's shield.

Dahey and Finder stood face to face. Dahey's eyes widened. Finder hadn't hesitated. Hadn't thought about it. He had put Dahey first. After all of it. After everything.

Dahey had been wrong. His court had supported him, yes, but it was Finder who had really been there for him.

Finder slowly released his fist from Dahey's chainmail. "I don't know if I can forgive you for what you've done."

Dahey took a step back. Ever since Dahey had been a child, Finder had been there for him. He'd loved him unconditionally. It was his own fault he had lost Finder. As though he had reopened an old wound, regret poured through him. He had been wrong to do this. It had taken him up until this point, up until this battle to realize that nothing was worth losing his brother's love.

"You don't have to," he whispered. "You don't ever have to. But for what we had—for what we had before I ruined it. For the boys we once were. It has taken me a war to realize that boy is still inside me, and he needs his brother." Dahey's voice broke at the word.

Finder looked him over, and Dahey felt stripped bare under his scrutiny. But when Finder looked up, his eyes were gentle.

"I love you, Dahey. I always have. And I love you still."

80

LARKEN

Airodion

The soldiers lowered their swords and spears, pressing closer.

No. They had not survived their fall just to be impaled by human soldiers. She balled her fists. Fynvarra curled around her, growling, but the Weeping Metal bolt had pierced his neck, rendering him unable to use his flame. And his wounds were still serious and needed a healer, or else he would bleed out.

Fynvarra snarled at the humans, lashing out with his tail. Larken pressed her palm into his shoulder. In the end, they still had each other.

She closed her eyes.

Fire exploded behind her closed lids. Her eyes flew open, blinded by the piercing light. She lifted a hand to shield her eyes.

Fire engulfed the Weeping Metal soldiers. They screamed, and the frost took them next, then the air vanished from their lungs. The earth trembled, opening into a gaping pit to swallow them.

In massive ranks, they fell, subdued by the court rulers' magic. And when more of the soldiers had cleared, Larken saw Finder and Dahey, side by side, arms lifted and moving in tandem as they channeled the fire.

385

"They did it," she whispered, and Fynvarra gave a faint rasp of a roar. She sagged against him. "They did it."

81

DAHEY

Airodion

Dahey took hold of the golden chain in his mind. But he didn't pull—he merely held it. He felt the faintest pressure at the other end—Finder had taken up the other end of the chain.

They turned to look at each other and nodded. As one, they held the chain between them. For a moment, nothing. Then the magic exploded within him.

The chain was not meant to be pulled one against the other. It was meant to link—to bind. And when they opened themselves fully, the magic came to their call. Dahey's heart beat faster and faster as the magic filled him with ecstasy. But Finder was there to ground him on the other side of the chain. They didn't pull against each other. Not once. They held on together.

Dahey's hands moved, and the flames leapt to answer. They raged at his call, at his direction. Finder did the same, the fire sweeping around him like a storm. They crushed the soldiers, their magic working together with Isra, Valakais and Etain to destroy them. The magic sang to them, pulsed in their bones, and they let it pour through them like conduits. And still, the steadfast chain linked them.

Ziegan's forces fled, pushed back by the remnants of the calvary. The firedrakes roared their triumph as the winged beasts fled.

Dahey twisted his hands, mirroring Finder's movements. No pain. Only joy. This is what he had thought the powers would feel like. What they should feel like. And when he looked at Finder, a small smile touched his cousin's lips. He felt it too.

When, at last, the wind and water died, and the earth had swallowed up the last of the soldiers, they let their flames go out. Dahey and Finder lowered their hands, and even the firedrakes' flames turned to smoke. He clasped Finder's shoulder, and his cousin gave him a nod before tearing off to find Larken.

Dahey watched as Isra disappeared to care for her wounded.

Valakais gripped him by the shoulder, his gaze dark. "We will speak at length about what you did," he growled. "But consider yourself lucky that you both were able to use the powers. Next time, you might not be as fortunate."

Etain studied Dahey with an expression he couldn't read. Valakais put an arm around her shoulders, helping her back towards Shadeshelm. They were too weak to portal home, but Dahey was sure they would leave as soon as they were able to return to their people.

Fear trickled down his back. What would happen now that he and Finder could use the powers together?

He shook himself. That had to wait.

They had lost many. The bodies of Autumn Court soldiers littered the ground, as did the broken bodies of the firedrakes who had plummeted from the sky and had not had Valakais to save them. Ziegan's forces lay scattered throughout, and some of the court fey who fought for him. But they had won. And pooling their strength had been enough to push Ziegan's forces back.

There would be battles to come, Dahey was sure of it. A war. But together, they had been able to turn the tide.

Dahey lifted his head to the sky and gave a shaky laugh.

They had won.

82

LARKEN

Airodion

Larken stood with Finder amongst the wreckage of Shadeshelm. She tried not to stare at Isra and Roone, where they sat together on a flight of steps. They had their heads pressed close together, Isra healing a deep cut on Roone's arm. Still, she wondered what would happen between Roone and Saja now that they were each other's *laithnam*, but from different courts.

Finder had healed Fynvarra's wounds, and the drake now lay resting in the rubble.

"How are you feeling?" Larken asked Finder as they walked, risking a sideways glance at him. It hadn't been easy for him to join forces with Dahey. But they wouldn't have won without it.

"Better," Finder said. His voice was husky.

"Did using your powers make you want them back?" she asked tentatively.

Finder nodded. "In some ways, yes. I don't miss the pain of using them, the guilt, but after visiting Raharney, they don't feel quite as painful anymore. I've always complained about them being a burden, but having them taken from me made me realize they are a part of me. I want my powers back. I know now that it is both my burden and blessing to handle. Dahey is untrained and untested, and on the eve of war, there is no time to teach him, even if he did find a way to take the rest of my powers without killing me. But for now, we must settle on using them together."

They walked on through the decimated city. Though it had taken a hit, it was still standing. For now, they had stopped the spread of Ziegan's forces across Airodion. She wondered how Dahey felt, knowing he had released such a blight upon Airodion. Saja had punched him square in the jaw after the battle, and Dahey had done nothing to stop him. Still, she knew that they had a lot of healing to do. All of them did after what Dahey had done.

Larken glanced up at the sky, overwhelmed at the thoughts of what was to come. Ziegan would be back.

"What will we do now?" she asked quietly.

"We need to see what the court rulers are capable of together. That will give us a better idea of the odds we face. Then, we must rally allies from wherever we can find them. Ziegan will be growing his forces. We must as well."

"And what about the humans? The Popes sided with Ziegan, but the humans don't have a choice. They'll do whatever the Popes tell them, even when it leads them straight to their deaths."

"Dahey claims that rumors grow of a human girl who defies the Popes," Finder said. "They say she has defeated several creatures that have plagued villages in Ellevere, and that her army grows by the hour."

Hope flared in Larken's chest. Could her parents have reached that resistance? She knew they never would have sided with the Popes. Perhaps this girl could lead her to her parents. "We have to send word to her, letting her know what's happening here. Maybe she can help us."

Finder nodded. "This is her war now too—all of the humans' war. Ziegan will not stop until he has taken both our realms, and who knows what he has promised the Popes in exchange for their armies. The humans will suffer, that much is certain. If this human girl joins forces with us, we stand a better chance." He looked tired.

Larken raised a hand to his cheek. "We still have each other. From the moment our souls touched during the life debt, we have had each other. We will not face this alone."

Finder pressed his lips to her brow in answer. They walked back to the great tree together as dawn spilled into the land, pinks and yellows and oranges lighting up the sky. Once the sun touched her face, Larken turned her face upwards, and the night finally ended.

They had much to do before the war to come.

83

DAHEY

Airodion

Dahey walked into the kitchens. He longed for a mug of the warmed spiced wine that was a specialty of the Autumn Court.

He turned the corner into the kitchens and stopped as he beheld Finder sitting at the table, nursing his own cup of wine.

He and Finder used to come to these kitchens after every tough lesson, every time they returned from battle, or whenever they just had a long day. They came late, after all the servants had gone, and they would talk about anything and everything until the kitchen staff rose early in the morning and shooed them away.

"Finder," Dahey murmured.

"Dahey," Finder replied, lifting his mug ever so slightly. "It seems you had the same idea as me. It doesn't seem right to survive a battle without spiced wine to celebrate."

Another jug of wine was already heating on the coals. Dahey poured himself a steaming mug. He hesitated, almost sitting at the table opposite Finder, but then came and sat beside his cousin.

"Thank you," Dahey murmured. "For today."

Finder shrugged. "It was to save Larken," he said simply.

They drifted into an awkward silence, a vast emptiness stretched between them. Dahey glanced at his cousin out of the corner of his eye, a fierce ache building up in his chest. How many times had they sat at this very table and debriefed after a mission?

Dahey thought about all he had done. He had sworn to protect Finder and then broken his word. Stabbed his kin and wrapped him in chains. Bound their powers together.

He had done it all—and Finder still loved him. Loved him when no one else had.

"You felt it today," Finder said suddenly, startling Dahey out of his thoughts. "You felt what the fire is meant to feel like."

"Yes," Dahey said. He remembered what it felt like when they had joined their powers together, when they had stopped pulling on the golden chain. He hadn't tried to use the powers since—nor had Finder. It seemed they were both afraid to go back to how things were, with either of them pulling on the end of the chain, and the pain that accompanied it.

"What did it feel like?"

Dahey hesitated. "It felt like pure joy. It felt like finally coming home."

Finder nodded. A small smile touched his lips. "That's exactly how I felt. It's always felt good to use them. Like the fire was made for my hands to wield." He shook his head. "My power over death is the same. It brings me the purest joy—but the greatest terror. For I know the destruction both can cause."

"I understand," Dahey said. And for the first time, he knew how Finder felt using the powers. All along, he had scorned his cousin for not wanting to use the magic. He had always wondered why Finder kept them locked away. But what he had felt today was undeniable pleasure. He could imagine setting fire to the world and letting it burn forever until the flames consumed him, too, just so he could feel that joy until the end.

Finder gave him a true smile then. "I've never been able to talk to anyone about the powers," he said. "Uncle never wanted to speak of them once they left him, and the other court rulers don't know exactly how my powers feel. But you do."

"What do they feel like without the chain?" Dahey asked.

Finder frowned, thinking. "Similar. But instead of a chain, there are three separate currents. One for the fire, one for glamor, summoning, healing, and portalling, and one for death. All of them bring me that same joy—but I keep them locked away because I know what they can do." Finder lowered his head. "It's agony. For them to bring me such pleasure and such pain." He looked up at Dahey. "But I'm glad I have someone to share them with." He gave Dahey a small smile that tore Dahey's heart in two.

A tear rolled down Dahey's cheek. He stood up from the table. Finder startled to his feet as well, looking at Dahey in concern. Not fear—but worry. After all this time, he was still worried about Dahey. Was willing to share his powers when he should have wanted to kill Dahey and take them back for himself. It would be what Dahey deserved.

Dahey sank to his knees before his cousin. "I'm so sorry," Dahey said. "For all of it. I was wrong about the powers.

"I never thought you deserved them. I thought you didn't appreciate them. But feeling them today... I can see what a burden they can be. It was the first time they didn't cause me pain—but it was the first time they frightened me. And if I didn't have you there to tether me on the other side of the chain, I don't know what I would have done. I would have surrendered to that pleasure and let the world burn to ash."

Finder stood before him, dumbfounded, but Dahey couldn't stop the words pouring out of his mouth. "I know the words I spoke to take your powers. I know the word I misspoke. To take. If I say the inverse... it should mean to give."

Finder's eyes widened.

"I'm not sure if it can be done, but I want to try. I want to try to give them back to you."

Finder shook his head. "It's too dangerous, Dahey. You could misspeak again, and we could both die."

"We could use the powers together, but not at full strength," Dahey said. "We will need someone with their full powers in the war to come, and that someone is you."

Finder paused, and Dahey held his breath. Finally, Finder spoke, his voice barely more than a whisper: "I thought I wanted them back, but here, faced with them, I'm not certain."

Dahey stood. "That joy I felt? It was nothing compared to yours. Because I tried to take them. They never wanted to be mine. They wanted *you*. I thought I knew the burden of the powers—but I don't. My father never did either, but you do. They chose you, Finder."

Finder met his gaze. Then he nodded.

Dahey clasped forearms with Finder. He breathed in deeply, then began speaking the words. A pulsing beat twisted in the air. The words poured out of Dahey, faster, louder. Darkness crept in at the sides of his vision, but Dahey shoved it away, gritting his teeth as he spoke them.

The channel of magic opened inside him. He felt the golden chain between him and Finder grow taught, tighter and tighter until, finally, it snapped in two. Both fey were flung backwards, hitting opposite walls of the kitchen, and then Dahey knew nothing more.

Dahey's eyes fluttered open. Finder staggered to his feet across from him. Dahey reached into himself, searching for the golden chain in the current. It was gone. A deep sadness welled up inside him. "I no longer feel the powers," he whispered. "Do you?"

Finder reached out a hand, and flames burst to life. He closed his eyes, a small smile on his lips.

Dahey bowed to the King of the Autumn Court.

84

KAISA

Ellevere

The Pope's men fled the city in a matter of hours, torn apart at the seams by the news of Pope Sersius's death.

Kaisa wanted nothing more than to sleep, but she returned to the building where she and the Pope had fought. She found the table where Pope Sersius had been talking to someone when she first entered the building.

On the table lay a strange orb. It was obsidian black with a peculiar, mirky substance swirling inside. With cautious fingers, she reached out to touch it.

Searing pain tore through her mind, and she felt as though her presence brushed up against another being's entirely.

She released her fingers, gasping. But through some strange urge, she placed her fingers on the orb again, this time placing her entire palm over the surface.

Less pain this time, only the strange feeling that her mind was brushing up against something.

Was the orb somehow sentient? She hadn't seen anything about it in

397

her book, but there was some kind of presence there, she could feel it. And it hadn't responded to the Pope when he had made his demands, so perhaps it would respond to her.

Nothing.

She released the orb, disappointment spiking through her. She was about to turn away when she saw the orb grow darker. Curious, she placed her hand on the orb again.

"Who are you?" a clipped voice asked. He—for it was a man's voice, was beautiful but sharp—like a weapon.

"My name is Kaisa," she said, her voice echoing strangely through her mind. "Who are you?"

"Where is Pope Sersius?"

She paused. If this was an ally of Pope Sersius, then perhaps she shouldn't be talking to him. But again, she thought about how the orb hadn't answered Sersius.

"Dead. I killed him."

A pause, and she could swear she felt shock ripple through the orb.

"You are an enemy to the Popes? To Ziegan?"

Again, that name. "Yes," Kaisa replied, trying to keep the venom from her voice. "Ziegan's monsters attacked my people. I've been trying to keep them safe. The Popes have abandoned us, siding with Ziegan, so they are enemies to me. They say their armies are headed to war in the faery realm. I have an army of my own, and I wish to join forces with those who fight against the Popes and Ziegan." She held her breath. Had she said too much?

Another shocked pause from the orb. "I am Dahey Fairburn of the Autumn Court. The courts and their allies stand against Ziegan. Will you and your army join us?"

Kaisa smiled. "Tell me how to find you, and my army and I shall come."

Tarrio found her sometime later, asleep in the warehouse, curled around the orb.

"I know you need sleep, but your people await your orders," he said.

Kaisa nodded. "We go north. To Airodion."

ACKNOWLEDGMENTS

Reaching the end of this book is so bittersweet and I couldn't have done it without the help of so many people.

To my parents—thank you is an understatement. You've supported me through it all and I truly can't thank you enough. I love you!

To Lauren Elliott, one of my oldest and dearest friends, your friendship means the world to me. Annie, Pauline, Camille and Gabby—I couldn't have done it without you. To Anna, Kourtney and Caitlin—your support is endless and I freaking love you. And a special, special thank you to Lindsey, Réka, and Madeline. I love you girls!

To MJ and Ally, you both have supported Autumn's Tithe (and Traitor) since day one. I'm so thankful to have you in my corner.

To my family, thank you so much for your support. I'm so incredibly lucky to have a family who encourages all of my creative endeavors. And to my barn family, thank you for always being there when I need it most.

And finally to Jinxy, Tater, Happy and Niko, my soul animals. I love you all!

PRONUNCIATION GUIDE

CHARACTERS

Brigid: Bridge-id
Finder: Find (like kind) -er
Dahey: Da (like law) -hee
Saja: Sa (like law) -ja
Madden: Mad-in
Remira: Ree-meer-uh
Rosin: Rose-in
Imogen: Emma-gin
Ainsley: Ains (like gains) -lee
Etain: E-tane
Asphalion: As (like has) -fey-lee-on
Aleea: Al-lay-uh
Embryn: Em-brinn
Givrain: Give-rain
Toma: Tow-ma
Maeve: May-vuh
Kaisa: Kai (like die) - sa
Isra: Is-ra

Sersius: Sir-see-us
Roone: (like dune)
Osiron: Oh-sir-on
Ziegan: Zee (like he)-gan
Valakais: Val-uh-kais (like ice)
Saoirse: Sear-sha
Ishan: Ee-shan
Fynvarra: Fin (like sin)-var (like far) - uh
Tarrio: Tar (like far)-ee-o
Koalin: Ko (like go) -a-lin (like sin)

PLACES

Airodion: Air-row-dee-on
Ellevere: Ell-vere
Ballamor: Balla-more
Shadeshelm: Shades-helm
Augrim: Aw (like saw)-grim
Barrensmere: Barrens-mere
Inniskeen: In-is-keen
Raharney: Ra-har-nee (like knee)
Tellaridge: Tella-ridge

OTHER

Dornán: Door-nan
Laithnam: Laith (like faith) -nam
Cynyada: Sin-ya-da
Arobhinn: Arrow-vin
Rhylla: Ra-la
Bresel: Bree-sell
Basiog: Bass-ee-og
Fomari: Foe-mar-ee
Furyon: Fury-on
Sorreno: Soar-ay (like hay)-no
Bean Sidhe: ban-shee

ABOUT THE AUTHOR

Hannah Parker was born and raised in Oklahoma. She holds a Bachelor's Degree in English Literature from Oklahoma State University, and her fiction won overall first place for the Katherine Paterson Prize for Young Adult Literature in the Journal *Hunger Mountain*.

When not writing, Hannah can be found drinking coffee, reading, or competing in the hunter ring with her horse. Hannah currently lives in Oklahoma with her cat, dog, and horses.